faking it

faking it

Amrita Chowdhury

hachette
INDIA

First Published by Hachette India 2009

ISBN: 978-81-906173-2-1

Hachette Book Publishing India Pvt. Ltd
4th and 5th Floor, Corporate Centre,
Plot No. 94, Sector 44, Gurgaon - 12203, India

Typeset in Meridien 9.5/12.3 by
Mindways Design, New Delhi

Printed and bound in India by
Manipal Technologies Limited, Manipal

For
Sumit, Shoumik and Aishani

Aamar Shokol Rosher Dhara

❧prologue

I enter the polished dark wood and glass interiors of Amaya in London's Knightsbridge, barely registering the hushed glamour of the discreet chandeliers and the press of its hip crowd. Still in a daze, with Gul propping my elbow for support, I walk towards the table where Apurva Mehta is waiting for us.

Gul's friend, Apurva, art advisor to galleries and independent curators, and specialist in South Asian art, rises grimly to greet us. There is a stern pity on her face. One look at her and all the arguments that have been burbling in my head for the past week die, unarticulated. An enlargement of a photograph of the Amrita Sher-Gil painting I have purchased lies on the table; no doubt from the picture I have scanned and emailed Gul.

'I...uh...have...the authentication certificate somewhere at home...' I blurt without preamble, forgetting all niceties.

Gul lays a warm palm on my arm. 'Hear her out first, Tara.'

'The style, the style is totally Sher-Gil,' I protest. 'The intense colours, this midnight blue, this red...'

Apurva shakes her coiffed head. 'Of course, I should see the actual painting first, but it's just that several elements seem all wrong to me. Look at the central figure, for instance...'

Ah. The Woman in Red! *I steal a glance at the enlarged print of my treasured purchase, the trophy item in my collection of contemporary Indian art, an untitled painting by the Indo-Hungarian legend, Amrita Sher-Gil! At once strong and poignant – a slight figure draped in red robes looking with intense eyes straight at the viewer; utterly alone in the market crowd around her.*

I identify with her completely.

'She's a typical Sher-Gil. What about her?'

I have grown obsessed with Sher-Gil's life before buying the painting. Tales of her flamboyant and troubled youth have appealed to me as much as the long lean silhouettes, the elongated limbs and the open-eyed candour of the brooding figures she painted.

Apurva takes a moment to sip her Scotch. 'Exactly. This style is reminiscent of Amrita Sher-Gil's early phase in India. Doesn't it remind you of the figures in The Bride's Toilette *or* The Brahmacharis *or even* Hill Women*?'*

I nod furiously.

'Now look at the backdrop,' Apurva continues. 'The detail of the market scene is typical of her later period, when she became influenced by the miniature style, and her figures became less prominent. These thick black outlines – Sher-Gil did not use them. The painting is really a clever juxtaposition of different elements from her work, with some add-on bits.'

'It could be an intermediate phase…' I try again. 'And the find was so well publicized. A huge Amrita Sher-Gil found in a derelict haveli in a small town in North India, that sold for crores…'

Apurva says, 'Wasn't the hue and cry about another, bigger canvas?'

'Yes,' my voices curves upward, appalled by how unreal I sound. 'Mine was found in the same haveli, just weeks after.'

Apurva is kindly. 'I will give you the names of some friends in India who can evaluate the painting for you. I strongly suggest you meet them.'

My heart sinks at this point and I fall back into the thickly cushioned chair.

And my mind goes back to where it all began.

part 1

❧one

The plane did a mini-dip somewhere above a Baltic state, just hours after take-off from London, sloshing insipid airline gin and tonic on the pages of *The Book of Answers*, my current cope-with-life manual. As I wiped the trail of liquid off the open page of inspirational text – '*Those things that hurt, instruct*'– a sigh pirouetted into existence like an applause-hungry diva. I thought: *I am in for much learning, then.* After all, this bizarre change of plan, this sudden move to India, did hurt like hell.

Rohan, my four year old, lay on the seat beside me in a red-eyed glaze, glued to the mini-screen, his curly hair ruffled, sated on cola and cartoons. Flanking my preschooler on the other side, Raj, my husband, sat half splayed on his sky bed, a day-old fuzz blurring the bullish thrust of his jaw as he watched the acrobatic leg-twists and tight-ass kicks of some oozing-from-the-top Hollywood stunt queen. How could he blithely watch a film, knowing I was seething inside?

Washington DC had been left far behind; and with it, my career, my contacts, my dreams, and my life as I knew it. I was on my way to live in Mumbai. Mumbai, that Raj maintained, was a fabulous opportunity, a once-in-a-lifetime chance he could not pass up. A chance to start a new India Fund! Hah, what was so fabulous about international finance in some far-flung outpost of emerging markets? Off track – *that's* what *I* would call it.

'It's a great movie, Tara. You must watch it. Channel 22,' Raj turned to me and beamed, oblivious to my anger. Then, happy as ever, he upped the volume on his headphones and went back to watching the film.

Bubbles of hysteria rose within me. Damn Raj! The only movie I wanted to watch at this moment was *How to Murder Your Husband*. But of course, nothing like that was playing on the in-flight video-on-demand. In fact, come to think of it, a movie by that name didn't exist. Maybe, *that's* what I should do while in Mumbai, I brooded dangerously. Make a Bollywood film on the subject, complete with a dagger dance set to hip hop as with a Shakira-esque shake of her booty and a roll of her eyes the gorgeous scorned wife considers her brainless spouse – to live or let die!

God, I *so* knew I was going to hate it.

As yet un-thumbed copies of *Shantaram* and *Sacred Games* lay in my carry-on bag; farewell gifts on my last evening from colleagues at work, wide-eyed about the underworld Mumbai they had read about. 'My Mumbai will be very different; far from the gritty reality of these books,' I had told them bleakly. Till two days ago, I had been a highly paid, well-respected, senior economist at Phoenix Advisory Board, specializing in economic and market research. At my hastily organized farewell party though, I had downed a couple of martinis and managed a brittle smile, feigning a blustery confidence I did not feel. I was still reeling from the shock of a three-week pack-and-move across the world, and fuming inside at ultimately – *always, always, always* – having to do the

Asian woman thing, i.e. chucking up your own life to follow your spouse dutifully around the world, after years of being your own mistress.

Now, on the plane, as I gazed out of the window, another sigh escaped me. Was it just three weeks ago, that life had been near-perfect? That perfect crisp winter Saturday that Raj had broken the news to me was still vivid in my memory...

A mild sun had broken through the clotted-cream clouds on Saturday morning after a whole week, melting the kerbside snow and bringing with it the euphoria that only sunshine after days of murkiness and gloom can bring. With Raj away on a business trip, I had woken Ro up and we'd dressed in layers of warm fleece and running shoes, mitts, beanies, and scarves. Ro had slid down the banister, despite my screams. I'd loaded Ro's little red bicycle with its training wheels onto the back of my silver Range Rover and driven the few short blocks to park at the end of M street. Then we'd wheeled his bike down to the narrow bike path along the C&O Canal. Ro, his curls trapped in his beanie, his naughty red-cheeked grin shining through its woollen confines, pedalled his bike while I ran after him, laughing, exhilarated by the bare branches trellised overhead, the sudden rush of water at the step-up locks, the occasional duck gliding through the grey semi-frozen sheets on the canal, the joggers and bikers we passed – strangers all, but happy to exchange a smile to commemorate this lovely day.

After a sluggish start to the century, global markets were on a jig and a roll. My work analysing markets and economies demanded grit and time, but come weekends, I was happy to forget it all and live for myself, and for Raj and Ro. At thirty-two, after six years of marriage, Raj still made me giggle, at the world and at myself; still made me go weak in the knees. Thinking of him I glanced at my watch, and realized it was 10am – he should be getting into National Airport about now and driving home in an hour. I couldn't wait to see him.

So we'd headed back, with me huffing a bit as I lugged both bicycle and boy back to the car, my son being too tired to pedal any further. On the drive back I'd spotted an empty one-hour parking spot near Dean & Deluca – too lucky an omen on a Saturday morning to ignore! I had quickly parallel-parked the long Range into the tucked-in spot. I remember I had picked out an artichoke pâté, a Cabernet-soaked pear tart, a chunk of Brie and a crusty French loaf for lunch, when I'd spotted a pile of imported pomegranates. Oh, how gorgeous on a winter morning! I had to have some. We were to attend a desi potluck party in McLean that evening, at the house of an ex-colleague from the World Bank, and I was picked to make mattar-paneer for forty. At least the anaars would get some *real* appreciation.

Then I had driven home to the red, double-brick detached Tudor house we had moved into some months before Ro was born. We still had to finish up the basement, but I loved the little period details – the crown mouldings, the cute niches, the carved fireplaces, and the cherry hardwood floor, perfectly polished to mirror the tall, wide windows. Not to mention my burgeoning but modest collection of Indian art, the centrepiece of which was a large oil on canvas, a swirl of reds, apricots and buttercups, abstractly hinting at female forms, which riveted everyone's attention. It was by Chitrita Goswami, an artist whose sensuously suggestive works had begun capturing the public imagination some years ago, and who was now very highly regarded.

So, that was home – just streets away from lovely row-houses and lively cafés and boutiques, yet quiet enough to hear the chickadees pip. In summer, the doors would open onto a garden full of hydrangeas and the sprawling lawns beyond.

Soon we'd heard a car come up the driveway. Rohan and I ran out to watch Raj emerge from his black BMW Z3, devastating in his black cashmere turtleneck and Armani jeans, armed with the loveliest two-tone, orange-beige, long-stemmed roses. 'Just flown in from Bogota – I picked them up from the Flower District early this morning,' Raj had smiled, kissing me and tossing Ro up in the air.

We had moved inside, a young family, happy to be together again. Soon the morning sun would slink off westwards and it would be perfect to get a log fire going, eat the cheese and bread, drink some merlot and lazily chat, before preparing for the evening's party. I was mentally ticking off my chores for the evening when Raj said:

'I have a surprise, Tara,' a barely-concealed sliver of excitement in his voice. 'Ellerman Jones wants to start India operations. They want me to move to Mumbai immediately to start and head the India Fund.'

Now I glared at Raj as a fresh surge of bitterness burnt my insides. My reaction had been intense. *How? Why?* I had reasoned with Raj. To uproot ourselves, when we were settled here, leave our home and friends and cars and school behind? It made no sense. But Raj was adamant. BRIC economies, he enthused. I knew. I was one of the economists who had pumped and primed BRIC notions, but to *invest* in, not to *live* there!

How *could* Raj? No, this was not right! He would have to pay for this. There was a smouldering hole right in my centre. Inhaling deeply, I ordered another gin and tonic.

The smiling Business Class airhostess who served my drink eyed my dark bootcut Seven denims and trendy Diesel top: 'You look so young, not like a mother at all.'

I smiled, despite myself. After all, I took great pride in how I looked; in striving to be the non-typical, desi married woman, sweating kilo-cals as I jog-pushed the stroller. White colleagues were always commenting on my large dark eyes and my golden-bronze skin – an effect *they* achieved by spending large sums of money in Solariums – while thin-lipped white women eyed my naturally-full, collagen-fillers-free lips, with a certain envy.

Feeling better already, I took a long sip and flipped open an airline magazine. A self-portrait of Amrita Sher-Gil caught my eye. Her vivacity shone through the darkening pigment; even the veining of the once enamel-like colours could not dim the sensuality of form and expression.

Bet *she* would never have changed her life around for anyone, I thought darkly.

I looked for a while longer at the self-portrait of the artist, remembering the sketchy details I knew about her. Behind that dazzling animation, somewhere in the deep recesses of her mind, hidden under those long dark tresses, had lurked a manic silvery skein that had found expression in wide exploration. She had struggled to establish her style in the face of mental and financial instability.

Western art and Indian art were such distinct orbs in those days, I mused – one young, energetic, based on a few centuries of vigorous experimentation; the other still in the shadows of centuries'-old tradition. Such mad fearlessness then, to attempt to move the orbs closer, to create that overlap of ideas and practice; but they had done it – Nandalal Bose, Abanindranath Tagore, Amrita Sher-Gil, and many others. What a core of steel they had.

I read:

Amrita Sher-Gil, known for defining the idiom of modern Indian contemporary art, is a coveted artist. Given her untimely death at the young age of 29, her limited body of works is always in great demand. In 2005, an Amrita Sher-Gil painting was sold through an Indian auction house at a staggering amount of 6.9 crores. As Amrita Sher-Gil's works are considered items of national heritage, her works cannot be sold to overseas buyers or taken outside India after purchase.

The article went on to describe the rising popularity of Indian art. Collectors of Indian art across the globe, the article informed me, were scrambling to get their hands on prized canvases. I knew. I had bought paintings myself, before the Indian art market had exploded to these hysterical heights.

I flipped the page. There were pictures of paintings by other artists, some bright and primal, some poignant, some too distorted to have any poignancy. A small boxed paragraph accompanying the article said:

Auctioneer and antiques dealer Roy Jordan is the latest entrant to join the Indian art bandwagon.

A specialist in rare art, Jordan is moving to India to source Indian masterpieces for his clients in the West. He talked about the tremendous movement in secondary markets, as evidenced by the sale of Amrita Sher-Gil's Village Scene *and the 70s and 80s vintage Raza and Souza works making headlines in international auctions.*

Hmmm.

All at once, sitting in the dim shadow of the overhead bin, among the overspill of Rohan's broken crayons, transformer star fighter planes and half-chewed books on hungry caterpillars, I knew what I had to do. So Raj thought the Sensex swoosh was too lucrative to ignore? Well then, I thought fiendishly, there would be more than enough for compensation, wouldn't there?

Fired with a new ambition I took out my pocket-sized leather notebook and began to write as neatly as it was possible to in a wobbling plane:

How to Get Even with Your Husband:
Buy art
And changed that to:
Buy contemporary Indian art
Then I thought some more:
Buy contemporary Indian art by noted and upcoming artists
I reflected a little longer and then wrote finally, with vicious glee:
Buy contemporary Indian art by noted and upcoming artists and blow huge holes in your husband's wallet.

❧two

'So what's your plan for the day?' Raj asked, as he buttoned his shirt, trying to smile at me from the extra-large gilded bathroom mirror over the double marble vanity in that casual we-are-a-happy-family way.

It had been a week since we had arrived in Mumbai. He had been trying all this time to be extra nice to me, hoping for a thaw in my mood, but now the effort was showing. I was still in no mood to be nice to him. Not in private, for sure. Not when nothing in my life was working out, and seven days in Mumbai were enough to show me that it might easily take seven *months* for matters to stabilize. I scowled at the mirror. 'Get my life organized. What else?'

'God, can't you let up for a second? Will the world end if you smile once?' said Raj, suddenly losing his temper and slamming the bathroom door shut behind him.

'Yes, it *will!*' I shouted through the closed door as I continued to apply my mascara. I had nothing to smile about. *Nothing. Nyet. Nada.*

My agenda had been made abundantly clear in the anxious pre-arrival moments before we had landed in Mumbai: find a good school for Rohan; find an apartment with a sea view; find a mini-battalion of maids to run the house. Only *then* would I be able to start looking at *my* life. But I had made zero progress in all spheres thus far.

Living in Mumbai was proving to be more expensive than living in Washington DC, or even Manhattan. I had never ever imagined this sitting in DC. Leaving the US, I had felt like something of a pioneer – among the first to ever negotiate the reverse trek to India. But now I realized that NRIs were swarming back to India from every corner of the globe, like flocks of migratory birds hovering over fields of fresh wheat. Not just entrepreneurs and bankers and senior folks in industry, but newly minted graduates too – hoping to sell French cosmetics and German turbines, or tap into cheap, educated labour pools. All this translated into tough competition for the posh end of rental properties. And the lease was hard to come by. Real estate prices made broadsheet headlines – conjecture today, reality tomorrow. Rumours abounded. Everyone was tight-lipped. It was frenzy on auto loop. Agents were upping their margins and real estate barons were laughing all the way to their Swiss bank accounts.

And so *we* were still ensconced in our luxury suite at the Taj Wellington Mews in Colaba.

Earlier this morning, my daily self-help calendar had helpfully suggested *'Focus'* as it lay on the dark teakwood of the bedside table, today's page open to a picture of a bottlenose dolphin leaping across a backdrop of blue. It said: *Avoid distraction. Be resolute and purposeful.*

Hello, this was Mumbai.

After Raj left, grim-faced, for office, I handed Rohan over to Cara – (the white housekeeper-cum-nanny who was part of the luxury package, a little something from Raj's company to cushion our landing in hostile Third World terrain; she had since taken up permanent residence in the guest bedroom) – and left to check out yet another school. My last hope! I seemed to have exhausted all options. Apparently no 'good' school in Mumbai was willing to give admission to Rohan; they needed him to be registered at birth!

I stepped out armed with a newly-published copy of the *Eicher Mumbai Road Map* that neatly detailed every road and apartment building but failed to warn the reader that the actual signs on roads and buildings had long since eroded away, or were covered by fluttering fragments of tarpaulin, or that street names might simply have changed. After several attempts, getting lost and being driven around in circles in the bylanes near 'Hutatma Chowk' (better known as Flora Fountain) I finally reached my destination: a grim, dark, stone building behind a grim, dark, iron fence.

A school with the shuttered look of a fortress.

Naturally I was denied entry by the uniformed guard. 'You cannot go to the office, Madamji,' he admonished.

'Okay, then can I please see someone to make an appointment with the principal?' I asked, quite reasonably I thought, wondering whether or not I should slip him a few hundred bucks in broad daylight. Principals in Mumbai were better protected than criminals in Tihar jail.

'No, Madamji.' The guard stood up, ready to throw himself at me and bodily prevent me from entering the school, in the event that I lobbed a grenade and attempted a run inside.

This school had been my last hope, and I could not even get past the security guard! It was as if every elementary school in Mumbai was zealously protecting its few slots, like a mother dragon guarding her eggs. I walked away, cursing. So, now I was at this *karmanye vaadhika raste* moment: *Keep trying. Do not worry about the results.*

But try *what?* Of course, an online city guide listed hundreds of schools, but then what self-respecting NRI can possibly send her child to the local neighbourhood school? I shuddered at the thought.

Climbing back inside the car, I hyperventilated into my Trésor-scented handkerchief, attempting to eliminate the stench of unwashed body odour from my nostrils as the rental company driver lifted his arm to close the car windows and flip on the weak air-conditioning. I needed an air-freshener right away. This was all too depressing.

All Raj's fault, obviously, that I had to deal with uncertainty *and* rank armpit smells.

I peered out at the shops as the car inched forward, avoiding pushcarts and pedestrians, wondering whether a stint of shopping might help get my mind off things. That's when I saw a yellow signboard for The Bombay Store, highly recommended by the guidebooks. They would have some nice costume jewellery, I thought. I was about to alight from the car when my phone buzzed.

Who could be calling me? Not Raj for sure. He had called me a sum total of one time in the week since we had been in Mumbai.

A woman called Lola was on the phone, the wife of one of Raj's newfound acquaintances who had moved back from the US a few years ago. Maybe Raj had asked her to chat me up. Her husky voice crackled over the congested network. 'Tara, are you free, darling? What are you doing now?'

'Oh, just trying to go to The Bombay Store to buy some costume jewellery.'

Lola let out a carefully modulated mini-shriek. 'Oh, but no one shops for jewellery *there*. Let me tell you about this store behind the Taj. And if you want the real stuff, there's this *luscious* little store in the Taj Arcade. You just give them my name and they'll take care of you. But where *are* you, sweetie? I have a solution to your school situation. Can you meet me right away?'

How could I say no to that? Thus lured, I quickly agreed to meet Lola at Indigo Deli. And after innumerable halts every hundred yards to confirm and reconfirm the convoluted lefts and rights, I finally reached my destination.

The unassuming street frontage of broken stones and crumbling masonry housing magazine-wallahs, paan-stalls and the occasional starved baby being passed around among equally starved women in search of pity-money, almost hid Indigo Deli from view. I entered through a smart wood and glass door, and heaved a little sigh of relief: I could order a proper latte here, I just knew it!

I spotted two expensively dressed women sitting at a corner table, one looking trés chic in a Pucci print kurti with sequins and silver zari. As I moved towards them she rose to greet me. I looked at her closely. Hmmm, this must be Lola. She was plump, but well-trussed. I couldn't guess her age. Mid-forties? The chunky stone rings on her raised hand were fiery daubs of carnelian, topaz and amethyst. Looking at her in her finery I mentally added *shopping for ethnic clothes* to my to-do list. I bent to air-kiss her cheek. 'Hi, you must be Lola!'

'Lopamudra, actually. But whoever wants to be called that?' Lola giggled, and introduced her friend, a Canadian who had come to Mumbai after expat relocations in Addis Ababa, Tokyo and Hong Kong. 'And this is Maddy.'

'Short for Madhulika,' Maddy trilled in her Canadian accent. 'But nobody calls me *that*.'

'Luckily my name is too short to shorten,' I smiled at Maddy, my attention caught by the delicate manner in which her jaw balanced the sparkling pink, champagne and white diamonds of her chandeliers. Mumbai dressing was totally alien to my style.

'And what is your name again, darling?' Maddy said with a cultivated air of casual boredom, flicking back her tousled hair as a row of pomegranate-seed sized rubies winked from her skinny wrist.

'Tara Malhotra,' I said and sat down beside them. Soon we were swapping key details of our NRI status: the nationalities on our passports, our troubles adjusting to Mumbai, and our lack of 'belonging'! There were questions on Raj's role in India; on his position in the company; on his antecedents. Where I had studied or what I did before I washed up in Mumbai was not of interest.

There was a momentary lull in the conversation. 'Love your necklace, darling,' Maddy cooed. 'It's obviously not from here.'

I looked down at the wooden beads around my neck. Obviously not! Had it been from *here*, there would be at least one blingy pendant dangling from it.

I decided to get down to business. 'So you know of a school I can talk to?' I finally asked.

In a voice huskier than that of a chawl-dweller in the grip of dengue fever, Maddy started talking about this *wonderful* school her child attended – a rare blameless white amid the chocolate brown of schools that abounded in South Mumbai. The École Nouvelle apparently combined the best of the Swiss finishing school tradition with an emotional intelligence development programme better than Monsieur Goleman's. As for the traditionalists who still trumpeted the virtues of the three Rs in these days of soft skills and abundant choice, well, they were quietened by the thought of the 'holistic cognitive development' of their offspring.

'But will they consider me?' I fretted, plagued by the thought of yet another school refusing me entry at the gates. It was all too much for my ego to take. This was especially difficult after living in the West – with its refined notions of gender, racial and ethnic balance inside each private school room. (Of course, being a willing, high-fee-paying South Asian did help getting a seat in a white majority classroom too.) 'I'd thought having a foreign passport would help in India,' I whined to the ladies.

'Oh *that* sort of criterion cuts no ice in Mumbai anymore,' Lola scoffed. 'There are just too many NRIs floating around Mumbai school corridors these days.'

'Don't worry, darling! Of course, École Nouvelle will meet you, I'll call them up.' Maddy waved her hands about again, very aware of the scintillating glow cast by the ransom of rubies on her wrists.

Mumbai goons, apparently, still had much to learn from the Robin Hoods of the dalit regimes of the North. They were much too slack going by this flagrant display of wealth. They chose instead to focus their energies on the preservation of statues of party leaders, dead and alive, and the banning of magazines for the blasphemy of putting in ads featuring Maharashtrian wine labels.

I mentally thanked Lord Shiva, the local impresario, that there possibly was at least one school which would not reject me because I had not pre-registered my child in-utero, nor had a three-generation family history with the school.

As we chattered on the waiter brought our food – cous cous upma, egg-white omelettes, pancakes, fruit and filter coffee. Taking a bite of my upma, I turned to Maddy. 'So what do you do, Maddy?' I asked politely.

She looked me straight in the eye. 'I exercise, darling,' she said.

I stared at her in disbelief. Mumbai was indeed a brave new world, nowhere close to the India I had grown up in, with its middle-class academic aspirations and work ethics. I needed a *map* to get around here. I had already bought all the possible Mumbai guides: Food, Fashion, Nightlife, Kids and Mums. But had anyone written *The Idiot's Guide to Living in South Mumbai*? Where was the nearest bookstore?

Maddy glanced at her glittering watch, exclaimed about running late, and gathered her Gucci bag to leave, promising to call me after talking to the principal.

Lola and I finished breakfast, and Lola told me all about her daughter who attended college in the US, their secondment to India, and Lola's giving up her job (she was in the pharmaceutical industry) to follow Dipankar to Mumbai.

Was it an Asian Woman syndrome then, I wondered, *qualified career women giving it all up to become trailing spouses?*

But Lola didn't seem put out by this. She talked of all the things I could do while in Mumbai – the local travel, the shops to frequent, the classes to attend (from Bollywood dance to databasing). 'You can even join Indian cooking classes, you know,' Lola smiled, enjoying her newfound role as my benevolent guide to life in Mumbai. So even cooking was not something to be learned in Mum's kitchen anymore, but to be done as a weekly social encounter with well-coiffed ladies, instructing their maids to stir the ingredients just so, under the guidance of some celeb pot-stirring expert.

Lola said, 'I am thinking of starting a tapas bar here. Then again, I could open an art gallery.'

I laughed, wrinkling my brow in confusion. She wasn't for real, I thought, as she continued, 'Or, even a Comedy Club. Probably an ad company to make corporate videos would be a great idea too.'

'Yes, well, that's so India, isn't it?' I said.

'Opportunities everywhere. You just have to pick the one you want,' Lola smiled and then asked, 'What do you plan to do?'

'For now, I am helping my son find somewhere to school. And ourselves somewhere to live.'

But, as with everything else in Mumbai, the apartment I went to check out after lunch was a dud.

Even as the car stopped in front of the peeling greenish building on Cuffe Parade, where Oily Sid, the agent, waited, I knew it would be no good. We walked through a dimly lit lobby, done in a kind of streaky marble that had gone out of fashion in the seventies, then up a rickety elevator playing piped Jingle Bells muzak. (What *is* it about India and its fetish for Jingle Bells?)

Oily Sid continued his monologue on the state of the property market in Mumbai. 'The market is absolutely booming, Madamji. Why, yesterday only I am taking NRI couple for property purchase meeting and realizing they had to go back to Dubai the next day, the builder is increasing his total by a crore.'

I gave the slightest snort. No wonder I couldn't find a decent house even with my super-sized expat budget. I was competing with these sheikh-sheikhina type Dubai-based owners, who had all been spoon-fed *Rich Dad Poor Dad* concepts with their gripe water, and were making their investments work hard by eking out extortionist rents that made Manhattan rents seem absolute value for money.

There must be more real-estate millionaires in South Mumbai than in all of the US Mid-West combined! Though what those millionaires got in lieu of their millions would make Cabrini-Green dwellers feel privileged. Buildings that sprouted mildew, eccentric plumbing that worked at will, dark, greasy kitchens, and scenic views of the neighbours' weekly wash hung out to dry over moisture-streaked walls and rusted iron grills.

We reached the ninth floor. Oily Sid led me through a dim hallway and a dark wood door. Inside was a View: Marine Drive lay stretched in afternoon stupor, and the greyish water of the bay looked as if it had sprung out of Middle Earth. But standing closer to the window, the unlovely melodrama of slum life in the Koli colony down below urgently brought India back. I shuddered, not being able to imagine myself living there. It was time to reassess.

'This is not what I want, Sid. In fact, none of the apartments you have shown me so far will do.'

'Then you have to up the budget, Madamji.' Oily Sid smiled ingratiatingly.

There went all my visions of cheaper living and higher savings in India! It seemed nothing less than a three million-dollar apartment in South Mumbai was halfway decent. But one had to live in the present. I said recklessly, 'Increase the budget, by all means.'

I would have to tell Raj, of course. But what *could* Raj say? After all, having forced me to come all this way to Mumbai, he simply couldn't expect me to live in a dump for the next few years!

❧three

'Oh tell me, tell me, that you'll help me?' Rimli, my childhood friend said, her eager face offering no clues about what she meant.

My mother – who had been calling from Bareilly every hour, on the hour, for the last two weeks since our arrival in Mumbai, hungry for updates on my daily battle with the city – had given her my number, hoping an old friend in a new city would cheer me up. And so now here I was, having lunch with her at a restaurant in Phoenix Mills.

Listening to Rimli plead like an excited eleven-year-old, I braced myself. Another one of her harebrained schemes? Rimli was quite famous for those back when we were pigtailed comrades in mayhem. Though we were meeting up after fourteen years, she looked every bit as weird as she did back then – in an edgily cut purple tunic with a shocking pink strand in her otherwise black bob. I broke an edge of a crisp dosa. 'Of course, but what help do you need?'

'It's for my first solo show in Mumbai!' Rimli chirruped in a high voice, and her blunt, ala Catherine Zeta Jones in *Chicago*, shook as she spoke. After quickly dispensing with my life – ('So, tell me na, about life in

DC, Tara. And, your husband, Raj. I remember all the aunties oohing and fluttering their pallus and getting all giggly at your wedding at the sight of him. How does he look *now* – has his hair fallen out yet?') – we got around to discussing hers.

Rimli was an artist. She had moved to Mumbai last year after studying art in Baroda and working a short stint in Delhi. She had not changed much – she was still voluble and volatile. But all our eager talk could not mask the yawning separateness of our lives; a decade of traversing different paths in different countries and chasing different careers. I knew next to nothing about her dreams and struggles – or even her art style. All I had was a fragment of hand-me-down gossip from my mother, about a broken engagement, six years ago.

'It's been a struggle, Tara,' Rimli confessed. 'I did not want to take any help from Mom and Dad.' Her parents were well-known surgeons back home, the same as mine. 'There were months on end when I could barely pay for the food and rent, but at least I had my art.'

Not enough food? I stared at her, aghast. My life was *so* cushy in comparison! Even now, as I whined about being in Mumbai, I could barely hide the facts: that I was living in a five-star serviced luxury suite, struggling to find a multimillion-dollar apartment. While this poor girl was fashioning a career in art from a shared one-bedroom sublet in some reeking, rat-infested suburban back alley.

'I've had several group shows and two solos, all in Delhi. That's why this solo show in Mumbai means so much to me.' Rimli looked quite undaunted, full of earnest resolve.

I looked at her quizzically. 'But what help do you need for this show, Rimli?'

'Look, it's just an idea! A friend who is a newspaper art critic is helping me with the show catalogue. But maybe you could write for it too. You love art – I know you've bought your share in the US – and you always have a lot to say.' She shrugged. 'Look, tell you what, there is this Legends of India art show tomorrow. I'm not going but I can give you my invite. Why don't you and Raj attend? It will give you some idea of the Indian art scene.'

I looked at Rimli sceptically. I had told her that I was interested in contemporary Indian art. I had bought many paintings too. But no major museum-quality pieces, really, apart from the Chitrita Goswami. I thought of my friends back in Washington who bought paintings from Sotheby's and Christie's auctions all the time. Now those guys were the real naffy art collectors! 'I'm not sure, Rimli, if I count as a serious collector from the US.'

'Oh, don't be silly. I don't need some million-dollar collector to back me up,' Rimli scoffed. 'Just write anything, talk about how the idea of art collecting is gaining momentum among young Indians overseas. The art market is expanding at all levels, not just the top-end, that sort of stuff.'

I grinned at her, and agreed. 'So what's your style, Rimli?' I asked. 'Is it abstracts? Do you do oils or acrylics?'

Rimli looked at me in a pained sort of way. 'Didn't I tell you I do sculpture?'

The diner had filled up with well-endowed ladies in fancy salwar suits, gold bangles and streaked hair – a kitty-party brigade. We decided to escape and explore the shops. After a quick peek at a large supermarket where harried housewives were queuing up behind dhoti-clad shoppers pushing unwieldy trolleys laden with twenty-five kilos of onions towards the two meagre checkout counters, we opted to go to the couturiers instead. Once there, I glanced lustfully at the beautifully detailed handmade finish of the clothes on display. Discreetly I scanned a lovely Surily Goel churidar set in peach for the price tag. It was several hundred dollars and I would probably wear it once or twice. I went through the entire rack, checking inside each neckline for the price tag. They were all up there in the stratosphere.

'People usually come here in the monsoon sales,' Rimli said, sensing my dismay at the prices.

I looked at the counter. A plump woman was fishing out a Gold credit card from her extra-large Louis Vuitton bag, while a shop assistant packed some half a dozen chiffon creations, carefully wrapping each in self-embossed tissue paper, and slipping a silver ribbon around each bag.

The monsoon was many, many months away. Plus Raj, I thought, could very well afford these dresses, even at the regular price. So, I picked up the peach churidar set without a second thought. Then, with my own gift-wrapped outfit lovingly placed inside a handmade paper box, I left the shop.

The next evening, clutching Rimli's invite, I decided to attend the Legends of India art show she had recommended.

My car swung into a derelict-looking mill compound somewhere in central Mumbai. 'We here, Madam,' the white-uniformed rental company driver announced and stepped out to ceremonially open the back door of the battered silver Honda.

We were outside an imposing old door of crumbling wood and wrought iron, ornate against the fading limewash on the wall. Oblivious to the pile of broken bricks and assorted dirt and dry leaves that lined the short path to the door, a chic couple alighted from a silver Mercedes ahead. The area around could have passed for the site of a recent bomb blast, the kind shown on television. Or a rubbish dump. Red dust and rubble mingled with plastic wrappers, dog excrement and crumpled condoms.

Why would anyone host an art exhibition *here*?

It had been an interminably long ride from Taj Wellington Mews. Two weeks in India, still jetlagged and without bearings, I had insisted on attending this art show that Rimli had sent her invite for. But Raj had demurred claiming work. So I had cobbled together an outfit from the limited selection in my suitcase – the rest of my clothes were still in storage – and stormed out without him. Thankfully, Cara, my imported-for-the-month nanny was still around and I could leave Ro with her without much fuss.

Before I'd alighted, a few minutes before the car had drawn up, I'd pulled out my compact, dying to check my makeup in the tiny mirror. But a decade without servants and drivers and I had forgotten how to ignore their presence. Instead, only too conscious of the coconut-scented gaze of the driver in the rear-view mirror, I'd put the compact back inside my bag. Now I fumbled to adjust my stole around the décolleté of my fitted and flared dress. Then deliberately letting my eyes go out of focus, I stumbled out of the car.

It was depressingly hot outside, especially after the pre-spring freeze in Washington DC. Looking at the wall of the building up close, I realized the peeled look was deliberate. A dull teal top coat had been scratched to reveal a mottled layer of ultramarine underneath. A liveried and red-turbaned usher stood upon a threadbare patch of red carpet and opened the door for me.

I stepped inside.

Wow!

It was like being transported into another world: a thousand diyas floating in wide bronze containers. Tall bamboos and cycads in enormous planters with tiny up-lights casting shadows on the walls around. Mumbai's gorgeous milling about, admiring the entrance space, talking to each other, strutting their stuff. I noticed an inscription on the wall, a carmine seepage of ornate script on aqua. *'The temporal perspective of contemporary art in India is a lucid stylization of complexity and sophistication, free of colonial hangover and manifest with philosophical, theological, sociological and scientific concepts.'* The quotation was attributed to a Lillian S. Cole. I goggled. It was like being accosted by *The Economist* inside the covers of *Hello!* magazine.

It was hard to imagine a shy and scruffy artist behind the type of art this Lillian woman was raving about. But then, with art prices being what they were, perhaps Indian artists didn't need to be scruffy and shy anymore?

There was more jargon on the opposite wall. I walked towards it: *'A repeated insistence on eclecticism and the collusion of hybridization and imitation within the postmodern can serve to elide the stagnancy of image, provide a diachronic sense of Choate multiculturalism and thus ease the edge of historical choice.'* The words were attributed to Latika Khanna, art historian.

My eyes were still dollishly glazed when I felt a firm hand on my shoulder.

Looking tall and trim in a charcoal suit and smelling as if he had spilled a whole bottle of Ralph Lauren Pour Homme on himself, Raj handed me a glass of champagne. He had been waiting for me in the foyer. Obviously, he was trying to make up with me. But I was still mad at him. I was going to be mad at him for the rest of my life. I was prepared to make concessions, however, to be overtly polite – we *were* standing in a public place, after all – and stiffly took his proffered arm. 'Let's go.' He propelled me forward, a shuttered look coming down on his face as he sensed my continued animosity.

He's brought it upon himself, I thought as we rode up arm in arm (polite smiles pasted on our faces), in a manned, wood-panelled elevator, to the buzz one level up, where the Legends of India art show was being exhibited.

More than the art on the walls, the hall was a lavish assortment of glittering ornaments and designer handbags! It would seem the entire handbag selection at Saks in Tysons Galleria had flown across the globe to dangle from the diamond-laden wrists in this hall in Mumbai. No matter that the unsubtly logo-ed baguettes and clutches and totes completely didn't match the colour and style of the accompanying dresses. The bling factor was dangerously high in Mumbai, higher even than found at the annual Ball hosted by Raj's investment banking firm. And the dresses! I had somehow imagined a sea of saris. Instead, in the spectacular Technicolor hues typically expected of India, glittering with beads, sequins, gold threads and Swarovski crystal, were an assortment of spaghetti strap chiffon tops and silk bustiers, short skirts and low-rise denim that would look totally in place on Miami Beach, and were worn with serious panache here. A sari was to be spotted here and there, but the minuscule blouses on the toned and curvaceous torsos – even with their sheer overlay of embroidered chiffon, the current rage – were definitely more *Sex and the City* than *Mother India*.

And to think I had worried about the demurely plunging neckline of my dress!

We wove through the press of prince coats and torso-hugging tees, ducking the kisses and waves of manicured hands as Mumbai art mavens greeted one another, and squeezed through the general commotion of paparazzi flashes and television camera lights that focused more on the celebrity attendees than the prized displays on the walls.

I moved up with Raj as he headed towards the hostess-of-the evening, glittering in a floor-length crystal-studded dress. Her husband – the consort-of-the-evening – was lit up too, with solitaires in his ears, a flashy bracelet of fire that shone every time he shook hands, and a slim row of crystal beads embroidered along the neckline of his suave bandhgala suit. But it was the chief-guest-for-the-evening, a Cabinet minister's wife, who must have single-handedly made the fortunes of many a Zaveri Bazaar jeweller. She moved about, shaking hands and exchanging hellos, resplendent in a bisque Kanjeevaram sari which perfectly set off the plump diamond and emerald choker that pushed out through the fat rolls on her neck. The Queen of England, rigged out in all the booty from the Tower, would have dulled in comparison.

I blinked, blinded by the twinkling trio, and muttered a congratulatory word about the successful exhibition. I still had to see a lot of the artwork so I turned to Raj hoping to hurry him on and was momentarily struck by my husband's lithe, groomed, good looks, more evident than ever when all the men around him were bulging at the midriff and had shamelessly pasted their thinning hair across their scalps. *But he is a selfish moron*, a voice thundered inside me. I turned away.

While Raj lingered, exchanging pleasantries, I moved away from the blaze of that inner orbit, into the coolness of the camera-free zone, to circle the rooms and anterooms and admire the drama, tension and texture of colours and strokes. I spied a particularly striking canvas. Reds and ambers luridly transposed, like the spillage of corpses and corpuscles in a Bond flick.

I snaked closer to the walls.

After centuries of perfecting the two-dimensional beauty and controlled emotions of miniature painting, the Indian art scene had exploded with bold experimentation and a latent passion – the confluence of Indian sensibilities with the techniques of the West. The global dispersion of people and ideas that had begun in the previous century had left their mark on the Indian art scene. Now, more than a half-century later, in art salons and studios from Mumbai to Paris to Rio, Indian artists were livening canvases with imagery and abstraction, dripping and knifing and brushing a riotous palette of experiences and influences, all thrown into further frenzy by the escalating demand for Indian artwork among collectors in India and amid the NRI diaspora.

Raj found me in the crowd, only to stop again to greet another business acquaintance. As the men chatted about stock ratings, mutual fund inclusions and private equity ventures, I slipped away towards a canvas that reminded me of Gauguin in his Polynesian phase, all pouting brown-skinned women and heaving bosoms.

'So banal, isn't it,' said an intellectual-looking woman in pink-rimmed glasses to no one in particular as she moved on. I moved on too, past a gorgeous female artist gushing to a reporter from behind the half veil of her super-straight hair, 'It was like, omigod, so exciting to be included in this show... modelling is fun but this is, like, where my soul is...' she shifted on her impossibly long denim-clad legs. Her painting was a subtly boring creation in beige.

Further on, a small crowd stood in front of a Jogen Chowdhury painting, its textured tones bright, like a swirling galactic spread against an inky eternity. Taking a peek above the bald and balding heads, I squinted at the price, trying to decipher the long string of zeroes and mentally recalculating the figure in dollars. *Wow!* It sure was worth a stash!

Next to it hung an austere Ganesh Pyne sketch: dark, detailed and expensively not feted.

In an alcove between that room and the next, a frail, elegant lady in a chiffon sari was perhaps explaining her canvas to two glamorous smoky-eyed society ladies of an uncertain age. There was enough kohl between the two glamazons to make a five by five foot charcoal sketch. I gasped as I recognized the woman.

Chitrita Goswami. One of my favourite artists! Her painting was a centrepiece in my living room in Washington. I had bought her work from Jehangir Art Gallery. Then, she had been an upcoming artist, and Raj and I had been young purchasers, trying to look like knowledgeable genuine buyers.

I walked up to her, but the talk was not of art. 'So sorry to hear of your son's death,' one of the glamazons was saying insincerely as a look of infinite sadness descended on the pale features of Chitrita's face.

I decided it was best not to intrude.

*

There you are, Tara,' Raj said with only the slightest hint of frost in his voice, as I was moving towards a Lalu Prasad Shaw canvas. 'Meet Dipankar. Lola, you've already met,' he waved towards my new friend from a week ago. 'They came to Mumbai three years ago, from New York.'

Tall and stooping, Lola's husband Dipankar stooped even lower to shake my hand. 'I hear from Lola that you studied economics in London. So did I. You must join the alumni group in town,' he said.

I beamed at Dipankar. London was one of my best-loved memories. It was before I had moved across the Atlantic to a high-pressure job dealing with heavy-duty financial analytics, before I had met Raj and fallen in love. 'I would love to.'

'Raj tells me you used to work with the World Bank earlier, and then in equity research.' Dipankar sounded impressed. 'We are always on the lookout for talented people. You must call me when you are ready to start working here.'

I smiled gratefully at him. I may have lost my Geography, but not my History. Someone recognized my past credentials. Someone still considered me a good hire.

'Stop tormenting the poor girl, Dipankar... she has just landed,' Lola interrupted. 'He is always trying to poach everyone he meets,' she said turning to me. Then she smiled. 'Forget the tapas bar, darling, I think I want to start my own art gallery! Have you bought anything yet? I have put red dots on five paintings already.' She explained the red-dot system where potential buyers expressed an interest in a piece of art and the organizers put a red dot on the item to indicate 'potentially sold'.

'I hope these paintings have all been authenticated,' I said sagely. 'I heard there have been some forgeries of Indian art recently.'

I thought of the news clipping in the in-flight magazine. There had been a couple of highly-publicized discoveries recently, erupting from inside the cloak of respectability and sending an electric shock along the global arc of the desi art grapevine. A signal of market maturity, said the critics. The gold rush of art, the financial papers claimed.

Lola shrugged dismissively. 'Oh, don't be silly. This is one of the most prestigious art shows in the country. I am sure they have a mechanism for vetting each painting. Plus, forgeries of Indian art are not as common as the newspapers make them out to be.'

Dipankar started talking with Raj about the pre-IPO valuations of preferred class-A stock of one of the companies he was currently promoting, and Raj responded with the pompous acuity of an Emerging Markets Fund promoter. Well, sort of. His salary represented the top-line item in the expense sheet of Ellerman Jones' India operations, but to hear him talk of it all, it would seem *he* was their top-line item.

Leaving Raj and Dipankar to chat, Lola and I moved on to look at the paintings: 'This is so grandly orchestrated, Lola. Such amazing prices, too. I remember the first art show I went to in DC, just six years ago. It was a different world then.'

It *had* been a different world, indeed. An innocent time, when well-put-together chiffon-and-pearls type aunties from Defence Colony in Delhi sourced art work from the subcontinent to display in Georgetown townhouses on visits to their US-based children. Young desi professionals like us went to them for our first lessons in art appreciation. Prices had been just about affordable. Raj and I, newly married after a year's whirlwind romance, had joined these shindigs and made our first art purchases together.

Success needs its own shehnai, and back then, in the US, it had included owning a large Husain oil, along with a mansion in Georgetown, a boat moored at Annapolis and children enrolled in National Cathedral. Even those still clawing their way up the NRI success ladder could afford a smallish Husain line drawing. Not of the seventies or sixties vintage, mind you. Not a serigraph either. Just a modern day doodle, of the type Husain twirled on a paper napkin, waiting for dinner. Enough to name drop. I had one of those Husain line drawings in my collection too – a small piece, the broken torso of a horse etched in a few strokes of graphite, duly framed in thick white matting and a broad black frame. Now, of course, exhibits of Indian art dotted the Manhattan–DC–Los Angeles–San Francisco landscape in closed packed structure, like transistors on a microchip. Auction houses focusing solely on Indian art did brisk global business, and art had its own Index. And the prices! By some estimates, art prices had grown at rates double that of the Sensex!

'By the way, I just saw Chitrita,' I said, suddenly remembering my glimpse of the famous artist.

'She is having a solo show in autumn. Do you know she has cancer? Terminal stage,' Lola whispered. 'And her son, who had Down's Syndrome, died last year. Imagine.'

I turned back to where Chitrita stood, elegant in a printed chiffon sari and cropped white hair. Chemo! I remembered her long hair had been in a stylish bun when I had first seen a photograph of hers, years ago.

I bade goodbye to Lola and wandered off alone, in search of a mauve or purple or lilac hued canvas to go with the planned décor of my would-be den. But an architectural composition in oil and torn paper and photographs accosted me – nowhere close to the colour purple, in fact as bleached of colour as possible, by an artist I hadn't heard of before. I liked it anyway. It was experimental, with that *diachronic* edge Latika Khanna had crowed about. Like something I might find in a tiny gallery in Soho! The price was gorgeous too – just above two thousand dollars. I was still thinking in dollars, and I had a collection to build. Couldn't let any opportunity pass, could I? So I sought the floor salesman to put a red dot against it.

'If you are the highest bidder for this Bhola Prasad painting, Madam, you will get it in two weeks,' the salesman told me.

'A good choice.' I turned around to see a tallish man with a dark European complexion in a black suit accented by a Paul Smith-type bright stripy shirt, a yellow silk tie patterned with elephants and a matching yellow pocket kerchief. Who but a middle-class Indian bridegroom in an in-laws-sponsored suit ever tucked a silk handkerchief in his breast pocket, I thought. What was this style, Indian motif meets gay-Brit fashion?

He introduced himself as Roy Jordan, an art auctioneer and dealer from the UK. Wasn't he the man who had been quoted in that article on Indian art in the airline magazine? My eyes studied his face for a brief second – his eyes were the deep blue of bottomless lochs in summer. He caught the look, cocking an eyebrow in this Daniel Craig way.

Disgruntled, I turned to focus on his tie, at about the same time he waved to summon one of the wine waiters milling around. 'You can't talk art without a glass of wine. It's sacrilege,' Roy said, smoothly taking the empty champagne glass from my hand and replacing it with another.

I took a large sip of bubbly, happy to finger the coolness of the glass in the heat and throng of the room.

'So tell me,' Roy asked conspiratorially, a little dimple on one cheek adding a devilish charm to his striking persona, 'do you understand all this?'

'Not in a "distilled essence of occidental inspired ethnic multiplicity" sense,' I said, and was gratified by his smile. 'But I do love art and I know what I appreciate from afar and what I would like for my own collection.'

'What painters do you collect?' He leaned back to look at me appraisingly.

I mentioned a handful of artists, wondering what he would think of both my taste and my budget. So without stopping to wait for his response, I questioned him about his background. I was as curious about auctioneering as a teenager about the Kama Sutra. Illicit pleasures or preposterous careers – anything with the touch of the forbidden held a certain kick of enchantment. It was the first time I was meeting an auctioneer socially. It seemed a floaty sort of career, indulged on endowment money bequeathed by grandparents. Personally, I just knew the straight types – bankers, doctors, engineers, lawyers, managers; still in the aspirant category.

'Which auction house are you with?' I asked Roy.

'I am independent now, Tara. But I spent my grounding years with one of the charm brigade hammer smiths.'

Charm brigade? What was that, big or boutique? I cocked my head. 'Do you handle Indian art?'

'I started with British antique books and curios. Then, interestingly I got hold of an old cap and jacket of Polly Umrigar, the legendary Indian cricketer. Do you remember him?'

I jogged my limited knowledge of Indian cricket in the pre-Gavaskar days. I didn't recall ever hearing of Umrigar. But I nodded intelligently, as he spoke about auctioning Umrigar's cap in London, thus launching a sports memorabilia speciality. He talked of caps and bats, batons and balls, and players like Peter May, George Headley, and Len Hutton, sports legends of their time, but names that a cricket-challenged idiot like me would never have heard. Nonetheless, it was an interesting story.

'From there I moved onto coins. I've just recently got interested in Indian art. I came to India five years ago to trace my roots – my mother was Anglo-Indian, you know. I was born in Lonavala but my parents moved back to England when I was three. I source Indian art for clients around the world,' he confessed. 'In fact, I am here to set up my own auction house, focusing on Indian art but mainly for western buyers.'

'Wow!' I exclaimed. 'Quite some competition you will have though! Sotheby's is in the space now, as is Christie's. Osian's and Saffronart, the Indian auction houses, are quite big. Between them, they have got quite a foothold in the market.'

Roy did a smug half-bow, winked and said, 'There's room for more, sweetheart. Plus, I am not aiming for one of those "of the Indians, for the Indians, by the Indians" art ventures. I want to foster serious dialogue across the India–West divide, give serious overseas collectors exposure to the Indian scene. Anyway, my line is more in antique and rare pieces. I'll find a niche there.'

'How interesting...'

I was about to ask him about the Sher-Gil painting he had commented upon in the magazine, when Raj suddenly appeared. He put an arm around my shoulder, in that silly proprietary way guys do to stake their claim, and I stiffened instantly.

'Darling, a friend wants to meet you. Let's go say hello.' It was the longest sentence he had uttered to me in a week. Then as quickly as he had appeared, Raj disappeared, leaving me to wrap up my conversation and follow him.

I said my adieus and Roy took down my mobile number. 'Maybe we can catch up some other time,' he flashed a big crinkle-eyed smile, punctuated by those deep dimples. 'After all, to set up my auction house, I'll need a rich patroness.'

God, I groaned inwardly. Was nobody subtle anymore? But a giggle escaped me. I was a new convert – from career wonkie to fluffball. I did not mind the mild flirtation. I could even enjoy this, I thought. 'I don't know about being a rich patroness,' I said, 'but it'd be lovely to see your collection!'

*four

Maddy called the next morning. She had used her connections to get me an appointment with the principal of her daughter's school later in the day.

It was past nine and Raj had already left – an early meeting, he had mumbled on his way out. I made a string of calls on Raj's mobile, but he did not pick up. When he finally answered, I was already seething, only to get even more livid when he claimed urgent meetings with a client delegation from Belgium. 'But it's a school admission interview, Raj. This is important,' I said through gritted teeth.

'You handle it. In any case, I can't come.'

I switched off the phone, not even bothering to reply. To say that I was fuming would be an understatement.

Nonetheless, at the appointed mid-morning hour, I stood outside the crumbling Art Deco mansion that housed École Nouvelle. It was a monstrosity, complete with a round cupola and carved pillars and years of grime anointing its dilapidated exterior. Jasmine grew on top of the peeling plaster and weeds erupted from every crack, creating a lace of shoots on the wall. Past the sentry at the door, I was led into the inner office from where the school principal, Ms Reynolds, a regular Pol Pot of Scottish origin, managed her campaign of parent massacre. She was in India, Maddy had told me, on a short term assignment from Scotland.

Ms Reynolds inhabited a large sunny office. Behind her desk, glass French doors led to the piece de resistance of this school – a grassy enclave, hemmed in by rickety buildings on three sides. There was a coloured climbing frame on one end, a football net on the other. A school with a yard in South Mumbai was about as rare and endangered as the Ganges River Dolphin in the foetid waters of the holy river.

Ms Reynolds' tone, as she spoke to me, was starchy enough to stiffen a nine-yard cotton sari. 'So Mrs Malhotra, you will be happy to know I can give your boy a seat. There is a seat available in August.'

August? That was four months away. What would my poor boy do till then? More importantly what would *I* do until then? If I had to spend one more day watching Playhouse Disney with Rohan, I would pull my hair out. But August was the best offer Ms Reynolds had.

My blood pressure rose instantly! But would it really help if I burst my aorta and collapsed face down on Ms Reynolds' desk across her obsessive-compulsively arranged paperwork? No, I told myself. Calmness was the creed of the moment. I remembered the friendly advice of my current self-help reading material, a little book with heavy words called *Don't Sweat the Small Stuff.* Silently, I counted to ten, decided to 'Choose my Battles Wisely' and put on a sugar-sweet smile to tell her about how bright Rohan was and how he would *love* to be at École Nouvelle.

Stepping outside, an overdose of Dior *Poison* assailed me. I turned to see Maddy sweep down the stairs in a lovely noodle-strap top and a tiered skirt in some swishy material embroidered with lots of mirrors. Definitely designer.

'How did it go, Tara?' Maddy crooned like Celine Dion with a sore throat. 'Any luck?'

I wrung my hands hopelessly: 'No vacancies till August.'

'Well, then you have lots of time for lunch,' Maddy smiled and whisked me off to her club where she was meeting her friends. It might distract me from all these school worries, I thought. Or perhaps someone might have a solution to my school woes. So I went off with Maddy, instructing my driver to follow her car.

Maddy signed me in as a guest, and we proceeded past the croton pots and tumbling arrays of pink and orange bougainvillea to the Club House. As we climbed up the stairs to the veranda overlooking the turquoise of the big pool, observing the toned bods spread-eagled in salute to the mid-day sun, the gaggle of diamante-encrusted shades in mauve and amber, and the assortment of cleavages peek-a-booing from tankinis and kurtis, I was certain of one thing:

This was *not* the India I had grown up in.

We joined some ladies sitting at a long table, and after brief introductions, the conversation settled down to the new Robbie Williams and Avril Lavigne releases and *Desperate Housewives* tapes, holiday plans in Amalfitana and the latest kurtis on sale in Neemrana. Beyond the emerald lawns, the Arabian Sea stretched endlessly, briefly bordered by a ragtag row of white buildings on one side, till the buildings grew greyer and fainter and were finally swallowed by the distant smoggy translucence where the sea melded with the sky.

'Let's do Maldives next month, girls, a moms' weekend away,' a plump woman said. 'I have a friend at the Sonesca resort there – I can get a discount on the water bungalows. Massages, manicures, mambo on the beach! Mmmm.'

'Oh that sounds gorgeous!' Maddy shrieked.

'What about the kids?' I croaked, obviously out of my depth. Mom's night outs, I loved. I had been away on many business trips myself. Who would complain about the downy comforts of room service and video-on-demand after a hard day's work, instead of going home to wipe nappy poo and loading the dishwasher? But a ladies' pleasure trip?

Maddy shrugged her shoulders, eyeing me suspiciously. 'Maids...?' she said, and that one word sufficed in highlighting my unsettled reality. It was one more thing to sort.

'Have you found a place to stay yet?' asked a large woman called Rose, in a heavy Brit accent. Then Rose started to tell me about her last six years in India. I was struck by her similarity to the sari-and-sneaker type aunties I knew back in the US. At how little they both had assimilated into the country they lived in, sometimes even after decades of living there. How very different from my generation that had studied and worked and assimilated with such ease. Rose, after six years in India, had not acclimatized to anything Indian. Except, maybe, her maids.

A woman who introduced herself as June passed me a slim glossy pamphlet about a school she ran for slum children.

'I don't know how you can go into those rat-infested alleys, June,' Rose shuddered. 'I used to work for a kid's NGO in the UK. I simply can't do it here.'

June sipped her coconut water and smiled, 'Someone's got to do it. There is a lot that needs to be done.'

June told me she had been a lawyer in a big Boston firm once. On a chance off-site retreat in the Adirondacks, she had fallen in love with the hotel manager. Only, he had turned out to be the scion of an Indian hotel chain business family, slumming there for the quintessential New England work experience before returning to his home and hearth. June had chucked her budding legal career and flown eastwards with him. 'I love it here,' June said, her clear grey eyes bright and positive. She was quite lovely in a downy way, all shorn fair hair and long limbs. What charmed me more was the earthiness of her mien, the way she connected with her environment and empathized with the unfortunates.

'How are you coping?' June asked me. 'It is a hard location, but my Indian friends seem to have more trouble settling in here than us.'

Us? As in 'us whites' as opposed to 'us browns'? What about 'us pseudo-whites' with our non-desi pretensions, our 'I'm-from-abroad' airs, our posh foreign degrees and our fancy work experience? How were we to deal with the overdose of melanin that pigmented our skin? Where did *we* fit in?

If I was an NRI in the US, holding on to a tiny fraction of India, tinier than the generations of immigrants before me, then in Mumbai I became someone else, a DCBA, a Desi Clueless Back from America, desperately clutching the arc of newly-adopted Americanism, asking identity questions in the country of my birth.

I cancelled the plan to see more apartments for the day. Then finding an unexpected afternoon free, I rushed back to Wellington Mews, to play with Rohan and watch cartoon reruns on the big plasma screen. We must have fallen asleep watching TV, because I woke up with a start, when my mobile phone rang, to see Rohan sprawled on the carpet between an empty pizza box and Cola Cola bottles.

'Hello?' I mumbled into the phone, massaging the crick in my neck.

'Beta! How is it going?' It was Mom, sounding all too fresh on the phone. I looked at the clock. It was past ten. She must have just come back from evening surgery. 'Have you found a place? You didn't call for the last two days, so I thought I would find out. When are you coming to visit us?'

The thing about my hometown Bareilly is that not many people had heard of it till Priyanka Chopra happened to get herself crowned Miss World. But people who know the city can appreciate how interested its inhabitants are in each other's lives. So a party at home and meeting all of Mom-Dad's friends would also mean listening to their take on the significance of my return to India, hearing the news of their sons and daughters becoming Vice Presidents for Microsoft, General Managers for American Express, Neuro-Surgeons or Space Scientists, located everywhere from Arkansas to Washington, and answering questions about why I had left my fabulous job in America, with its two-inch title, and how I planned to tackle my unemployed status.

I wasn't sure if I was ready for it; I stalled: 'Let me get settled down first, Mom.'

Then Mom asked after Raj, her voice softening instantly. Truth is, my mother is a desi feminist, the sort who totally espouses the 'earn-your-income-but-fast-for-your-husband' philosophy. She has the biggest soft corner for my husband and is always admonishing me to do right by him. 'And...' Mom started again, a little hesitant this time, 'I was thinking... now that Rohan is almost five, have you thought of the second one? You are thirty-two already...'

This was rich, coming from a lady who had only one child herself because she was so busy with her career! Had I not done my duty by producing a child well before hitting the thirty mark? Abruptly, I claimed sleepiness and put the phone down.

It was only after I put Rohan to bed and glanced at the bedside clock, that I realized it was past 11pm. Raj was not yet back from work, and he had not even called.

I thought glumly of the days ahead. No new apartments to see, no other schools left to contact. I must create new choices. But I was exhausted already. It was not a huffing and puffing, heart-sinking, limbs-flailing kind of exhaustion. This was all mental. I could not read, could not even *look* at, another self-help book. The last one I had started, a big thick volume called *Romancing the Ordinary* talked of baking fresh bread to connect with the magic of the ordinary. But what *was* ordinary? There was a ground shift in my life and everything ordinary had changed places with the extraordinary. Time sat heavily on my hands. No chores, no spring mulching, no commuting to office, no spinning deadlines. Instead the days yawned, mumbling options of spas and shops, making me feel lethargic.

Then, there was the emotional vacuum.

Was it just a few weeks ago that Raj and I had been friends, discussing everything from office politics to international politics, sharing glances over our child's head and waiting for a sizzling moment alone?

Raj, ah Raj! Seven short years ago, at a noisy Friday evening party in Foggy Bottom, our eyes had first connected across a roomful of people! And a sudden incandescence, still so vibrant in my mind, had lit up the moment...

The party had been hosted by a friend I had recently met at one of those NetSAP events where newbie South Asians congregate to meet others of their ilk. Newly minted from the London School of Economics I had transplanted myself across the Atlantic to join the junior ranks at the World Bank. So there I was, in a navy silk halter dress, learning to mix peach martinis, and listening to the internet jokes doing the rounds among a group of preppy VC types. It was the turn of the millennium, excitement shimmered in the air, the markets were a thrilling joyride offering the confidence of promising tomorrows.

I'd looked up on a sudden impulse and seen a tall trim guy enter the room, dapper in a buttery soft Nappa leather bomber jacket and black jeans, his strong jaw hinting at utter confidence. He had walked across the room, holding my gaze for an instant, and then stopped midway to join another group, curious eyes darting towards me once more, before looking away. I had responded by airily walking over to a group where some Indian-American lawyer turned political aide was holding forth on Bibi's polemic policies and the rise of Ehud Barak.

I had felt his gaze upon me, time and again, all evening as I moved to different clusters, introducing myself, joining in on conversations about Capitol Hill, the destabilization of the Baht, transport woes on the Autobahn, the best towns to rent a villa near Sienna, and the latest Pedro Almodovar film.

An hour, two martinis and one pepper tequila shot later, I gave up pretending to ignore him and walked up to him.

'...7000 animated creatures in that amazing ground battle scene,' he was saying.

'Do you know the animators spent two years on just Jar Jar Binks,' an eager buck-toothed bloke responded.

Jeez. Episode I! Typical guy-glee over some computer-animated creatures.

'Too much focus on animation, not enough on characterization,' I said, shamelessly butting in. They all turned around to stare at me. But I looked straight at the tall trim guy and extended my hand, ignoring the rest of them.

'Hi, I'm Tara.'

He smiled. 'I'm Raj. So Tara, what do you do when you aren't mixing martinis or beating up a poor guy for liking animation?'

Soon the rest of the crowd dispersed and only Raj and I were left, chatting about life in DC and, between bites, divulging details about ourselves to each other. But even more than his words, I was checking him out, very aware of him, the sharp angles of his cheeks, the soft side-twist of his smile, the slightest softening of his eyes as he smiled, and of myself, of the rise and fall of every shallow breath I took; that faint tingle along my spine. Raj told me about his undergrad days in Maryland on a squash scholarship, his time in Wharton and his role at Ellerman Jones, the pressure of managing some tens of millions with Emerging Markets exposure given the constant winds of changing fortunes in international markets, from tumbles in Asia right when he had graduated from B-school to Real-whipping in Brazil now. I told him about myself, my family, my education in Delhi and London.

After that we had met again in group outings – dinners in Asian fusion eateries in Dupont Circle; foreign films in Georgetown; art stops in Sackler and Freer; beery laughs in comedy clubs off Connecticut; business mixers hosted by TiE. Our glances collided intermittently and our laughs were that extra brittle with awareness. But he was playing it safe, wasn't he?

Then I – literally – ran into him at an utterly boring economic conference in NW, where my boss was speaking un-rivetingly on *Local Dynamic Stability Using Non-Stochastic Hyper-extended LM Framework: The Future of Economic Progress in Botswana*, and I had been up half the night, adding human-interest pictures of Ndebele tribal children and antelopes in the Okavango Delta to a boring slide show about an even more boring macro-economic theorem.

I was running around with the boss's four-pound ugly laptop, hoping there would be no last minute snags connecting it to the projection paraphernalia, when I had turned into another endless carpeted corridor, almost snagged my heel in the red, diamond-pattern double pile and tottered into the person coming from the other side.

'Hey,' Raj had exclaimed softly, using both arms to steady me. 'Tara! Wow, what are you doing here? You okay?'

I had nodded, too rushed to stay and chat, and yet loath to move.

Raj held me a little longer than strictly necessary. 'Meet me after,' he whispered at last, reluctantly letting me go.

As expected, the boss's speech was a colossal bore. The audience, mostly ageing theoreticians, nodded sagely, while the young interns fiddled with their hair or conference papers, in an attempt to ward off sleep. After lunch, while the boss went for a closed-door discussion on World Bank policies in sub-Saharan Africa, I sat in on the Latin American discussion where Raj was speaking on Bovespa stocks and Real futures and emerging market tools. Though the subject matter was not much more scintillating than what my boss had to offer, I was mesmerized. I couldn't take my eyes off Raj – the way he stood at the podium, wide-shouldered, that casual tilt to his head as he looked straight at the audience. I noticed his hands, broad and brown and strong, as they sliced the air, accentuating points. I loved that disarming grin, a side-twist revealing perfect white teeth. By the time he was toasting an imaginary caipirinha to the Brazilian future, I was practically drooling.

We met in the lobby at 4pm and escaped the confines of the decadent Victorian hotel. It was a lovely autumn afternoon outside. We walked towards the Jefferson Memorial. Trees brilliant in the red, orange and gold of autumn hues, reflected in the calm waters of the Tidal Basin. The wind was crisp, and we sat under the trees hugging our suit jackets, chatting about his dreams and mine, his childhood days as an army brat in border towns and Delhi, and mine in small-town India...

'It's awkward with a desi girl,' Raj had confessed suddenly, holding my cold hands in his warm clasp. 'Too much pressure, you know; too much protocol.'

I could only smile. Ruefully! I mean, here was this gorgeous guy I was attracted to, but he felt he had to stand off and follow some mysterious protocol? I had removed my hand from his and grinned, 'Look, Raj – no pressure.'

*

No friends expressed surprise when Raj had proposed to me a few months later; our parents were totally *non-de trop* in their lack of opposition; and within a few months, I had visited India to marry my best friend.

Best Friend! Such a happy phrase for a marriage partner! I changed my job, which involved travels to sub-Saharan Africa in the World Bank, to financial research in a boutique financial advisory firm in NW, and Raj moved up the rungs at Ellerman Jones, rapidly expanding his portfolio.

Raj got his citizenship and, tagged along with him, so did I.

From then on, each little step we took together had been a conscious choice: of blending in or standing out, of going mainstream or reverting to our subculture. The target was clearly visible – an integrated approach to life, an intermingling of ideas and ideals, the pleasures of the melting pot, the dynamic excitement of constant change. It involved those extra steps – going out of our comfort zones, again and again, adapting and recalibrating our accents and our cultural icons, our work behaviour and social networking, eating patterns and talking patterns, holiday destinations and hangout joints.

With none of the usual dilemmas and confusing tugs faced by couples whose parents were in town and country, expecting them to be a certain way or not, we made our own choices, rejecting or accepting what we deemed best, without the need for rebellion or creating a counterpoint to our parents.

Together we travelled around the world, our shopping forays expanding from Banana Republic to Burberry, and my repertoire of cooking evolving from Chhole to Chianti stained pappardelle with porcini and lamb ragù. Contemporary Indian art, a shared new-found love, brought agreement to our usual at-odds natter on politics and fashion.

Soon Rohan toddled into our lives, changing the tilt of our weekends from shops and museums to picnics in the park, grassy concerts in Wolf Trapp or hikes along the Potomac. I had revelled in the potent combination of being in control and being taken care of, happily taking important decisions like which suburb to buy in or which preschool to apply to, and letting Raj fuss over Ro and me.

Six years of love, of experiencing life together.

And now this.

Best Friends! Hah.

My phone rang and I dove across the sofa to pick it up.

'Tara, I'm sorry for calling this late.'

My heart gave an inadvertent lurch as I recognized the voice.

It was Roy. He asked if I had managed to procure the Bhola Prasad painting I had selected at the show.

I had. The show organizers had called just this afternoon inquiring about the method of payment – a banker's cheque I needed to send to their office, and then the painting would arrive within the week.

Roy told me about some other art shows in town: a solo show at Jehangir, that famed art spot, and a group show of women artists, where, I was surprised to learn, Rimli was exhibiting too; she had not mentioned it to me.

'It's been on for a month, and tomorrow is the last day. I was planning to go. Want to come along?' Roy said.

Immediately my dark mood lifted.

'When and where?' I asked. It was something to do, something other than talking about fashion and travel.

Roy mentioned a gallery behind Rhythm House. 'Meet me at Jehangir. Tomorrow at ten. We'll walk over.'

❧five

Outside the Jehangir Art Gallery, despite the fierce midday heat, a curious crowd had gathered around a street painter as he sprinkled coloured sand to create a short-lived masterpiece on the grimy sidewalk. Moving through the crowd I sidestepped him and climbed up the wide staircase, glad for the shade inside.

Raw splashes of colour assailed my senses as I walked into the main hall. Huge canvases hung high and low; furious brushwork in neon tones leaving it all to the imagination. *What was this?* A sinister tropical jungle, full of myth and mystery, hinting of rapacious beasts and predatory birds? What about those bright primary gashes, overpowered by deeper overlays in earth tones?

Thousands of globes of high wattage lit the room, focusing their intense beams on the paintings. The weak cooling system could not cope; it was hotter than Brazil. A lady in white-and-pearls shrieked, 'It's so deep and intense, isn't it?' in a piercing voice. At the far end of the room, a television camera focused on a painting, raising the temperature of the room further. A pretty young TV reporter looked blindly into the camera, and trilled: 'Upcoming artist Vikram Shinde, graduate of

Parsons Schóol in New York, who has already exhibited in Berlin and Perth, is holding his first solo exhibition in India. Reporting for ETV Live, this is Namrata Bhavnani,' into a cordless microphone,

I hurried out of the hall and crossed the lobby to the other side, where a larger hall had been partitioned to display the debut works of three student artists. It was marginally cooler in here, thank God. The white walls were covered with art of varied styles. The first section had a series of runny watercolours. I consulted the little pamphlet. *Metaphorical exploration through colour,* it stated. The next section had half-blurred photographs, close-ups of streetscapes and siestas on sidewalks, their eternal Indian poignancy reduced by a clichéd approach. The last section had some grotesque nudes, males and females, with twisted limbs and spilling intestines. I walked out disappointed, and almost immediately bumped into Roy as he strode in, looking cool in a crisp white linen shirt and jeans.

Roy smiled suavely and led me outside, a short walk along the side road, with the sun beating down upon us through thinly leaved trees. My kurti immediately blotted up and stuck to my sides.

We walked up to an old building with a new dark teakwood door and a tiny brass plaque that said: Galerie Moon. A freestanding poster announced the ongoing show in crisp red and blue lettering on stretched white paper: *'Female Forms: Divine Power Within.'* 32 women artists from all over India were being showcased, the byline informed us.

Roy said that Pushkala Kanojia, the curator for the show, was a renowned art historian and the owner of the Earth Gallery in Delhi. 'She's written two art books and contributed to countless others,' he said as we entered the hall.

Inside the cavernous whitewashed space I was pleasantly surprised. The first impression was of rich congruity in a spare setting, just the mix of voltaic drama and restraint that I would have expected of a top-of-the-line show. 'Pushkala certainly has a good sense of display,' I said, looking around.

'Oh, she's big league!' Roy agreed.

Suddenly Rimli walked in. She looked a bit surprised to see me with Roy. 'Tara? What are you doing here?' she blurted out, then put her heavy bag on a chair to cover the awkward pause.

'Roy told me you were exhibiting here so I had to come,' I said quickly.

'Come, see it then.'

Roy shrugged good-naturedly and the three of us walked towards the far end. Each of the paintings reached out to me from the wall, they were hung with lots of creamy space between them. Two security guards stood around in wraith-like silence. There were no viewers apart from us. 'Hmmm. Interesting work. But it's so quiet in here. Where are all the other visitors?' I asked looking around.

'It's the last day of the show,' Rimli laughed. 'What do you expect? Pushkala will be here soon enough.'

We reached the far side of the room. Rimli pointed towards the corner. 'That's mine.'

It was a mixed media sculptural installation – forged metal pieces pierced a wooden plank and contorted into an army of curving, interlinked figurines. Scraps of wool hung about them, deep red and deep blue. Below it, in a white sand alpana, a brilliant sun spread out its rays, floating in a sea of yellow rice, ringed with black.

'What do you think?' Rimli inquired anxiously.

What could I say? It was a bit strange, and I didn't quite understand it. But it was Art. And she was one of my best friends. 'Very interesting,' I ventured. 'Inspired. Different, for sure.'

Rimli beamed at me. 'I'm so glad you like it.'

Uh-oh!

And then I heard myself say, 'Why don't you take me to your studio sometime? I'd like to buy one of your pieces, maybe commission something.'

And I thought, What would I *do* with a sculptural installation? Where would I put it? In an apartment I didn't have?

A gasp escaped me as we approached the next piece – delicate reds and blues mingled and arced in a thin stalk, upon which sat a jewel-plumed parrot, feathers individually collaged out of patterned and textured emerald papers. There was much understated drama. But what was that little spill of carmine on the violent mating of mauve and fuchsia? I drew in my breath, trying to decipher shapes and meaning in the fusion of colours.

'It's so refreshing,' I said, commenting on the sheer wash of pale colours, compared to the other oils and acrylics with their thick layered spatter and flat-brushing and knifing of oil and acrylic.

'Well, it's an interpretation of rape,' Rimli said in a matter-of-fact way.

I was shocked! I scanned the painting again and Rimli traced a spot where the faintest jut of blue darkened to a rim of cobalt, and minuscule cobalt flecks gathered in the shaded pink and peach folds below. I wouldn't have guessed.

'All the paintings in this show depict female energy and life – conveying how banal and ordinary it appears on the outside, but look within, and you can spy a skein of violence, of tragedy, of death and sorrow.'

I turned around to grin at Rimli, but she was completely serious.

I looked around the room taking in the fecund, desolate interpretations of the female energy. Suddenly, each work reeked of death, tyranny, sodomy and rape.

Then a haunting image of unusual luminosity caught my eye – a goddess figure, her lean patrician face defined by a hint of mystery, the sculpted folds of her lips arcing in benevolence, while the weaponry around was suggestive of some violence in the air. A beautifully scripted signature on the shaded and blended background said Shyamolee Ray. The next painting, as near as possible in emotion, juxtaposed a pantheon of Phoolan Devi lookalikes against an assortment of rifles, knives and spears. The artist had added a series of chopped arms which, bereft of their bodies, seemed disturbingly alive as they jumped hypnotically out of the canvas. Like Miró's eyes. What were they doing – begging for mercy or scavenging for the spoils?

On and on the paintings went, each suggesting an invasive use of force. They seemed poised on that moment when all hope is extinguished, when everything seems bleak, except for one thing – that last spark, that elemental, guttural rise of female energy. *Adishakti, Kali, Bhadrakali, Mahakali.* The serpent-like rise of the aggressive kundalini, fierce and fearsome, splayed on canvas or board, in whirls, furls and figures of sombre and intense shades.

But where was that divine power of positive hope? I wondered. Not just the hope that vanquished tyranny, but explored the way forward? Not just the hope that annihilated past injustices, but created positive ideas and modalities? The power that made women into messiahs against social evils, but also made them equal creators of a world rich in health, education, happiness, money and even the arts? There was an Indian Madonna in the corner, with a little baby in a hammock. But did motherhood sum up all that could be said about the creative urge?

'What if someone walks in now and wants to buy a painting?' I turned to Rimli, curious whether violent female art had any takers.

'They will be disappointed,' Roy gave a laugh as light as a watercolour brush on handmade paper.

'What do you mean?'

'The show was sold out on day one.'

'Really?' I was amazed.

'You really don't know much about how galleries work, do you?' Roy sounded a touch condescending. 'Most works get pre-sold. Days before an exhibition opens.'

Rimli told me that her work had been picked up by Pushkala's friend from Jalandhar. To be displayed in the lobby of a newly built hotel. Shyamolee Ray's work was sold even before it was put in the catalogue, Rimli told me. Apparently some buyer wanted to pay top dollars for this old piece and Pushkala had convinced the owner to sell it, but put it in the show before sending it to the buyer.

Just then a tall lady in a stylishly cut beige linen suit, long ropes of green beads clicking as they swayed from her neck, tottered over to us on impossibly high hot pink sandals. She was accompanied by a petite short-haired woman. 'Hi, Pushkala.' Rimli rushed up to air-kiss the tall woman. 'How come you are late today?'

'Oh, I just had to meet Karan in Juhu. He wants to buy some paintings.'

'Karan as in Johar?' Rimli squealed.

'Yes.' Pushkala shrugged with posed insouciance, which really implied she was ready to hoot out loud and do a tabletop dance announcing it all. K-Jo, after all, was Bollywood's rainmaker. Bigger than the biggest art dealers in town! 'He even mentioned doing an art special on *Koffee with Karan*.' She fingered the beads about her neck smugly.

Yeah, *right*.

Pushkala introduced her friend as Shakuntala Khanna of Khanna Gallery in Delhi, and I blurted out my name, mentioning several art purchases from Khanna's both from their Delhi space and online.

'Yes,' Shakuntala's eyes widened in remembrance, and she smiled more warmly. 'I recall the name from Washington DC.'

I basked in the warmth of that smile, balm to the ego, sensing a rise in estimation in Roy's eyes, feeling every inch the global art collector, known by name and by location to global purveyors of contemporary Indian art.

'Not last year though?' Shakuntala asked lightly.

She'd found me out. With prices being what they were, I hadn't quite made it to the recent sales. 'The move…' I grinned at her. 'But I am looking to collect even more, now that I am in India.' Then I turned to Pushkala, congratulating her on the amazing exhibition.

We hung around talking about the paintings for a few minutes when Pushkala announced, 'I must rush again. I am meeting with a Board member of Tata Sons about his personal collection.'

Wow, this lady moved! And in the top-most circles. Art, especially high-end art, attracted bigwigs from every sector of life.

*

Over lunch at Samovar – the legendary eatery that has fed every Mumbai celebrity from Husain to Bachchan – Rimli, Roy and I sat under angled wall fans in the narrow, corridor-like space. The heat was something else. I sat back despite the drumming in my head – suggesting that a migraine would start soon – and talked of art valuations and margins commanded by dealers willing to risk investing in upcoming star artists. It was a pure hedging and betting game; simple arbitrage against expected price, higher risk leading to higher gains.

I looked at Roy uncertainly, placing my elbows on the table, cupping my fingers around my mouth. 'So when Pushkala resold that old Shyamolee Ray, which the buyer had probably bought for a pittance years ago, how much would she have made?'

'A fair sum,' Roy shrugged, enigmatically.

Rimli fell quiet for a moment as she pondered the margins. 'Not less than a crore. It is a big piece. The margins, even on commission, will be huge.' She shook her head. 'I tell you, I am an artist because I love to sculpt. But if I had any sense, I would be a dealer.'

I could see that. It was creating value out of nothing. It was true entrepreneurship. The perfect business proposition – buy low, sell high. Unlock potential which did not exist until now. Amazing.

'Maybe that's what I should do while in India...' I looked into the distance thoughtfully. 'Become an art dealer. Open a gallery.'

'Maybe you should,' Roy grinned as he daubed his mouth with a thin paper napkin. 'And when you do, don't forget my margin for giving you the idea.'

Laughing together, the three of us dug into our food.

*

My mind was heavily laden with art when I arrived home, a pastiche of snippets culled from offhand conversations, recent and past, an impressionistic melange of hype and madcap reality and fragmented perspectives sewn together inchoately to create one bold image: art was hot; art was happening; art was money.

Rohan came whooshing at me as I reached home, and I played with him absent-mindedly, putting together Lego blocks, my thoughts still focused on that last conversation with Rimli and Roy, about starting an art gallery. The idea had really caught my imagination. To say that a few weeks away from gainful employment was making me restless was the least of it. It was also the idea of experimenting with my life, of reinventing myself, as others around me dallied with new brands and new travel destinations and new pastimes. Art was not new to me. I had been a collector for years.

I was dying to talk to someone about it. Trouble was, I didn't know whom to talk to. It couldn't be my mom and dad. They would simply freak out. Art was too out of the ordinary for them. My friends back in DC would not have a clue either. And Raj? I simply could not be bothered to share anything with him.

But then who?

I sat back against the bed and switched on the bedroom television, skipped through the channels and, somehow, zeroed in on a CNBC India segment where a smooth-haired, malt-voiced lad was talking about art prices and an upcoming by-invite-only preview of a special collection at the Taj on Friday evening.

Suddenly, art was everywhere. The social pages were always full of heavily made-up socialites hugging each other in front of paintings, shaking hands with the artist, at gallery openings everywhere. The accompanying reports read something like:

> *Alpa Virani, looking savvy in a white figure-hugging kurti, exchanged pleasantries with artists Shyamolee Ray and Bhola Prasad. Pinky Batlibhoy dazzled in her peacock coloured sari, a look different from her usual Western style. Kitty Kushagra, always up-to-the-minute in her dressing, was seen in a slim belted black dress and chunky ruby choker. Anil Roy came in a red sherwani. The art community was represented by artists Harinakshi Dey and Mangal Pandey.*

There was never any mention of the art.

I picked up the *Business Times*. After flipping through pages and pages of bold typeface about 'Amazing India' and an Indian-owned company trouncing a European giant in a merger bid, I turned to the back pages. Sure enough. There was an article about Art Funds – that were doing great business at the moment.

> *'I only buy art as investment,' a Delhi businessman said. 'I have been constantly buying and selling paintings for the last seven years, and I have made on average 130 per cent returns. This is what prompted me to start my Soigné Art Fund. We have a million dollars in the Fund now, invested in works by emerging and established artists.'*

Well, that beat the market rates, fair and square!

I put the newspaper away and braced myself to tear Rohan away from the television for his evening bath. There were tears and tantrums as expected. Barely did Rohan doze off that Raj arrived, strangely early by his standards, announcing a last-minute invitation to join a group of new business contacts to check out a new lounge-bar in town.

'Now?' I asked sarcastically, looking at the clock. It was 9pm already, but Mumbai was the eternal party town. I decided to go, suddenly wanting more than night cream and a book in bed.

The lounge-bar was a cavernous space with tinted orange lights and slate-blue leather banquettes. In a motley crowd of young bankers, consultants and minor industrialists, the conversation revolved around the best places in town, weekend plans, travel and real estate, Indian designers and Indian stocks. But somehow when the lights dimmed to trance music, Raj linked his arms about me, drawing me close, his breath soft on my hair, to join other couples as they took to the dance floor.

For that moment, trilling on three champagnes, swaying to electronica, my mind euphorically empty of rational thought, memories of slow-dancing with Raj in the years gone by taking precedence, I was glad to be in his arms again.

'I want to start an art gallery,' I confessed to Raj as we danced; my defences tipsily down.

'If you must work, why not do what you are good at, like financial research?' Raj stiffened immediately.

What, no deviations allowed for anyone, except Raj? I exploded: 'So only *you're* allowed to chase fads?'

India, after all, was his flavour of the moment, the biggest fad of our times!

'At least I'm chasing a fad with positive returns...' said Raj abruptly leading me back to the table.

As soon as we got back to the Mews, Raj walked into the study and slammed the door behind him. The slam was like a hammer. There was a gash inside me.

I would show him, I vowed. I would start an art gallery without his help.

six

Speeding through the post rush-hour calm on Marine Drive, still nursing my anger from the previous night, I headed for a charity sale in June's house. Set in the slapdash skyline of Walkeshwar, between ugly buildings overrun with rusted exterior plumbing and knotted masses of electrical wires, June's house – a low lying independent bungalow – came as a surprise.

A uniformed guard manned the gate. Down a short flight of stairs, a dark woman in a white apron opened the double doors and ushered me inside. 'Downstairs, Madam,' she said, as I took in the tall carved ceiling and expansive sitting room lavishly decorated with paintings and statues and dark teakwood antiques.

Downstairs was another living area, already filled with clothes racks and mounds of costume jewellery, which a flock of women were browsing through. Beyond them, I could see double glass doors and a green patch. A *garden* in Mumbai?

'Hi Tara,' June came out from somewhere behind me and gave me a warm hug and a kiss.

'You have an amazing house, June,' I gushed.

She smiled and told me to check out all the stalls in the bedrooms and clattered upstairs to check on things.

One bedroom had brocade bustier tops and embroidered dresses, and an improvised changing area behind a white sheet screen. Another room had piles of satiny lacy lingerie and mounds of silk robes and teddies. The ladies were using the attached bathroom to try things on. In the main hall, one table was stacked with beaded silk stoles and another laden with silver jewellery set with lapis, malachite, red jasper and lacy agate. I bought a pair of earrings – swinging ones studded with amethysts and garnets. A cheese supplier had set up a tasting corner with salty crackers and a variety of imported Emmental and Brie and Gruyère, alongside chorizos and saucissons. Next to him, two bearded, light-eyed fellows were selling pashmina and Kashmiri carpets.

This is the life, I thought. If one must suffer Mumbai, this was the way to do it.

Beyond the glass doors, the lawn looked very inviting. I walked outside to take a breather. Palmyra palms shaded the grass and chequered it Klee-like in hues of olive and moss. There were established trees and flowering bushes. There was a glass fence and beyond it, the sea and Marine Drive. Unbelievable! Garden chairs were set up in the shade. Two grey-haired ladies were relaxing on cushioned cane easy chairs, sipping weak coffee, their purchases lying on the grass in bright faux-organza carry bags.

June walked up to me. 'Too much haze today, no? Nariman Point is so blurred. I am yet to see perfect blue sea in this city. Oh, how I wish I was back in Boston…' she shrugged her shoulders. 'Yes, it's not often that I wish I were home. But then, we all have our off days… Now tell me, have you bought anything? All the sellers are contributing to raise money for a home for slum kids.'

I showed her my earrings. 'I still have to look for more things, I just took some time off to admire your garden.'

Maddy emerged from the lingerie room, clattering on four-inch-high beaded sandals, carrying a large handmade bag. 'I was *so* out of swimming things after the Maldives trip. Clothes just fade out in Mumbai and become boring,' she pouted, and swung her bag. 'I found de la Renta and Marnie swimsuits today.'

'Come now, taste the Banoffee Pie quickly before there is none left. It's amazing,' June said ushering us into the living room. The famed dessert turned out to be a baked foamy fluff of banana and toffee in a pie. Absolutely divine.

The room was buzzing now and the sofas were full of shiny ladies, drinking coffee and forking tiny bites of quiches and cakes into their mouths. Maddy asked June to show her a painting she had recently purchased, and I followed them upstairs. In the far corner, beyond the tan sofa and teak table, was a 3D painting in earthy reds and browns. Thick slaps of paint had been gouged away to create a sunken Shiva, chipped in parts and stippled with shadowy craters. June mentioned the name of some new artist of whom we hadn't heard.

'It is so clichéd!' Maddy shuddered as soon as June was out of earshot.

It was indeed a ghastly specimen of Indian painting, the type to appeal to matted-hair tourists on shoestring budgets or pot-bellied paise-counting businessmen who wanted to appear 'kaltured'.

We walked around the room, taking in the other works of art. There were wall-sized works by Tyeb Mehta and Souza, as well as exceptional canvases by everyone from Charan Sharma to Vaikuntam. My own collection, which Raj and I had been so proud of in DC, paled in comparison.

The doorbell rang and June's maid ushered in some more guests. It was Alessa, one of Maddy's friends, who greeted us and introduced the others – the tan one as Gul Dastur, and the pale freckled lady as Charlotte Caldwell, both expatriates from the UK.

Gul Dastur looked at the Shiva painting and made a face. 'Is this June's latest buy? I am amazed June actually bought this. She usually has such good taste.'

Charlotte pointed to the Elephanta-type torso of Shiva, arrayed plastically across the canvas, with that vacuous smile of beatitude one expects of a calendar deity. 'Look at it – it has nothing new! It has no passion. Frankly, I find most Indian art like this. Not much deviation from the expected. Static. Loosely derivative,' Charlotte said.

Wow, I thought. This woman talked like an art folio. I looked around to see if the others could comprehend what she was saying.

Gul winked at me. 'Charlotte is an established expert on art history.'

'Yes.' Charlotte accepted this with a straight face. 'I wrote a book on the art of British officers' wives in the pre-Battle of Plassey days. I spent a lot of time in Delhi researching the book and met many so-called celebrity Indian artists. None of them boast of the cutting edge, the real spark, when you compare them to international celebrity artists!' she said baldly, every inch of her thin frame stiff with derision.

'Really?' I had not thought of Indian art in these terms. 'What about the Progressive Artists' Group? I thought they sort of changed the face of Indian art.'

'Hah!' Charlotte snorted, in a supercilious way, her long thin nose quivering in her long thin face. 'They, even more than the others, showed no originality, no growth. They blatantly copied from Picasso and Matisse. Then they did not evolve their styles, they stagnated. Typical Indians!' She gave her long neck a shake. 'Do you *really* think they would have been this popular had their buyers been knowledgeable enough about global art?'

Not that I knew much about the intertwining of inspiration across the global art cosmos. But Charlotte's opinionated stance annoyed me. For one moment I forgot my American passport and my NRI status and slipped into auto-defence mode on the shaky foundation of bookish knowledge gained from coffee table books.

I said loudly, 'But surely there is nothing absolutely original ever? Okay, so the Progressives were inspired by Picasso, but Picasso himself was inspired by African tribal art and by Diego Rivera. Rivera, in turn, was inspired by indigenous Mexican art, which has its roots in African tribal art. In fact, all tribal art has similarities – look at Australian aboriginal art, at the Madhubani paintings from India, at Kokopelli silhouettes and North African cave paintings. Each one takes inspiration from the other. So?' I challenged

'Picasso, as you rightly pointed out, took influences from many sources.' Charlotte looked directly at me. 'But he took the *spirit* or the feeling of these paintings, not actual compositional elements. It's tough for laymen to understand,' Charlotte condescended. 'But Picasso's style underwent constant metamorphosis. If you study his paintings across the decades, you will see that his style morphed. It returned to exploration after each stage, to something new, something built upon previous experiences. There was constant ground breaking. The Indian Progressives did not budge from their original oeuvre.'

Oeuvre? Who the hell used words like that in a conversation? I looked around to see Alessa looking very bored, as was Maddy. But I had an argument to win, I couldn't back off.

'You cannot make a generalization,' I exclaimed.

Alessa excused herself and wafted down the stairs, lifting her dress to reveal maroon stilettos with maroon silk ribbons that laced around her ankles. Maddy followed her, exclaiming over Alessa's shoes, 'Are they Jimmy Choo or Manolo?'

'Balenciaga,' Alessa said, before they disappeared.

'It's not so either or, Charlotte. The Progressives had a brief inspired phase. But look at the younger crop of artists. They seek inspiration from everywhere, from Indian masters to western art, from mythology to films to comics and graffiti. Look at Subodh Gupta. He is simply so unexpected. Look at the younger lot. They experiment a lot. Their work is not what you would call "Indian",' Gul joined the debate.

I looked at Gul gratefully.

'Then why do you think, Gul, Indian contemporary art has not found interest among serious Western collectors and galleries?' Charlotte waggled her finger at me accusingly: 'It is because despite all these cross-cultural influences you talk about, the overall mien of the art lags by about five decades.'

'What are you talking about? I thought the whole hoopla about art was created because Indian artists are doing so well in auction house salesrooms!' I said.

Gul looked at me. 'The thing is, Tara, the people who buy Indian art at those high prices are mostly

Indians living abroad. Plus, the prices are woefully low compared to even Chinese art or Jewish art, let alone Western art.'

'Exactly,' Charlotte said triumphantly, ignoring me now and looking at Gul. 'These Indian buyers just want to trumpet to the world that they are successful. That they too can buy art. It has nothing to do with the inherent quality of the art. Tell me, are major Western galleries and museums buying Indian art? In ones and twos possibly, but in quantities?'

Gul shook her head quietly, and Charlotte answered her own question. 'Most Western collectors find Indian art caught in the figurative realm which went out of fashion half way through the previous century. Even installations which recycle everyday articles have been a done thing for decades.'

I didn't quite know how to respond. I had reached the deep end of my knowledge.

But Gul held her stead. 'I disagree, Charlotte. Indian contemporary art is at a development stage. It does not have its arrays of critics and marketers as art in the West. But times are changing fast. New artists are collaborating with museums and art workshops abroad. Perception shall follow soon.'

'Well, we are not going to resolve this today,' Charlotte said. 'Let's see how it shapes up.' Then with an abrupt offhand wave, she walked off towards the stairs.

When she left I turned to Gul. 'You know a lot about Indian art!'

Gul smiled. 'I studied art, you see. But I am not very talented. So I gave it up, and ended up in luxury jewellery marketing.' She raised the crimped curtain of her hair, and tucked it behind her ear. 'But now that I am in India for the next many years, I want to market Indian art. Start a gallery. Do something.'

'Hey, I have been thinking along the same lines,' I exclaimed automatically. 'We should talk.'

Promising to get together soon, Gul and I exchanged cell phone numbers. Then Gul stopped to talk to a friend, while I happily spent ten minutes debating over a lilac pashmina stole, or a demi-bra confected of blushing mauve silk and lace. The stole won in the end – what use did I have for a demi-bra meant for display? What would I do with it? Parade in it semi-naked for Raj's viewing pleasure? Never!

Consolidating my plans for setting up an art gallery involved exhaustive groundwork. To this end, I met Ravi Uppal in his home office in a spacious penthouse on Cuffe Parade. June had given me the goss on Ravi, about how he had turned defunct family mills into captive upholstery spinning units for Italian fabric designers, reversing the slide of his family fortune. His art collection was legendary, his knowledge and contacts in the art world, unparalleled.

'Any friend of June's is my friend,' said Ravi, a grey-haired, pot-bellied man in his sixties, his crisp Lucknowi kurta bright against his leathery jowls. He threw open the doors of a cupboard with deep shelves revealing stacks and stacks of paintings. 'Are you looking for pleasure or for investment?'

'For pleasure,' I said, taking in the mind-boggling collection.

Ravi pulled out three small canvases: an old Ramkinkar Baij watercolour, a colourful pop-art piece by Vishnu Shastra and a charcoal sketch by a mid-twentieth century artist – three very different styles

– and talked about how well he knew the artists. My eyes were drawn towards the piece of pop-art – clean lines and glowing colours and quite comical really, with animals on a boat.

Ravi wrote the price on a piece of paper. 'For a friend,' he said.

I counted the zeroes. I did not know whether to bargain or not; so I didn't. Hah! My second painting bought without consulting Raj first. But then he had planned a whole continent move without consulting me first.

So there!

The next day I called Rimli. She had just finished a big piece and excitedly invited me over to her studio to see it. I told the driver the address for Rimli's studio. He looked at me askance, as if I had suggested a trip to planet Zurg! But I could see what he meant when he dropped me in a rubbish-infested lane in Bhuleshwar saying the car could go no further. The narrow lane that ran between the shops and crumbling chawls was lost in the confusion of cycle carts, pedestrians, ragamuffins, rag-pickers and cows. The stench of rot and refuse overcame me. I quickly covered my nose with a folded handkerchief and breathed as little as possible. Asking for exact directions, I arrived at a ramshackle building and climbed up the cracked wooden steps in a dim stairwell to the second storey door.

Rimli opened the door, in glue and paint spattered denim overalls, her hair scrunched up into a high ponytail. 'Welcome,' she smiled, and her nose ring glimmered in the dark.

I entered, welcoming with deep gasps the heavy scent of Padmini incense lingering in the small shuttered room. The room was smaller than my kitchenette at Wellington Mews. There were some old wooden crates topped with colourful cushions and one squishy sofa-chair to relax in. The rest was work stuff – a long dirty table with clay and bits of scrap metal and all manner of strange tools that looked more suited to a Tata sheet metal factory, than an artist's studio. Several sculptures – bent intertwined forms in wrought iron and steel, adorned with fretwork and wood and scraps of fabric – were placed on the floor. Rimli had told me the last time we had met that she layered her work, each little bit or scrap was infused with some meaning, so that the whole piece was a story in itself.

'This is lovely,' I beamed at her, meaning it. 'Which is the new piece you have finished?'

She led me through a small corridor to another, even smaller room. There was a big oven-like thing there; an autoclave, Rimli told me. The room had a dirty rectangular table with metallic legs topped with more scrap metal, tongs and pincers blackened with use, and a pair of heavy-duty gloves. On the table was a sculpture, a bit different from Rimli's usual pieces.

'I've been experimenting,' Rimli said, yanking the band off her hair. Her hair tumbled down to touch her shoulders, straggly and spare. Her deep pink shock of a lock had been coloured again – it was purple now. Clearly, she had been experimenting with other things too. As I stared at her sculpture, I exclaimed, 'It is gorgeous, Rimli.' It was, in an edgy sort of way. It was a large ceramic head that had been painted in a million jarring shades of primaries and metallic, out of which metallic curls and strips angled out in all directions, with those signature wool threads hanging on them. Colourful bindis dotted the top haphazardly.

The whole thing rested on a black metal base. I didn't know what it meant. But, somehow, the overall effect was startling.

'I'd like to buy it,' I said impulsively.

Later, as Rimli made tea with teabags and an electric kettle set on the windowsill, she asked me what I had wanted to talk about. So I told her how I wanted to start an art gallery and how I was scared because I did not know how.

Rimli abruptly stopped stirring her tea and looked me in the eye. 'I know we had joked about it, Tara. But why do you want to get into this?'

'Because... because...' I fumbled for an answer, offering loads of reasons – how I loved art and how I had been collecting art for several years and how it would be fun, how it would alleviate boredom and also fulfil my desire for creative pursuits and alternative business ventures. There was a fractional truth in all of them. But, somehow, I sounded absolutely unconvincing even to myself. Why had this suddenly become so important to me? Because, at the centre of this vortex lay one fact. Something I did not want to divulge to anyone. I wanted to start a gallery out of pique. Pique at Raj. Pique at Raj's words. Other emotions were involved too. Anger. Pride. Resolve. I had to, *had to*, show him.

Rimli leaned against the window, and picked up a box of Camel Lights from the ledge. 'Okay, let's say for reasons unknown you have decided to start an art gallery. What is the problem?'

I slid my empty tea mug under the cot and clutched my fingers nervously. 'It's just that I don't know how to – how to source art, how to start an art gallery, how to sell art – I don't know anything. It seems so hard...'

Rimli snorted, half amused and half impatient. 'But you have fancy foreign degrees in Finance. So what's so hard?'

'Yes... but...' I spluttered again, because therein lay the problem. Financial research and valuations were a very different sort of finance from the financial mechanics of actually starting and running an operating entity. I was actually scared of playing with my own money. 'There is so much I don't know,' I confessed to Rimli, a darkness gathering within me. 'Sourcing, selling, running the gallery...'

Rimli laughed, a loud uninhibited expression of mirth, shaking the ash from her cigarette. 'The demand for sculptures is less than that for paintings, so I've taken a slower path to my present. But promising young painters can choose which gallery to go with. So a commission-based model won't attract them as much as outright purchase by a gallery. Of course, that means having deeper pockets to invest and taking the risk. Just get enough stock for the first four-five shows and then keep going from there.'

We talked of finances. Rimli suggested an infusion of cash from Raj, which I ignored. 'I could always go to banks, or find angel investors among friends,' I said, thinking of Dipankar, and June's husband, and even my own savings to use as seed capital.

'Will you have any partners?' Rimli prodded and I mentioned Gul Dastur, though I still had to talk to Gul.

'All you need is gallery space. The rest – the marketing, the display, the catalogue, the selling and follow-up – is hard work, but sheer mechanics. There is enough demand out there. You just call up *your* friends and they will call *their* friends and' – she clapped her hands – '*Ta da!*'

I looked at her askance. Was anything ever that easy? 'But will they buy? And finding a space in Mumbai has to be the toughest task of all!' I wailed.

Rimli arched her eyebrows wryly. 'Babe, you have posh friends, and art is a happening trend. Send out fancy invites, make some personal phone calls, host a nice cocktail reception and keep prices reasonable. You'll sell out.' She lit another cigarette. 'Don't worry too much, Tara. As for space, you aren't looking at some expansive pad with a sea view. Just get a big enough space, ideally near the art precinct in Kala Ghoda, slap on some cream paint, and you will be ready to go.'

I looked up to see Rimli eyeing me, lids narrowed, brows raised, proving a point. 'So what is the problem?'

'I am scared,' I said again in a small voice.

Because, to tell the truth, putting money down – my own or anyone else's – for my own venture was outright scary! I mean, I knew about money matters. I had advised global institutional clients, but always with the safety netting of a big company behind me. But my own venture! The list of *what ifs* that could go wrong was endless.

'Scared?' Rimli stubbed her spent cigarette against the window sill. 'Then you might as well give up the idea right now.' She paused for effect. 'Or gather courage. Look at me.'

Look at her? I was appalled. Look at *what?* At this tiny studio in a smelly alley? At a shared apartment in Borivali? The daily train rides to get to a studio as close to the Art District as possible? I mean, Rimli was a friend. I couldn't say all this to her. But being out on a limb did not seem fun to me. I had grown soft on steady salaries, backyard rose-beds and airy hotel

Gul asked about the paintings I owned and, very conscious of her amazing collection, I rattled off the names mechanically – the Husain line drawing, the large Chitrita Goswami, the newly bought Bhola Prasad and Vishnu Shastra and many young artists.

'Chitrita?' Gul said. 'I just had an email today about an art event she's hosting to raise money for children with Down's Syndrome.'

'Well, now that I'm in India, I want to buy a Husain or Raza or Souza oil.'

'You're kidding, right? A trophy piece at today's prices?' Gul looked at me incredulously, eyebrows raised.

I simply smiled back serenely.

'I have a gallery name in mind,' I told Gul instead. 'Saloniere Star.'

When I reached home I got a call from École Nouvelle. 'We have an unexpected vacancy. Are you still interested in admitting your child to our school?'

Was I still interested? What a question!

Gaining a sudden belief in divine intervention, I rushed to the school to sign the papers and pay the hefty dollar amount, before they had a chance to change their mind.

Saloniere Star was going to change my luck!

seven

It was the day of the Amrita Sher-Gil special commemorative show opening.

Roy had sent two passes. But, of course, Raj was not around. And even if he were, would I still want to spend an entire evening with him? Instead, with Gul away for the weekend and Rimli down with the flu, I asked Lola to accompany me.

A couple of gorgeous women alighted from the cars ahead of ours to the honky-tonk of car horns and the stiff-moustached, baton-wielding admonitions of a tired traffic policeman. Seeing their scooped, slit and sequinned dresses, their in-vogue stiletto sandals of dizzy escalation, and their extra-large totes of Louis Vuitton and Fendi vintage, I was glad I had taken care to glam up. I was dressed in an old red and taupe leather skirt, a red chiffon top with trailing ruffles, and a modest floribunda of antique rubies glinting in my ears.

I was about as ready as I ever would be.

I glanced at Lola sitting beside me and smirked. Gosh, she was a darling, but today she was popping out of her clothes like Britney, in one of those gold-spangled, bosom-enhancing, shaped and flared kurti-tops with a slew of champagne-coloured stones about her throat and ears.

'Are these real diamonds?' I asked Lola, despite myself.

'Champagne diamonds, darling,' she said.

Of course they would be. Mumbai jewelleratis took themselves quite seriously.

We were getting our purses searched by the security guards, when Roy emerged from inside, looking very dapper in an open-necked, body-hugging black silk shirt and a black diagonal striped suit. As he stood there greeting us with that deep-throated laugh, he could have been pegged as having an alternative persuasion, but for that intent man gaze and the lingering way he looked at me. He leaned forward to kiss my cheek, his hands resting on my arms with easy familiarity. 'Hubby-less again, Tara?'

'He's away... in Brussels.' I said, very aware of his hands on my bare arms. 'So I brought a friend instead. You've met Lola, haven't you?'

'Of course!' He turned to Lola, and raised his hand to cover his eyes theatrically. 'My God, woman, you dazzle.'

Lola simpered coyly and Roy led us indoors, his broad palm warm against the sheer chiffon veneer on my back. Then Roy excused himself and disappeared to talk to someone.

The main hall of the museum had a Guggenheim-like staircase spiralling upwards, where the permanent collections were housed. But it was on the main and the mezzanine floors that Amrita Sher-Gil intently presided over the cocktail cognoscenti. Flanked by banks of Sher-Gil's photographs were paintings from the government coffers in New Delhi, broodingly evocative, despite the hint of cracking veins across their lacquered surfaces. It was difficult to say what was more striking – the seductive wide-eyed gaze of the pouting dark-lipped artist, hinting at the tempestuousness beneath, or the haunting stare of her starkly etched silhouettes.

I stared at Amrita Sher-Gil's picture.

'My God, doesn't she look just like Frida?' Lola exclaimed, as we stood, champagne flutes in hand, in front of an intense portrait of young Amrita – her centre-parted hair and thick eyebrows accentuating her artistic ferocity.

'Oh look at this one,' I pointed to another captivating close-up. Sher-Gil's eyes looked straight at the camera, a demurely drawn sari pallu over her head belying the torrid promise of her bee-stung lips.

'She was supposed to be really attractive,' Lola whispered in awed admiration as we stared at her picture.

Then Roy came back to our side, and steered us through the crowds, as much aware of whom we passed as of the paintings. Between Roy and Lola, they seemed to know the entire room. They kept up a steady commentary as we moved along.

'She's a well-known art writer and promoter,' said Lola pointing to a lady in a large maroon bindi and resplendent temple-bordered sari. 'A doyenne of the Indian art scene.'

'That's the Hungarian Ambassador,' Roy pointed to a tall blond man, deep in conversation with a graceful lady in white. Apparently, he was the co-host for the evening and had flown in from Delhi for the event, while the minister who had inaugurated the show had already left to open a Dalit rally somewhere else in the city.

'That's the Honorary Consul for Denmark,' Roy whispered as we approached a straw-haired man with a totally different aspect ratio – as short, as the Ambassador was tall. He was unusually florid, like a beach ball with a straw mop, a regular Humpty Dumpty.

'Hello, dear Henrik.' Roy moved up to shake Humpty Dumpty's hand.

The Consul appeared honourably confused, as if he could not quite place Roy but found it embarrassing to admit so. Roy reminded him that he had helped him source a rare yen from Japan a few years ago when the Consul was posted in Kuala Lumpur.

'Ah yes, yes, I remember now,' the Consul dithered. 'It has been many years... It was a seventeenth-century coin, wasn't it?' Then he added with a twinkle, 'Quite expensive too – were you the dealer? You must have made a fortune!'

'Well, I was your agent's agent. I knew the Japanese family in Kyushu who owned the coin. We met briefly, you and I, when we had first shown it to you.'

'So what brings you to town?' The Consul asked Roy.

Roy spread out his hands dramatically and said, 'The search for the next big thing.' Then Roy smiled and his voice rose fractionally as he went on to elaborate: 'My obsession with finding rare things appears to remain unabated. Why, just yesterday, an old contact of mine from Varanasi informed me that he has stumbled upon this old family from Tanda who claim to have an early, undiscovered Amrita Sher-Gil in their crumbling kothi...'

I gasped, almost choking on my drink!

I did not know much about sourcing major artworks, but discovering an Amrita Sher-Gil was a major coup!

Roy rubbed my back gently, his fingers like gossamer, tingling every nerve, an amused smile playing on his lips.

'Tanda?' Henrik lisped. 'Cold?' He sounded amazed and intrigued.

'No, no, Henrik, a *place* called Tanda. It's a really off-the-map sort of place in Uttar Pradesh.'

'How did a family in such a small village chance upon a Sher-Gil?' The Consul voiced the question that had been about to roll off my tongue.

'It has a bona fide provenance, Hendrik,' Roy explained. Apparently, the old zamindar family had helped Amrita Sher-Gil's husband, Victor Egan, set up his medical practice in nearby Gorakhpur. The painting had been given to the patriarch as a gift. Not realizing the value of the painting, the family had forgotten about it. There it lay, in a crumbling village mansion, probably covered in a blanket of dust and warped by decades of scorching summers.

'One of the young descendants of the family, on a visit to his ancestral home, suspected its lineage and called in an expert – an acquaintance of mine – from Varanasi. This guy just called me yesterday,' Roy said. 'I had helped him sell some other bits and pieces overseas.'

'My God! This is sensational!' I exclaimed, overcome at the thought of a Sher-Gil no one had seen. 'What does it look like?'

'I have only seen a picture,' Roy said. 'But my man tells me that the painting is particularly evocative, three lean female figures, one with a child, in deep shades of moss, cobalt and peat.'

I was lost for a moment, wondering what it would feel like to be the proud owner of a Sher-Gil. I couldn't imagine! This was serious stuff. The sale of her *Village*

Scene by an Indian art auction house had broken all records of return on investment in art. Rumours floated that gains on Amrita Sher-Gil's painting were higher than gains on Infosys stock in the same period.

It was all news to me.

Where had I been living?

Because everyone else seemed to know about this sensational find.

As I moved with Roy the entire room eddied around us, asking questions, offering comments.

At the heart of this maelstrom, Roy stood unfazed, grinning as people came by: envious dealers and salivating gallery owners, fashionista dilettantes and sage collectors, each one aiming to uncover some unsaid secret about this newly discovered find. Just as Roy turned to me, whispering in my ear some silly detail about a fat balding gallery owner, I saw a flashbulb wink. The paparazzi had dived into the melee as well.

As we were winding our way to the table, a lady in a black top, black trousers and a heavy black unibrow walked up to us. 'I'm Ramya Ramchandran,' she introduced herself.

I nearly gasped in awe. I had heard of *her*. She was a former specialist of South Asian treasures at the Smithsonian in Washington DC.

Ramya spoke candidly in true Yankee fashion, her unibrow a squiggle of black furrowing her forehead: 'This blows the lid off the event, young man. By the way, the Sotheby's Indian art expert from New York is here in the room. Do you know her? I will introduce you two, I'm sure you will have much to talk about.' She fiddled with the bright pashmina stole slung on her shoulder. Then she looked at Roy again. 'We've met before, haven't we?' she frowned, as if trying to map Roy onto her mental topography of art dealers and curators around the world. 'I knew all the guys who were handling South Asian art in London. Weren't you doing something different back then?'

Roy was smooth but evasive. 'Lovely to meet you, Ramya. I have heard so much about you.' Then he gave my shoulders a squeeze, and said, 'By the way, this is my friend Tara. I promised this lovely lady some champagne. So if you'll excuse us?'

'When did you promise me champagne?' I teased Roy, as he propelled me towards the exit.

'Don't know about you but I'm ready to escape,' he said, looking into my eyes. There was none of the wandering eye eagerness of before, and his usually taut facial muscles drooped softly now, making him look tired and old. 'We can go to Dome for that champagne I did not promise you. Humpty Dumpty and his friend are coming too.'

'Hang on, let me find Lola first,' I said.

But Lola didn't want to come. 'Oh, but, darling I need to go for another cocktail reception, hosted by De Beers,' Lola demurred when I went up to her. 'No doubt there will be a lovely display of jewellery to sigh over. And buy! You guys carry on.'

Later, overlooking the linear carat shimmer of Marine Drive at night, an empty bottle of Veuve Clicquot downed between us, the four of us lay half splayed on the sinking sofas of Dome. A jazz saxophonist played live, and the candle on the low table did a frenzied flicker to the deep wailing licks of the instrument.

I rested my head lightly on the plump cushions, and massaged my head with two fingers, wishing I had gone home. My mind was awhirl with the news of the Amrita Sher-Gil discovery. There were so many questions I wanted to put to Roy. But the drink and guilt were getting to me. Blue circles throbbed to the alto tones behind my partially closed eyes.

Around me, the conversation followed the usual cadences of economic buzz, culture shock, household help, the friendliness of locals to expats compared to, say, in Melbourne or Jakarta, the gorgeous parties, the roadside filth, the trauma of poor sickly children and hijras begging for alms. Standard expat fare. I had sat through so many of these conversations that I couldn't muster the enthusiasm for another one. Not with a splitting headache.

Roy's phone rang. He turned away slightly and spoke softly in sharp syllables. German?

'Girlfriend?' I half teased as he put the phone down, my interest heightened.

'A work colleague,' he said, not elaborating further.

'By the way, Roy, I can never afford a Sher-Gil but I am looking for a Husain or Raza or Souza – midsized, in oil or acrylic, not too outrageously priced,' I said, feeling small about not being able to even consider the Sher-Gil, and utterly drained by the hot evening.

Roy's warm brown fingers lightly smoothed the dull ache from my head. 'I'll keep a lookout for you, Tara,' he promised softly.

The next morning Roy was all over the morning papers. Even the *Business Times* talked about rising art prices and the recent Sher-Gil discovery. The pulp-happy writers of page three, of course, went on overdrive about Roy, about his Anglo links to India, the event from last night and the newly discovered Amrita Sher-Gil.

And there, under the article, was half a picture of me, with Roy whispering in my ear! *Wow*. I read on avidly, sipping my morning tea.

Pressmen speculated about the connections between Amrita and the zamindar from Tanda. The story talked about the rift between Amrita's parents and Victor Egan – her Hungarian doctor-husband and cousin; about how the young couple had escaped to an ancestral property belonging to Amrita's paternal relatives in a non-descript village called Saraya. The unemployed Victor had begun helping out at the local dispensary. Apparently, the young zamindar had befriended Victor over a tiger hunt and later helped him financially. After Amrita's death, when Victor had set up his practice in Saraya and Gorakhpur, he had continued with this friendship. The painting could have been given to the zamindar as a gift in lieu of the help.

There was even a quote from Roy, saying: *'This is a significant find; it also opens the possibility that there may be other works by Amrita Sher-Gil, lying around, undiscovered.'*

On Sunday evening Raj arrived back from Brussels, laden with gifts that delighted our child but did little to appease me. Raj was excited about the bond market shifts, which were making investors friendlier to risky emerging market equity. I listened disinterestedly, refusing to share his excitement.

Of course, folks overseas were getting more excited about India than they had been in twenty decades. For sure, the China-refrain in business circles was expanding to India-China. But it was all more hype than reality. All created by the Indian media. Raj had been absolutely brainwashed by the *Business Times*. I couldn't remember there ever being this much furore about India Shining in the *Wall Street Journal* before.

'Anyway,' Raj continued. 'People kept asking me about current FDI in India and market movements over the past year and projections.' He was at the dresser, putting away his cufflinks in the box with the rest of his collection. 'I tell you, it is a hot area–' he paused– 'Who's this?'

I looked up to see Raj frowning at the newspaper photograph I had cut from the paper – Roy bending into my ear; my hands resting on his arm, part of my face cut off – I knew it looked a tad cosy. Nothing to it, of course.

'Roy Jordan,' I shrugged casually. 'You met him at the Legends of India art show, remember?'

Raj drew a blank. 'I don't remember,' he huffed with instant animosity as he placed the box inside the dresser and slammed the drawer shut. 'You didn't tell me...'

I cut him short. 'You don't need to know about *everything* I do. What you do need to know is I've found the apartment I want.'

❧eight

Two weeks later, Raj and I sat among the potted frangipani trees on the open-air terrace of our new home, in an uneasy truce after months of bickering, swirling golden Moet against the purple twilight.

A lone star glittered dimly in the diffused gauze of the sky, but I took it to be a lucky omen for my life.

My life! I shook out my hair and laughed softly to myself. I couldn't think of it as *Our Life* anymore. It was My Life and Raj's Life. Separate entities.

Still, we had stood together on the top floor of Om Deep earlier that evening, exhaling a deep sigh at the sight of the grey swells of the Arabian Sea. So this was it, home, an oasis of sanity in this mad city, leased after a month of listless negotiations. I had fallen in love with the apartment on first sight – with its large rooms, its marble parquet floor and expansive views of Marine Drive and Back Bay from a double-height wall of glass.

Later, we fell into bed. I don't quite know how it happened. Maybe it was the slow kiss under the stars, maybe it was the soft trace of Raj's hands on my back, maybe it was the vacuum in my own mind, maybe it was the alcohol.

In the morning I kicked myself for losing control, and by the time Raj woke up, I was po-faced again.

By ten the sky was already a clear blue, brilliantly lit by a scintillating disk of gold. From my new home in Om Deep, with the air-conditioners whirring, I surveyed the blue-grey expanse of the sea and the whitish buildings along Marine Drive.

No one really knew of my plans to set up a gallery, except Rimli, Gul, her husband Pheroze Dastur, and me. Between errands, I met up with Gul and went to meet Pheroze's lawyer to iron out the legalities.

After all, the gallery, though it sold art – where emotions must preclude purchase, where compositions must touch hearts before minds – was nonetheless a business, a start-up, for Gul and me. Our money would go into it, so there needed to be a clear plan on how the business would emerge, chrysalis-like, from the pupa of ideas. It had to be more than just a string of casual shows with no real plan for sustainability.

Whenever Gul said that the art we picked would matter the most, I worried about the details. We debated the location: the premises had to be swanky enough to attract collectors who prided themselves in nurturing new artists, but were accessible enough to younger buyers.

'I wouldn't want to be snooty, Tara,' Gul insisted, very solemn. 'Not to my artists, not to my clients.' I couldn't agree more.

Then there was the choice of the art itself – a broad sweep of possibilities from paintings, sculptures and installations to prints, and bric-a-brac.

'None of those doe-eyed village maidens, they make me puke!' Gul said, wrinkling her nose.

'No dewy Krishnas, and no Buddhas either,' I said, adding my own list of absolute no-nos.

In the afternoon, while I was running around sourcing curtain fabric from Yamini and Atmosphere, Raj called. When I answered he was miffed that I hadn't answered on the first ring. He told me that we were invited to a surprise birthday party for Lola that evening. So I stopped at Aza on the way home to buy a dress for the evening. The Manish Malhotra wedding collection glimmered with crystal, beads, gold and platinum thread. A babe-like shop assistant trailed me through rows of satin-padded hangers, saying that Manish's new collection was selling out fast. I left with a swirling chiffon creation by Anamika Khanna.

Raj arrived home early and Rohan excitedly clambered all over him. He joined in the game Rohan and I were playing and I was confused about how to behave. How could I be playful with my son and cold with my husband, all at once? Raj picked up a sheet of paper on which I had doodled possible names and logos for our art gallery. 'You are still serious about this gallery business?' His voice was soft.

I ignored him.

When we arrived at Lola's house, the maid ushered us into her spacious living room where quite a crowd had already gathered. Lola was not home yet; apparently Dipankar had taken her out on some pretext, and would be bringing her in shortly.

I took in Lola's high-ceiling apartment and the extra large canvases in every imaginable colour. It was amazing that I had known Lola for two months and I was coming to her home for the first time. For sure, she was an avid collector! A large red and blue Raza dominated the dining area. A silvery-hued floor to ceiling piece boasted the signature of Akbar Padamsee. There was a small but gloriously colourful Paresh Maity, a stark work in black by an artist whose scrawled name I could not decipher, and many others.

'I can't reconcile the Rolls Royce showroom in the mall with the beggars at the street corners,' I overheard a red-haired firang comment. The latest *Forbes* stats on Indian millionaires and billionaires was out. 'What do you think of Indian stocks?' he asked a tall swarthy man sipping a single malt on ice.

'A bubble,' his desi companion responded, touting Hold stance and Gold Futures.

I spied some known faces. A white jacketed waiter handed me a glass of sparkling wine. An arm snaked about my waist, and startled, I looked at Raj, very aware of the fit of his shirt on his lean torso: 'Come meet a friend of mine.'

We went up to a silver-haired man, who greeted Raj with an embrace. Raj introduced him as Vijay, a lawyer, financier, and art collector, who had started an Art Fund. 'Tara wants to start an art gallery,' said Raj, introducing me to him.

'Art is the way to go, I tell you,' Vijay wagged his index finger knowingly. 'It's all economics! Look at the prices. Anything half-decent has become unaffordable for the average investor. Newer artists are always a gamble. The only way out is to spread the risk. Volume buy and volume sell, on pieces that are sure sells. I decided to start this fund last year, and within two months I had 30 crores put in 50 paintings. Every day I get calls from more investors.' He thrust out his chest in that swaggering, over-confident manner that I had begun to identify as a trademark of the aggressive new

Indian businessman. Whatever happened to the shy, retiring desi of yesteryear? Probably, driven away by the bullish stock-market!

Vijay said, 'You must be a collector as well, Tara. What artists do you plan to sell in your gallery?'

'Emerging artists,' I told Vijay. 'I want to bring art to the masses.'

'No money in that,' Vijay said dismissively. 'Nothing but Tier 1 artists, I say. All this lower price, emerging bandwagon is pure bullshit, I tell you.'

'Yes, but an Art Fund? Come on!' I retorted. 'What would a person say, "I own one-twenty-eighth of a Husain?" Where is the passion in that?'

'If you seek passion, Tara,' Vijay's voice was grizzly with scorn, 'don't enter the art business. Art is economics!' He was most emphatic, his suave face transformed, the churlish bully beneath coming to the fore. 'You have to intuitively understand current trends and hedge your bets.'

I felt my hackles rise. My God, the man was a boor! 'I don't agree, Vijay. A true collector buys from the heart, and not for immediate gains. Of course, all art rises in price eventually. But how can you guarantee returns in an Art Fund? Where would your returns be if you cannot sell?'

'But aren't there more collectors than ever?' Raj jumped in, alarmed that the conversation was not going the way he had hoped.

'Most collectors, Raj, just pick up rubbish!' Vijay opined.

'Really?' I said, arching my eyebrows.

'Really! Unless you have really deep pockets, unless you are a hotshot industrialist or a fancy money-man, you cannot buy anything worthwhile. Not even one-twenty-eighth of it.'

There was a sudden hoot from the door. Lola arrived and there was a chorus of felicitations. She looked fabulous. 'I cannot imagine being forty,' she sighed dramatically.

(I knew for a fact that she was forty-five.)

Late that night when I was in bed my cell phone rang and I groped for it in the dark. Roy's low, husky voice came on.

'Roy!' I whispered delightedly. 'I only see you in the newspaper these days! Have you sold the Sher-Gil yet?'

Raj woke up when he heard me exclaim so I got out of bed and left the room.

'Straight to the point!' Roy put on a wounded tone. 'Can you talk?'

Then, in a brisker tone, he apologized for calling so late and told me that the Sher-Gil was in Mumbai. Its provenance had been authenticated, its insurance done. Its new owner lined up.

'Come over to the Yacht Club tomorrow if you want a look,' Roy told me.

When I came back to the room Raj had turned over to his side and was feigning sleep.

The next morning I headed for the Yacht Club as soon as Raj left for work.

Roy looked deliciously casual in a fitted tee shirt and short shorts. Smiling, he ushered me into an old world suite, with shuttered windows, dark wood furniture and deep earth-coloured cotton fabrics. The air-conditioner was on full blast, and long stemmed fans hung low from the overhead wooden beams shuffling the frigid air in an arctic blast. 'There are no humidifiers here,' he explained. 'It is an absolute must to store paintings properly in Mumbai. This damp sea air makes me worry. I shall rest easy only when I move the painting to a friend's storage facility.'

Alone in the room, I was very conscious of him. Aloud, I said, 'I can't wait to see the painting.'

He led me to the bedroom. I walked reverentially towards the Sher-Gil painting set on two oversized easels. It was gorgeous – a massive five foot by six foot canvas, dominated by hues of deep teal and maroon red. There were three figures on the canvas, with a beautiful doe-eyed, long-limbed woman with a baby in the foreground. Going closer, I could see the even brush strokes, the moody shading of deep hues as they cut deeper and deeper. But the eyes of the woman struck me as odd. Proud but full of misery.

'It's so like *The Bride's Toilette*...' I whispered, afraid to speak loudly and disturb the regal presence of the painting. *An Amrita Sher-Gil, rediscovered!*

Roy's hand brushed mine as he leaned over to switch on some more lights, flooding the room with the bright yellow halogen glow of down-lights. I came out of my reverie, instantly aware of him standing close, almost feeling the warmth of his form. 'This is so fabulous, Roy,' I said, as overcome by the magnificence of the painting, as by him.

'Yes, the provenance is clearly established, the expert in Delhi has endorsed it as an original. I have been flooded with inquiries.'

'But how is it possible,' I turned towards Roy, 'that a genuine Amrita Sher-Gil went undiscovered for six decades?'

Roy shrugged, and I could see the muscles stretch and ripple in his black tee. 'They were just not looking for it. It was found in some godforsaken village, for Christ's sake. No one there knows a thing about art...'

Then Roy's voice changed its register and he looked me right in the eye. 'But it makes me think, Tara, what else is out there – undiscovered, unrecognized, unappreciated?' He was leaning so close he was almost touching me. I froze, my back stiff, my nerves on high alert. If I wanted to I could have let him touch me. Would his touch prickle and burn?

Instead I gave him an extra bright smile, and moved towards the living room, murmuring, 'I should make a move.'

He followed me, his eyes now a deeper blue. 'On me?' he teased. Then sensing my discomfiture, he changed his tactics. 'Lunch?' he suggested in a rough-edged voice and I suddenly felt very warm, despite the air-conditioning.

I knew I should have declined, but Ro was at school and I had a free afternoon.

So I didn't.

Sitting in Indus, over beer and club sandwiches, I told Roy all about the gallery I wanted to start and he told me about the auction house he wanted to set up. Then we spoke about ourselves. He told me how his parents had met. His mother was an art student. His father, an officer of the 6th Poona Division, had been photographing the sculptures in Ellora, when his Leica had chanced upon a slim pale form bent over a sketchbook, glowing like eggshell tempera on bas relief in the dark grandeur of the caves. It had been love at first sight.

It was a lovely story; and he told it even better. I listened, mesmerized.

Roy smiled, a potent flash: 'Now, that Progressive Group painting you want to buy, Tara, what's your budget?'

I raised my hands to my face, feeling a blush coming on. Here was a man who dealt in crores. My budget was laughably low. '40 lakhs,' I heard myself mumble.

He held my hand in his over the table. 'I'll see what I can do.'

✤nine

There were still a million operational details to sort out to make the gallery a reality. We had to worry about sourcing, transporting, packaging, framing, hanging, installing, cataloguing, online presence, marketing – not to mention finding an appropriate gallery space. All of which had then to be fit into financial metrics to create a Plan.

'Go with the broad brush-strokes, Tara,' Pheroze had laughed at his own joke when we'd met with his accountant at his office to sign some incorporation papers.

But it was easier said than done. In another place and time, I would have fretted for a few months over financial assumptions and projections. Now I was expected to put my own money down on 'broad brush' calculations? The chasm between theory and practice had never been wider.

Financial planning proved especially tricky. No matter how I slashed cost projections and jacked up prices, the cash seemed to drain away. The real estate costs were especially killing. The only way to make it work was to sell high-priced, high-margin works by established artists, which is precisely what we did not want to do, even if we could cough up the initial amount needed to acquire such art.

'I have news,' Gul said excitedly, walking in that moment. 'You have to thank me, darling. I have just solved your problem.'

My problem? She didn't know the least of them!

She told me that an old family friend in the property development business had a proposition for us. We needed to meet him right away. 'Oh and can Raj come too? His presence would really help. Is he in India?' Gul inquired.

'Oh, he's in India, I think,' I replied in my most disinterested voice.

Gul laughed, 'Like *that*, is it?'

And I felt a flicker of annoyance. I knew what it was like. Still, I didn't want Gul to be amused by the dismal state my marriage was in. I wasn't. Besides, Raj was actually being quite conscientious this week, leaving text messages about his schedule, even when I didn't pick up his calls. I knew today, for example, he was at some *Business Times* sponsored forum on 'Sebi Rules for FII in Debt-funding Tools'. Dry stuff, if you ask me. He was welcome to it. Because, it was like this: he could have been in *Marrakesh* with *Mallika Sherawat* being flown in for a *belly dance* and dinner at a symposium on Emerging Market Derivatives for the Luxury Retail sector, and I wouldn't have cared *less!*

At the Sea Lounge in the Taj, Gul's friend, a tall, fit-looking fellow in a white shirt and Gucci shades perched on his head, was waiting for us. He rose from the sofa chair, thrusting forward his chest. 'Gul, lovely to see you...' He gave her a bear hug and turned to me. 'Hello, I'm Sudarshan Malkani,' he smiled, revealing dentist-perfected teeth.

'Tara Malhotra,' I said, and mentally checked a snigger at his old-fashioned name and his silvery hair, so at odds with his hot-bod looks and attitude.

'Call me Sud,' he said and suavely flicked a finger to beckon a waiter. 'My office is just behind the Taj, I use this place as an extension of my office. So...' he paused, looking condescendingly at the two of us, 'I hear you ladies want to start an art gallery?'

Gul nodded and leaning forward in her chair began to explain our plans of starting an art gallery that focused on the works of emerging artists.

Sud heard her out and then said, 'Here's the deal.' He owned a place in Colaba. An old row house with lovely bones, now rundown and vacant. 'If you like it, you take it for free for the first year. Renovation costs are yours. After that, I take a part of your proceeds. Say 20 per cent?' He drummed the table, impatiently.

A million thoughts crossed my mind – that he was as brash as he was dishy; that he knew nothing of our plan; that I knew nothing of his business rep. He could be a shark. He looked feral. That 20 per cent seemed obscene. Then another annoying thought crept in – that until recently I never used to notice other guys. Guys other than Raj, that is.

Sud was looking keenly from Gul to me.

Gul turned to me. 'Twenty per cent is a lot. But here's what I feel – what is 20 per cent of nothing? Nothing. So if we take it up as a challenge, to make it big, then 20 per cent of something big should not hurt us.' She turned to Sud, a sharp, assessing look on her face. 'But there has to be an end date to the contract, no? I mean we cannot sign ourselves up for 20 per cent for ever, year on year?'

I felt compelled to say something too. 'Suppose we do like the place and spend money to fix it up, then we need to amortise that amount from our payments over the next few years. So does that take a few points away?'

Gul stared daggers at me while Sud could barely cover his smirk. *Gosh.* I shut up, mortified. Given he was a Mumbai property king, this guy probably cobbled together five deals like this before breakfast every day. 'We should cap the rate and dollar amount.'

Sud took a bite of his melon salad, and looked at me appraisingly. 'If you agree in principle, we'll let our lawyers worry about the details.'

Our lawyers? That meant we needed to get one right away! I sipped my lime soda, fighting for time, feeling iffy about making money-related decisions off the cuff. It would be saner to flip open a spreadsheet, and play around with scenarios and see the optimal possibility. But this was reality. The guy was across the table, expecting quick answers. I slowly put my glass down and hesitated. 'I will be okay with 15 per cent.' I looked at Gul.

Sud snorted. 'Okay, 15 per cent sharing for three years, starting after your first year of operations.'

My American nanny was clamouring to return home.

At June's house, bent over in dhanur asana to Shambala Shop music and the nasal twanged instructions of a California-dreaming yoga guru, I asked for help.

'You must lower your standards,' June advised. She had much trouble with maids in her first year in India, she confessed, so much so that her mother-in-law's priest had given her a brownish stone to counter bad maid karma! 'Once I lowered my expectations of local maids, I coped better,' she explained.

I thought of the women I had interviewed thus far. It had seemed such an easy exercise, given India's trodden hordes. But I had seen the Mahar-bai types with their all-knowing street-smart talk; the weeping widows sent by a church in Byculla; the barely-teens, looking like they could barely manage themselves, leave alone my house. Not that my American girl was tops, but she was clean and could read bedtime stories. So when June's maid brought me her cousins from her village, I decided not to analyse too much, and hired the untrained girls on the spot.

I organized play dates with Rohan's new buddies from École Nouvelle and I learned how to manage life in Mumbai – which playgroups to join, the best places to buy imported Italian Pecorino or pots of kesar kulfi, what kid shoe brands were acceptable among the discerning. I learned the carefully orchestrated ins and outs of gathering food supplies in Mumbai – of little speciality shops from Colaba to Worli, some of which stored certain cheeses, others certain cereals. In DC, I would have happily driven fifty miles to source samosas. Here, I was happy to be chauffeur-driven fifty kilometres to source smoked Gouda.

Maddy invited me, with extra passes, to a spa opening. I braced for disappointment as we entered a derelict-looking building in Kemps Corner. But up the elevator, as we entered a dimly-lit frangipani-scented minimalist room, I gasped in surprise. Champagne was on offer. Beautiful skinny women milled about, sampling grilled mushrooms and polenta, only too happy to spend even more time making sure they looked even more stunning.

'Welcome to Rudra,' the hostess said as I signed up for a complimentary Ayurvedic massage and blow-dry. After a delicious ylang ylang and cardamom-scented massage, I was a soft target when the spa owner accosted me. A thousand dollars, I calculated backwards. Not bad for unlimited services for a year!

This part of Mumbai, I had to admit, I could easily get used to.

India was not bad, if experienced from a five-star perspective.

Just don't tell Raj I told you so!

Late Thursday night, after Rohan was asleep, I sat on the bed with my laptop working on the gallery plan. There was too much to do. A fuzzy lump in my chest gained definition till it became big and heavy, and full of imminent threat. What was I letting myself in for? I felt none of Gul's nonchalant airiness.

The door to the bedroom creaked open and Raj walked in, looking unreasonably fresh for someone who had been up and at it since five am. 'Waiting for me?' He walked towards the bedside, gently closing one arm around me.

I stiffened instantly. This was what I hated about Raj. Our relationship had become so cold I didn't talk to him unless I absolutely needed to. But then he had sent me two cutesy text messages last week, to which I had not responded.

'What are you doing?' He peered at my laptop.

I wriggled away angrily and saved my document. 'Just making plans for my art gallery.'

'What art gallery?'

I told him of the plans I had been making with Gul. Let him make what he wanted to make of it.

'Why, may I ask?' He sounded annoyed.

'Because I love art! Because I don't have a job anymore! Because I gave it all up so we could come here!' I shouted, angered beyond measure.

'But why an *art gallery*? God, didn't you hear what Vijay said that day? What do you know about running an art business, anyway? Why not work in an area you know something about? There is too much hype about art now!'

Raj ranted on about researching art and investments needed and target markets, barraging me with questions, as if I had not successfully managed my own career for so many years. Had I not been asking Gul the same questions?

Had I not been trying to answer the same questions?

✧ten

And so a gallery was born – on paper, anyway – when Gul and I registered it legally. *Saloniere Star* – a space to launch the careers of future luminaries of the art world. Of course many more long-worded documents would have to be signed in triplicate and many more sums of money sent to government offices through cumbersome demand drafts, before it was official. But, thankfully, our lawyer and accountant would take care of those details.

Now that we had a space, Gul and I sat down with the dossier our architect Jai Bhavnani had sent, minus cost approximations, which he said he would give us when we met.

'It's quite a list,' I said finally, perusing the renovation plans. Jai had suggested caving in a couple of walls to create some arches, updating the bathrooms, creating a false ceiling to instal fancy Italian lights, redoing the kitchen space, designing an entrance lobby portion and creating a storage loft. All of which translated into a lot of dosh and several months of work.

'We must ask him to simplify the plans,' Gul said resolutely.

The next day we arrived in Jai's office and were asked to wait in the reception area. Sipping the machine-made, extra-sweet coffee provided by his assistant, I flipped through a catalogue of his previous commercial works. 'Wow, look at this,' I showed Gul a picture of a vineyard gallery Jai had designed in Western Australia: a fabulously modern elevated cylindrical creation in Tasmanian oak, glass, and steel, joining the winery with its famous restaurant and tasting room, with barely-curved walls and curved ceilings and futuristic space balls strung on messed-up, wire-mesh-type lighting fixtures.

Gul made a face. 'He must have made that on an unlimited budget!'

The door opened just then and Jai beckoned us inside. On the ammo of the super-swish design we had just seen, Gul started off on the thing worrying us the most – the money. 'How much will the reno job cost, Jai?' she asked worriedly.

'I can ball-park a figure,' Jai stalled, and smilingly asked if we wanted more coffee. As we shook our heads, he chuckled. 'So tell me first, did you like the proposal? We can discuss the money later.'

'The thing is,' I cleared my throat and looked him straight in the eye – I was slightly defensive about being on a budget, yet ready to state it: 'We have a budget for the renovations, Jai. So knowing costs even approximately will help in determining work specs.'

'I appreciate your frankness,' Jai smiled smoothly. 'Let me assure you first. You are expats. I will create something for you to match your international standards, something suitable for the type of clientele you would expect. I will give you a completely finished, furnished space – all you will need to do is add the paintings.'

The consternation must have shown on our faces, because Jai went on to say: 'Less than thirty lakhs, I assure you.'

'Thirty lakhs!' gasped Gul. 'We need to halve that cost. Look, these bathrooms and the kitchen, we don't need those for a gallery.'

'A bathroom for your high society guests, surely?' Jai raised an eyebrow.

'Well, maybe one,' Gul grudgingly acquiesced.

'Okay, I will rework the ideas and give you a detailed plan.' Jai assured us he would deliver some drawings and a revised quote in a week.

I snorted. Knowing the pace of work in India, Jai would take two weeks at least.

Back in Om Deep, Gul and I sat glued to my laptop working out the maths. But gallery costs continued to be worrisome. There was the renovation cost of the gallery, the cost of acquiring the artworks, as well as the initial marketing and operational costs. Given that the renovation cost was going to be significantly higher than the couple of lakhs Gul and I had allotted for it, we were already stretched to the limit.

'We need an infusion of extra cash,' I said.

Gul nodded solemnly. 'But how can we do it without diluting our equity further?'

'How about a loan, Gul? Go for debt funding instead?' I thought of the hundreds of unwanted telemarketer calls I received every week, pestering me with their offers of personal loans, no guarantors or security needed, that too in a market where verification was a joke. It couldn't be so hard then to get a business loan, I figured.

I called my bank manager and after some explaining of our business idea and some hints about typical art margins, he easily agreed. 'I can give you a personal loan of 15 lakhs in 48 hours.'

'But wouldn't a business line of credit be at a lower variable rate?' I asked. After all, we didn't need the cash tomorrow, and we would have to pay an extortionist interest rate on a personal loan.

'It will...' he hesitated. 'Look, normally to qualify for a business loan, you need to show me profit and loss statements for two years. What's the annual income of your gallery?'

'We are just starting,' I said, a bit flustered now, as I tried to remember all the business finance mantras from my earlier life. So no one would give a business loan to a non-entity even in these laissez-faire times when banks were pimping credit like the freshest femme fatale on the streets?

'But look here, Mrs Malhotra, I know Mr Malhotra banks with us,' the bank manager cleared his throat, and I could at once see a young twenty-something guy on the other side, flicking back his gelled hair, as he dreamt of weekly targets. 'If he acts as guarantor, we might consider giving you a business line of credit. But rates will be high because you have no cash flow history. Maybe half a basis point lower than the personal loan.'

'What about giving me a personal loan on a line of credit basis?' I said. We could save interest payments if we were charged for only as much of credit as we drew upon.

'It's not something we normally do,' the young banker responded. 'But I will ask.'

It was just eleven, too early for lunch. So Gul and I sat for a while, drinking coffee, and discussing other options. Some fifteen minutes later, the phone rang. It was the bank manager.

'You're in luck, Mrs Malhotra,' he said solemnly. 'We can give you a personal loan, which you can use as a line of credit; in essence you pay interest on the amount you use. So, should I send my man with the forms tomorrow?'

Ravi Uppal's private sanctum atop a Nariman Point highrise was a handsome den with deep cherrywood panelling and a view of Marine Drive. This was the life! I admired the huge FN Souza dominating the reception area. A Chitrita Goswami hung above the water cooler, a large Ravinder Reddy sculpture stood by the door.

The secretary led me into the inner room. Ravi rose up to greet me. Behind him, a gigantic Raza Bindu spiralled inwards in shades of blue. 'Looking to buy more paintings, Tara?' Ravi smiled affably.

I told him about our plans for Saloniere Star.

Ravi was amazed. 'Wow, quick work, Tara. You've just arrived in Mumbai, and already you are starting an art gallery!'

I said, 'Well, my business partner Gul Dastur has been in India for a few years. Do you know her?'

Ravi crinkled his eyes, '*Noo...*'

So I told him all that I knew about Gul.

'My rule of business is, Tara, don't ever take a partner,' Ravi said emphatically. 'Employ people, give them a cut as needed, all of that. But since you already have a partner, let me not scare you.' His thick lips parted to reveal pale yellow teeth. 'So what can I do for you today?'

'We need your help, Ravi,' I said.

He nodded sagely. 'You want me to invest in your gallery?'

'No, no,' I said quickly. 'We may come to need angel investment later. For now, I just need contacts and advice. Kind of like a mentor.'

'Ah, yes,' Ravi said.

He talked of his recent trips to Paris and Montpellier to meet with designers and couturiers and fabric suppliers who wanted to outsource a part of their manufacturing to India. It was an expansion from his outsourced yarn manufacturing units in Surat and Thane. He sighed loudly as he pressed the intercom to order cold coffee. 'Look, I would have personally introduced you to my artist friends. But under the circumstances, given how busy I am at the moment, I can just give you some numbers. Will that help?'

I was delighted. This was already more than what I'd expected him to do. He flipped open his diary and rattled off a list of names – all luminaries of the Indian art circuit, already established stars in their own right. I asked him for newer artists. The current luminaries might already be too big to go with a new gallery.

Ravi promised more introductions in a few days. 'But don't be scared of established artists. Many of them are trying to carve a bigger name for themselves in the international circuit. If you can help them seek wider audiences, through art fairs and biennials and fellowships, they will sell through you.'

There was more to think about. *Art Fairs. Art Fellowships. Exchange programmes.*

Ravi started to look distracted again, so I quickly mentioned my wish to find an oil painting by one of the Progressives. Ravi looked at me with interest again, peering over his glasses till I mentioned my price range.

'You realize you will find only a mediocre Progressive piece for that price?' Ravi said.

'I know.' But everyone I knew in Mumbai seemed to own at least one painting from that genre. That need to belong had grown each day, further increasing with each visit to a new friend's house, aggravated daily as I spent time in Gul's gallery-like home, like a craving feeding on itself, a scorpion biting its tail or an endless chase along a Mobius strip, on and on, never reaching that finish line. I must have one!

'Have you heard of the Cancer Foundation art auction?' Ravi asked. 'They will be previewing soon. I think they may have a small Husain and Souza in there.'

My attention was piqued. It sounded perfect. A small Husain, or Souza, bought in aid of needy children. Better than buying a small Husain or Souza merely for the sake of owning one! I was hooked to the idea. I needed to know more about this Cancer Foundation art auction. Ravi promised to get me in touch with the organizers.

Saloniere Star was slated to open in late August. There was still a lot to be done and Gul was getting kind of frantic. 'We have no pipeline, Tara. I'm really nervous. Now, Muthuswamy, this amazing young painter in Munnar I have been in email contact with, who I had thought could be one of our first finds, is suddenly talking to a gallery in Chennai. Let's go to Munnar on Thursday and check him out.' She then also suggested flying to Baroda thereafter.

I stared at her. *In three days?* How could I leave my nascent household upon two untrained maids and scuttle off in such haste? There were social engagements – the usual toggle – a birthday party at India Jones, an opening night for a new show, a Wine Night hosted by one of the Consulates. I could easily give them a miss but Raj was travelling to Dubai – some conference on

Asian equity portfolios. Of course, he was not going
to cancel for me.

'Let me see how I can manage it,' I told Gul, loath to
say no again. I had to do what needed to be done.

I reached home worried. I was at a loss. How could
I go away? Couldn't quite ask my friends, and my
mother could not be expected to shut her clinic at such
short notice. I made a flustered call to my mother-in-
law. Thankfully, she agreed to come spend time with
her grandson. Feeling infinitely lighter I prepared for
our first visitor to Om Deep and asked the maids to
air the guest room and stock the tiny guest bathroom
with toiletries.

'We're on for Thursday,' I called Gul, asking her to
make flight arrangements.

That afternoon I picked up Ro from school after
his taekwondo lesson, grabbed a large tub of chocolate
ice-cream, and sat him on my lap. While he gobbled
the ice-cream messily, I gave his little head a rub: 'Dadi
is coming to see you, Ro.'

'Really?' he said excitedly. 'Dada too?'

'He'll come later. But when Dadi comes, Mommy
has to go away on work. For two nights, maybe. You'll
be a good boy for Dadi?' I said, half wondering at the
wisdom of trying to explain it to a four-year-old.

Better to leave quietly and deal with the tantrums
when I returned, no?

Gul was hyper when we met at the airport early
Thursday morning, and frantically waved a sheaf of
papers quoting the results of Sotheby's latest auction in
New York. 'The art market is going soft,' she wailed, as
we walked towards the check-in counter.

I had not seen the results yet. Sotheby's auction results were something I gathered from magazines when they created headlines. Now, of course, as a gallerist, I would have to keep closer track. I grabbed the sheaf from Gul and went through the printout as we waited for the lady at the counter to check us in. Once past the security gates, we sat on the drab plastic tub chairs, waiting for our flight to Kochi to be announced.

'These numbers are all in tens of millions!' I told Gul, yawning a bit, as I looked around for a Café Coffee Day counter. 'What's the problem?'

'The problem?' Gul looked at me incredulously. 'The problem, my dear Tara, is that most paintings sold below reserve prices! I was talking to friends in London and some dealers in Mumbai too. I fear the market may be softening. Is this the right time to enter?'

I had no answers for Gul. But who set these reserve prices anyway? And who decided that a painting with a reserve price of eighty-five million, when sold for eighty million, was indicative of the market softening? It seemed pretty bogus to me!

'We'll be fine,' I assured Gul. 'India is always a few years behind the US in market maturity. Our Mumbai billionaires will continue to demand their trophy art for a while yet!'

'We don't deal in trophy art, remember?' Gul snapped.

Munnar was lovely – cooler and greener than India's financial metropolis, and despite the thick coating of red dust that dulled the sheen of the overhead foliage and the strong heat that baked the black roads, had a magical timelessness to it.

We crossed Munnar town, with the usual dilapidated shops and odd relics from the British era, drove past a well-maintained golf course, and reached a tiny cottage in a cul-de-sac off a lane leading to a tea estate, overlooking slopes of tea plantations and red ginger shoots and cardamom trees. Here we finally met Muthuswami a young bearded artist with intelligent eyes, ready to connect with his audience.

'Welcome to my shack,' Muthu greeted us. While he prepared coffee, he talked about growing up in Munnar, studying art in Trivandrum and then coming back to Munnar to house-sit the lovely holiday home of an old schoolmate who had gone on to join the diplomatic corps. 'Inspiration is everywhere, and my friend is seldom in India. It's perfect.' He gave us thick coffee in little steel glasses.

His paintings were stacked against the wall. They were monochromatic layerings of paint and texture and materials, suggesting green fields, brown rivers, blue skies. The images, abstracted with much gutting and layering of primer and colour, made the third dimension palpate with mystery. Mauve peeked from behind a ridge of brown, a hill of blue had specks of carmine and primrose. It was a seminal moment – we loved his work, we loved the way he explained his vision, and he liked us.

But: 'Let me think about it, Gul,' Muthu said. 'I had already been talking to a gallery in Chennai about this lot when you called.' It was an artist's prerogative after all, to choose whom to go with, especially if he or she showed any promise.

Muthu seemed eager to make his mark, but he wasn't committing then and there.

As dealers, we couldn't seem too eager and give away our advantage. We didn't press him much, but over a simple lunch of Kerala fish stew, reddish broken rice and yoghurt, prepared by a cook from a nearby village, Gul put forward her reasons why we, with our global outlook, would be a better choice to propel him to international stardom and how much harder a new gallerist would work for a new artist, compared to an older, established gallery. Leaving him with these thoughts, we drove back to Kochi to spend the night at a hotel, before taking the morning flight to Baroda.

The next afternoon we were in Baroda. Ravi Uppal had arranged for us to be met by his friend, Alta Deb Pal, who met us at the airport.

'Hope you are not too tired,' Alta, a large woman in a red salwar-kameez and a big bindi, said. 'You have such a short stay in Baroda, so I have lined up some quick meetings.'

We first met a young artist, Nayan Doss, whose sharply etched figures and darkly hued backdrops were in direct contrast to Muthu's works. Nice, but not extraordinary. We drove on, to arrive at the tiny studio of Arghya Akhouri. The name was tough to pronounce, and the art might prove tougher to sell, unless one aimed at high-end tourists looking for souvenir art. His huge canvases typified India in a calendar art way; with ripe-bodied, full-lipped women, their heavy lidded eyes drowsy in divine orgasmic ecstasy, alone or in groups, with deities in the backdrop. Gifted brush-strokes adorned the figures in blues and reds and greens, but the entire effect was too lush – pimping the other India of erotic spirituality and the Kama Sutra. 'Not quite our style,' I smiled apologetically at Alta as we left.

We drove for a bit after that, past shops and battered automobiles, along streets that could have belonged to any small town of India, lined with milk booths and shops selling plastic buckets and steel canisters and saris and giddily gilded puja items. The maze of small lanes led to a larger road leading away from the city, and the Hyundai Santro dodged bicycles, trucks, cars and pedestrians to finally arrive at Space Studio, a refurbished pharmaceutical factory which the owner loaned to artists in exchange for a piece of art. Alta parked the car, and we emerged, re-energized by the serenity of the place in the late afternoon light. Once inside, the calm of the well-lit individual studios seemed to blow away the dust and devilment of a city that mixed the ancient with the industrial.

We walked around the place admiring the artwork which mixed urban design, graphic design, metalwork and traditional paints. The space had a village-like feel, as artists hung out in each other's cells, discussing how to source material or the latest film, or walking out to smoke a joint. Alta introduced us to a smallish soft-voiced man, Pulak Parikh, who created massive sculptural paintings. His two-and-a-half dimensional metallic abstracts, signifying fear, joy and rage, churned the sea of psychedelic canvas around them, drawing the viewer into their depths.

'These are great,' I enthused.

Gul spoke to Pulak for a bit. He had graduated from MS University five years ago and had already had solo exhibitions in Bangkok and Berlin through exchange fellowships, but not many in India. His pieces were priced a bit high, but we knew we would come back to him, if not for our first show, then later.

*

By Saturday morning, when I arrived home, I was exhausted but excited – the trip had been a success.

'Mummy...' Rohan came running to me and clung to my legs. I hugged him tight, glad to hold his little self in my arms. It was like pinning down a butterfly and within minutes, he was fluttering around, free, jumping off the sofa, talking nonstop about some birthday party he simply had to attend.

'What's happening?' My mother-in-law rushed in, adjusting her cotton sari and I offered her an appeasing smile. We lingered over mid-morning coffee and onion pakoras, while the maids pussyfooted around, dusting in the background. 'Do you know how much onions cost in this city?' My mother-in-law exclaimed in surprise. 'Double of Delhi! Even more than onion prices in America when I had visited you.'

After dropping my mother-in-law off at the airport, dressed in a silky halter dress from Kimaya, I left home again.

The birthday party turned out to be an amazing extravaganza in the Crystal Ballroom at Taj President. An entire big-top circus tent had been rigged up with clowns and jugglers parading about, while a contortionist performed tricks and games stalls offered a myriad activities. Pouf-haired mothers tottered about on three-inch heels, waving their diamond-laden wrists, commanding sullen ayahs to run after their tots. I took Ro to line up near the tattoo artist. Then after a humongous meal from stalls serving assorted Chinese, Italian, Chaat, South Indian and North Indian dishes, we staggered home, laden with return presents.

On the way back, I scanned my phone for messages from Raj. Was he back from Dubai today or on Sunday? I couldn't remember. That's how connected we were these days.

❧eleven

Raj arrived home on Sunday in a jovial mood, having struck a deal with some Middle East institutional investors at the conference, and unloaded a plethora of toys for Ro, bought from Dubai's retail abundance. His mood lasted the week; he came home early every night to play with Rohan. We spent the evenings sullenly together, meeting his new friends in one trendy nightspot or other.

The days, meanwhile, continued to be devoted to the gallery. Gul and I continued to work in a frenzied manner. The summer deadline loomed nearer and nearer and we got more and more manic as we detailed the to-dos. The list was appallingly long. We needed to quickly finalize our first couple of shows, so that we could go ahead with the operational and marketing details of actually acquiring and framing paintings, creating the catalogues, marketing the shows and pre-selling the works.

Panicking, we called Muthuswami and convinced him to exhibit his paintings for our opening show. We focused on our credo of promoting future stars and after much pandering to his artistic ego and some delicate negotiations over terms, Muthu agreed. His last show in Kochi had been a sell-out and several galleries from around India were courting him. The refreshingly inexperienced artists from the FFA in Baroda proved easier to convince; they were to be the focus of our second show.

Muthu sent us images of his paintings via email and we selected the ones we wanted to display. Framing was crucial, and we visited the better known SoBo framers as well as some dusty footpath shops in Oshiwara to see what was available. Gul got excited over some dusty railway track plates, and I had to literally drag her away. We tracked down printers in grubby little alleys in Colaba and Fort, but the printed brochure samples were unimaginative and the colour schemes clashed. Finally someone recommended a quality printer in Parel. We spent hours fiddling with the logo design for Saloniere Star and by Friday, had our business cards printed.

Gul and I started attending gallery openings, meeting patrons and connoisseurs, artists and dealers, trying to talk to as many people as we could. People took our announcements in their stride. *A new gallery?* Why, yes, it was a great time for the art industry. *A focus on young artists?* Of course, with spiking prices for established artists, the emerging sector was clearly the growth area.

But the pace of the art world was blistering. There was a show opening every evening of the week, interspersed with double-duty days of auction previews, art talks, art fashion shows, art curated by bankers, art created by film stars, art to raise funds for NGOs and art created by NGOs. No sector of the city remained untouched by the tentacles of contemporary Indian art.

To attend these shows after a full day's work of liaising with suppliers and customers and to be in best sales mode all the time, was taxing to say the least.

By midweek, Gul had to threaten and bully me to visit another gallery. I couldn't believe there were enough buyers for all this art.

Gul said some of it was the pre-monsoon frenzy. 'But, yes, there are enough buyers in the city.'

Thursday evening, we were at an edgy found-art installation exhibit by a young Chelsea College graduate. Video images and sound footage focused on a structure made with rope, fishermen's nets, coloured rice and rusted car wheels. No one mentioned rupees or dollars, but there was talk of dismantling it and shipping it to an Art fair in Manhattan. Apparently, it had that kind of a 'feel' to it.

Gul accosted the delicately boyish artist, Neil Prakash, suave in his Armani Exchange black fitted tee and red-rimmed eyeglasses. 'This is fabulous, Neil. My God, the buzz in this room reminds me of the Damien Hirst show I had helped organize in London.'

I looked at Gul, my eyebrows rising of their own volition and I quickly tried to make my face as neutral as possible. What was she on about? A Damien shark-in-formaldehyde Hirst show? I had never heard of anything like that from her before.

But Gul coolly flashed our business card at Neil, and introduced our gallery, and held Neil's hands in an affectionate, motherly clasp. I was tempted to giggle. *My God, do I know this woman?*

What in the world was she doing? Surely, Neil was not falling for any of it?

But Neil seemed suitably impressed. 'Damien Hirst...' He whispered, awe lacing his voice. 'Wow. I'd love to talk to you some more.'

'What were you on about?' I giggled to Gul later.

'All true, I assure you,' Gul winked. 'I once worked for a PR firm that handled a Damien Hirst show.'

Meanwhile, I stalked my own prey. I zeroed in on a grey-suited guy loudly telling another grey-suited guy about some big-ticket VS Gaitonde painting he had bought recently. Gaitonde, now that was a painter whose work I had seen. I squared my shoulders, flicked back my hair, and confidently walked up to them.

'I couldn't help overhearing you mention Gaitonde...' With a sweet smile I told them about the Gaitonde in the Sotheby's auction in New York last year, sighing over the delicacy of its form, the drama of its hues. 'It was sheer poetry on canvas. I've always felt he is under-appreciated...' I stopped as I sensed my audience overwhelmed by this unexpected paean to Gaitonde. 'I am an art dealer, by the way. Tara Malhotra,' I smiled, extending my hand.

My palms were ice-cold. Would they know that I was exaggerating big-time? I had only *walked* through that auction preview and the only thing I could afford had been a two-inch bronze statuette of nineteenth-century vintage. A full-sized, contemporary Indian painting, in this over-blown Indian art market? Forget it.

The man looked at me unquestioningly, accepting my statement at face value. He probed nothing. He did not ask what I had bought at the Sotheby's auction. He did not even ask if I had been there representing anyone. Emboldened, I offered him a Saloniere Star card.

'Amazing! New galleries are opening in this city by the day. The way the art market is going, there must be room for a lot more,' the man said, pumping my hand. 'You must be a big collector too? Whom do you buy personally?'

There it was again, that assumption, that if I was selling art, I must be a *Big Collector*!

I had to do something about that.

Sheets of morning light impinged upon the double storey glass windows of my living room, and despite the heavy-duty blinds and air-conditioning, autoclaved it. I was feeling as hot and bothered as the day outside. I had been up since dawn, compiling a list of art contacts we had made, annotating it with remarks, a cheat-sheet to remind me who they were later. Then, Gul called, all freaked out: 'Tara, get here immediately. It's an emergency.'

It turned out to be the latest cost estimates from the architect. Despite cutting down on a bathroom and the false ceiling, the price continued to be horrendous. There wasn't enough time to find a new architect and go through the specs process again.

We went over the line items listed in the architect's proposal, discarding several suggestions. Did viewers really need Arne Jacobsen Egg chairs or a Jean Prouvé daybed to sit in while pondering a possible purchase? But the cost still remained higher than what we had planned. We had already promised to fork out advance payments to the artists, a slightly higher than anticipated rate for Muthu to get him to agree, not to mention all the operational costs of shipping, framing, displaying, cataloguing and marketing.

Gul slumped into her sofa chair. Worry lines furrowed her forehead. 'We could stagger payments to Jai, I guess.'

I paced the room, back and forth, back and forth. 'We need more starting capital, even to stay afloat in the first year.'

With much trepidation, I called up the relationship manager at my bank, and asked about extending lines of credit. The manager had his customers to keep. He agreed to extend the loan limit. But for the extra credit, the rates he offered were near extortionist.

'I could ask Pheroze,' Gul said, 'but he has his own business balance sheets, and I have always prided myself on running my own show.'

I did not even want to *ask* Raj. 'We need that infusion of capital,' I said gravely. 'Ravi Uppal had offered...maybe he will offer a better rate than the bank?' I let my voice trail off. Did we have that many choices given the tight timeframe?

Money was just that touchy thing that we couldn't approach friends with. Business had to be kept on strict book-keeping terms, separate from personal spend and friendships. An angel investor was called for.

We called Ravi Uppal. Fortunately, he wasn't travelling that week, and he said he could see us for a few minutes, if we reached his office at once.

Once in Ravi's office, I explained our case quickly. Then Gul spoke about herself and her knowledge of art while I provided our plans for the gallery.

After hearing us out Ravi agreed to provide capital without batting an eye – it was loose change for him. He discussed his terms – no expected returns in the first year, but a rising expected return on investment for the next three years. Plus a chance to buy paintings at cost.

We agreed; better to have cash flow, than a little less autonomy. Ravi was too busy with his own businesses to intrude upon us much. Plus he had so much experience in business and part-time art dealing.

'Provided I get a say in the running of your gallery and can tell you when I think the gallery needs to be steered in another direction. Like if I wanted to sell something through you...'

'No,' Gul emphasized. 'We can definitely consider it, but not guarantee it.' She spoke of our vision, and the need for autonomy in finalizing shows.

Ravi did not press the matter. 'We can take it on later,' he said magnanimously and called his assistant to formulate some documents for us to sign, after which we all shook hands on the deal.

Just as I was getting my blood pressure in order, Raj called to say he had to make an urgent overnight trip to Delhi. Some SEBI organized event with the Finance Ministry bigwigs that he could not slip out of. Not that it mattered whether he was around or not. But then, just when I thought the day couldn't get worse, I got a call from school. Rohan had misbehaved in class – for the second time that week.

Emotionally worn-out, I rushed from Gul's place to the school, hair messy, face barely made, in daggy old jeans and a plain shirt that was already looking crumpled from all the agitation of the morning. The hot weather did not help; two minutes outside air-conditioning and my hair frizzed up and my skin sprouted warts.

I rushed to Rohan's class to hear his teacher tell me he was stressed out. At *four* something?

'Could it be a lack of attention?' his teacher asked.

A catalogue arrived by courier, a slim glossy volume titled *A Half Century of Masterpieces – The Cancer Foundation Charity Auction*. There were 40 lots, each with a museum-print-quality photograph and a brief description of the artist, the painting and its provenance, all from the post-Independence period with an estimated pre-sale price below 40 lakhs.

I flipped through the catalogue. There, somewhere in the middle, between a Guernica-inspired Alphonso Doss and a quintessential Raza Bindu, was a full-page photo of messy, muddy brown strokes on a bluish-brownish background, and hidden in there, if looked at closely with imagination, was a female form, a little darkened burnt cocoa shade suggesting the side-view of a pendulous breast, thick flat-brushed strokes going lengthways to suggest hair.

The adjacent page said:

Lot 24
M. F. Husain b. 1915, (Pandharpur, Maharashtra)
Untitled
Signed in Devnagri (upper left)
Gouache and Acrylic on canvas board
25.4 x 30.5 cm 8 x 12 in)
Rs 3,600,000 – 4,000,000
$ 82,000 – 90,000

I was so still, my heart thumped loudly in my own ears. Should I bid for it? It was more expensive than any art I had bought before. It was not very inspiring. On the positive side, it was not a line drawing on paper, and it was not a horse! And there it was, that signature in Hindi: Husain. *Who's sane?* I laughed to myself. That's what I was paying 40 lakhs for – that thick black scrawl on the messy taupe-teal background.

❧twelve

I arrived at Gul's apartment to find her on the floor of her guest bedroom, like a lily afloat on a pond of multi-coloured art folios. I was dying to show her the auction catalogue. But Gul was too worked up about the gallery as she showed me design ideas for catalogues and talked about some PR agents her friends had told her about. She talked of PR gimmicks and I immediately imagined a Bollywood starlet swanning in to open our gallery for some exorbitant fee. 'A waste, isn't it?'

But Gul had other ideas – starting with an agent to help bag interviews in rag mags and slots on television. She talked of landmark PR coups staged by others before us – a post party at Enigma; invites sent with caviar tins; belly dancers on opening night. Tacky, jazzy, classy, brassy, anything would do.

'PR costs more money.' Money, or the lack of it, was the bane of our business life! Gul, who was usually so self-assured, was suddenly worried. The must-have wants of the cognoscenti were a Fendi baguette or a Ferretti yacht or a Raza Bindu. Without a splashy do, would they even come to buy the work of an unknown painter from an unknown gallery?

So when I finally showed Gul the auction catalogue, she looked at me as if I had grown two horns. 'Don't be crazy, Tara. This painting is not worth 40 lakhs. Don't buy it.'

I didn't know what to say. I looked around her guest room. A massive Jehangir Sabavala seascape amplified the headboard space above the guest bed; a large Sudarshan Shetty sculpture stood next to the desk. I knew the painting I proposed to buy was not high art, but then I was not in the market for crore-plus art either! My gaze inadvertently strayed to the door leading to Gul's lounge, where her wall-sized Souza and Gujral oils on canvas were hung. Her in-laws' room had Pichwai and Warli and Tanjore style paintings. Now, that was what being a real art aficionado meant. Gul had the right credentials to sell art to others. Me, with my Chitrita Goswami and my Bhola Prasad, where did I stand?

As if she could hear my thoughts, Gul said, 'You know when I bought my paintings donkeys' years ago they weren't priced like they are now.' Her voice trailed off, and became stern again, 'I would not pay to buy that painting.'

Hot outrage blazed inside me. Not much happiness or peace came my way these days. When I had finally found happiness over one thing, completely at ease with what I was choosing to buy, Gul had to go and spoil it for me with her pious speeches. I still had to deal with the melodrama of telling Raj what I proposed to do. I couldn't not tell him – a 40 lakh purchase was like buying a BMW or putting the down payment on a mortgage – couldn't quite slink it onto a credit card statement.

With Gul's admonitions trailing me, I walked out feeling desolate. What had I hoped – to be lauded for purchasing a bad piece of expensive art?

*

I reached home to find the cook throwing a tantrum and engaging in a shouting match with the maid. The last thing I needed. I screamed at them both. I hated India for this intrusion of people in my space, for the confusion and the chaotic infrastructure that always demanded help. At best, life felt like a television soap opera enacted for the viewing pleasure of my maids and drivers. At worst, it needed constant management to allocate and reallocate duties and provide daily reminders for basic jobs. I stormed out of the kitchen.

That night Raj made a rare appearance at the dinner table. 'I signed on the Research Head from BNP Parisbas in Zurich to join us in a month. Quite a young guy...' Raj proceeded to make some silly, straight-from-the-*Business Times*-type hot air remark about foreign currency convertible bond issues and cross-border takeovers by Indian firms. I saw red. Why was he so sanctimonious all the time? And this sudden jingoism – he was not even Indian by passport anymore!

'I'm buying a small Husain painting from the Cancer Foundation auction. 40 lakhs,' I told him baldly, changing the topic.

It went as I had expected, with Raj acting like a rap singer on crack – basically as belligerent and violent as imaginable. In response, I hurled a magazine, Frisbee-like, across the room, knocking down a vase full of thick-petalled oriental lilies. There was water everywhere, and as if reflecting off the watery surface, Raj's voice was loud and slick with anger.

He suggested investments, the usual harangue of infrastructure funds and precious metal hedging. I didn't hear a word of it – he already did enough of that stuff.

'Why a Husain, Tara?' he screamed. 'You won't even get a great piece at that price. It's a sheer waste of money!'

I felt a chilling thrill down my spine. I'd got him. I had. 'Because *you* brought me to Mumbai, and everyone I know here owns fabulous art!' I said in my snootiest snarl.

With perverse pleasure I realized that the more Raj raised his voice, the greater my resolve to buy this piece became. Till he shivered with rage like the sea in a gale and said, 'Don't waste my money on buys like this!'

My money? MY MONEY? Just because we had joint accounts, and for the last four months I had not put anything in it, didn't make it *his* money. And whose fault was it anyway that I had to resign from my job?

That did it! I would show him. I had to do it on my own. I must. My voice sounded utterly surreal to my own ears. 'I will not touch *your* money. I shall take money out from *my* 401k and *my* E*Trade.'

'What does that have to do with anything?' Raj said agitatedly.

But 401k was like a mantra I could not get out of my mind. I had parked large chunks of my salary over the years in my investment account. The amount seemed a lot in rupees, but doable in dollars. My investment in art might even double in a year. It was like a sudden revelation. My money, my decision! I wanted an MF Husain painting and I would have it!

I wanted to meet the curator for the Cancer Foundation auction collection, and in true Mumbai fashion, Ravi Uppal connected me to a dealer who knew a collector who knew the curator-auctioneer, Tushar Kripalani. In the Hilton lobby café, over mocha lattes, with a pianist tinkling away in the backdrop, Tushar told me about the provenance of the paintings in the *Forty under Forty* collection, gathered like scattered nuggets from the private boudoirs and locker safes of his clients in Mumbai and Delhi and London. He touted the Husain as an excellent buy for an acrylic gouache work by the artist. 'Come for a personal look before the official preview,' he said, as he unfolded his tall stringy self from the sofa.

As I was leaving, I saw Roy emerge from the elevator with a lovely girl stuck close to his side, but they disappeared before I could reach them to say hello.

Later that evening Roy called. 'Was that you in the Hilton lobby, Tara? I'm sorry I couldn't talk to you, I was with a client.' Sure didn't seem like just a client, but I said nothing. Roy told me he'd been away in Europe the past two weeks. When I told him about the Husain in the Cancer Foundation auction, he said quickly, 'An amazing Jamini Roy has just come in too. You will like it – all darkness and drama. See that before you bid.'

Thursday evening, after a repeat visit to the renovation site to confirm that the size of the arch carved between the two halls was neither too small nor too large, I met Roy in his temporary office – a set of high-ceilinged crumbling rooms on an upper floor of Dilkhush – an Art Deco mansion in Fort – owned by some friend of his. Up a dusty curved staircase, the shabby paintwork and frayed woodwork of the hall was livened up by a couple of ultramodern leather sofas.

'Tara, lovely to see you,' Roy said, looking debonair in a peach coloured shirt, the piquant smell of his aftershave filling the room.

Dilkhush, said Roy, was a place he used mainly for storage, while the unique pieces he found awaited private sale. It was an interesting set up.

'To whom does this place belong?' I asked again.

'A rich industrialist friend who bought a couple of paintings from me,' Roy said.

'And your auction house plans?'

'Are going too darn slow,' he answered. 'There is so much activity through private sales at the moment, I need a breather before moving on to the auction house idea.'

Roy led me through a corridor, past rooms full of dusty rosewood and teakwood furniture culled from old houses across the Coromandel Coast, to a small air-conditioned room, where a line of deep-set cupboards opened up to reveal a stash of brilliant artworks hung sideways on wire frames.

Roy pulled out a small framed work. Dark oil pigments glistened in the light. There was a slight fading in the corner. But the subject itself, a toothy hag with intense eyes that stared out knowingly, was hard to ignore. The painting was signed in Bengali, and pasted behind the canvas was a picture of the seller – a distinguished looking old man clad in white dhoti and silken kurta, from some time-forsaken village in Purulia, holding the painting.

'I wanted to show this to you,' he winked, 'just in case you changed your mind.'

He showed me some other pieces he had acquired. There was a large lovely oil painting by a student of Ravi Varma, but I was beyond symmetry just then; I only liked painters who broke the symmetry, smashed it to smithereens. There were water colours of Himalayan peaks and portraits of bejewelled, semi-clad women and charcoal sketches of knobby-boned men, by artists like Khare and Hayden and Bankey Behari, whom I had never heard of before. Roy confided he was talking to Christie's to put up the Bankey Behari for their Fall auction. 'There is amazing movement in secondary markets. I have clients calling me from as far as Copenhagen and Helsinki.'

I was impressed – a piece to be sold through Christie's, no less. We returned to the main office, and I told him of my plans for Saloniere Star, and how, despite the trouble of getting a space ready and trudging out of town to talk to neophyte artists, it was fun in a way that drafting the 20th edition of the prospectus of some top Red Herring touted stock had never been.

'It's amazing!' Roy absently reached out to flick my hair away from my eyes and tuck it behind my ear, startling me, making me intensely aware of him and me, and the silent space around us. 'Galleries have such an important role to play in developing primary markets, Tara.'

I basked in reflected glory. I loved my new role as a nurturer of the fine arts; it sounded so good and meaningful. Roy showed me catalogues for some upcoming auctions in Dubai, talked about an Art Fair he'd attended in Prague last month, and this cool new gallery he'd seen in Lisbon.

Later he suggested dinner, and I agreed. Rohan was away at a friend's place – a special weeknight birthday treat for his newest best buddy and would go to school tomorrow from that child's place. I glanced at my watch, it was only seven. I would be home by nine thirty.

We took my car. Roy picked up some friends on the way – Jeet, the spiky-haired scion of a chemicals unit, his lovely scooped-dress wearing wife, Geetu, and their relatives from the UK. We all hopped venues in Lower Parel, eating wasabi-miso-soy infused tempura and lettuce-wrapped garlic pepper pork, drinking endless caprioskas and dancing to nineties mix and Bollywood trance. We didn't talk much, but it was great fun. So much so that when Roy and Jeet and Geetu invited me for another night about town, testing out some new restaurant on the Juhu waterfront, I happily agreed. I was all for making new friends.

When I dropped everyone home, and got into my apartment, I looked at my watch again. It was nearing midnight. Raj was already asleep in the bedroom.

When I put my mobile on the charger, I saw that there had been eight missed calls from him.

On the dance floor, I hadn't heard a thing.

❧thirteen

The preview of the Cancer Foundation auction collection was a glittering affair in a chandelier-lit room of the Oberoi, bursting with newbie collectors and experienced dealers, deeply drunk on the business of buying and selling art, and on cheap Mahabaleshwar wines.

I had, of course, seen the painting before in a personal preview, when I had stood for several uninterrupted minutes holding the tiny framed Husain in my hands, not knowing whether to feel awed by the fact that I held 40 lakhs of hard cold money or dismayed that the painting did nothing to make me feel rapturous. Anyway, the signature was there all right – on the front, and on the back as I had been told. There was even a hologram slide stuck to the back, with the painter's signature on it. All bona fide, collectible material, I was reassured.

I had gathered as much information as I could about the process of bidding, trawling art sites and past auction results of Christie's, Sotheby's and Bonham's online. Gul dug out an Osian's catalogue which conveniently listed some of the past Indian art auctions, complete with pre-auction prices and final bid amounts. 'If you have made up your mind to be so foolish, Tara,' Gul had said to me, 'you might as well do it properly.'

Raj, of course, had been avoiding me in that way celebrities avoid the paparazzi – pretending to steer clear and yet not quite being able to control the odd caustic remark.

Anyway, I was at the preview to get into the mood, feel the vibes and get the pre-buying buzz. I bumped into a collector-friend of Ravi Uppal's, who said, 'It's good there is no buyers' premium for this charity auction.'

Buyers' premium? What the hell was that?

I hurried over to Gul's house, not sure whom else to expose my gross inexpertise to.

Gul gave me a stern look, her best don't-do-it dissuasion, and said, 'Buyers' premium is a standard practice when buying an exorbitant item at an auction, and then getting slapped with an extra odd 20 per cent in commission for the agent.'

Like they had not made enough commission from the sellers already! Thank God for small mercies then, that the price would be the auction bid, with no extra hidden payments needed.

The next evening, I was back at the Oberoi. A knob of disquiet had settled in my belly. There was a subdued excitement in the room. Waiters moved around carrying trays of drinks and canapés. Posh svelte women hung onto the arms of pot-bellied men. I gave my head a belligerent shake. I didn't need Raj hanging about next to me.

But before I could huff any more, an arm slipped into mine. It was Roy. He handed me a glass of wine, 'I thought you might welcome some company.'

I felt a bit tickled, and just a tad disconcerted. Were my troubles this obvious? Was it *such* a well-known fact that Raj would never be around to give me 'company'?

Soon the Master of Ceremonies rounded people up and urged them to take their seats. I put my untouched glass of wine under my chair, and watched, slightly distracted, as an earnest looking woman talked about the Foundation. The auctioneer was introduced. A thin woman in headsets stood nearby, probably to take in phone bids. Two men, dressed in black, carried in Lot 1 and in a clear, dispassionate voice, Tushar introduced the artist, Umashankar Pai, as an unsung hero of the pre-contemporary movement in Indian art, and described Pai's works as *'the idyllic lilting figures laden with reverie and melancholia, delicacy of brush-work and colours that merge into a vortex of lyrical cadences'* – words straight out of the catalogue.

Tushar changed the cadence of his voice as he opened the bidding at a low amount. Paddles went up across the room, an array of headstones marking wallets about to be buried under heavy art purchases. But as the auction continued and the price escalated, the paddles dropped off. Finally, two bidders competed for another round, till the price settled just below the estimated maximum.

Not a bad start then, I heaved a sigh of relief, glad it was not going crazy and felt the faintest stirring of excitement. Paintings kept coming in, some going a little over and some a little below. Paddles rose with slower frequency now, only serious bidders in the fray, while the rest watched. In between each round of bidding, waiters walked around with champagne bottles, quietly topping up glasses.

By the time Lot 23 came up, I was feeling utterly relaxed, swimming in the good stuff. 'Lot 23,' Tushar

said, and described the painting and the contributions
of Maqbool Fida Husain to the cosmos of Indian
contemporary art.

The men in black brought out the painting and
put it on a stand.

I was poised on the edge of my chair, my feet on
tiptoe even inside my three-inch heels, ready to raise
my paddle as soon as Tushar stopped speaking. But
before I could raise my hand, someone from the back
offered 40 lakhs.

'What, what?' I spluttered. It had already gone up
to the stated price! There was a sudden bustle in the
room, as people rose from their torpor, and swivelled
around in their chairs to look at the man brandishing
his paddle. Someone whispered that he was a dealer
from Miami, someone else whispered he was an ace
collector from Dubai.

Tushar was loud. 'Do I have a bid of 41 lakhs for
a rare acrylic gouache Husain?'

Rare? Was it rare? Was there something I didn't
know? It had already gone to the limit of my budget.
Maybe I could squeeze in a lakh more. I raised my
paddle.

The room went quiet, anticipating unexpected
drama. Tushar picked up a tiny silver gavel, gave it a
wimpy little bang on the podium and raised the bid
by another fifty thousand. The man behind must have
raised his paddle because the bid rose again. Before I
realized it, all eyes were on me and the unknown man
and we were both engaged in a bidding battle.

Half way through queasiness hit. What was I doing?
How did I arrive at this point of silliness, at this irrational
paddle-popping mania?

'50 lakhs and 75 thousand,' Tushar was saying,
looking at me meaningfully.

I could feel the eyes of the attendees boring into my back, piercing me from the side, curious about my next move. But my arms felt swollen, like balloons full of hot air. I could not exhale. I could not raise my paddle. To go up any further was impossible. I was already *way* beyond my limit.

My paddle remained lowered.

'Lot 23 to the gentleman in the back,' Tushar said. 'Congratulations, sir.'

I went into hiding.

The bedroom had never been so appealing. I lay in bed with the blinds down and the air-conditioner on and a soft downy blanket to curl up in and forget the auction fiasco! Gul called me several times about gallery work. I sent her a 'not well' sms. I couldn't believe how badly the auction had gone. The price had gone 20 per cent above the expected maximum!

Then Roy called in the evening. A condolence call I thought, reluctant to pick up the phone. But the ringing persisted so I took the call. He didn't mention the fiasco of the previous night. Instead he urged a meeting in Shamiana, talking of a surprise, much nicer than yesterday's Husain. My interest was piqued.

I arrived at the Taj early. Behind the lobby counters, the reddish panels of Husain were fresh reminders of my loss. Roy was waiting. His voice was sweet as he kissed my cheek, 'Don't worry about a silly auction, Tara. Buyers bid. Some win, some lose. Happens all the time!'

I resented his cheery tone. That was easy for him to say; today I could have been the owner of a Husain acrylic gouache on canvas! Instead half of Mumbai, including potential customers from my gallery, knew I had lost the bid! I could taste the bitterness in my mouth.

'Look at it as a blessing in disguise.' Roy's eyes were soft blue. 'I just came across an unusual piece this week. Much more unique than the Husain you were bidding for.' He paused: 'An Amrita Sher-Gil.'

'Amrita Sher-Gil?' I whispered in awe. 'I don't understand. I thought you had sold it. I read in the paper...'

'So I had.'

For a high seven-figure dollar price, I remembered. I flashed him a look of exasperation. 'It was in crores.' Was he making fun of me?

'No, this is another one, Tara.' Roy leaned forward. 'It's a much smaller one, found in the same haveli. It has just been authenticated by my friend in Delhi today.'

Amrita Sher-Gil! I gasped in awe. To unearth a rare find in a forsaken feudal house was one thing, but to find two of them – 'Amazing,' I gushed. 'You found *another* lost painting?'

'Well, lost paintings find me,' Roy gave an affected wave.

I leaned forward, my own travails forgotten, eagerly remembering his off-hand anecdotes from the past, of finding old masterpieces in empty privy-pursed coffers, and relics of ancient establishments eager to pawn off dusty oils for the rustle of new notes. As a debutante dealer, I had personally not met this type of seller. I didn't even know how to find them, all I had access to was young talent.

Roy talked about the Sher-Gil paintings found in Tanda, and the current day landlord, who had been running a failing potato cold storage operation, till his discovery of the first big Sher-Gil in his ancestral haveli. 'Turned his head, I tell you,' Roy spooned a delish cloud of cocoa-cream into his mouth. 'He went looking through that haveli of his, examining every odd bit of brass and every two-penny rendition of his waxed moustached forefathers and his heavy-breasted "foremothers" and kept sending me pictures. Most were worthless. But then he found this one in the bottom drawer of a rotting chest.'

'And the painting itself? What is it like?' I asked eagerly.

'It is a 1.5 x 2 foot canvas, Tara, a mini treasure, in earthy red and midnight blue, with the slightest crack in the left upper corner. But let me assure you, that does not take away from its beauty. In fact, the crack adds to the texture.' Roy leaned back, a thoughtful look in his eyes. 'You have to see a painting, Tara, breathe in the impressions it creates, marvel at the textured striations, absorb the play of colours and shadows. It will simply sound banal if I just describe it inch by inch.'

The painting was arriving from Delhi in two days, Roy said and we fixed a late evening meeting for three days later.

I love the word *banal*. Of all the monstrosities tossed around in the art circuit, amid tongue-twisters like 'triptych' and 'pastillage', the word *banal* stands out. Short. Simple. Abrupt. Its beauty is that it can be sprinkled quite liberally, even in normal conversations.

So instead of focusing on *banal* work, I rushed home to rifle through my collection of art folios and look at works by Amrita Sher-Gil. I wanted to talk to Gul about the painting I would soon see, but her displeasure over the Husain was fresh in my mind and I wanted to still hold this one close to my heart.

So I just looked at books instead. There were paintings in private collections, and works sold in recent-year auctions. I noted the tall slender figures, full of athletic grace of form and ascetic detachment of expression. I took in the pathos of a dark-skinned village woman and the wrinkled form of a bearded old man. *Conflict*, art historians wrote, abounded in Sher-Gil's works, and in the way she attempted to blend the formalism of Western aesthetics with an Indian atmosphere. They talked of her Hungarian mother and her Sikh landowner father. They talked of her *'lucid stylization'* and paintings constructed as a *'stiff tableau'*.

I found Sher-Gil's biography and read through it. Then a quote made me pause. Mulk Raj Anand, the writer, talked about Sher-Gil's perception of India:

> *She seems to perceive, even when they were in a fair, that each one of them was alone; especially the women who were segregated in both rich and poor households. And she brought an ambivalent attitude in tune with the ambivalence of the people: Together and yet alone.*

Oh my God! This was exactly how *I* felt, some sixty odd years after Sher-Gil had lived and painted – ambivalent about my life back in the country of my birth. Together with so many old relatives and newfound friends, yet alone – totally, completely, utterly alone. It dawned on me then. I loved Amrita Sher-Gil. She painted what I felt, what I had become. An educated, modern, globetrotting woman, who was not yet free!

I was still communing with the spirit of Sher-Gil when I left to meet Roy.

❧fourteen

My head was like a ball of wet cotton, sodden with thought, when I arrived at Roy's makeshift office. Looking heartbreakingly handsome in a two-day stubble, he led me to the storage room where the painting waited for me, displayed on an easel.

I was prepared to be impressed. Instead I was shocked. If ever a painting could so totally reflect all that I had been feeling, it was this one. It was *Destiny*, I was meant to meet this painting. If I lost out on the Husain, it was because this moment was pre-ordained.

Reverentially, I floated forward and found myself growing alternately hot and cold. There was a girl, draped in deepest burgundy red, squatting beside a wheelbarrow of vegetables. Behind her were silhouettes of tiny faceless men and women, buying and selling pots and potatoes, leading bullock carts and carrying wicker baskets on their heads, the ground dark, the sky darkening. A village market in the evening. It was her face – sad and determined; it was her eyes – vacant and white in a dusky face – that drew me. She was in the market. She was surrounded by people. She was alone. I raised chilled fingers to my face, and absorbed the colours as they sang to me. A million shades of blue, leavened by a hint of black, a touch of grey, a trace of brown. Lighter shades lit up in spots – a cart, a stall, a sari, a kurta. Deepest wine spilled in the centre.

'It's…' I couldn't trust myself to speak further because if I did, I would gush and burble and lose any edge in negotiation. 'It's…' I started again. I cleared my throat: 'It's lovely.'

Still in a trance, I followed Roy back to the main room, where he showed me an authentication document – a laminated sheet with a picture of the painting, a brief description, and a statement of authenticity, dating the painting to the late 1930s, signed by Daniel Leibowitz of Haute Artefacts, Valuers of Fine Art, Prague and New Delhi. Roy said that Leibowitz authenticated all his paintings for him.

I didn't know what to say. Should I ask the price? Maybe I should wait. Absorb the moment, first. I studied the certificate for a long time, carefully observing the watermarked back, the circular seal in the front, but said nothing.

Later we went out to the rooftop of Indigo. The air was warm and dense and the sky starless. An industrial-sized fan blew hot air, cigarette smoke and frenzied chatter towards us. Roy asked for a bottle of Margaret River Shiraz and then turned to me.

'Something on your mind, Tara?' Roy asked perceptively. 'You seem…quiet.'

'No, it's just…' I sighed. I had been holding it all in for four months. 'It's just that woman in the painting. How solitary she looks… It's how alone I feel these days.'

'Ah, Tara…'

Did Roy sound guarded and indifferent, or full of sympathy? I could not gauge. But my emotions were at bursting point; impossible to contain. They spilled, they gushed, they poured out. Every charged moment of the past four months, especially all the incidents with Raj, and how each little spat moved us further and further away, was revealed. Even more than the quarrels, our silence, that stunned hush, thoughts and joys and fears frozen dense, locked in motion, unable to escape their confined pressure, the chill rising and rising further, in a numbing fog of despair, was getting to me.

I cringed at my own words, recoiled from this impulse that made me confide in Roy, when I had not uttered a word to Gul or June or Lola or my friends in DC or even my mom. Especially my mom. But the words were out.

Roy leaned forward to clasp my hand, his fingers warm upon mine, his thumb tracing little patterns on my skin. He had rolled up his shirt sleeves, I noticed. His forearms were thick, wrists broad; sailor's arms, not an artist's. Around us, people continued to clatter cutlery and talk loudly, lost in their worlds. I slumped into silence like a wrung dishcloth, all emotion drained.

In silence, we walked downstairs and on along the broken cobblestoned path, past the colonnaded walkway of the Taj, to the foreshore. It was past midnight but it was strangely alive – family clusters walking noisily, couples cosying up on the wall, street sellers peddling trinkets and toys, the Gateway in the distance. We went to the edge, a low parapet separating us from the darkness beyond, unrelieved by the lights of distant boats.

There was a deep rumble in the heavens somewhere. A silver crackle shattered the sky, veining down to the anthracite sea. A breeze picked up, lightly playful, bringing out the smell of the damp earth and offshore waste. A raindrop struck my cheek and slipped down. Roy raised his hand to my face, but before he could wipe the lone drop off, the rain came down, sudden and hard. People started dashing about to find shelter, cars honked, and water flowed down fast along the sloping edge of the road.

We ran across the road, holding hands to dodge the skidding cars, away from the people huddled in front of the lit shop windows, and stopped in the dark shadow of a square column. I turned to Roy, my eyes glittering, exhilaration as fresh as the rain coursing though me, full of a lightness I had not felt in weeks. The glow from the shops reflected off his white shirt, but his face was in the shadow as he bent, his lips a soft brush across mine. And suddenly we met in a fierce grip, lips fused, his hands on my back, warm through my clinging clothes, and warmer still as one palm curved around to the front. Sheets of water enclosed us from the street, liquid curtains hung from scooped arches, skittering as they fluttered against the dusty pavement. Rivulets sloshed around our feet. Somewhere in the distance, laughter echoed under the shuddering sky. A car honked and I sprang away, shocked at the mindlessness of my action.

The pre-monsoon had arrived.

❧fifteen

I woke up the next morning in a rush of memories: Last night...under the eaves at the Taj...one passionate kiss...Roy and me...a moment's madness till the honking of a car split us apart.

Oh God, Oh God! I sat up. How stupid! What had I done? Would my indiscretion be found out? Was there a mark brandished on my forehead? A mark which shouted: 'Seeker of Extramarital Thrills, Spiller of Marital Secrets'? Not that anything had really happened... Just a kiss! A brief bout of stupidity! Still, wasn't that bad enough?

I raked my hands through my frizzy hair, trying to scour the embarrassing memories, trying to drown out my thoughts. Recklessly, I rushed through the day, only half-absorbing the morning chatter of friends at the school drop-off – the usual yada yada about the weather, and countdown calendars for summer trips – and spent the morning desperately overseeing the work in the gallery and debating with Gul on the emulsion colour for the walls: Classic Ivory Matte versus Sand Dunes. As the best backdrop for the paintings, it was a crucial choice, but I could not concentrate.

There was a string of text messages from Roy.

Sent: 1:33AM

You were amazing!

Sent: 9:27AM

Good Morning. Can't stop thinking about you...

Sent 2:38 PM

I have to see you again. Let's meet.

How was I supposed to respond to these? Any word I uttered was open to misinterpretation now! I just ignored the messages. Instead, Gul and I went to a canvas stretcher in Kurla, Muthu's rolled canvases in tow, and negotiated prices for urgent delivery. Ravi Uppal had introduced us to a television art correspondent, and we talked to him about pre-publicity.

Raj came home by nine, after an early dinner with clients who were flying back to Dubai by the night flight. I was staring distractedly at the television, half absorbing the intricate goings-on in a new crime drama on Star World, my mind firmly on the night before, on how easy, how mindless that step had been; and on the coils of marriage and how the light-heartedness and easy camaraderie that had trimmed every moment of our days in DC, edging tough routines in happiness, was irreparably tarnished.

Raj sat down on the sofa, shrugged off his jacket, and sighed; a mark of contentment or maybe tiredness. 'Tarun, that Research Head I hired last month, is good. I presented the first India Report for our fund tonight.' His voice was deadpan as he described the sheikhs and their Boston-bred financial handlers. 'They loved our analysis.'

I looked at Raj, taking in his lean profile, and the sparkle in his eyes as he spoke of the economic analysis of market activity in India, and the clients he had lined up, from Brussels to Qatar City. His first real conversation with me in weeks, and he spoke of business.

Once, I would have shared his excitement – once, even when talking finance, his arm would have been around me, his eyes filled with laughter, as we joked about the loops in financial reporting. Now, it was news to me that Tarun had already relocated from Switzerland and started work for the Ellerman Jones India Fund. I wondered about his family, what they made of this move from Zurich to Mumbai. As for what was happening in my life, what energized me, what caused me to despair, Raj hadn't a clue.

'So,' Raj turned to me, cricking his neck, giving me the steady eye. 'How was your day? What expensive stuff did you buy today?'

I shook my head. Was that his idea of a joke?

'Nothing,' I said. Where could I even begin? There was so much I wanted to tell him, but so little I could say. What should I say about what was happening to us – him and me – and our lives together? What should I say about the botched auction? What should I say about the Sher-Gil? What, indeed, *could* I say about Roy?

Rimli came over early next morning, just as I reached the gallery, visibly strained, dejection weighing her usual sprightly demeanour, waving a newspaper article about some young artist who had committed suicide in Baroda. I had never heard of the artist, Manasi Sheth. Art was a hard taskmaster, especially for those who didn't succeed. But Rimli was especially forlorn because Manasi had been a graduate of her alma mater, MS University in Baroda, although many years her junior. She showed me a clipping:

Bharat Times
Western Zone Edition
June 1

*Baroda. In an act of summer madness on a searing
49 degree Celsius day, young artist Manasi Sheth, a
graduate of the Faculty of Fine Arts, committed suicide
in her tiny Fatehganj flat. While no actual note has
been discovered, an empty bottle of Calmpose found
next to the body suggests drug overdose. Fellow young
artists suggest that lack of recognition as an artist may
have prompted Manasi's actions. Paintings bearing
signatures of eminent artists Bhupen Khakhar and
Binod Bihari Mukherjee were found among Manasi's
artefacts.*

'You are doing a noble thing,' Rimli told Gul and me.
'Helping young artists reach their true potential.'

Nobility was the last thing on my mind. Lines of
credit coiled around like shackles, binding down noble
intent. The business of buying and selling and making
margins to stay afloat removed the floaty veneer of art
touted for the sake of art. Of course, I believed in Muthu
and the Baroda artists I was talking to. But there was
more to it. Somehow, now, commercial viability came
first. We had to make the gallery succeed.

But I said none of this to Rimli.

Gul and I went over the day's tasks with the
foreman, and then left for Gul's house. Over coffee,
Gul, Rimli and I continued our discussion on the need
for deep reserves of self-belief in an artistic endeavour.
Rimli spoke of her plans for her next shows, the gallerists
she wanted to work with and her struggle to survive as
an artist. I remembered that day in Rimli's studio and
how emotional she could be about art.

After Rimli left, we emailed Gul's friend Apurva, sending her information and photographs of Muthu's works, and waited for it to be a decent time to call her in London. The printer emailed the Saloniere Star draft catalogue with write-ups, and we edited it, deleting a superfluous word here, adding a comma there. Then we dashed around looking for an art photographer to take digital photos of Muthu's canvases for the catalogue, and watched him fuss around with his reflectors and light-absorbing backdrops like an ingénue fussing with her makeup boxes.

In the evening, I rushed Rohan to extra practice for a school swimming event. Then my mother-in-law's cousin's niece-by-marriage called all of a sudden, announcing an unplanned visit from Amritsar. I was rushing around getting the fridge stocked and the guest room ready when I got another sms:

A collector is interested in Sher-Gil. What is your plan?

What? Where did a mystery buyer appear from? Of course, a dealer like Roy would not show a piece to just one potential buyer at a time. But it flummoxed me. Just when I was dwelling on the embarrassment of contacting Roy again, on what I would say, on what he would reply, the situation had turned around.

Quickly I texted him back:

Like painting. Let's talk.

Almost immediately, the phone rang.

'Hello, stranger.' Roy was on the line.

I cringed at the amusement in his voice, but before I could respond, he said, 'A businessman from Delhi is interested in that painting. If you want to buy it, you must decide quickly.'

'We haven't talked about what it's worth...'

'Meet me this afternoon,' Roy said. 'We can discuss the price.'

So in between business errands and Rohan's swim class, I met Roy for a quick coffee. A brief uncomfortable meeting in a cramped coffee shop in a hotel lobby, with Roy looking at ease, insouciantly draping his arm on the back of my chair, while I kept looking at my watch, very aware of him, of the divine musk-menthe smell of him, and squirmed. It was surreal. That evening outside the Taj was on my mind, I knew Roy knew it was on my mind, but I pretended it had never happened, and studiously avoided his gaze.

'The price...' I began.

'Depends, Tara,' Roy grinned. 'Last week I would have said 50 lakhs, now it is 60 lakhs.'

'As much?' My eyebrows jumped up. 60 lakhs! It was much more than the Husain.

'It's a good piece, Tara.' Roy withdrew his arm from behind my chair, all cool and composed. 'A rare original! Husains, you can find more easily, he's put out such a prodigious amount of everything from serigraphs to line drawings. But a real Sher-Gil, Tara, not many people own one. Who knows where the price might end, once my friend from Delhi starts bidding?'

'Bidding?' What about me, I felt like squeaking. Did I get first right of refusal? Obviously I was not clued in to the way high art worked, despite all my efforts at getting an art gallery going.

'Look, it's nothing personal, Tara.' Roy was all friendly again, his voice softer, patting my hand with his warm palm before I could snatch it away. 'But it's business...' He paused, 'If he offers a higher price, I will feel compelled to accept. You've had some days to think it over. This guy just called me yesterday. He stopped by on his way to Hong Kong to see the painting. I need to tell him soon.' Then he changed tack as his hand moved further up my arm. 'And we have some other unfinished business...'

Suddenly I felt small, exploited and overwhelmed, a small fry in the global art market, bravely trying to gather resources to buy an expensive work of art, while highflying businessmen zipped across the world, making quick stopovers to pick up luxe art, nonchalantly scrawling their signatures on lump sum cheques, before going on to seal some other multi-million-dollar, global, money-moving deal.

'I need the weekend to think,' I told Roy. There was much to think about.

Mumbai felt more claustrophobic than ever. Nothing worked as planned and every small job required intervention – maids who forgot instructions within half an hour; plumbers who left behind leaky pipes; two-bit computer geeks who could not manage the erratic internet connection; shop assistants who trailed me around asking multiple questions – everything was making my anger spill over levels of control.

I longed to escape this chronic inefficiency; I longed for a system that worked.

Then Roy called Tuesday, sounding chillier than a pot of kulfi. 'Have you decided about the painting?'

I dithered. I knew I wanted to buy it. But to decide single-handedly to spend 60 lakhs was very tough.

'Come see the painting again, if it will help you decide,' Roy offered curtly. 'Otherwise I have another offer.'

So I went over. Roy was cold and polite when I met him but the painting drew me like a magnet, the colours more vibrant than in my imagination, the scene more poignant every time I gazed at it.

'I am flying to Vienna tomorrow. I want to close the deal before that,' Roy said.

I gazed at the canvas. There was a crack in one corner. Would the paint chip off or the canvas rip? 'What of the longevity of the painting?' I asked, staring at the red-robed woman. Why was I so drawn to her? Was I like her, a distinct node on internet chat rooms, linked through nodes to thousands across the globe, and yet alone? So deeply, unbearably alone that there was no one to listen to what I really clamoured to say?

'There *is* aging, Tara,' Roy's voice rose behind me. 'Oil paints will age, and varnish will yellow over time, that is a given. The primer may loosen, the stretchers may crumble, the canvas may desiccate, anything is possible, Tara. There are no guarantees against aging – you must understand that.'

That bit I did understand. In theory. There were many elements that could make a painting disintegrate over time. There was dust, dirt and humidity affecting the surface of the painting. Varnishes were organic liquids and disintegrated over time, making them yellow, masking away the depths. The quality of paints used mattered too, some faded away faster, the tints losing their glow. Where thick, paint could chip. Where thin, paint could crack. The primer used to seal the threads of the canvas itself was a glue-like substance and it could congeal, crumble, warp or flake over time. The canvas was cloth after all, and unless well-preserved, it could quickly fray. The stretchers in the back, the material used in the frames, was wood – and subject to rot, dampness, insects, and other pests. A million things could go wrong.

But this particular painting, how good was it? There was the certificate and all that. But would that piece of paper tell me if the painting was about to fall to pieces the next day or next year?

'Where does this painting stand?'

Roy picked up the painting and turned it around. 'See I had to have this one restretched – the painting had started to sag.' He flicked a finger against the wooden frame at the back. 'The front obviously has some aging – the colours were probably more radiant fifty years ago. You could get the quality restorers in. But to scientifically assess the aging damage and to restore the painting is an expensive proposition, Tara. Not worth it for a small painting in a private collection. It is okay as it is.'

What banal questions I was asking, I rebuked myself, even as the air around me felt thinner and more still and difficult to breathe in. Why worry about restoring a small painting? But the key question was this – at a moment in time, when relatively unknown new painters were commanding tens of thousands of dollars in overseas auctions, was I willing to spend 60 lakhs on a Sher-Gil? The combination of size and stature was unique.

'I have an offer, Tara. The guy is ready to pick it up today, but I felt you should get first right of refusal.' The thinning air snatched up Roy's words making them appear faint and distant.

Oh God, oh my God. For an instant I was back in the auction room again, about to lose out to some unknown last-minute bidder, and I stopped breathing altogether.

'I'll take it.'

'Done,' said Roy.

There was a secret in my heart.

That is how I wanted to keep it, under wraps, till money had changed hands and the framed canvas was on my wall. I didn't tell Raj, I didn't rush to pick up the phone to call any of my numerous friends who collected or dealt in art. There would be time enough for unveiling my treasure, when friends would come over and admire my new acquisition. Not now. Not till the money actually changed hands. The dismissive gasps and unwanted advice when I had been trying to buy the small Husain were all too fresh. I didn't need it all over again. For now, I called my bank in DC to give them the details of Roy's bank in London, and waited for the transaction to eventuate.

I didn't even tell Gul! Actually, it just so happened that there was no time. With just over a week to go before she flew to London, pressures were high and tempers were higher, and we were constantly screaming at the canvas stretcher and the graphic designer.

On a sudden impulse, I finalized my summer holiday plans. And the money seemed to flow as I made reservations for a weather-beaten, one bedroom, cottage-shack in New Hampshire, booked a car from Boston airport, sent emails to those whom I planned to meet and snatched free moments to buy gifts for friends. My credit card bill was going to be huge. Then, there was all the shopping I was dying to do in the US. But I ignored the thought and continued the virtual spending.

I was off in ten days! Escape to unconfined spaces. Hurrah!

On Wednesday evening, a prosaic message arrived from Roy:

Is the fund transfer happening?

No more ribbing and flirting now, it was all cut and dried financial transactions. I responded immediately, apprising him that I had called up the bank and made the transfer. I'd even sent a faxed signature and had been told that the international transfer process would take up to three business days.

Roy was getting restless now. He called in the early hours three days later, annoyed that the money had not reached his account yet. He was at the airport. 'I am back to Mumbai on Saturday,' he said. 'Hope you can sort it out by then.'

'It shouldn't take that long...' I mumbled feeling guilty. I was flying out to the US on Sunday night, so it was a small margin.

'Who was that?' Raj asked, waking up from sleep.

'Just a dealer. About a painting,' I replied, taking in his tousled hair and sleep-softened eyes. He knew nothing about what I was up to, I thought with a pang. There was so much I had to tell him – the Sher-Gil painting I was buying; Saloniere Star opening in September; and most of all, my plans for the summer. But I needed to pace my disclosures. I couldn't have him gagging on too much information. The Sher-Gil would be disclosed later. After all, I was paying for it from my own account. And Saloniere Star didn't matter to him. That left the summer.

'Raj...' I cleared my throat warily.

A cautious look came in his eyes and he sat up, alert, while I apprised him of my summer plans. The air thickened as I talked of New Hampshire, Boston, and DC. 'You can join us later, when you find the time,' I added and left it at that; he had to come to terms with the fact that our travel plans could no longer match, that Ro and I needed this time away.

In the same way that I had to accept so many things.

On Thursday evening, Roy called, back from Vienna, sounding cheerier than before, saying the money transfer into his account had happened on Wednesday. I felt a tremor of anticipation. The painting was finally mine.

'Congratulations,' Roy said, echoing my thoughts. 'I'll have it delivered tomorrow. Do you know where you will put it up?'

Where would I put it? Why, I hadn't paid a single thought to the matter. I wouldn't even be around to enjoy the sight of it, as I would be leaving the next day.

I waited up for Raj that evening, and told him about having bought the Sher-Gil and that I had paid for it from my 401k savings and my old E*Trade account.

Raj simply looked fed up. 'It's your decision. It's your money. I hope it makes you happy.' He slammed the door behind him, ending the conversation.

The Sher-Gil arrived on Friday before noon, by courier. I glanced through the paperwork, to see the invoice receipt and certificate of authentication, and then put it away to watch them unpack the painting.

When the painting was unveiled I gazed mesmerized at the red-robed woman all over again, and reached out my hand to touch her. I wasn't dreaming. She was really, really mine. She had cost a mini-fortune. But she was worth it.

After the delivery guys left, I called Gul.

'*What* did you buy?' she squealed on the phone.

She turned up in twenty minutes, completely agitated, alternating between solicitous felicitations and angry accusations. 'What's this? You bought a Sher-Gil? Wow. Congratulations. But *where* did you get it from? *Whom* did you buy it from? You never mentioned a thing. You...' she was silenced as she caught sight of the painting. Gul took a few steps closer, and an involuntary sigh escaped her. She said softly, as if in a trance, 'I don't know anyone else who owns a Sher-Gil. Do you...?'

I shook my head triumphantly.

'You *have* got it authenticated and valued and all that, haven't you?' Gul asked.

I showed her the certificate Roy had given me.

'But did you show it to an independent source?'

Obviously, I hadn't. I had kept the whole thing under wraps, and I'd wanted the painting desperately.

Gul tut-tutted: 'You are a gallerist, Tara. Follow process, even if it's a formality.' She took some digital pictures on my camera. 'Email these to me. I'll show them to Apurva when I'm in London.'

I waved her off cheerily and began packing for my holiday, home to the US.

❧part 2

❧sixteen

I entered the polished dark wood and glass interiors of Amaya in London's Knightsbridge, barely registering the hushed glamour of the discreet chandeliers and the press of its hip crowd. Still in a daze, with Gul propping my elbow for support, I walked towards the table where Apurva Mehta was waiting for us.

Gul's friend, Apurva, art advisor to galleries and independent curators, and specialist in South Asian art, rose grimly to greet us. There was a stern pity on her face. One look at her and all the arguments that had been burbling in my head for the past week died, unarticulated. An enlargement of a photograph of the Amrita Sher-Gil painting I had purchased lay on the table; no doubt from the picture I had had scanned and emailed Gul.

'I...uh...have...the authentication certificate...' I blurted without preamble.

Gul laid a warm palm on my arm. 'Hear her out first, Tara.'

'The style, the style is totally Sher-Gil,' I protested. 'The intense colours, this midnight blue, this red...'

Apurva shook her coiffed head. 'Of course, I should see the actual painting first, but it's just that several elements seem all wrong to me. Look at the central figure, for instance...'

Ah. *The Woman in Red*! I stole a glance at the enlarged print of my treasured purchase, the trophy item in my collection of contemporary Indian art. At once strong and poignant – a slight figure draped in red robes looking with intense eyes straight at the viewer; utterly alone in the market crowd around her.

I identified with her completely.

'She's a typical Sher-Gil. What about her?'

Apurva took a moment to sip her Scotch.

'Exactly. This style is reminiscent of Amrita Sher-Gil's early phase in India. Doesn't it remind you of the figures in *The Bride's Toilette* or *The Brahmacharis* or even *Hill Women*?'

I nodded furiously.

'Now look at the backdrop,' Apurva continued. 'The detail of the market scene is typical of her later period, when she became influenced by the miniature style, and her figures became less prominent. These thick black outlines – Sher-Gil did not use them. The painting is really a clever juxtaposition of different elements from her work, with some add-on bits.'

'It could be an intermediate phase...' I tried again. 'And the find was so well publicized. A huge Amrita Sher-Gil found in a derelict haveli in a small town in North India that sold for crores...'

Apurva said, 'Wasn't the hue and cry about another, bigger canvas?'

'Yes,' my voice curved upward. 'Mine was found in the same haveli, a few weeks later.'

Apurva was kindly. 'I will give you the names of some friends in India who can evaluate the painting for you. I strongly suggest you meet them.'

My heart sank. *Oh God, Oh God.* I wanted to escape. Our first show opened in a month. And, now I, an art dealer who was supposed to advise clients on expensive art purchases, had supposedly bought a fake! I got a grip on myself. 'But I know Roy. He would not do this to me,' I said emphatically. 'What about the certificate of authentication he gave me?'

The certificate itself lay in my house in Mumbai. But I remembered the scrawled signature under the verification statement. *Daniel Leibowitz.* I had heard Roy mention his name, his valuation expert friend in Delhi, who had also verified the big Sher-Gil painting.

'Leibowitz? I haven't heard of him. I'll ask around. Is he based in Delhi?'

'Wasn't there a mention of a Delhi-based foreigner in a forgery case last year?' Gul sat up.

I didn't know. I didn't know anything, it looked like.

'The money you paid...' Apurva started softly.

I stared numbly at Gul and Apurva.

My money! I had fought with Raj to buy this painting. I had emptied my personal retirement savings account for it! Note-bills spread across my mind, a garland smirched in red, mocking me, mocking my stupidity.

Apurva's eyes narrowed. 'There is more.' I noticed the veins undulate in her neck.

More? I thought frantically. My life was a mess. My finances were finished. What more was there?

'A friend heard something about Roy Jordan. You should meet her. We can go straight from here, I've spoken to her already. She lives close by.'

Lady Barbara Stewart, an ageing Barbie doll, pink-tipped and pink-lipped, in a lilac linen suit, wife of a former Ambassador, part-time art dealer and author of the book *Anglophonic Paradoxes in Postcolonial Postmodern Indian Art,* lived in a period townhouse in nearby Soho. She met us in her opulent study. Satin trimmed chintz curtains ballooned in the bay window behind her.

'I am not the expert on Sher-Gil' – Lady Barbara pronounced it 'Shire-Gil' – 'but there are rumours about Roy Jordan.' She fingered her triple strand of pearls.

I stared at her as she spoke of a forged signature on a soccer ball sold a decade ago in Milan, and the missing golf link of a famous dead punter soon after some money had exchanged hands with much fanfare. There was also talk of an abrupt dismissal from an auction house after a short stint years ago – a clash of ideologies, they had claimed officially.

But, but, I stammered in my mind, Roy Jordan – the dealer turned friend; Roy had been in the papers in India so often. He had to be bona fide. Surely news reporters in India would have unearthed these details?

There were more mysteries surrounding Roy Jordan, Lady Barbara said. She talked about the whisper of a swindled inamorata, a widowed middle-aged countess from Lichtenstein who had later been forced to retire penurious to a small property near Marseilles.

How could I have known Roy for six whole months and never learned of all this? I could picture him so clearly, so sure of himself in that laidback way, full of jokes and flirtation.

I wanted to tear him apart.

Claw out that dimpled smile.

Destroy that suave air.

The plane trembled mid-air. The clouds below resembled frozen froth. Barren rocky terrain was visible through the tears in the curdled cloud layer. Baltic Asia in summer. A journey I was making again with my son, six months after moving to Mumbai, returning via London from an abruptly truncated holiday in the US. And I was more troubled than before. Just this time around, there was no Raj to blame.

This time the mess was of my own making.

I had to face it: my expensive Amrita Sher-Gil canvas, with an exorbitant per square inch rate, was in all probability a fake. What if I confronted Roy directly? Would he refuse to admit anything? Had he fled the country by now? The scoundrel! But other than bitter teeth-gnashing, there was no denying the fact that I was easy prey – a disgruntled wife giving into his charms, not bothering to verify credentials.

Then there was the other angle – of the credibility of Saloniere Star. The news would eventually leak out, somehow, that I had bought a dud piece of art. Who would then believe in the authenticity of works of art sold through my gallery or believe me when I offered advice on the purchase of a future luminary of the art world?

Where was the way out? Not only had I lost a lot of money – all my retirement money, – but once word leaked, I would lose my chances as a gallerist too. An open confrontation with Roy was out of the question. He would only deny matters – after all what proof did I have? There would only be further losses if buyers shied away.

On the wall behind Gul, in the grey light of the day, the warm glow of yellow overhead-lights cast a mysterious penumbra upon the jewel-toned flats of a large Satish Gujral, lending it a depth and shadow unimagined till now.

'Cigarette?' Rimli offered around her pack of Camel Lights and Gul took another. We had gathered in Gul's house – Gul, Rimli and I, to confer about what to do about the Sher-Gil painting.

I had not spoken to anyone else.

'What next?' Rimli asked. 'Have you spoken to the experts Apurva suggested?'

'How much will you disclose is the question, Tara.' Gul looked at me pointedly.

'What should...what should I say?' I spoke for the first time in half an hour.

After all, any expert, however well-referenced through a friend, was bound to ask for details. Like: Have *you* bought the painting? Like, what did you pay for it? Then the word was bound to spread.

'How could you, a gallery owner, be so naive? You have to give away as few details as possible,' Gul sank into the sofa, and tugged at her hair, as if pulling at it would provide some answers. 'One way out might be to somehow expose Roy, and to show that there is a scam going on. I am sure you are not the only one duped here. A person like him would be systemic in his approach to art crime.'

Art Crime. The words stung like a poison-tipped needle and the venom spread instantly, blackening everything it touched inside.

'But if word gets out now, it will seem as if you are the only one,' Gul said.

'I'll come with you, Tara. Where is this art expert?' Rimli patted my arm, reassuringly.

'Delhi.'

'Who is he anyway?' Rimli asked curiously.

'Ram Ojha, a Director of INTACH in Delhi.' I dug out the name Apurva had emailed me.

'INTACH?' Rimli sat up. 'Those guys restore masterpieces. I know because a friend from my art faculty went to work for them.'

Rimli explained that the Indian National Trust for Art and Cultural Heritage was a key organization set up for the conservation and protection of Indian cultural artefacts, including the restoration of art. 'Are you sure you want to talk to him? He may be well connected to government and private resources in art, and then news will spread, no?'

I agreed, feeling faint. This was all getting too complicated.

Rimli came to the rescue again, suggesting we speak to a retired professor from the Faculty of Fine Arts in Baroda, who was an expert on Sher-Gil. 'He lives in Delhi now. He won't have the latest testing technologies at hand, but at least he will not know the current set of dealers and buyers of art.'

The evening was gloomy. Grey clouds stooped low almost touching the glistening treetops. I too was swollen with regret, a puffy mass of if-onlys – except the time for prudence was well past.

I could not bear to look at the Sher-Gil painting. It hung there, alone and accusing on a wall in my living room, the lady in red, like a mad-eyed witch, entrancing me with her intense gaze, mocking my stupidity even as she cast spells that dispelled common sense.

I got up and took the painting off its hook. But what could I do with it? I could not just put it in the rubbish bin. In the end, I dug out Raj's toolbox and found a spot in the bedroom, in a corner cordoned off by deep coloured drapes. I held the nail against the wall, and directed all my anger, all my frustration in the hammer as I struck it against the nail.

Except I hammered my finger.

I flung myself across the bed, howling at the sting in my finger, tears erupting from deep within in a deluge. Raj walked in at that moment, home early on advance warning of further downpours. Seeing me cry, he gathered me in his arms.

And I told him about the Sher-Gil, that it might be a forgery, told him again how I bought the painting with money taken from my personal savings and retirement accounts in the US – my individual E*Trade and 401k balance stood at zero now – and how Gul, Rimli and I thought the best way forward was to find out more about Roy, unveil his forgery scam.

As I confessed the events of the summer and my motivations to buy the painting, my heart thudded – what should I say about Roy? My heart did a cowardly backtrack, a sort of escapist palpitation. *Nothing happened,* it said, *nothing really happened. Don't tell Raj,* it grovelled, going into contortions. In the end, I just rambled on about Roy's shady history as a dealer, the wicked sullied-sales in Europe and mentioned nothing of that fleeting, crazy kiss.

Guilt gnawed at my own treacherous omission.

Raj listened in silence and remained quiet long after I had finished telling my story.

A window was ajar. The wet wind carried in the mayhem of car horns mixing with the steady falling of the rain. Rohan was in the next room, on his PlayStation, and occasional hoots of joy echoed through the door. Raj's silence was further highlighted by the evening rain song.

'Say something…' I whispered to Raj, desperate for a connection now, wishing he would say something, anything, even if it was only a deprecating word.

Raj sighed deeply. 'What's there to say? It was your decision to buy the painting; it is your decision to turn art crime investigator now.' He was cool, utterly detached. He lifted his shoulders and his eyes turned up to the ceiling, and then to the window to look at the fogged-out curve of Marine Drive; everywhere but at me. 'All I can say is Good Luck.'

With that he got up to go towards the study, and without looking back added in his chilliest voice, 'I'll catch up on my emails, I think.'

I remained on the bed, frozen in my loneliness. It was not possible to feel more alone than this. I covered my face with my freezing hands, clamping down the hysteria.

Alienated from my business partners, misunderstood by my family, dismissed by my husband, set apart from the revelling crowds of friends by an act of foolish impulsiveness – where could I go from here? Who could I look to for consolation?

To myself. I would have to take care of it.

On my own.

✲seventeen

Rimli and I drove in straight from the Delhi airport to Rimli's art professor's Paharganj residence.

Professor Manoj Bakshi lived in a tiny third floor apartment of a building whose façade was almost entirely hidden behind billboards advertising Dr Jhatka's Male Infertility Clinic, Dr Bhalla's Smilecare Clinic and Dr Batra's Gynaecological Centre.

We panted up the staircase and pressed the bell. A mild-looking gentleman with a rim of white hair around a bald head graciously received us. Rimli had told me that he used to be a regular tartar in his days, slashing unskilled brush-strokes with the sword of his verbal lashes, insisting students learn formal perspective and traditional proportioning before they tried to break it with experimentation. Now, he looked like any other mild-mannered geriatric.

Inside the incense-scented living room, we sat back in red-cushioned cane sofas enjoying the chai and hot jalebis that his wife had organized for us. The walls of the room were lined with small framed watercolours and oil paintings – a few his own, but most of them gifts, tributes to his past as a teacher from many student artists now of greater repute than himself.

The professor reminisced about his days in Baroda with deep fondness and remembered students who had done well in the rapidly on-the-move world of Indian contemporary art. 'So what brings you here, Rimli?' he finally asked, after we had discussed Baroda and Rimli's career and rising art prices, and Professor Bakshi had lamented his isolation from the art world since his retirement five years ago.

Rimli cleared her throat and introduced me. I unwrapped the thick swathes of carefully packed layers around the Sher-Gil painting. It had been small enough to fit in the overhead bin of the plane. But then who puts some 60 lakhs worth of fragile canvas and paint without protection in an overhead bin? I had insisted on clutching the large wrapped parcel in my lap all the way from Mumbai to Delhi, refusing to even drink water lest I spill a drop. Now it lay on Professor Manoj Bakshi's coffee table, a tablet-size profusion of intense colours.

Professor Bakshi bent low, his eyes shining with excitement as they paused upon the signature, a snaky black *S* with the words *'India, 1938'* scrawled below it. He lifted his bifocals a tad and peered at the painting again. 'Is this supposed to be Sher-Gil?'

'That's what I want to know...' I said softly, watching his brows knit and un-knit as a look of intense concentration came upon his face. Then he raised his head slowly, focusing on us. 'Why do you want to know?'

'A dealer brought it to me,' I said, leaving it open-ended, letting him come to his own conclusions. I wiped my upper lip. The lack of air-conditioning was really getting to me now. What was I thinking, acquainting myself with non-AC-cooled India in the oppressive August heat?

'I wrote my thesis on Amrita Sher-Gil and conducted a lot of research on her life and works thereafter,' Professor Bakshi said. 'But I have not come across this painting, or any mention of it. Plus, I have never seen such a small Sher-Gil canvas.' He shrugged.

I told him how it was found in a forgotten haveli in the village of Tanda, near Saraya where Amrita had lived with her husband Victor Egan.

Professor Bakshi nodded, 'That seems plausible.' He acknowledged that the painter indeed had lived in Saraya, so it was technically possible to find an undiscovered work of hers in the nearby areas. Of course, given her fame it was unlikely that the owners of such a work would not have cashed in on it till now. 'Plus, she painted with passion, with animation. I cannot see her pouring that passion into such a small canvas. I would say it's probably a fake.'

'Are you sure?' I heard Rimli asking.

'Surety is a variable quality, Rimli. You should know.' Professor Bakshi went into a sort of intellectual trance, his voice strident and authoritative: 'The way big painters nowadays add their signature to large canvases conceptualized by them, and then painted by their apprentices. What is an original then, Rimli?'

He went on: 'It has been done for aeons. Picasso is said to have said that he would happily add his signature to an excellent forgery. Renaissance masters had large schools of art, and added their signatures to works produced by barracks of apprentices. Is a Giacometti sculpture really his, or an artist-endorsed fake masquerading as an original? During the Renaissance, those paintings might have been sold as works of apprentices, but then centuries later they turn up and get attributed to masters. What then is a forgery, Rimli, when the artist himself has accepted it, given it gravitas?

'In India, too, in recent times, there have been cases of families peddling fakes as originals or refusing to acknowledge the originals if they stood to make no profit from the sale. Artists have died poor and it's only now, when secondary markets for their works are in such a tizzy, that new masterpieces are being discovered, again and again, from some forlorn kothi or ramshackle godown. Assistants have copied masters, and masters have employed assistants to actually paint the works they merely conceptualized. Stories abound. Apprentices and students offer convenient provenances when all else fails. So what is fake and what is original is a complex question.

'Then again, if you want to be sure, you have to subject the painting to physical tests. Take it through X-ray radiography to check the lead content in the whites used, and see if the absorption through this lead layer is similar to lead absorption in other Sher-Gil paintings. Do an infrared analysis to see if she did charcoal drawings underneath, which may indicate that she had sketched prior to painting. You could even scrape a sample of the paint and study it under a scanning electron microscope. You could study the canvas to detect its age. All this will take time and money. Even then tests may prove inconclusive. Are you prepared for it?' Professor Bakshi looked at us quizzically from behind his moon-shaped glasses.

'What is your considered opinion, then?'

'That it is not a Sher-Gil.'

'But the style...'

'Is clearly a pastiche,' the professor completed my sentence, sounding very sure of himself. 'Look at the elements here, Tara. A strong central character, yes, looking like others done by Sher-Gil, just like the figures in *The Bride's Toilette*, but it is surrounded by this miniature-inspired backdrop detailing. These were from different periods. Even if she mixed periods, why would she pour so much passion and such experimentation into a small painting? It does not add up, Tara.'

'But the dealer has offered provenance papers...'

Professor Bakshi shook his head, and took off his bifocals. His eyes were blue-grey with cataract. Omigosh, what *could* he see, I wondered for a second.

'I would love to see these provenance papers. But what does paperwork really mean in terms of Indian art? It is all in a shambles. There is no data bank of information. There is no paper trail of documents handed down from original purchasers, the zamindars and the maharajas and the intelligentsia. No, the concept is still not fully understood by modern artists, leave alone artists of Amrita Sher-Gil's days. It is just a buzzword thrown around to fool the buyers. Pfff.' His lips curled in distaste. He looked at me critically. 'Any one can write up provenance papers with no proof. I would suggest you meet the original seller, check his background, see if there is any truth in his words.'

Can't we go meet the original owner?' Rimli asked, as we left the Professor's house and sat inside our hired car.

I gulped in the air-conditioned coolness and set the painting on the seat between us, a 1.5 x 2 foot brown paper parcel, a testament to imprudence. 'No,' I exhaled slowly, but the breath stuck inside, a sticky unguent of air, choking me. I let go, cleared my throat, yet I failed to feel lighter. 'I don't know where the owner lives in Banaras now. I don't have a contact name or a number.'

'Doesn't the paper mention the name or the address?'

I took out the paper Roy had given me, the watermark a joke when there might be no truth to its content. 'This states just the name of the seller's ancestor – *From the original collection of Rao Bahadur Murali Thakur, of Himmat Kothi in Tanda.* We could always take a dusty road trip to the village and ask around for the current location of the modern-day thakur.'

'What about the man who signed the authentication certificate? Would he know?'

'Maybe...'

Daniel Leibowitz, the authentication expert who had signed the paper giving credence of validity to my Sher-Gil, had also gathered proof and provided documents for the multi-crore Sher-Gil canvas Roy had sold earlier. If he was a friend of Roy, would he tell me? Did he himself know anything?

Rimli gave me a nudge, and I started back into reality. 'You have the address for the authenticator?'

The document listed an address in Vasant Vihar, but could we to go to this Leibowitz unannounced and ask for details? I gave Daniel's address to the driver and sat back again, lost in thought.

The car moved slowly at first through the congested lanes of Old Delhi, but speeded up once we were on Ring Road. The Sikh car driver wove in and out between lorries and jeeps and kamikaze motorcyclists. Used to slower Mumbai traffic, I shook in fear with every swift swerve and every sudden lane change, until an hour later, when the car took the exit for Vasant Vihar. We arrived in a posh residential neighbourhood of whitewashed bungalows, stacked in closed packed arrangement, each shielded from the dust and deprivation of the streets by large iron gates and high, thick, brick walls. We reached a cul-de-sac, at the end of which stood a cream stucco bungalow, hidden from the road by a profusion of bougainvillea along the boundary wall, their fuchsia tones brilliant in the afternoon light.

'What now?' I sat in the car, peering out of the tinted window, trying to squint at the third floor of the bungalow, which was the address I had for Daniel Leibowitz.

'Let's go see him,' Rimli tugged at my hand and extended her arm to open the door. 'Let's go meet this guy, see what he has to say.'

'Wait,' I held her arm, stalling her. A white Honda City, parked along the kerb, suddenly started up and drove to the gate. A khaki-uniformed guard opened the gate of the bungalow, and two men and a woman, all strikingly tall and fair, strode out toward the car.

One of them was Roy.

I didn't want him to see me here.

'Oh God, duck!' I hissed at Rimli, pulling her down with me to crouch upon the floor of our car. 'I saw Roy.' I hoped no one noticed us.

We inched up slightly so that only our eyes reached window level. Roy was accompanied by a blond man, possibly Leibowitz. Who was the pale woman? We slid down again, as the doors of the white Honda slammed shut and it moved out of the cul-de-sac, towards us. Did they see us? I huddled down further, curling up as much as I could, till a wave of dizziness engulfed me, and I jerked up to get some air. The white car passed by.

'Follow that car,' Rimli told the rental car driver, and he looked at us in a slightly bored fashion not sure whether he should follow such a ridiculous command. Nevertheless after a moment's delay he did, and the car jolted as he swerved and veered along the narrow residential roads chasing after the white Honda.

'Keep your distance, keep your distance!' Rimli kept shouting at him, clearly energized by this pursuit sequence, as we hit a road bump and bashed our heads against the ceiling of the car.

The driver had clearly seen his share of bad car-chase sequences in Hindi films because he kept up a steady commentary: 'What Shah Rukh did in *Don*, waah ji waah. Bas, I will take you just like that,' he assured us as he went full throttle up a narrow bumpy road. It was a short chase, mercifully, and just as I began feeling the jalebis from Mr Bakshi's house ride back up my alimentary canal, the white car slowed down outside a gated bungalow, and our car halted abruptly three houses away.

Armed sentries stood at a tall sheet metal gate, which opened up to swallow the white car. We sat at a distance, looking at the double-storey bungalow fronted by a high boundary wall and the impressive brass plaque on the side of the gate.

I got out of the car and walked to the gate. The armed sentry stood up from his chair, holding his AK47 swaddled in its own belt like a baby, ready to stop me if I dared barge in without permission. 'What is it, Madam?' he asked in a surly voice.

'Just reading the plaque,' I said. The brass plaque was emblazoned with an insignia, and beneath in crisp etched lettering it said 'Embassy of Romania'.

'Visa queue in morning,' the guard informed me, assuming I was there to get travel documents for Romania.

I nodded and turned back to our car. *Romania?* I was puzzled, not quite able to make the connection between Roy and the Romanian embassy. As far as I knew, he had a British passport and Anglo-Indian antecedents. Though he did mention sales in Prague, and Bucharest was just a hop from there. Could there be some connection? Was the mystery woman a buyer or someone in on the plot?

Our return flight to Mumbai was next evening. It may well require a couple of days to follow the Leibowitz angle and we had not even started. But by now I was dying for a bathroom break and, unfortunately, it could not be any bathroom, not even in an emergency, not unless it had toilet paper and sparkling floors – *another* fallout of having lived overseas for a decade! So we told the driver to take us to our hotel.

The Imperial, a posh behemoth in Lutyen's Delhi, had Mercs queuing up in its driveway, bringing in the evening revellers. Somewhere behind the white exterior of the hotel building, the sky was a gilded pink.

We escaped into the marble lobby to check in, observing the women with their oversized Marc Jacobs handbags and thick diamond bracelets and the men in their sharp business suits. Much like any hotel lobby in Mumbai, apart from the hotel staff, there was not a single sari or kurta in sight. Nor was there an ounce of ungainly adipose gained from oodles of ghee-laced delicacies on display. The patrons all looked uncannily alike in their svelte sleekness. It seemed the whole of India had had a makeover in these past few years. From a nation of Sanjeev Kumars and Moushumi Chatterjees, it had metamorphosed into a nation of Enriques and Shakiras. Where were the people who inhabited India five years ago?

Rimli and I took the lift upstairs, past the corridors of heavy-framed art and flower-filled vases. The room was as delightful as promised, with tall windows overlooking the palm-dotted lawns. Rimli had admonished me about staying at The Imperial when I should have been cutting costs. But she too was enamoured enough not to say anything and I was glad I had heeded Lola's advice about staying here.

Despite the circumstances of this visit, the stay would be memorable.

After freshening up, we went down again, and in the splendour of the potted-palm-studded Atrium, by the hum of the central fountain, we tucked into a selection of fancy pastries and mini sandwiches, choosing to decline the usual English cup of tea and opting for a glass of crisp Sula white instead.

Rimli took out a tiny diary and flipped through the pages, moving her finger down names and numbers inscribed in a minute font. 'I seem to know only aspiring artists...' she rued, as she continued to turn the pages. 'Aha! I have it. This woman was my senior in Baroda, but she is an art consultant now. She may know Leibowitz. It's an old number, I hope it works.' She called and managed to get her friend on the line, and made an appointment to meet her next morning.

As we sat out in the late evening, nursing our drinks, Rimli giggled suddenly.

'You did well today,' she said.

'Well?'

'You didn't once complain about the heat and the dirt,' Rimli raised her glass and grinned cheesily. 'You are getting used to India.'

Shefali Mirza, Rimli's senior from Baroda Art School, occupied a handsome one-room office suite in a lane behind the South Extension shopping area, a few steps away from the ancestral house she shared with her lawyer husband and his brothers. Large canvases in heavy frames lined the walls of the spacious room, and a glass Phillipe Starck bookcase housed an enviable collection of art folios.

Shefali gave Rimli a hug as she greeted us. 'It's been ages, Rimli. I really admire your decision to pursue art as a career. I could never be a painter, it's too hard! But I read the notices of your show here last year, something else was happening that day...' She looked away for a second, trying to recall what had been on her calendar. 'Maybe I was travelling.'

Rimli asked Shefali about her art advisory business.

'Well, I got married straight after Baroda.' Shefali fingered her straight long hair with one fair bejewelled finger. 'My husband's family owns businesses and farms, but they were always big art collectors. So I started advising my husband's business colleagues and clients about art for their offices. Now, of course, I am an independent consultant offering art advisory service. I have many big MNCs as my clients.' She mentioned names, eyes as bright and intent as the diamonds on her hands as she waved them about gracefully, looking every bit the successful businesswoman. 'So what brings you here?'

Rimli brought the conversation around to Roy and Leibowitz.

'Roy Jordan? Isn't that the guy who discovered a Sher-Gil in some old haveli?' Shefali adjusted the pale pink chiffon dupatta on her shoulders. 'Yes, I remember reading about it in the papers. After that auction of *Village Scene*, Sher-Gil is such big news. You know, they say the businessman who bought it ten years ago made 6000 per cent profit on the sale. I expected to hear more about it in the papers... like who bought it.'

'There hasn't been much news after the new Sher-Gil sold, has there?' Rimli said and mentioned the small Sher-Gil, the untitled *Woman in Red*, without saying that I had already bought it. It might just take a phone call or two to connect the dots, but I was hoping that Shefali would be too busy to make those connections.

'*Another* Sher-Gil you say?' Shefali made a face. 'Hah! I am not sure I would believe it. Sher-Gil paintings are not ripe tomatoes that keep dropping off plants. Come on! Two in a row! Nobody can be that stupid.'

As I realized now, any sane person would have discussed a Sher-Gil purchase with her friends, gathered the requisite background information from experts and then approached the matter with caution. 'Leibowitz?' I asked her, trying to deflect my mind from going into further self-berating.

'I have never heard of him. Let's Google him.'

Shefali turned on her computer and Googled '*Leibowitz Delhi Art*' – something we had not thought of doing. But nothing useful came up. 'That does not mean much. Maybe he goes by his first name or middle name. Many people associated with art do. Maybe he is just new to town. I move about in the art circles in the capital a lot. So I will ask. What does he look like?'

I didn't know for sure what Leibowitz really looked like. Roy's companion yesterday had been tall, lanky, sandy-haired. Was he even Leibowitz? I gave that sketchy description to Shefali.

'Suppose we wanted to show the painting to someone...?' Rimli butted in, without completing the question.

Shefali lightly touched the pearls around her neck as they glowed and blushed, nestling against the pink chiffon of her kurta. 'Verification, Rimli, is a bit of a joke in this country. I know there has been a lot of big talk about it. Osian's is getting into art verification. Everyone is more aware of the need for paperwork. But – and it's a huge BUT – there are gaping holes where provenance information was never collected and preserved. So obviously it's easy to fake paintings. Still, for living masters you can always apply to them, and ask the painter if a painting is one of their creations or not. Sometimes painters don't claim their own paintings, for whatever reason. Maybe it's a piece unworthy of their current name. Maybe they don't like the seller who is trying to make money off it. For artists who have died recently, you can try to contact their families, friends, colleagues, or even apprentices to check if they have ever seen the painting. It is a complicated process, and requires immense time and patience. There is no guarantee that credible information will turn up. Mostly buyers just buy on instinct if the price is not whopping, and hope for the best.

'But for Sher-Gil, I don't know...' She thought for an instant: 'She has been dead for decades. Her paintings have been declared national treasures, and there has been a ban on selling them overseas. You could do what you would do for a Picasso – ask his family for verification. You could speak to her family. Maybe the family has some idea; some old papers, an old letter perhaps, which connects Sher-Gil to this painting. I could introduce you...'

I looked at Rimli, a message in my eyes that said I definitely did not want to come into the open right now. Talking to Amrita Sher-Gil's surviving family would be akin to that.

We drove back to Vasant Vihar, and arrived at the sleepy cul-de-sac again. Only this time we proceeded past the uniformed lathi-wielding guard to the flat three flights of steps above the tiny garden.

A man-servant opened the door, and showed us into a spacious room with taupe leather couches, colourful Fabindia cushions and beige, tailored drapes. Smart, but impersonal, except for two large paintings and a messy table along one wall. The table looked like an artist's jumble sale, littered with paints, masking tape, various palette knives and a white box with knobs.

Leibowitz walked in. He was the tall, sandy-haired man of yesterday. What I did not gauge from the distance though was his impressive presence – shoulders that spanned over two feet, even in an old tee shirt, and grey eyes that looked inquisitively from behind wire-framed spectacles. 'Hello?' he said, at once greeting and questioning us.

I introduced myself and Rimli, and mentioned Roy. 'You've signed the Amrita Sher-Gil painting I purchased from Roy Jordan. Sorry to come in without an appointment, but I was in town so I just decided to drop in.'

'Yeah?' Leibowitz sounded unconvinced. 'Call me Daniel, everyone does. So what brings you here?'

'Look,' I laughed a little shrilly, 'we just decided to stop by on a whim, just to connect a face to the name of someone involved in the sale of my beautiful Sher-Gil.'

'Involved?' Daniel's mouth curled into a lop-sided smile, like an arc etched by an unsteady hand. 'That's an interesting word! I hope you are enjoying your Sher-Gil?'

'Very much...'

Conversation floundered for a second. I was at a loss as to what to say next.

'What are those things?' Rimli asked, pointing towards the objects on the table. 'Do you use them for authentication?'

'I do,' Daniel said. There was still a trace of hesitation in his voice.

'I'm quite curious, you know,' Rimli smiled innocently. 'I am an artist myself, I do sculptures, installations and the like, and I give out certificates for my works when some galleries request that I should. But most galleries don't ask for certification. Earlier artists obviously left no certificates. So how do you do what you do?'

'You are after my trade secrets, then,' Daniel smiled, but his eyes remained cautious. 'I do empirical studies – style match, material match, signature match. I talk to the seller. Then I run some tests. Basic spectrometer analysis is the first option. Infrared analysis, X-ray screening and microscope work can be used for a more thorough analysis. Depends on the value of the painting.'

The terms were not new to me. I had learned about these things through Professor Bakshi and read about them online after meeting Apurva Mehta in London. The authentication of paintings in the West – especially with the longer European history of art preservation –

was a more established procedure where provenance was checked, and visual discrepancies like signature mismatch, new stretchers on old paintings, the types of wormholes in the stretcher wood, old nails or mounting marks on the back of an old painting, all were carefully noted, before further testing. Carbon dating or white lead dating was used to trace the age of objects. X-ray methods were used to detect additional layers underneath the painting and to look for evidence of tampering or to check the pigment content. Ultraviolet and infrared analyses were used to detect anomalies, while technically sophisticated atomic spectroscopic methods were used by museums to study paint compositions. Small spectrometers were used to measure reflectance and absorbance of light from paint surfaces, especially white pigments, which have varied greatly in composition over the ages, from lead-based to zinc- or titanium-based.

This was done for major works selling through auctions and being picked up by museums or private collectors. Despite this, forgeries abounded. Even experts could get fooled and sometimes inventive and knowledgeable forgers could fake masterpieces that passed through a battery of tests.

There is a world history of art hoaxes, and sometimes forgers admitted to having created fake masterpieces to expose the art world. Dutch painter Han van Meegeren created a fake Vermeer, and colluded with art historian Abraham Bredius, who gave it a stamp of authenticity. Elmyr de Hory had confessed to having forged a thousand Chagalls, Matisses, and Modiglianis through his career. John Myatt created bogus Renoirs, Picassos and Modiglianis in an attempt to create near-perfect art. New York dealer

Ely Sakhai had flooded international markets with fake Impressionist, Post-Impressionist and Modernist paintings, selling fakes to Asian collectors and originals to galleries in the US.

In recent times, dealers in forged art had shipped fakes from one country to another, paid duty on worthless fakes, and then used customs documents to establish provenance and sell paintings for millions later on.

'Wow. That sounds complicated.'

A guarded look appeared in Daniel's eyes. Did he sense that I doubted him? He couldn't suspect that yet. Not when I was still trying to find out what had happened. I fumbled around for another train of thought – something to deflect his suspicions. 'Are these tests usually invasive?' I asked. 'Could there have been any damage to my painting due to these tests?'

Daniel said, 'Imaging is usually not. Spectrometers are my starting point. If you scratch the paint, yes it's invasive, but we know how to take the minutest trace of paint for labwork. It is essential for further restoration work.'

'You do restoration work as well?' Rimli bent forward showing interest.

'That was my forté, yes. I have been an art restorer at museums in Europe,' Daniel answered looking from Rimli to me, trying to assess what we were about.

I had to ask him, I had to. 'So you ran these tests on the Sher-Gil as well?'

'Some.'

'And...?'

'And...' Daniel spelt out with a sigh, 'pigments don't lie under a spectrometer. The paint had higher lead content, similar to paints used in Sher-Gil's days.'

The pigments matched? I goggled, confused. How could they match, and yet be fake?

Daniel stood up, and put his hands in his pockets. 'Look, I'd love to sit and chat, but I have to meet someone. I am sure I have the exact results filed somewhere. If you are really interested, make an appointment and come back. Other than that, I can assure you, everything matched up.'

He moved towards the door, reached one long arm to open it, and stood there as we filed out.

❧eighteen

Sheets of dark rain greeted us as we landed at Mumbai airport. The rubbish on the roads – which eddied upon the wind on dry days – became sodden and bloated, forming into mounds along the sides of the rain-ravaged roads. But the next morning was clear and sullen, only the water in the potholes a vague reminder of the heavy showers of last night. Then Gul called to ask if I would visit the gallery.

Gallery?

I had barely had a chance to think about the gallery in the few days since I had returned to India. But Jai Bhavnani's people had completed their work while we were away, and with the first show opening just two weeks from now, the place had acquired a buzz.

'I'll be there first thing,' I assured Gul, feeling guilty for not putting in my bit into our partnership, for not just being distracted, but for also proving to be the source of the distraction.

So after Rohan was off to school, and after a futile monologue with Raj – trying to tell him what had happened in Delhi – I went to Colaba.

*

The door to the gallery was unlocked; Gul must have arrived.

Stepping inside the thick old-wood and brass door, I took a moment to take in the free-standing light sculpture in the spacious lobby space. It was all bent fibreglass and moulded plastic and steel rods. Such a messy process to get it imported from Italy via Dubai – Jai had to get a special delivery, it had taken much longer than expected, but it looked every inch worth the trouble.

Beyond the sculpture lay the renovated space, an expansive viewing zone of rooms connected by scooped arches, smelling of fresh paint and lit by the criss-cross of new down-lights on the ceiling. Gul was standing near the back wall, and my eyes locked in at a spot behind her, where the wall had sprouted what looked like a fat white cabbage with layers of high and low scabs and scales, concentrically petering out. Damp from the monsoons; the walls had held out for long, but then last night's showers had probably tipped the saturation content.

Gul said gloomily: 'Last thing we needed now. I just phoned the architect.'

Frantically, we waited for Jai's foreman to show up, who assured us that he would take care of it in two days. Two entire days of waiting for workers to scrub the wall clean and repaint the entire section and letting the paint dry, while Muthu's canvases were held at the framer and eagerly invited previewers were informed of a delay. This damp could not have happened at a worse time.

'We cannot have any delay. Please!' Gul's pleading tone could reduce a robot to tears.

The foreman was not so immune. 'Two days. Pukka,' he promised.

After that we got busy informing those who needed to be told, rescheduling dates for the delivery of paintings and moving some preview appointments to later dates. It was mentally exhausting and the day turned worse when Sud stormed into the gallery, in a swirl of questions and a surge of comments, eager to sweep up quick financial profits from his investment in Saloniere Star. 'The gallery looks great, ladies,' he remarked. Then the questions began – action plan, margins, buyers, cost calculations, the lot. 'Presold any?' he asked astutely, hitting upon the issue heavy upon Gul's mind.

We had no easy answers for him. We had done extensive pre-marketing, and despite my recent slackness, Gul had been very professional, pitching Muthu's canvases with the avidness of a star saleswoman. But we had no committed purchases yet, and two weeks to go before the show.

'Uh-oh,' Sud said. 'Better get cracking then. Let me see what I can do.'

Ravi Uppal had left us alone till now. No more than an occasional checking-in to see if we needed a soundboard or a contact. But soon he would demand answers too, want returns for the money he had put in. He would not be pleased to learn of my Sher-Gil purchase either. He may even threaten to pull his money out. I couldn't afford to be doubly bankrupt.

'Tara...' Gul caught me by the shoulder as Sud left. 'Just get this Roy episode out of your mind. At least till the opening.' There was panic in her voice.

The next couple of days were frantically busy; because patrons would not come to us, we went to them. We took our laptops along wherever we went and over endless coffees and chats, showed an endless number of prospective clients digital slides of Muthu's canvases, talking of his passionate style and his concerned world-view, and answering endless questions about the investment potential and lasting value of his works.

A different mindset prevailed in collectors interested in emerging artists, I learnt. They were not talking of rate per square inch appreciation and dollar gains. They did not have investment at the back of their minds. Collectors of emerging artists spoke instead of how they had bought a particular painting because it sang to their senses, or how the colours danced in their eyes, or the stories they saw in the artist's paint-splattered shapes.

It was a clean sweep of heart over mind, emotion over moolah. It was these collectors we could get enthused about Muthu's paintings.

At the end of a long day, I was quite glad to come home to a house that seemed to run by itself – a luxury India provided – where you didn't have to rush for school pick-ups or scramble to buy groceries or cook. The basics carried forward unaided, with minimal supervision. Provisions were ordered, clothes got washed and ironed, well-cooked Indian meals were served on the table, and my child was fed, bathed, clothed and picked up without fail.

I could perhaps rue the lack of variety in my meals. I could feel a desperate guilt for not being there to play imaginative games with Rohan or tuck him into bed and read him his bedtime story – so guilty, in fact, that I sometimes spent hours watching him sleep, tracing the contours of his face and absorbing the way his lashes shadowed his cheek, and how his breath felt upon my hand, soft, warm, laden with innocent dreams – but there was one thing I had to admit.

India had its advantages, and I was beginning to appreciate them.

Here the basics took care of themselves.

Roy called me two days later, just as I was readying to go to the gallery. For the first time after I had bought the painting from him, nearly two months back. 'Hi Tara, I just returned from Vienna.' He was expansive and chatty, full of enthusiasm as he talked of his meeting with some European collectors who were keen to expand their repertoire to include Indian art.

I didn't know how to react. The last time I had met him was at the coffee shop in the Oberoi Arcade, before his man had delivered the Sher-Gil to my house. There had been an awkwardness then – the memory of that mad moment by the Gateway clouding everything else.

But talking to him now, I could not stir up even a speck of that memory in my imagination. It was beyond thought that I could have liked this shallow man – this cheap fraudster – and had been taken in by his empty glossy words. *Who were these Viennese buyers*, I thought acidly – *more women?*

'Daniel said you had visited him?' Roy said suddenly, his voice petulant.

Oh, so *this* is what the phone call was about. 'I happened to be in Delhi on work, so I thought I would drop in,' I replied casually.

'And what did you think of dear Daniel?' Roy laughed. 'He is quite the expert, you know. He has worked with the national museums in Warsaw and Budapest and Prague, then he even did a stint in Boston, at a gallery housing a private collection!' Roy threw in names for emphasis.

I didn't know much about the museums in the countries once behind the Iron Curtain, or even their artists. But Boston I could picture: a Corinthian-pillared grand mansion rising off snow-banked pavements, containing Baroque and Renaissance and Impressionist art in large, gilded frames under ornate ceilings.

Daniel Leibowitz worked in museums like *that*? I didn't know what to believe.

Rimli phoned the gallery the next day. I learned that Shefali Mirza had called from Delhi with news of Daniel Leibowitz, confirming all that Roy had said earlier. Rimli said, 'Daniel is new to Delhi, but supposedly quite the pro – a master restorer from European museums, even one in Boston. He's been in the capital for the past year, consulting on art conservation, giving lectures. People know of him, Tara. I am confused.'

There was a long pause as Rimli and I tried to digest this news. It was a dead end. There were no trails ahead. 'Well...' I exhaled softly, not knowing what to say. 'I should focus on our opening for the moment.'

Sluggishly, I went through the day, supervising the work. It was my responsibility to make sure the catalogues were finalized and I drove out to Parel to approve the final printed proof. It was four by the time I emerged from the printer's, with an 8-page glossy brochure, combining pictures and write-ups and a lyrical introduction by Apurva; the result of weeks of back and forth with the designers. No point reaching the gallery at six in the evening. Instead, I decided to break off early for a spell at the spa, an afternoon of low music and lower lighting and deep shiatsu strokes.

*

I left the spa renewed. Outside, the clouds of the past weeks had broken through, and thin strings of sunlight were turning glitter-spun rakhis in street-side stalls into discs of amber and golden fire. I could not help asking the driver to park on the road, and dawdling by these stalls, touching bits of silk thread and spangle and ornate crystals, and swinging back into the past, to my teenage years when I had last seen such shops. Joy renewed itself, and I reached home happier than I had been in weeks, confident that it would all work out.

Dinner? I texted Raj, and he responded immediately: *New stock inclusion in portfolio. Dinner good.* I made a teppenyaki booking at Wasabi, knowing how much we both enjoyed it.

For once, the evening didn't end in histrionics or half-silences. There was a new truce between Raj and me. There was much we avoided saying, and yet the conversation fluttered lightly like a windswept butterfly. Not bad after six months of constant tussle and rancour.

'You've changed, you know...' Raj said, putting a shrimp tempura into his mouth with chopsticks.

Changed? For good or bad? 'What do you mean?' I asked quietly, fingers pausing around a tiny sake glass, watching the Japanese teppan chef chop vegetables and meat with the precision of a surgeon.

'Not quite the girl I married...' Raj scrunched his eyes trying to put into words what he wanted to say, while being wary of my reaction to his words. 'Different. Lovelier somehow; you dress better, you take care of yourself, you spend more time with Ro than in DC, you've organized our home so well...and yet...and yet...you're different.' He put his chopsticks down and traced a pattern upon my fingers with his finger, a barely-there sensation. 'Prickly at times, not a straight-shooter like before... I'm not sure what's on your mind...'

How was I to respond to that? Did I know myself what drove me anymore?

I was quieter for the rest of the meal, hesitantly telling Raj about Muthu and the Baroda youngsters, while Raj spoke of his 100 million committed funds and the search for the best ROI-generating investments to park the remaining cash collected from global investors. 'The market's just right. We're going nuts keeping pace,' he gave me a hesitant smile.

After an amazing Wasabi Crème Brulee, we left the restaurant, sated on good food. The driver was waiting for us when we came downstairs. As we drove off, Raj took my hand in his hands and held it tight. I could feel the driver's eyes upon us, I could sense his amusement, but what the heck – it was legit.

Reaching the cusp of Marine Drive, Raj suddenly said, 'Stop the car. I want to walk back.' Stepping out onto the walkway at Marine Drive, partially reconstructed with large flagstones and tree-saplings, we told the driver to go home. 'We can take a taxi back. Come,' Raj drew me towards the parapet separating the walkway from the sea.

We sat on the wall, legs dangling, the sound of waves lashing against the rocks coming from beneath our feet, our posh clothes incongruous with the surroundings and the homely families clustered around. 'That must be our house,' I pointed to the end of the long curve, where a congregation of vertical lights twinkled dimly.

A fresh late-monsoon breeze blew from the sea, laden with the teeniest trace of moisture, cool against our damp skin. There were no stars to be seen, hidden behind the last of the monsoon clouds. We sat there for a long time, taking in the atmosphere, the unknown people around us, the night riders on the Victorias.

Raj bent to place a kiss upon the back of my neck, the barest press of warm lips, and I shivered – that little gesture more sensual on Marine Drive than making out on the Mall in DC – and remembered old times, the magic of 'before'.

'I love you,' the words came out involuntarily.

'I love you too, babe,' Raj placed a finger lightly upon my lower lip, getting the most delicate kiss in return.

I smiled. 'Let's walk,' I said, swinging my legs up, away from the sea, and sprang down onto the walkway.

We walked, hands held, and after a few minutes, I took off my high-heeled shoes, holding them by their thin straps, and walked barefoot, matching Raj stride for stride.

The next day was a big one for Saloniere Star. Gul had appointments with several collectors of emerging artists. By lunch time, three fashionistas had blazed through the gallery in a swirl of embroidered skirts, perfectly tousled curls and blob-sized diamonds, muttering 'Nice,' 'Very Nice' at Muthu's canvases. But no cheque-books were opened, no promises were made.

Gul clutched my hand. 'Oh God, Tara, what if no one buys?'

The question remained in the air, a formless presence, hovering like a ghost.

Ravi Uppal telephoned in the afternoon, sending us in a tizzy, and we looked for the subtext in his call. Had Sud been talking to him? Was he going to threaten to pull out on us? I was doubly scared: what if Ravi had heard of the fake Sher-Gil? But Ravi simply referred a potential client, a new buyer he had vetted for us.

Come mid-afternoon, a solemn looking young man in an open-necked white shirt and a dark grey suit that fell perfectly upon his lean length, came in. He handed us his business card and spoke earnestly of his newfound passion for Indian art.

Kiran Kejriwala then asked us for details of Muthu's background and his inspiration, and walked around the gallery slowly, seeking to find meaning in a flat stroke of vermilion here and a daub of umber there. Then he turned to Gul and smilingly shot off a barrage of questions about her antecedents, her personal choice in art, and our future shows.

'My grandfather owned jute mills outside Kolkata, then after jute collapsed, my father moved to Bombay to start a cotton mill. The mill is defunct now, and I started this technology business,' he gestured at his card. 'But no one in my family was ever into collecting art.' Kiran talked of the young painters from Kolkata whose works he had collected. 'Kolkata art prices are so underrated,' he mused, and spoke of galleries he had discovered on business trips to that city.

'It's a barely kept secret, isn't it?' Gul agreed. 'The big art markets remain in Mumbai and Delhi. But one or two big auctions in Kolkata is all it will take, and prices will rise there too and the market will change.'

Kiran liked two very different works. One was a reckless spatter of green. In the dense verdure, like wild animals hiding in jungle grass, were tiny daubs and dashes of green – evident, yet subtly hidden. The other was a wash of boundless blues. There were materials stuck on it – paper creatively cut, ropes intricately twisted, pictures of floating whale carcasses, all glued in place.

Kiran went back and forth between the two canvases, staring at them entranced, taking a half-step back and a step forward as in a shadow dance, pulled by strings of inspiration. After some half an hour of mulling aloud, while Gul and I shivered in a silent agony of *'Will he, Won't he?'* he surprised us.

'I'll take both,' he said.

In the evening, Rimli came over for dinner and after Rohan was asleep, we scoured the internet for stories on art forgeries. There were any number of sites offering advice and caution on art purchases. There were stories of rogue dealers and villainous painters – a Picasso sold over Wal-Mart's website that was later proclaimed a fake by his own relatives; anonymous masterpiece copiers and restorers who could not resist that last flourish – of adding the master's signature; paintings that supposedly disappeared during the Nazi regime only to resurface later with the slightest cloud of doubt attached to them; paintings declared real finds by serious auctioneers only to be dismissed as fakes later. There were more recent stories too – newly rediscovered Jewish artefacts and art masterpieces, carefully created in modern times, then shipped as originals via Eastern Europe to create a trail of provenance, paying thousands of dollars in duties, and then being sold in the US for exorbitant amounts.

The value of contemporary Indian art was nowhere close to that of Western art. But who was to say that current price levels were not attractive enough to inspire nefarious schemes? There was cheap labour arbitrage in every other line of business, so why not in art? Why not use poor struggling artists, pay them a pittance in rupees to create fakes aimed at the hundred-grand or more market, and sell them to rich buyers in dollars? Especially given that information and documentation about Indian art barely existed.

Rimli recounted stories of assistants who faked the master artists and established painters who were equally willing to add their names to works executed by able assistants in their signature style. Tame stories, indeed, compared to the master-minded accounts of selling forged European Masters from remote places on the Continent to plush buyers in America.

But who was the guilty party in my case?

Roy alone?

Or Roy and Daniel working together?

Rimli and I were outside the Yacht Club the next morning hoping to catch a glimpse of Roy Jordan, when my phone rang. And suddenly it was all claptrap and hi-voltage drama as Gul screamed in my ear: 'Where *are* you? Five days before our show opens you disappear? It's our investment you know. I understand you are troubled, but there are limits! This is sheer negligence! How irresponsible of you! There are a zillion phone calls to make!'

Gul vented for several minutes without let-up, howling like the summer loo, sending hot gusts of guilt my way. I had been most remiss, focusing on my follies and on how to undo past mistakes, rather than working on the gallery. I gave up my foolish notions of playing chase-the-crook, and raced to the gallery, asking the driver to drop Rimli to her studio after he had dropped me.

The mid-week opening of Saloniere Star was a glittery affair, largely ignored by television media, but the presence of the print paparazzi with big flashbulbs added to the dazzle of the evening. Thanks to the extensive referrals by Ravi Uppal and the endless pre-marketing phone-calls we had made till our voices gave, fourteen paintings from the lot of twenty had been pre-sold. Gul and I had kept two paintings each for ourselves, so while anxious to field more queries for the four remaining paintings, we could actually relax enough to enjoy our big evening.

The collectors attending the show were the usual mix of investment bankers and businessmen's wives, young cash-flush buyers with confident I-have-arrived airs, catching up with each other and engaging with the few art dealers circling the room. Raj was not there yet, his flight back from Hong Kong had been delayed.

Muthu and his coterie of long-haired artsy young-guns added a certain edgy tenor to the evening. Clients who had bought his paintings were glad to meet the artist, shake his hand and get photographed with him, while his articulate explanation of the motivations behind each painting and his varied style impressed both new and seasoned collectors. Sud stopped by briefly, and Ravi Uppal stayed back for a lengthy chat with Muthu.

My new Mumbai friends were all present – June, Alessa, Lola and Maddy back from their summer jaunts across the world, happy to swill chilled wine on a warm Mumbai evening, to talk about summer stops in exotic destinations, and rue their return to India.

Maddy started talking of new musicals in Toronto, and Gucci saddle bags in Harrods, and July weather in Cinque Terre. Then Maddy caught my attention with, 'I'm off to Kovalam for the weekend. It's such a shock to the system to be back.'

I stared at her. Four years of living in India, and she was still stuck in the stage of ennui and rejection. Was this where I was headed? Unable to make the compromises necessary to belong to a place, and clamouring for an ideal that existed nowhere, but inside my own head? I moved on. I had art to sell.

It was nearly nine and the crowd had begun to thin when I heard Gul's voice whisper stiffly to me, 'Tara.' She indicated the door, where Roy stood, dapper as always in a dark grey shirt and trousers, scanning the room.

He gave me a jaunty wave as he caught my eye. It was the first time I was seeing him since I had been duped into buying my painting. I froze. He moved through the throng, smiling insouciantly, as if nothing was amiss, as he made his way towards me. My own feelings were somewhat violent: I felt I could hack him to bits if someone handed me a pick-axe.

But then I remembered where I was – at the opening of my gallery, Saloniere Star, surrounded by my clients. I willed my facial muscles into a smile as he approached.

'Congratulations, Tara, this place looks so classy,' Roy gave me a quick hug before I could move away. I noticed a dusky blonde at his side, clinging to his wide-shouldered, dark-jacketed frame. 'Ayesha,' Roy said cryptically, by way of introduction.

The woman offered me her skinny hand, 'Congratulations, this place looks lovely. Nice turnout too. I love that blue landscape,' she said, quite sincerely.

'Are you into art?' I asked her; she couldn't have been more than twenty.

'Well, sort of,' she simpered at Roy, gripping him even tighter. 'I've grown up with art. My dad is a big collector, and Roy has this amazing Hemendra that Daddy is buying from him.'

Hemendranath Mazumdar? I looked at Roy, feeling sick. More fake art for sale?

June grabbed me just then to say goodbye, and I talked to her distractedly, wondering all the while if I should warn the young desi blonde about what Roy had done to me. Should I tell her to get the painting checked out before purchasing it?

When June left, Gul came up to me. 'Does he only sell to women?' she hissed viciously, her eyes following Roy and his friend around the room.

'He is selling to her dad,' I said limply. Ayesha's presence only highlighted my own summer idiocy. What an ass I had been to be drawn by Roy's apparent empathy, to be taken in by his smooth style and suave words. It scared me to think how close I had come to losing control. And it angered me to think of the money I had lost. I could not let Ayesha make the same mistakes. I had to try and warn her. *I had to!*

I saw Roy and Ayesha laughing and chatting with Ravi Uppal. Oh God, how did Ravi know Roy? What if Roy told Ravi about my Sher-Gil in conversation and Ravi asked to see it? I had to interrupt immediately. Heedlessly, I walked up to the trio.

'Come, come, Tara,' Ravi beamed at me, clutching Roy by the shoulders. 'You know Roy? He's a master at finding masterpieces – the man to talk to for that Husain you were after – of course, I'd rather you find it through me.'

'I know Tara. I know her *very* well,' Roy purred, his teeth a hard slash of white in his tanned face. This was coasting too close for comfort. I got angrier at Roy for putting me in a spot. Did the others get what he was trying to imply?

I turned to Ayesha. 'So, Hemendra Mazumdar?' I put on a smile, aware that my eyes were sullen and angry, and that the smile barely curved my cheeks. I could not even pretend anymore. 'Who is the seller then – some old zamindar?'

'How did you know?' the desi blonde gushed. 'Actually, he is from this tiny village outside Kolkata. Isn't the man Hemendranath's grandnephew or something?' She looked up at Roy.

God, he was even using the same story! Was *I* this dumb? My mind was a red haze. 'Ah!' I nodded, a barely controlled, even keel to my voice, 'I would love to see the painting, Roy, just to see a Hemendranath for real. Is later this week possible?'

Roy's eyes narrowed, there were flints in there now, and no softness. 'Not this week, I'm afraid,' he said. 'You seem to have a thing for rare works, don't you, Tara?'

'I have a Hemen in my archives, Tara,' Ravi Uppal said obligingly, rubbing a plump finger upon his dark jowls. 'Lovely example of the Bengal School – it's a very realistic, life-like silhouette of a young married Bengali woman from his 1920s phase, inspired by the Romanticist period in Europe. Come see it any time.'

'Uh, sure, Ravibhai,' I nodded to Ravi.

'My painting is getting restretched,' Ayesha confided, and my eyes flickered towards Roy's face again; I caught a fleeting look of anger before he shot a glance at Ravi and masked it.

Suddenly I knew. The stretcher had to be in it! My Sher-Gil painting was also restretched. Desiccated stretchers, Roy had said. Did all the paintings he sold have desiccated stretchers? There had to be something to it. If we could trace the canvas stretcher Roy used, there might be some clues there.

'Well, I'll see you around,' I told Roy and went back to my other guests.

As the last of the visitors left, Gul and I locked up the gallery and went over to Joss for a cosy dinner after-party – just Muthu, a few of his friends, Pheroze and Rimli. It was such a relief. The opening had gone well, ending the months of uncertainty and preparation in starting our gallery. Pheroze Dastur raised toasts and we downed vodka shots, choking on the liquid heat as we toasted the rise of Saloniere Star.

I was on my third martini when Raj arrived, profusely apologetic, carrying an extravagant bundle of roses.

'Raj...' I exclaimed, surprised. I had mentally expected to see him at home, fatigued from his trip and crabby the instant I said anything about missing the opening of Saloniere Star.

Instead, he was all sweet and smiles, despite the obvious tiredness in his eyes. 'I'm so sorry, Tara. The plane was delayed. I know how important this was for you. What about a private tour for me?' he entreated engagingly.

So I took Raj back to the gallery and walked him through the paintings, pointing out a dramatic midnight blue canvas I had bought for my collection. He admired the lot, made some intelligent comments about the subtext in some of the works, and then, complimenting me on keeping the best piece for myself, drew me urgently to him. Pinned against the wall, in the luminous midnight glow of my newly acquired painting, I answered his need with equal passion.

Later at home, cosseted by the syrupy romance of roses and the private viewing of dramatic paintings, despite my indignation over fake art and its devious dealer, fueled by an inferno of desire, Raj and I reached for each other.

❧nineteen

Gul and Rimli were extremely relaxed when we gathered on the morning after the opening, ready to analyse and pick apart the previous night's show. 'Did you hear about Chitrita's latest show in Delhi, at the India Habitat Centre?' Rimli said, knowing how much I admired her. 'She raised 4 crores for the Down's Syndrome Foundation.'

'Really?' I exclaimed, only half-interested. My mind was still on Roy and the new Hemendra canvas he was selling to Ayesha's father. Rimli and Gul were shocked when I told them about Roy's latest con.

Gul rolled her eyes in distaste. 'Does Roy's entire business model revolve around selling to gullible and dumb women?'

Dumb? That included me.

'Come on, yaar,' Rimli laughed. 'He has to have a more robust model than that!'

'You'll be surprised,' Gul was scathing. 'Did you see how that woman was all over him last night?'

Ladies, I'm here, I felt like telling them. But then, they knew I was there and they knew I had been a bimbette with a loose purse. They knew everything, except for one last bit. They knew nothing about the kiss under the eaves of the Taj!

'We must find his canvas stretcher,' Rimli said.

'But there are so many canvas stretchers in town,' I wailed. It was like finding one particular beetle in the Hanging Gardens; a lost cause.

'There can only be so many professional ones used by the art world,' Gul said. 'Look at the standard of all services in Mumbai. I can bet you there are no more than three or four framers used by professional art sellers.'

Of course, there was no question of asking Roy directly. Instead, we made phone calls to people we knew, and got the names of three framers and canvas stretchers who offered fine finishing with imported woods and bulk rates – one in Kurla, one in Malad and one in Bhayander. We asked in Chemould, just in case. They hadn't heard of Roy. We stopped by in the grimy gullies of Khetwadi, at the roadside framers. It was hard to imagine fake masterpieces being put together in the open dust.

So after organizing for my mother-in-law to pick up Rohan from school, Rimli and I set off for Kurla in my car, a name and an address in hand. Savera Mill Compound, off the Kurla-Andheri Road.

It's amazing how difficult it is to track down an address in India, where even locals don't know the names of roads one street away, or the name of a shop two doors down. We had a mobile number, which I had called several times, but it was switched off. The streets all looked the same, endless ribbons of rubbish and monsoon potholes, lined with sorry-looking shops selling buckets and chiwda and cheap, shiny fabric. Ultimately, after some twenty stops to ask for directions, we arrived at a dilapidated compound in a by-lane. As usual, there were no signboards. An old cobbler – shrivelled skin stretched on bones – sat outside in the midday sun, waving the flies away from his grimy shoebox.

I lowered the car window. 'Savera Mill Compound?' I asked.

He pointed to the gate behind him. Rimli and I got off the car, and entered through the ramshackle wooden gate. There were framers and carpenters inside the compound, men who worked with wood. Didn't the rotted door bother them? Didn't they ever think that it reflected upon their craft as wood-workers? But how many in India had the luxury to care about aesthetics?

Inside the compound there were sheds with corrugated tin roofs and a couple of rundown buildings, and dark men in white kurtas and chequered lungis sawing and polishing. They watched us balefully. The smell of fresh resin filled the air. Rimli and I looked too conspicuous here, with our polished hands and glossy shades.

'Asgar Ali?' I inquired. But the men remain silent, staring at us, pretending not to hear, till one nodded his head, indicating a spot further ahead. At the last building, a heavy-set man pointed us to the back area.

The back of the building had been cordoned off with piles of wooden beading and sawdust all around. Was a real Hemendranath being restretched in these surroundings? I shook my head, and looked at Rimli. For all her street-smarts, she looked equally confused and uncertain. She pointed towards the open door.

We went in. It was a dimly lit space, two storeys high, but not very deep. It was somewhat cleaner than the rest of the surroundings. Thick hessian sheets covered oddly shaped piles. I lifted one sheet up slightly and saw a stack of stretched canvases. The walls were lined with tall racks, full of wooden sticks, tubs of dowels and rivets, trays of age-darkened tools. There was a workbench of sorts, and behind that a staircase, dimly sweeping up towards a half-mezzanine. Someone was up there, I could hear voices. What were they talking about?

We sneaked up the staircase, silently. *Rats*, I heard, and *barsati repair*. Something innocuous then. Rimli and I exchanged a glance. We climbed up the remaining steps. Two beady-eyed men sat on the floor, in the shadow of a large worktable, messy with callipers, gauges, bevels, dowels, hammers and saws. Their lunch was spread out in front of them, aluminium dabbas of cold crumpled rotis and heavily spice-scented curry.

'What do you want?' One of them asked.

'Asgar Ali?' I said.

'Seth is not here,' he replied in a surly voice.

'When will he come?'

The man was reluctant to answer, and after much prodding told us that Asgar Ali could come in one hour, or he might come later.

We went back to the car to wait. Some forty minutes later, a fat man rode a small motorcycle into the compound.

Rimli and I reached the asbestos awning outside the back door.

'So you want frames made, Madam? Canvases stretched? You are an artist? All this trouble, coming all the way – you could have just called, told me sizes, or I could have picked up the canvases and had the framed pieces delivered to your doorstep.' Asgar Ali squirted a jet of reddish spittle on the muddy ground. His pot-belly belied his tall frame, as he stood, back concaved, belly protruding even further, chewing paan.

'I tried calling many times...' I was stuck, there was nothing in particular that I needed, and yet I didn't know how to broach the topic of Roy Jordan and the Hemendranath painting without preamble. 'Can you stretch jute?' I asked lamely.

'Yes, Madam, jute fabric not available, but you give it and I will stretch it.' The man ballooned his cheeks, ready to spit again. Instinctively I stepped back, revulsed by the thought of an accidental drop of spittle landing on me. This was obviously going nowhere.

Rimli leant forward, and in her softest voice asked, 'Can you restretch an old painting for us?'

'Ye..es.' Asgar Ali looked quizzically at us. After all, restretching was part of his business.

'Can you handle old paintings? Fragile pieces?' Rimli continued.

'Speak clearly, Madamji, what do you really need?' The man swallowed, forgetting to spit out his chewed paan, looked shiftily around, and indicated to us to move closer to the inner side of the asbestos-roofed area. 'What do you want?'

'Can you find old stretchers for me? Something from old wood, like fifty years old, you know the kind that has worm holes?' Rimli was courting trouble.

Asgar Ali was quiet now, almost watchful, waiting for our next move before opening his mouth.

Rimli leaned forward again: 'I need work like you have done for Roy Jordan.' Then after a pause, she continued, 'That gora sahib? You have stretched paintings for him, haven't you?'

There was a change in the air, swift as the crackle of white-hot electricity in a dark sky. The man transformed from a paan-chewing stranger to a flinty-eyed opponent with a hint of ruthlessness about him. 'Who are you, Madam, asking all these questions? Why do you want to know?'

Rimli was loud, extra loud, obviously faking a bravado she did not feel. 'Roy Jordan may be doing something illegal. Once the police are involved, then you will get into trouble too. Tell us now.'

'Don't threaten me with the police, Madam!' He spat inches away from Rimli's foot. 'Go back where you came from. Go now if you value your life.'

He didn't move an inch, barely lifted up his hands, but I felt the life drain from me! If anything were to happen, if we were attacked, if we screamed, would a single man here come to our rescue? How did we get into a mess like this, thinking we could solve this alone? Especially me with my phoren-returned lifestyle? No one had ever threatened me before.

Urgently, I pressed Rimli's arm, 'Let's get out of here.'

For once, Rimli did not resist. We were too nervous to even swivel around, to turn our backs on Asgar Ali as we left, fearing he might strike us from behind. We took faltering steps backwards, with Asgar Ali's fierce gaze on us, till we reached the passage between the two buildings, just metres away, and sprinted along the dusty pathway to the gate of the compound to get into the car.

'Drive fast,' I told the driver looking back. But there was no one watching us.

Crisp samosas, fresh from the corner shop, and sweet hot ginger tea greeted Rimli and me when we reached home to collapse onto the sofa, after battling two hours of afternoon traffic from Kurla to Walkeshwar, still rattled after our encounter with Asgar. My mother-in-law presided over the tea with sweet ceremony, all in control, with Rohan fed and playing in his room, and the nutty-spicy smell of just-cooked dinner wafting from the kitchen. As she fussed over us, clucking about how tired I must be from work at the gallery, a wave of nausea overcame me, a cloying wish for simpler times, when all I could have been worried about was my work and Rohan's dinner!

I had lost heaps of money I could ill-afford to lose, I had been duped by a savvy conman, and I was living in this bizarre marital fugue where I did not know where Raj and I stood, and I continued an uphill struggle to adjust to the basics of living in India.

And now I was playing with my life.

You tried to threaten a goon?' Gul looked at us as if we were mad, when we told her of our adventure the next morning. We probably *were* mad, going on a crazy hunt across town, searching for men involved in the illegal trafficking of art.

'Well, at least we know that Asgar Ali has done some work for Roy. He knows something!' Rimli was all pumped up by our big discovery. She flopped onto the couch and made a face at Gul. 'The big question is – what do we do next?'

There was no clear path forward anymore. No stray bits of information had turned up about Daniel Leibowitz; there was nothing to follow up on. The framer was involved somehow, or so intuition suggested. He must have felt exposed, defensive. Why else would he behave in such a prickly manner? But it was a tricky trail. 'Maybe we can try asking the other canvas stretchers? Maybe I can follow Roy?' I said, clutching onto half straws and iffy ideas.

'Maybe you can concentrate on the gallery for now. We need to sell four more paintings. Our next show starts in three weeks! We need to start the whole photographing, cataloguing and marketing process for that show. There is so much to do.' Gul pursed her lips, annoyed.

But I couldn't let it go. No. Roy was not going to get away with this. I was going to do something; make him pay in some way, expose him, finish off his scamster days.

In the end, we decided that I would take one more day off – just one last day – to see the two contacts we had got in Malad and Bhayander, while Gul manned the gallery on her own and organized the shipment of paintings for our next show, to be air-freighted from Baroda to Mumbai.

Rimli was loath to let me go alone, but she had a deadline that week, to send a sculpture for a group show at Vaidehi Gallery in Chennai, who were hosting her solo show in three months' time. She had already wasted enough time with me.

It was the worst day I could have chosen to travel across Mumbai. Not having kept track of the festival dates, I was surprised when near Worli we got stuck behind a large truck carrying hundreds of blue-shirted revellers, coloured pink, orange and yellow, tossing clouds of gulal in the air.

'Dahi Haandi,' the driver informed me – an annual Mumbai tradition celebrating the birth of Krishna, when large groups of revellers travelled across the city in open-top trucks, scattering gulal, chanting slogans, and competing with other groups to bring down a pot of goodies dangling from garlanded ropes high above the crowds at road intersections, making circular human pyramids to reach the prize at the top.

The truck took a turn eventually and we coasted for a few minutes before getting caught in another procession of dancing young men, and then another – of raucous men, smeared with gulal, oblivious to everything but themselves.

It proved to be a futile trip in the end, an endless voyage along badly paved roads choked with fume-disgorging buses, frustrated honking cars and rattling rickshaws. The man in Malad offered no response to the mention of Roy Jordan. I had managed to cull a photo of Roy from an old magazine, and I flashed it around. But there was no flicker of recognition. I travelled on, another hour of bumpy roads, burping with road sickness, mad with the lurching pace, and reached a small road-side shop in Bhayander that was closed on account of the holiday.

When I reached the gallery the next morning, Gul took hold of my arm excitedly: 'Look at these!' She pointed to a consignment in the storage room – the paintings for our next show had arrived!

We stood in the storeroom and Gul began to unroll the canvases one by one, making me hold one side while she unfurled each artwork. The artworks, by gangly art school youngsters, all three in their late twenties, were in total contrast to the deep bright tones of Muthu's canvases.

The lot from the first painter was large, textured and pale: mauves, peaches, lilacs and creams. Ethereal washes of paint on canvas. My spirits soared just looking at the glowing gem-toned pastels.

'We will need a deeper background to highlight these paintings,' Gul said. 'Eggshell blue, that'd be the perfect backdrop.' Gul was right: these paintings would fade against cream walls, a coloured background would set them off to perfection.

Then Gul started to unpack the second box, carefully slicing through the packaging tape with a utility knife. As she unrolled the first painting, she laughed in amazement. I remembered the painter, a slim young man with Jamaican dreadlocks, and his one submission at that student art show in Baroda had been an instant hit. It was pop-art on pills, and this particular painting, with Indian figures in 1950s type silhouetted comic-book style, with speech balloons and an unusual pale pastel coloration – was a full-on Amar Chitra Katha on canvas, or a Roy Lichtenstein on steroids. 'We definitely need a pale background for this one. We'll need different rooms with different themes,' Gul giggled. 'Imagine all the write-ups we need to cover three artists!'

Suddenly it was too much to take all at once.

The gallery would have to remain open till late every day for the next few weeks with the Muthu show. A week's gap to get things ready and then the second exhibition – featuring the group exhibition of young Baroda artists – would start. The paintings that had arrived before the monsoons had already been framed. But the new lots had still to be framed, and the entire cycle of operations and marketing run through again.

'We'll get ten workers to repaint the gallery overnight,' Gul said, refusing to be bogged down, excited by the new cache of paintings that had come in. 'We may need later on to hire a man to do the running around, but for now my driver can take the canvases to the framers, chase after delivery and so on.'

'We need an art expert to do a write-up for the next catalogue as well,' I said.

Gul went through her diary, found the number of a consular friend from Delhi, who had worked as a Cultural Attaché in the Far East, and promptly called the lady. The woman was only too happy to write for our next catalogue, and we promised to email her pictures of the paintings soon. I thought: *Oh God, the wretched rigmarole all over again – photo shoots, catalogue design, pre-selling to a new set of buyers!*

My mother called in the evening to ask about the show, saying she wished she could have escaped from her busy schedule to attend and telling me about some endoscopy conference she was chairing next week. 'Are you happy with the gallery, beta?' she asked.

'Yes, Mom,' I whispered, feeling the unsaid strain of the distance between us, of our lives that had become mutually exclusive. I had spent no time with my parents since coming back to India. I was so busy chasing my own life I had no time for them.

After I hung up, Raj called from Hong Kong: 'There is news of turmoil in the domestic financial sector in the US and the Dow has slid again.' He feared that the newly formed India Fund might implode on itself if US investors decided to pull out of overseas investments. 'They think that Indian stocks are over-valued. We need FIIs...' He sounded quite perturbed, actually. 'I am flying to New York directly from here,' he announced.

Whatever.

I had no time to think about Raj's problems. We both had our own battles to fight. Separate ones. We couldn't afford the luxury of cosying up to each other or providing a strong shoulder to support the other. I mean, who had the time? Of course, it's another matter that during the last six months, annoyed by everything Raj had done or not done, I would have said: Who had the *desire*?

Well, maybe now I *did* have the desire, but....

The list of buts went on.

'Do what you must,' I said and handed the phone to Rohan, who was quite upset that his daddy was not coming back for the weekend as promised.

Later that night, my mother-in-law got a panicky summons from Delhi – my father-in-law's blood pressure had risen alarmingly. She had to take the next flight out. I quickly logged on and made an online booking for an early Friday morning flight to Delhi. Then, on a sudden impulse, I booked tickets for Rohan and myself to Delhi and then onward to Bareilly, for the same afternoon.

I was flying home for the weekend, I decided. I was going to meet my parents.

Time did countless counter-revolutions, and then stilled itself.

There was a power outage on the evening that I arrived home to Bareilly – a familiar phenomena in north India. Rohan was inside somewhere, playing a game of snakes and ladders with my father, in inverter-lit dimness, and my mother, just back from her evening rounds in the clinic, was supervising the chhole-puris in the kitchen. So I took myself out and sat in the garden. My mother's garden, redolent with late blooming tuberoses and night jasmine, cool and white in the hot twilight, took me back many years. I lay back in a canvas easy chair and stared at the stars above. So clear, they hung. Like silver confetti, they had silvered my childhood dreams too, on nights just like this, sparking my imagination, whispering shiny promises of good times to come. How simple life had seemed then, an inextricably linked chain of karma and reward. *Work hard. Do well.*

The electricity returned; there was a collective sigh from the neighbourhood, of people leaving their gardens to go back inside their houses. Behind me, something, some small creature of the night, a squirrel probably, or maybe a rat, scurried up the grapevine that crept up the pergola covering the driveway.

I sat up with a start.

'Tara,' my mother called from inside, and at the same instant, Rohan called out to me as well.

Wiping my eyes, I went inside to the cool whirr of ceiling fans, hot chhole-puris and sweet, elaichi-flavoured homemade kheer.

Comfort food, laden with carbs, as good as it gets.

'How is Malhotra saab? Did you call up in the evening?' My father asked.

I had stopped over in Delhi that morning, and my father-in-law, after an emergency visit from the family doctor the previous night, seemed much better. He was delighted to see Ro and sat him on his knee. When the doctor came to check his blood pressure it was much lower than before. 'See, I just needed my grandson next to me,' my father-in-law said, making me feel guilty about dragging my mother-in-law away from him for my own peace of mind and for having given in to his excuse of an upcoming bridge tournament to stay back in Delhi. I should have insisted that they both visit. Later, he had reluctantly bid goodbye to Ro as we left for the airport. 'I will call after dinner,' I told my father, tearing into my third puri. 'They were going for an ECG in the evening.'

After dinner my parents and I talked of Rohan's school and local gossip. We spoke of Raj's work, the state of the Indian economy and the current deluge of goings-on in the financial sector in India. No one asked me any questions about the art world or my gallery. I was glad, because I would really have nothing to report except that I had been screamed at by Gul for gross negligence when I'd told her that I was going away for the weekend.

My parents and I called up my mother-in-law late in the evening. The ECG was normal, thankfully, and the heart specialist had let my father-in-law go home with new medicines and some strict instructions.

Later, after Rohan had fallen asleep and the three of us sat on my mother's sofa, chatting and watching Doordarshan Samachar together, my mother absently running her fingers through my hair, just like she did all those years ago when I was growing up, my sense of homecoming was complete. Six months of living in India, sixty plus channels vying for my attention on television, and I was happiest watching Doordarshan again and being my mother's little girl.

'Oho, did you see that, Tara?' my father said suddenly. 'Some painter committed suicide in Kolkata. It is such a hard field – too much risk, too much frustration...' My father was using the news excerpt to launch into a little 'be careful with the art business, beta,' speech but I was staring at the television, riveted.

It was a small news item, with the camera fixed on an old Jamini Roy painting. Tarun Pal Sanyal, said the news telecaster in Hindi, a Kolkata-based artist, had been found dead in mysterious circumstances in his tiny studio off College Street, pooled in his blood, his wrists slit. A scrawled suicide note, about his struggles as an artist since graduating from Santiniketan, was found beside his body. But among his meagre possessions were two, large, high-value paintings identified as works by Jamini Roy and KK Hebbar. The Doordarshan camera abruptly panned from the Jamini Roy painting to a jowly, pan-chewing Inspector sitting at his desk. 'We are investigating,' Sub-Inspector Biplab Saha commented, looking officiously into the camera.

I sat up. *Jamini Roy? KK Hebbar?* Found in the tiny studio of an unknown artist?

Jamini Roy, the celebrated artist from the Bengal school, and *the* most faked artist in India! Maybe there was a remote chance that Tarun, a Bengal school artist, had drawn inspiration from Jamini Roy and sourced a Jamini Roy painting at a time when prices were more affordable, or had even inherited it from a Bengali relative or mentor. But KK Hebbar, the Karnataka-born legendary artist, known for his graceful lines and lyrical compositions, how unusual was that? How would Tarun have got hold of a Hebbar, when those paintings now retailed for crores?

Was it a clue? Were the paintings fakes, made by Tarun Pal Sanyal himself, commissioned by a seller of forgeries? The thought seized my heart. I was immediately restless. I wanted to pretend it wasn't a big deal, act like this news meant nothing, like it was not triggering hope again. But what if there was something to this death, what if this *was* the beginning of a trail of forgeries that ultimately led to Roy?

I had to find out.

I called Rimli long distance, after my parents had finally gone to bed, to confer with her.

'It might be something,' Rimli agreed. But she was depressed and subdued. 'It's too depressing – an artist committing suicide! Reminds me of my own struggles. I almost wish it were murder.'

Back in Mumbai I entered the secure confines of Saloniere Star, greeted Gul enthusiastically, and by way of appeasement sent the driver down to Indigo Deli to fetch us each a coffee. Then I switched on my laptop to show Gul the design layout ideas I had worked on.

After ensuring that she was in a reasonably friendly frame of mind, I told her about the news item I had seen on Doordarshan. 'Maybe,' I suggested hesitantly, 'I can meet some new artists in Kolkata, and identify some pieces for our future shows, and also dig up the dirt on Tarun Pal Sanyal if I make a short trip there?'

Gul was kind. 'Don't go in a rush,' was all she advised. 'Take time to identify your best picks from among the new lot of upcoming Kolkata artists, and pre-arrange some meetings.'

I nodded my head, and as I did a feeling of nausea swamped me; remnants of all the heavy, ghee-soaked chhole-puri I had eaten over the weekend. Besides there was no way I could leave in a rush. Raj was still away in New York and with my mother-in-law gone, Rohan had no one to look after him. I couldn't leave my little boy with the maids. My mother would come if I asked, but she would need time to reorganize her schedule and organize backup surgeons for her patients. No, I just had to wait for Raj! Three whole days! Anyway, I needed three days to get organized, to shortlist who among the emerging artists to see while in Kolkata.

*

Maddy called me mid-morning on Wednesday. 'Hiiiii,' she said cheerily, and talked about the fabulous new kundan rings at Moksha, and invited me to join her in the afternoon for the launch of the latest Wendell Rodericks collection in Kemps Corner. It was the time of the year when fashions changed and designers launched their festival collections. Every event organizer under the sun went into a tizzy showcasing a pantheon of clothes designers, jewellery designers, interiors designers, bag designers, shoe designers, and craft designers.

But I was in the middle of writing lyrical descriptions for the catalogue of the second show, and phrases like *'suite of paintings profiling the urban landscape of modern India and its inner intermingling with ethnicity'* hovered in my mind. For once my heart was not in shopping. 'Not today, sweetie, I have a spa appointment,' I lied to Maddy and hung up before she asked me for more details.

Rimli came in the afternoon, flashing a copy of *Get Gorgeous* magazine, an oversized glossy about the rah-rah set, and I could not help kidding her about it. 'I can't picture you, of all people, reading this mag!'

'It's a friend's,' Rimli said defensively and drew my attention to the centrespread. A glossy-haired woman, Natalia Balogh, wife of the Cultural Attaché of Romania in India, was pictured in a lovely sequinned dress next to a painting by Paritosh Sen. *The woman who had entered the Embassy of Romania with Roy and Daniel!* It was an interview, and we hurried through the five-page article, looked at pictures of her in a gorgeous bungalow with her Labrador Luca and attending various diplomatic soirees in Delhi, and read that she was a great admirer of Indian fashion and Indian art. The article went on to say that she collected contemporary Indian art and now her friends back in Bucharest and Braşov and Iaşi and those in diplomatic ranks around the world, impressed by her collection, were expressing a similar interest in both Indian fashion and Indian art.

'Is she just another ditzy buyer?' Rimli looked thoughtful. 'Or, is she part of the plot?'

The bloated feeling persisted. 'See a doctor,' Gul advised. 'You've been too stressed lately. It could, you know' – she rolled her eyes heavenward as if this too was a calamity for *her* to deal with – 'be an ulcer or something.'

So I did. My first trip to a doctor in India, and I can't say I was impressed.

I mean, I know medical tourism is riding high in India; or so the newspapers tell me. NRIs and foreigners were swarming into the country for every treatment possible – from bypass surgery and surgical fat reduction to a complete dental make-over; but it couldn't be to clinics like these!

After subjecting me to the usual probing questions and an undignified physical examination in a tiny congested clinic, with scruffy medical assistants who looked no better than street-side labourers as they stood by open bins overflowing with syringes and cauters, and while I was still agonizing over whether the surgical instruments were sterilized after each use, the lady doctor shook her head. 'Get these tests done. Maybe it's just a virus – a tummy bug is going around in the city – but we must eliminate the possibility of a hormonal imbalance.'

So I went to a dingily cluttered path lab, and sat on a hard chair in the glare of a harsh fluorescent

light while a young girl in a salwar suit and white
nursing coat pierced me with a pre-needled syringe,
transferred the blood into two tiny unlabelled phials,
and then closed them with rubber stoppers with her
ungloved hands.

Back home I sat in my living room after dark, in
blessed solitude – such a luxury in India – staring at
the bleak chain of lights along Marine Drive, misted
by smog. The subcontinent, South Asia, the Diaspora,
I thought, a myth surrounds these words, shadowing
identities, reviving longings for customs left behind,
conjuring images of an exuberant culture. I had
suffered a decade of nostalgia when I was away, yet
now that I was here, I could not immerse myself in
it. I found the rambunctiousness chaotic, that same
rootedness excluding. The economic significance of
the move back did not bother me anymore. The sense
of economic vibrancy was colouring my sensibility in
slow motion, like a clouded dawn, the hint of pink
blushing behind the cumulus of grey; weeks of listening
to the chest-beaters of the local financial papers and I
had forgotten the hard-nosed reality of *The Wall Street
Journal*. But other questions bothered me. The question
of belonging, of being a naturalized alien there and an
expatriate alien here, of being unable to compromise
on both ends, cavorting in the exosphere, hovering in
an unimaginable split, one leg here and one leg there,
stretching every tendon, every muscle to its limit. The
divisions remained. They just changed their type, from
skin colour there to the state and city and street of my
birth here. What would it take to belong?

Raj arrived late on Thursday night, when the
street below had fallen silent and the house was even

quieter, except for the hushed sounds of an American crime drama on late night television, which was on in the background, while I sat on the sofa, distracted, chewing upon a manicured nail, and inhabited an airy world mind-miles away.

'Hello,' he said uncertainly, setting down his suit carrier on the floor.

We stood there, mere shadows in the flickering light of the big flat screen.

Seas and oceans, he had crossed to return home; but the distance of my living room seemed un-crossable.

'I'm glad you are back,' I exhaled, as a wave of relief, of belonging, flooded me. *He was back. I will talk to him. Life must change.* We would deal with it all together. Moving forward, I hugged Raj, burrowing my head in his chest, feeling the light clasp of his hands, like a sponge soaking up my woes.

Later in bed, I told him about the Kolkata happenings and asked if he could manage Rohan for a couple of days while I went down there to investigate. 'I feel there is something to it. I feel it in my gut.'

I omitted to mention the trips to Malad, the scary sullenness of Asgar Ali, driven by the need to solve this puzzle, to clear my name, to lift this burden of misery.

'I would rather you forget about all this,' Raj lifted my face with one long finger, so I could see the deep flecks in his molten chocolate eyes, and my own shimmery concaved reflection in them. 'Make up for the money lost in other ways. Let bygones be bygones.'

'I must find out more, Raj. I need to clear my name.'

Raj was silent. But it was a warm silence, full of new possibilities.

*

Ravi Uppal visited Saloniere Star the next day, fresh from a trip to Parisienne ateliers to take in orders for made-in-India fabrics for assembled-in-China haute couture. Gul and I exclaimed in delight as he whipped out some croissants he had picked up from a boulangerie on Champs-Élysées the day before.

Biting into her croissant, Gul updated him on the goings-on at the gallery, and he looked at our plans for the next show, commented upon the catalogue, absorbing details of revenue projections and offering suggestions for shows later in the year. He was very much the hands-on angel investor.

Gul had been hinting for the last two days that I fess up to Ravi, show him my Sher-Gil, seek his opinion and ask for his help in unmasking Roy. But I was not sure. I was not ready to peel away the layers of control yet. As we wrapped up the session and I started closing the spreadsheets on my laptop, Gul gestured to me again, mouthing 'tell-him' but I ignored her.

'By the way, ladies,' Ravi said, as he got up from the back office room, and walked through the gallery, 'the margins are better for established artists. Why don't you sell works by already known painters? I can help you source them.' Ravi stroked the back of his thinning head of hair with his palm, and smiled at us encouragingly.

Gul and I let out a collective groan. The same dilemma – margin pressures versus upfront investment. We had been over this many times.

'We can't invest in pricey acquisitions just yet,' I said, stung by the crunch bug.

'Plus we are following another strategy,' Gul explained. 'To expand the entire pie of the art market, make art reachable to a larger number of people by selling affordable quality art.'

'You could always deal in established artists on the side, up your margins a bit, subsidize these young artists you want to showcase,' Ravi shrugged. 'In fact, I have an idea. Can you take a few hours off? I'll show you something.'

It was midmorning, not really the time when potential buyers and sellers traipsed in. There was work to be done for the next show – catalogue work, phone calls, the works. But no pressing appointments deterred us, and high on our croissants, we agreed to go with Ravi.

Out in the blistering sunshine, on a thrilling bouncy ride in a speedboat across the grey Arabian, coiffed curls madly fluttering in the brisk breeze, we headed towards Mandwa jetty. Once there, we walked the rocky path from the dock to the street and a waiting car whisked us the short distance to Ravi's beachfront property in Alibaug.

Beyond a brick and barbed wire fence, cypress trees and broad palms shaded the pebble-ringed lawn and large bungalow; testament to Ravi's standing as a successful businessman in the city. A manservant stood in the foyer to usher us indoors. The inside was captivating – designer sleek with Minotti designs rendered in glossy Burma teak, etched glass panels, recessed lights, rustic durries, thick white cotton upholstery, enormous urns filled with flowers and of course, art on the walls – extravagant pieces boasting famous signatures.

I admired the sea view beyond the glass French doors, a sleepy scene containing a lovely tiled pool and beyond it, a blue painted wooden canoe casually banked upon a ribbon of sand melding into the grey-green sea; it was unclear what Ravi had in mind when he had suggested this impromptu trip, but it was gorgeous to escape Mumbai to see this.

The resident maid walked in with mint caprioskas on a tray. 'Come,' Ravi invited, and led us to the downstairs level and through a corridor to a large windowless room, a haphazard holding area lined with open shelves that held thick stacks of paintings. A large air-conditioner hummed in low volume. Gul and I mouthed silent wows, exchanging amazed glances. Ravi flipped canvases at random. 'Art has been my passion for long.'

It was easily proved. Modern lots in one corner; older lots in another stack – Tyeb, Padamsee and Sabavala and their ilk; and another area with special one-offs – Meera Mukherjee, Abhanindra, and so on.

'Look, here's my idea,' Ravi started. 'I have old lots in my possession, which I want to sell off, rotate, and buy fresh. Why don't you take some of these – I'll fund you to acquire the paintings or you take the consignment on a commission basis – and sell them. In fact, I can lend you the money to buy the paintings, if you want. It's a bit of easy money on the side.' Ravi gave us a kind, reassuring smile.

There's a thought, I thought. *Easy money on the side, to make up for losses in other areas*. I walked up to a stack, absently going through the canvases, till I paused at one, a darkly evocative Bikash Bhattacharjee. I had seen this canvas just recently, in some auction catalogue – one of those over-the-top sales which send the gong beaters into a tizzy. Ravi must have acquired it lately, and at quite a whopping price. That thought gave me a start. Enough of a start to dispel any notions of easy money; landing me straight into the messy truth of insurance dramas, sale restrictions, heavy hustling, and late night vigils for pricey customers. Surely we had enough to handle.

'Maybe later, Ravi,' I exhaled.

'There's too much on our plates at the moment, Ravi,' Gul said, looking around, taking in the big temperature-controlled room full of paintings, probably having the same thoughts. 'It could be something to think about, to consider for a later date.'

Ravi backed off gracefully, and after a lovely early lunch of spicy channa, ghee-soaked parathas and rasmalai under a bougainvillea covered pergola overlooking the sea, we made the trip back to town on choppy waters.

We reached the gallery by two, and our graphic designer knocked on the door minutes later. 'I was meeting another client in this area,' she said. 'I thought I'd drop in to collect the new specs.'

I showed her my roughs and the three of us argued over cover and invite designs, flipped between Framemaker and Illustrator, cropping amateur pictures to get the perfect balance of image and text, playing with fonts, and nudging background shades point by point to find that perfect colour.

I burped in the middle, lethargy dulled my limbs and I wished I could put my head down and sleep. Heavy lunches did not agree with me, for sure. Still, I pushed myself to stay alert, eyes wider than usual to mask my sleepiness. After nearly two hours, what I had visualized on paper and Powerpoint was transported into rough graphics.

'I'll send you the final pictures after we get them from the professional photographer,' I told the designer as she was leaving, after promising to send a draft version by next week.

Exhausted from the session, Gul decided to take a walk outside to browse for gifts in a new curio shop which had opened nearby and I slumped into a soft leather chaise and absently flipped through folios and catalogues from Gul's collection, randomly at first, and then in hasty concentration, racing through the Bikash Bhattacharjees sold in the past few years.

There, in the catalogue of a Gorham's auction in London last year, I found the painting I had seen in Ravi's house that afternoon – the small glossy catalogue picture barely capturing the dark drama of the real thing. The price, with a few too many zeroes to assimilate, touched the crore mark! *So Ravi Uppal was trying to sell among other works, a painting he had bought only last year?* I was intrigued – was it because he did not like the work? Did he, maybe, need ready cash for his business? If so, then how could he offer to lend us money to buy and resell paintings from his own collection?

As I got up to leave, my mobile phone rattled against the desk. It was a text message, from Raj:

P-notes are pesky. Dinner tonight, my lovely?

I couldn't help giggling, as I sat up and typed back:

Foamy Finance, if you ask me. Dinner sounds good.

My drowsiness disappeared and I waited for Raj's text, which he sent promptly telling me he would make a reservation. I was flying to Kolkata tomorrow morning, but then my overnight case was already packed and dinner did seem something to look forward to. I could catch up on my sleep on the plane.

That evening, after putting Ro to bed, I dressed up again, discarding a fitted top and skinny denim combo when it felt uncomfortable – too many chhole puris and channa paranthas in one week. Vowing to up my exercise after coming back from Kolkata, I wore a red dress with a flirty hemline which swished around my knees when I walked. Raj was waiting in the living room, dressed in a stylish Narendra Kumar shirt I had bought on an impulse that evening, stopping at Ogaan on my way back from the gallery; I fingered the fine lawn, admiring the lean deconstructed look. He took my hand and we walked out to the lift and down to the garage. Raj drove, with the windows rolled down. The evening breeze and the privacy, sans driver, was heaven-sent.

The drive to central Mumbai was long, and just as I began wondering why we were pulling up outside a rundown mill compound, I went inside the non-descript building and was totally wowed. Plush mahogany pods enclosed cosy dining spaces around a dim-lit floor and tall video screens projected images in hallucinatory motion. Intricate guitar tremolos against the thump-thump of Afro drums set the low decibel backdrop to high decibel conversations.

'Some place,' I smiled, looking at the long brown menu with a jumping amphibian on the cover. 'Blue Frog,' Raj said. 'Feels like being back in the US, doesn't it?' There would be live music later! I settled back happily in the pod leather seat.

Raj smiled over his baked brie on little phyllo squares, pleased with the way his work was going. 'PE ratios can only go higher,' he said, hoping to get me interested again.

'Dipankar thinks the stocks are over-valued,' I laughed, flirting back. The *Business Times* mania had gripped me too; I was just teasing him.

'In pockets perhaps; but even cynics can't negate the basics – these companies are sitting on so much cash and so little debt; the rules are getting transparent, labour is plentiful, and investments are flowing in.'

The waiter brought our orders – linguini in a pistou of walnuts, olives and roasted apples and prime steak – perfectly presented on large creamy platters, calorific installations in a temple of gourmands. In between mouthfuls we animatedly discussed the news trickling in from the US, a blip perhaps, something that would not affect the Indian story, the local economists reiterated.

Our old amity went up in basis points as we talked of indices and credit influx, but the long-term reserves for our relationship – I wasn't sure how matters stood there.

'So you like it here now, Tara?' Raj changed the topic, and leaned forward, asking something I chose not to ask myself.

What could I say? So I told him about my day instead – the French croissants courtesy Ravi, the impromptu trip to Alibaug, the pressure of art sales, and how I had rushed after getting his text message, getting my hair done at the salon, picking up his shirt, navigating evening traffic to pick up Ro while talking on the phone with a prospective client, getting home to find the dinner ready in steaming pots – as per the menu I had stuck to the fridge this morning and the dining table set for three, feeding and bathing Ro, instructing the maids on the breakfast menu, before getting ready to start the evening.

Raj chuckled, his eyes crinkling, 'So very Madly Malabar, ain't it?'

'So very Madly Malabar,' I agreed, grinning back.

❧twenty

Kolkata! I stepped out of the airport, full of hope.

Amal Chatterjee, a contact of Ravi's and my local host in the city, was there to pick me up. He had a packed schedule ready, from artists in Bhowanipore, to galleries in Ballygunge, even a long day-trip to Santiniketan if I was game.

'Today we have three meetings in the afternoon. We start with an artist in Salt Lake, then go for a meeting near Kalighat, and finally near Dover Lane. But first I promised the proprietor of Nabojyoti Gallery in Salt Lake that we will stop by for a visit,' he said good-naturedly, his well-oiled, centre-parted hair framing a friendly round face, eager to introduce me to the artists I had pre-identified over the past three days.

'Let's go to College Street first,' I told Amal.

'But we have appointments,' he protested and looked at me quizzically, his round eyes getting rounder, gauging my seriousness as a gallery owner, turning the pre-fixed schedule upside down.

'Have you fixed a time to meet the Nabojyoti guys?'

'Mota-moti... Approximately...' Amal started.

'There is something I must check urgently,' I explained to Amal, not knowing what else to say, and told him that I had to trace Tarun Pal Sanyal, the artist who had died last week. I wanted to do this first thing in the morning, before our appointments in the afternoon.

Amal looked confused. He had not heard of Tarun Pal Sanyal, or of his death. 'Plus, if this guy is already dead, then why the interest?'

'He was painting something for a friend of mine on commission. I promised I will find out what happened to that work.'

Amal did not look very convinced by my answer, but he did not probe any more. 'Okay, give me the address and I shall tell the driver,' he said, offering to wheel the trolley with my suitcase.

I declined his offer, and followed him through the crowds to the parking lot. 'College Street.'

Amal turned back to look at me, and laughed. 'That's not an address. College Street is a long, densely populated area!'

'That's all I know,' I tried to not look as stupid as I felt.

Amal shook his head, his eyes proclaiming me crazy: 'How can you trace someone with no exact address? It's hard enough finding a place when we have the address. Whom will you ask?'

Now that was what I hadn't figured out. So intent had I been on getting to Kolkata, armed with just that brief news clipping, that I did not have a plan of what to do once I reached the street where Tarun Pal Sanyal had lived.

A long ride later, when we reached College Street, with its row upon row of tin-shed stalls selling books – new, used, and rare – and sundry kurta–jeans clad students milling about, I realized just how stuck I was. I had no proper address.

I got out of the car with Amal behind me, and walked along the street staring at the disinterested looking shopkeepers. They looked bored, and were busy dusting books or swishing brown-tainted mops in the air to drive away the flies. It was early in the day, and already the heat was intense and the flies plentiful. I paused in front of an old bookseller, his features softened by plumpness giving him a friendly air, and asked about Tarun Pal Sanyal, only to realize that he did not understand a word of what I was trying to say. I needed a translator.

Amal was not amused when I asked him to translate for me; it was dawning on him how tangential this whole wild chase was. 'Please,' I beseeched. Anxiety flecked my voice, in bluesy pointillism fashion.

Amal shook his head disapprovingly, but asked the plump man my question in Bengali. The man shook his head in reply.

Tarun Pal Sanyal, Amal asked a couple more shopkeepers, but they all shrugged their shoulders; no one had heard the name. We had no descriptions, no landmarks to go by. It was hot now, as the sun climbed up higher in the clear sky, scalding the tin roofs and charcoal path. I wrapped my dupatta around my head, but while it offered meagre shade from the sunlight, it stifled me too, shutting out the sullen air.

Even a mention of his recent suicide did not trigger any memories. One man lost among millions. With each shake of the head, with each incomprehensible gaze, my heart sank further.

I glanced around, taking in the locality. Away from these stalls was typical old Calcutta, a warren of time-stilled narrow alleys radiating behind one broader avenue, fronted by elaborately embellished buildings that had once known better times. They looked grimy, the dust of decades upon their carved bastions and filigreed iron balconies, a skirting of open drain at their feet.

I stopped Amal. 'Let's go to the local police station,' I told him. There was one name I could surely trace. The policeman, Sub-Inspector Biplab Saha.

Amal was incredulous. 'Police station? You want to *willingly* walk into a police station to find out about this guy?' The tone was of pure disbelief. Like no crime could be greater than willingly walking into a police station.

'Let's talk about this over coffee,' Amal suggested and led me through the thin morning crowd back to the waiting car. 'Coffee House,' he told the driver.

The car stopped in front of a dilapidated building with an intricately carved Victorian façade. 'Coffee House is a Calcutta landmark,' Amal said informatively as we walked up a winding staircase, as if I were a tourist on a Visit Kolkata mission!

Bangla rock music played through the thick cigarette smoke haze, dense enough to raise the particulate matter content of the room to hazardous levels. We ordered our coffees and grabbed the only empty table in the centre of the room. We had to shout to each other to be heard. 'If no one knows Tarun Pal Sanyal,' I yelled, 'then the investigating officer must.' There had to be a way to trace Biplab Saha, and through him Tarun, the artist.

'But this is crazy,' Amal barked. 'Who is this Tarun? If he was a good artist, capable of getting commissions from Mumbai collectors, why have I not heard of him?'

'Tarun Pal Sanyal was unsuccessful. Wildly so, *that's* why he committed suicide. But my friend knew him through family friends, so she gave him the commission,' I wildly embellished the meagre facts I knew, not caring if Amal saw through it all. But I was at a loss. There seemed to be no way other than walking inside a police station and requesting assistance.

'Tarun Pal Sanyal...' Amal drummed his fingers upon the table, impatient. 'But the police...' He shuddered in distaste.

'Excuse me,' a voice cut in. I looked up to see a man of middling years in a faded yellow batik kurta with long frizzy hair and a matted beard. Not the sort I would ever strike up a conversation with. I stared away, happy to let Amal deal with this one.

'I could not help overhearing... Tarun Pal Sanyal...' the wastrel said.

Suddenly I was all ears. Someone who knew Tarun Pal Sanyal! 'Do sit down, have a coffee,' I smiled at him, inviting him to pull up a chair, and noted with renewed interest his tall frame and the intelligence in his eyes.

'You are talking of Tarun Pal Sanyal, the artist who died, aren't you?' he asked, coming straight to the point.

I nodded, waiting for his next words. A lead, dropping right into my lap, it was divine intervention, blessed by the Goddess Kali herself. 'He was my friend,' said the bearded man in accented English, introducing himself as Sabbyasachi 'Sabi' Ganguly, a youth leader in a local party and a tenth year doctoral programme candidate in Political Science at Calcutta University.

Only in politics are *youth leaders* men at some unmentionable midlife moment, I smiled to myself. The real apparatchiks in positions of powers are the septuagenarians.

'Only in Kolkata,' Amal was saying proudly, 'will someone walk up like this, to talk of intense matters with strangers.' He smiled at the man: 'Some coffee for you, Sabi Babu?'

'This suicide... was it suicide, or was it something else...?' Sabi began, and I was hooked. 'I was surprised. We'd met at a party rally and struck up a friendship. This was a couple of years ago. Tarun always seemed so content. Wistful, yes, for bigger things, but he had come to accept that he was not going to make much money through art. He seemed happy enough with the occasional poster design, and sundry art work that came his way. Last year, I think, he found a mentor. He did not mention the specifics, but he hinted that someone was interested in his work. He'd started flashing his cash – splurging on kebabs and kachoris, cases of Old Monk, you know. So this suicide, it seems such a waste, so unnecessary when things were finally looking up...' Sabi looked troubled.

'Could you take me to his place?' I asked. 'Did he live alone?'

'Well... I am not sure of his family, they live somewhere near Burdhman. But he didn't live with them. No, he was not married,' Sabi answered, pre-empting my next question.

'Do you know much about his family?' I asked. 'The news report said he had a Jamini Roy and a KK Hebbar in his collection. Could it have belonged to his family?'

Sabi shook his head. 'Tarun was a moddho-bitto Bengali, you know, middle-class. In fact, his father died young and he was brought up in straitened circumstances. I cannot imagine his family owning Jamini babu's painting. Hebbar, now that's a name I am not familiar with.'

'Please...' I told Sabi, my fingers light upon the thin sleeve of his kurta. 'Can you take me to where he lived?' *And where he died.*

Amal paid for the coffees and we walked out onto the street and up to the car. As we drove Sabi told me more about Tarun. Mid-thirties, resisting family pressure to get married, no steady girlfriend after some woman dumped him in his twenties to get married to a respectably employed accountant. As for his art, Sabi claimed to be no purveyor with a keen eye for the goods, but Tarun did not seem to be making it big. Who knew if it was lack of talent or lack of English? Sabi mused. In a world where good marketing skills were essential for success of any sort, Tarun, it seemed, was particularly unworldly, insisting on works that the dealers did not want.

The car moved along the main road for a few minutes before Sabi instructed the driver to turn into a narrow winding alley, and then another, and another, squeezing alongside wide Ambassadors and rickety handcarts and children lolling on the streets, crossing sweet shops and chai shops, to end up in a lane of greyish, sun-starved, three-storeyed buildings, somewhere parallel to College Street. Clothes and towels hung out of the windows, fluttering like flags. Rusted iron bars guarded the windows from scheming monkeys and intruders.

'This building,' Sabi pointed to the middle of a non-descript row, and I strained my eyes upwards, at the dank premises, at the foot-wide strip of yellowy sky peeping between the rooftops, and tried to imagine the helplessness of someone living there; it would be enough to propel *me* to suicide.

Sabi instructed the driver to stop at a PCO booth and said that he had to call the agent who looked after the room Tarun Pal Sanyal used to occupy, explaining to us that the police had cleared the premises and the landlord intended to put it out on rent again. I offered Sabi my phone, and he made the call from the car. The agent promised to come in twenty minutes, an eternity to wait in those cheerless surroundings.

Then dismay assailed me; of course, the room would have been cleared out. It had been a week since the news of his death had broken. There would be nothing new to find there. 'So what's inside now?'

'There weren't many possessions to begin with. Just a few clothes, some art supplies – the police took custody of the paintings, his family in Burdhman was informed. Maybe they have collected them by now.'

'Would the Jamini Roy and KK Hebbar paintings have gone to the family?' I asked.

But Sabi hadn't a clue. 'Maybe the police have them. Maybe the family has already sold them to raise some good cash. Most probably they were cheap copies he had found from somewhere. I only got to know of his death the day after he died, and by the time I arrived the room had been emptied out. Maybe someone looted it. Maybe there was some mistake in identification.'

Half an hour later, a thin dark man with thick glasses arrived and took us upstairs to a room on the second floor, complaining that no tenant had come forward yet, probably scared by the superstition of the lingering spirit of a life interrupted. A dark room, with windows along one wall that probably let in some oblique sunlight for a very short period in the mornings, and a shared bathroom at the end of the corridor. Devoid of personal items, the room told me nothing. I might have to go to the police after all. The murkiness got to me; there were too many shadows here, and the air was too musty. Itchiness returned to rasp my insides. Water, I needed water, my head swam.

'Let's go,' I said and climbed hurriedly down the stairs, clutching the sidewall, swallowing deep breaths to dispel the suffocation. I spied a small tea and snacks stall across the road. 'I'll get a bottle of water,' I told Amal and Sabi and walked towards it.

In front of the stall, a fat man in a dhoti and vest sat on a makeshift table of plank and bricks rolling out small triangles of dough and filling them with a potato masala, making samosas for his evening clientele. He assessed me, a cunning look in his narrow eyes, as he handed me a bottle of Himalaya and my change. 'You came to see that babu who died? Why he lived here, in these poor quarters, I don't know...' He spoke in Hindi, in a lilting Bihari accent.

I ignored the man, not meeting his eye, thinking he was just another nosy Kolkata resident with time on his hands. His voice followed me as I uncapped the bottle and took a sip of water. 'With all those foreigners who kept coming and going to his place, why, he must be making lots of money.'

Foreigners? I stopped mild-gulp. 'Foreigners came to meet him?' I asked the man. 'To buy his paintings?'

'Buying! Selling! God only knows!' The fat man shook his head. 'Paintings, who knows? Drugs, more likely. Who makes money on paintings? This is the world for you. No one is as they seem.' The roadside samosa-maker gave me his two-paisa philosophy.

With trembling fingers I sifted through an envelope in my bag for pictures of Roy and Daniel Leibowitz, cut from a Delhi magazine. 'Him?' I waved Daniel's photo.

'Yes,' The fat man confirmed. 'He's the one! One Indian man was usually with him. They came even after Tarun Babu died, after the police were called in, and left with a large bag of his things. Stealing from the dead, Ram, Ram!'

There was nothing more to be done. I turned to Amal, who had followed me to the stall. 'Well then, case dismissed,' I said. 'Let's follow your schedule, Amal, meet the artists you have arranged for me to meet.'

We dropped Sabi off on College Street, thanking him profusely for his help with a couple of hundreds that he reached out for with amazing alacrity. Then I went through the rest of the day, meeting with new artists and their agents, assessing talent and portfolios, determining their potential for sales in the Mumbai market, clicking a prodigious number of digital photos and making notes. Two artists stood out in my mind. Gul would be pleased. Amal made quick stops at some galleries in Ballygunge and New Alipore, and I walked behind him noting the Paritosh Sens and Ganesh Pynes, fractionally less expensive than in similar galleries in Mumbai.

The next morning, after a lazy start since it was Sunday, Amal took me to the bylanes of Jadavpur to the studio of a young artist couple, Pinaki and Ruma Rai. Over chai and mishti, in a room full of plants and a few mediocre paintings, we talked about the psychology and history of art expression.

Pinaki, a stocky fellow with a large head, talked of how social realism still permeated the works of some Indian artists. This was similar to the phase of American art in the 1930s and 1940s when those artists had evolved themselves and their ideas beyond the diktats of European art to social realism and then broke away from social realism towards abstraction and post-modernism.

We had a lively conversation about art movements, its newer trends, and the role of private galleries in a country where the government did not have the resources or the mindset to invest in museums and art programmes. It was nearly one by the time we finished talking. 'You must have lunch. I insist,' Ruma said and left to check things in the kitchen.

After a simple lunch of rice, daal, a vegetable and of course fish, they showed me their paintings. The French-bearded Pinaki did these untitled post-modernist daubs of acrylic gouache on paper and board, and while there was tension and drama between the play of colours and empty spaces, the shapes could be construed to be anything, or not. Ruma, a petite woman with knee-length hair, made benign wash painting scapes, of the kind convent school girls did to please standard eight art teachers. Neither style was what I would want to sell in Saloniere Star, but their erudition on art and artists around the world, probably because of their other job as lecturers at the Government Art College in Kolkata, was impressive and I could not help warming to their easy hospitality.

Promising to keep in touch, I said goodbye to Pinaki and Ruma. As we sat in the car, I asked Amal to cancel the last appointment on the pretext of shopping. I dropped Amal off near Park Street before telling the driver what I really wanted to do in that stolen hour – visit the police station near College Street.

Arriving alone at the Jorasanko police station, I entered the gate and walked up the narrow steps leading to the rundown building.

'Yes, Madam?' The portly man on the chair near the entrance held a rusty rifle in his arms. Did he even know how to use it?

I told him I wanted to meet Sub-Inspector Biplab Saha, and he got up reluctantly, hitched his khaki pants up his ample girth, and waddled inside, still cradling the rifle. I followed him, past paan-pocked walls and tables heaped with piles of fraying paper. In the far corner of the room, under a dust-blackened ceiling fan wobbling on its long stem, Sub-Inspector Biplab Saha sat, rolling tobacco on his wide palm.

'Madam wanted to meet you, Sahib,' the portly gatekeeper grinned ingratiatingly and shuffled back to his spot near the door.

There were no chairs in front of Biplab Saha's desk, and I stood, very conscious of his oily curiosity and the loud slap of his palm upon his other hand as he rolled the tobacco some more and tossed it into his mouth. I told him that I wanted to know more about the suicide of artist Tarun Pal Sanyal and the possessions he had left behind.

'Artist's possessions?' Biplab Saha chewed his tobacco as his eyes lazily sized me from head to foot with a slow assessing look. 'Why, Madam? What's your interest?' His gesture was so Bollywood bad-cop, that, were it not for my disgust at this distasteful appraisal, I would have laughed out loud.

I said I needed an answer for a collector who had already paid for a painting that was never delivered. I asked again about the paintings mentioned in the papers. What had happened to them? Jamini Roys, after all, did not disappear into thin air. I mentioned the foreigners seen leaving the building with a large bag.

But Biplab Saha was a thorough professional. Not a twitch of a facial muscle gave any clue of the sums of money Leibowitz must have paid him to take the paintings. Or perhaps I had no way of extracting the information from him. I was about to beg and grovel for information, but the leer gleaming in the man's eyes undid me. Why willingly subject myself to this, for no end result?

'Excuse me,' I walked out of the police station, head held high, and told the driver to take me straight to the airport to catch the evening flight back to Mumbai.

The next morning, when I stepped out of the bathroom in a mid-length skirt and a cheery buttercup yellow top – with expertly applied makeup to mask my exhaustion – Rohan was up, pouting and commanding cuddles; his neediness for me growing in direct proportion to my preoccupation. No smiles here, just a litany of demands: 'Are you going to drop me to school today, Mamma? Why can't you pick me up like other moms? Why can't I buy the new Power Rangers watch on the way back from school? Why? Why?' He stopped in aggrieved silence.

By the time I acquiesced to the easiest of the demands – buying Ro his fifteenth Power Rangers toy that very evening – and got him into his morning clothes and at the breakfast table, Raj arrived back from the gym. School drop-off was impossible. Fifteen minutes was all I could grab from Raj's schedule, if timed right, and I needed to talk to him, to tell Raj about Daniel and the missing Hebbar and Jamini Roy, to get the mystery of the death of Tarun Pal Sanyal off my chest. Not that Raj would have any ideas, but I simply needed to speak to someone.

'Sorry, Ro. No drop-off. But I promise to pick you up,' I gave him an extra cuddle, and asked the maid to drop Ro to school, yet again.

Raj came to the breakfast table a few minutes later, hair damp and slicked back, adjusting the cuff-links on his white shirt, and sat down to a breakfast of omelette and toast. I told him quickly about my quest for Tarun Pal Sanyal.

'It seems a bit beyond you, Tara,' Raj was quite matter-of-fact, as he cut up his omelette with precision. 'Admit you made a mistake, write off the painting and move on.' He wiped his mouth with his napkin as he got up from the chair, and rushed off to meet with an asbestos manufacturer from Jharkhand who was in town to seek an FDI investment for his new factories.

I don't know what response I had expected from Raj. A hug maybe; or a soft reassurance that things would reveal themselves somehow. But this hurried casualness left me in despair. I squared my shoulders. I had dealt with bad bosses and the dotcom crash and bitchy colleagues. I could deal with one devious dealer and his nefarious racket!

Saloniere Star was quiet, the last unsold painting had been sold while I was away in Kolkata. Not that we were about to break even any time soon, given all the start-up costs we had accumulated. But a sold-out first show was a milestone. To be celebrated.

Gul was relaxed enough to suggest sneaking off to Indigo Deli for a hot cuppa, and for a delightful half hour, there was no mention of art, artists, or my fruitless Kolkata trip.

When we returned to the gallery, I showed Gul the digital pictures of the more promising works I had seen in Kolkata. 'Oh, let's simplify it this time. Let's just do one artist,' Gul exclaimed. 'I'm exhausted with the group show!'

This was true – the second show for Saloniere Star, the group exhibit of Baroda artists, due to open in another two weeks – was completely exhausting. With three young artists to cosset, three sets of art write-ups to edit, and three sets of logistics to be worked out it was quite a battle. Anirban Ghose, one of the Bengal school artists I had met, a tall frail young chap with long hair and heavy framed, large canvases, with loads of detail, mixing kitsch and cartoon and Bengali text with texture and tempera, seemed dynamic enough to be able to carry a solo exhibition on his own shoulders. 'Yes,' I agreed with Gul, and showed him a picture I had taken of Anirban and Amal posing next to Anirban's painting.

'Wow, look at those soulful brown Bengali eyes,' Gul laughed at the picture. 'He looks cute, he'll get some good press. Let's sign him on.'

'Anirban it is then. I shall talk to him.'

Once that was settled I plonked myself onto the leather couch in our office, my mind still full of Tarun Pal Sanyal and the missing paintings. Could Tarun have had a real Jamini Roy and real KK Hebbar in his possession? Were the paintings among the things that Daniel had picked up? Why did he take Tarun's things? What was the connection? Were the pieces forgeries, commissioned by Daniel and executed by Tarun Pal Sanyal? But if that were true, then how would the operation proceed now, with the forger dead?

'Tara! Your phone is ringing.' Gul's voice cracked through my thoughts alerting me to the trill of my cell phone. I quickly extracted it from my bag. 'Hello?'

'You getting too smart, Madam...' the voice on the phone was deep and deadpan.

'What...what...who?' I spluttered.

'Look, Madam. Stop chasing after dead painters and digging about...otherwise, we know where you live, where your child goes to school... You won't even find his body.' The voice let it sink in, a heavy cannonball of dark intent.

Omigod! I doubled up in alarm, clutching onto the phone. What had I unleashed? My poor, poor child!

'Who was that, Tara? Who was it?' Gul was next to me, squatting on the floor, holding me as I slumped onto the sofa, head lolling, limbs limp, face colourless as sun-bleached fabric.

I raised bleak eyes. 'Oh Gul, what do I do?' Even my tears froze in fear.

Gul bent low to hug me, conveying shock and sympathy, offering the soothing words that I had been seeking from Raj this morning. Nothing sage in those words, no guarantees that matters will work out, but just the fussing helped in energizing me enough to get up.

But the panic refused to go away; that gutless feeling that the fall from here was bottomless.

Whom could I trust anymore?

Were my maids in on it? Was the doorman a lackey of the goons? Had the driver been bought off?

No, I couldn't trust Rohan with any of them.

My stomach heaved. I ran to the bathroom, doubled up against the basin, and threw up. I leaned against the sink, choking on my fear, sobbing till the tears came no more and all that remained was an empty retching that wouldn't subside. I washed my face and emerged from the bathroom and told Gul I was taking off for the day and headed off to school to pick Rohan up early. But scared witless to go around the city shopping for those toys I had promised him, I took him to the club instead, finding a safe haven inside its guarded confines in a way that no home could offer. No unwanted elements could come barging in here. No riff-raff could drag Rohan away from within its sanctum.

While Rohan went happily for a swim, in the spare swim-trunks of his I usually kept in the car, I sat by the poolside watching him hawk-eyed, tears pricking my eyes behind my huge shades as he cavorted in the water totally unaware of the threat to his life. Such innocence! The thought tore my heart like a blade cutting through vinyl. I would do anything, *anything at all* to keep him safe.

My phone rang as I sat there. It was the doctor. 'Congratulations, Tara. The test results just came in. You are pregnant. Not something you were suspecting, were you?' I heard her chuckle, sounding quite cheerful at the thought.

Pregnant? No, I couldn't be pregnant! 'Impossible,' I told her.

'No contraception is foolproof, you know,' the doctor clucked.

I sat paralysed as the doctor rang off telling me to make an appointment for another check-up and sonography. This wasn't happening! Just when things were going so terribly wrong, they had to get worse!

A shadow fell on me, and I lifted my face up to see Lola standing there, showing off her summer tan in an electric blue swimsuit, looking like a bar of candy wrapped in a lurid wrapper. 'Babe, you look horrible!' she exclaimed, and pulled an easy chair to sit next to me. 'That Raj giving you trouble? Tell me all.'

I didn't know what it was, her naive openness or the abrupt irony of her statement, when I must have

caused Raj as much grief as he had caused me. I couldn't
stop myself and burst into tears. Horrible, plump tears
that erupted from deep inside. Eventually I stopped,
and amid hiccups and deep breaths told her the story
of that mad midsummer fixation that led me to buy a
forged painting and everything that followed thereafter
and the anonymous threat of this afternoon; everything
except Roy and my newfound pregnancy.

'You had better call Raj,' Lola advised awkwardly;
she had not been expecting such a detailed confession,
it was clear. But, then, I had not been expecting to
confess either. Except that it was done now and on
that warm orange afternoon, the setting sun a glowing
carroty orb upon a sheet of blue, I felt lighter than I
had felt in months.

I called up Raj, and he promised to leave office
immediately to come to the club. The sun set as Lola
left. Rohan wound down eventually, agreeing to an
early dinner and fell asleep in the cosy swag of the
easy chair after a quick meal. A gentle breeze blew in
from the sea and above me the stars glittered beyond
the crocheted stole of clouds.

I sat staring at the darkened sea, unaware of the
few patrons around, till the slightest trace of a finger
on the nape of my neck brought me back to inky
reality. I turned to see Raj standing there, concern and
kindness in his eyes as he bent to place a gentle kiss
upon my forehead.

In that gossamer night, brought together by the
shared concern over our firstborn and the excitement
over the unborn, Raj and I sat, his arms around me,
my head against his shoulders, drawing comfort from
each other, attempting to come to terms with the new
problem that confronted us.

❧twenty-one

It is probably an idle threat,' Raj said the next morning, when he returned after personally dropping Rohan to school. 'But then, it may not. We can't take a chance.'

'Can we go to the police?' I asked, knowing even as I said the words, that it was useless.

'Whom would you complain against?' Raj asked. 'You don't even know who called, and there is no proof against Roy Jordan or Daniel Leibowitz.'

Constant watchfulness over Rohan – that was the only way, we reckoned. Of course, there were work commitments to be managed. But one of us would have to be around for school drop-offs and pick-ups, diligently, every day. No tennis or taekwondo or chess for the poor child either. There would have to be a total embargo on all that. As for the time when he was home, well, there was no choice – we couldn't leave him alone with just the maids; but then, we could not babysit him all the time either.

Raj called up his parents and after some appealing, but without telling them the real reason why, he managed to convince both of them to come for an extended stay. Not the ideal solution, but then, what else could we do?

Softness filled Raj's face. 'I'm worried about you too, Tara. I'm worried about all of us.' He held me tight. 'I shouldn't have insisted on this move to Mumbai. You were right. You and I, we both need to end this madness, don't you think?'

Raj removed his arms from around me and moved back a step, looking at his wristwatch. 'I hate to leave you alone now,' he said, mentioning a meeting he would be late for unless he left immediately. 'But I promise you, I'll negotiate a transfer out of here.'

For months I had wanted Raj to promise me this, and now, when he did, I didn't know what to say.

Rimli arrived, rushed and bothered, just as Raj was picking up his laptop and moving towards the door. 'You won't believe this,' she was bursting with barely-suppressed excitement, not even bothering to greet Raj or me. 'Have you seen the paper this morning?'

I shook my head. I had not.

Rimli pulled out *The Times of India*, and opened a page in the middle. *'Fake Khakhar in London Auction'*, the small headline stated, and then went on to describe how someone had raised the alarm on a painting up for sale at a famous art house in London. Bhupen Khakhar had become the latest darling of the forgers, and questions had been raised about the antecedents of a few paintings in recent times. A morbid thought, but Death did that perhaps. Exciting bounty hunters to fake a collection that was suddenly made limited and invaluable by the demise of a famous artist.

'Wow,' I said, feeling hollow. More fakes. That's all I needed to hear.

'That's not all!' Rimli continued. 'I was so upset last night after you called with news that there were no clues to be found about the death of Tarun Pal

Sanyal, I couldn't sleep, and as usual, like I do when I am so restless, I decided to do a bit of cleaning. You won't believe what I found.' She pulled out a yellowing newspaper clipping from her appliquéd tote bag and spread it out on the table. 'Remember this article? I had shown it to you then, we had even talked about it?'

'What?' I frowned at the paper.

Raj stood up. 'I'll go to office then...'

'Wait, Raj. Look at this.' Rimli pointed to a small news item in the snippets section. It read:

> Baroda. In an act of summer madness on a searing 45 degree Celsius day, young artist Manasi Sheth, a graduate of the Faculty of Fine Arts, committed suicide in her tiny Fatehganj flat. While no actual note has been discovered, an empty bottle of Calmpose found next to the body suggests drug overdose. Fellow young artists suggest that lack of recognition as an artist may have prompted Manasi's actions. Paintings bearing signatures of eminent artists Bhupen Khakhar and Benode Bihari Mukherjee were found among Manasi's artefacts.

It was the article Rimli had showed me months ago, before summer, aggrieved about the death of a fellow graduate from her alma mater, the Faculty of Fine Arts at MS University in Baroda. Then we had been caught in the pathos of a young life snuffed out by the savage competitiveness in the world of art – by Darwinism in the Art Mart – as yet another artist, unable to cope with the pressures of competition and flagging public interest, ended her life.

'Sounds familiar, doesn't it?' Rimli asked, her face grim.

'Like Tarun Pal Sanyal...' I whispered.

There was a hardness in Rimli's voice now as she paced the room. 'There has to be a connection, Tara. I sense it. I have friends in Baroda. Let's check this out.'

She was right. There had to be a connection. Bhupen Khakhar, a long time Baroda resident, the artist who combined traditional art elements with contemporary themes, could surely inspire modern-day Baroda artists? It was possible that old paintings of his lay scattered with old friends or acquaintances, and had been bought by a young admirer at some non-stratospheric price in days past. But Benode Bihari Mukherjee, a Bengal School old-timer, what were the chances of finding *his* canvas with a young artist in Baroda?

'No!' Raj said suddenly, his voice loud and harsh in the momentary stillness. 'No, Tara. Don't do this please. It's not worth it.' He looked into my eyes, his own intense pools of brown.

So I told Rimli about yesterday's anonymous phone call, the threat to Rohan from some unknown man and in retelling her about how some coarse-voiced, horrid fellow had threatened my son, and warned against chasing after dead painters, my own terror mounted again. What could I do? *What*? If I fell silent now, made no attempts to find out anything more about Roy and Daniel, would my son be safe? Or was I a marked target now and forever, in the eyes of the perpetrator, regardless of what I did or didn't do? The mind of the Mumbai underworld, of those paying him to bump me off, was beyond my comprehension. I knew nothing but pure dread.

'This could be done quietly. I can just discreetly ask my friends,' Rimli said eventually. 'Get the police involved, expose these maniacs and let the law take over.'

'*What* law?' Raj thundered, suddenly beside himself. 'Tara, are you nuts? This is Mumbai. The police are complicit with those goons! Don't you read the papers, for God's sake? And this is Rohan's safety at stake!'

I always do what I have to do. *Always.* Not seeking permission, never needing to. But to be churlish at this point when Raj was so concerned and I needed every bit of emotional backing seemed wrong. 'Just this once...' I heard myself nevertheless, persuading Raj, obsessively drawn by the urge to unmask Roy, who had so completely humiliated me. Everyone in Mumbai would know by this week, courtesy my inadvertent disclosure to Lola, about my fake purchase. Questions may not be asked, but the smirks would be there. My buyers would know and my friends would know and I would have to front it all. If, if only, I could get one lead to expose Roy and his partners, why, I could face it all, head held high.

'Think of the baby at least, Tara,' Raj said quietly.

'Baby?' Rimli squealed. 'You're pregnant, Tara?' She moved forward to hug me and put her arm about my shoulders, one hand patting my head in compassion. 'What a horrible phase you're going through, babe. Should we forget about this then? Move on with our lives? I think Raj makes sense.'

'No.' I extracted myself from their cloying consideration, and looked up, resolve in my eyes, determination in my voice. Raj might be ready to write off 60 lakhs – and that was very generous of him, considering the fights we had had about not buying art as an investment – but I had to redeem myself in my own eyes; if not retrieve my money, then at least make that bastard Roy pay.

Raj frowned and knitted his brows together, looking ready to explode. 'Think of Rohan, Tara. Think of...' he trailed off.

'I *do* think, I *do*,' I said imploringly, pointing out that inaction and silence on my part didn't guarantee an end anymore.

Then Raj said, 'Nothing guarantees an end anymore, except packing our bags and leaving this country.'

My gasp was almost audible. It was not something I wanted, I knew suddenly. Offered three months back, I would have jumped at the chance. But now I was not ready to pack my bags and move back to my old life in a hurry. There were things I had to do and experience in my new city; there were bridges I had to mend. I held my ground.

'One last time, then...' Raj said gruffly, opening the door behind him.

'One last time...' I promised, making a pact with him, and with myself.

Baroda was festive with pre-Navratri hysteria. Crinkled gold and red foil garlands clashed with the assorted sales banners in shop windows. Rimli and I were here to find out more about Manasi Sheth, while my in-laws held fort at home and kept an eye on Ro.

A hired car had picked us up from the airport. I had asked Ravi's friend, Alta Deb Pal, who had helped Saloniere Star source Baroda paintings on our earlier trip, to meet us at the airport and she sat in the front seat now, next to the driver, as we drove towards the downtown hotel, the only half-decent one in town apparently, where Rimli and I would stay the night.

'You should have come next week. Navratri in Gujarat is very special,' Alta said. She pointed to a large field where preparations were underway to erect a gigantic frame of bamboo to create a dance marquee. 'That's the garba enclosure.' Used to dandia festivities and desi glamour in air-conditioned suburban reception halls in the US, the very thought of dressing up and dancing in this searing outdoor heat seemed outlandish. I let the thought pass, and shifted forward in my seat, closer to Alta. 'Do you know anything about an artist called Manasi Sheth?'

Alta frowned, 'Manasi Sheth? Isn't she the one who died a few months ago? I thought you were here scouting for artists and sourcing for your future shows?'

'I am, I am,' I nodded my head furiously, hoping it distracted attention from the shakiness of my voice. 'It's just that someone I know had expressed an interest in her. Maybe some of her work is available somewhere?' After my Kolkata experience, feigning professional interest in Tarun Sanyal's work, fabricating fresh stories of the same kind came easily to me.

'I'll ask around,' Alta shrugged. 'Now I have a few young artists you could meet.'

'I really am only hunting for a Manasi Sheth this trip.'

Alta did not look too glad at the prospect. A dead artist, and that too, not one of her protégés! There went any commissions and referrals! 'I don't know...' her voice trailed off. 'It could be a wild goose chase across the city with no results. I don't think Manasi was that great an artist. I can't recall her work, just the news of her death.'

Nevertheless, Alta gave us some numbers for artists and art teachers who might have some leads on Manasi and left us to get on with our day. Rimli and I left our luggage in the hotel and set off to meet one of Rimli's old art school friends. On the way, on a long car journey along twisting roads, I called up the numbers Alta had given me. The first person was an artist, Shruti Pethe, and she was hesitant to answer any questions saying she barely knew Manasi anyway.

The second contact, Uday Mansukhani, an art critic for the local newspaper and some art journals, totally trashed Manasi Sheth's works. 'There's just one word for her works – puerile! No depth. Though I must say *she* was quite pliable and quite hot-looking too! If she did nudes of herself, perhaps they would have sold!' he added bawdily.

The third number was for Ramendra Singh, a lecturer at the Faculty of Fine Arts started by Maharaja Sayajeerao at his eponyously named university in Baroda, the raison d'être of Baroda's place of prominence in the Asian art scene. No one picked up the phone, so I decided to try again later.

We entered a suburb of Baroda where the alleys remained narrow, but the houses became grander with plots of land around them. Finally we reached the house of Rimli's friend, Disha Aggarwal who, Rimli told me, worked as a fabric designer for her family textile business, combining a melange of ethnic and cosmopolitan influences to create upholstery fabrics for export to the Middle East. For every art student jostling for space amid the pantheon of Art-Gods, there were many more who took the eventual sidestep, into teaching, into commercial art, into the steadiness of routine work.

Disha greeted us in her plush home-office on the ground floor of a high-walled, white stucco bungalow with a view of an emerald lawn and rows of rose beds, painstakingly maintained in this hot clime and more exquisite for it.

'Hey, Disha,' Rimli hugged her old friend who was dressed in a pale peach Kota cotton sari that swelled about her spreading hips, 'You've grown fat!'

'Two kids,' Disha laughed good-naturedly. 'What do you expect? But *you* look like the poster-child for the eccentric artist! Look at that hair.'

'She changes her hair colour almost every week,' I laughed, as we sat down.

After catching up with each other's lives, Rimli asked, 'So how is work?'

'Sometimes I rue giving up art, but this is good too – I get to be an artist and a businesswoman,' Disha shook her head, and adjusted the pallu of her well-pinned sari away from her shoulders. 'You tell me...' she said, offering us tea and biscuits brought in by a liveried servant on a glass and pewter trolley. 'What brings you folks to Baroda?'

Rimli said something about a collector looking for Manasi Sheth's works. I was glad Disha did not ask too many questions about why some Mumbai collector was trying so hard to locate works by an unknown and mediocre Baroda artist.

Disha drummed her fingers against the elegantly fluted handle of her teacup. 'Manasi Sheth? Was she also from FFA? She must have joined after we graduated.' She looked into the distance, and knitted her brow, trying to think back. 'You know, on second thoughts, the name *is* familiar. Not for art, though. No, what comes to mind is gossip – she was found kissing her Anglo boyfriend in a public place. It might not be much for you Mumbaikars. But that sort of stuff makes big news in Baroda. But, who with, what, how, don't ask me, I don't know. I could find out for you if you like. Shouldn't be that hard! It was quite the talk of the town for a while.'

Anglo boyfriend? Big deal. Unless… Rimli and I exchanged glances, struck probably by the same thought. Could there be a connection to Roy Jordan and Daniel Leibowitz?

'Oh please, could you find out?' I leaned back into the cushiony sofa, momentarily easing my back.

Disha sighed and pulled out a diary from a drawer in her pristine desk, with nothing on it except a white iMac, and scribbled some names and numbers on a paper. 'Try these people, they might know something,' she said, getting up and glancing at her watch. 'Now, if you'll excuse me. I have to go to the factory, but I too will make some phone calls on my way, and if I find anything, I will let you know.'

In the car on the way back to town, I called Ramendra Singh's number again. This time the lecturer picked up. He could not recall much about Manasi Sheth beyond her suicide. 'I teach mostly chiaroscuro, I don't remember Manasi being in my class. But the news of her death had rocked the faculty.' He paused, and added, 'There is a show opening tonight; the works of some of my ex-students. Maybe someone there might know. Why don't you come?' He gave me the name and location of a gallery.

We called up the other numbers given by Disha. No one seemed to know Manasi Sheth particularly well. But a general verdict emerged – that she was extremely good-looking, that she was not a promising artist, and that she was seen hanging out with a white guy.

The afternoon was hot, and I was only too glad to retire for a siesta to my hotel room after a heavy Marwari thali lunch, to escape the mid-day sun and mull over the emerging picture of Manasi Sheth. Did she forge the painting that was found in her apartment when she died? Or did she know the forger? We were still no closer to any answer. There was an address I had for Manasi Sheth, her home-cum-studio. But three months later, what clues would it offer? I lay down on the soft white sheets, softly massaging my belly. The last thing I vaguely heard before I dozed off was Rimli talking about photographs – Roy's and Daniel's photographs – culled from the newspapers.

It was dusk when I woke up and a warm honeyed sunset filtered in through the curtains that had been half-drawn, gilding everything in sight. 'Rimli?' I called out, stretching on the bed, and she came out from the bathroom, freshly showered and dressed.

'The art show opening, remember?' she reminded me. 'Move it, Preggy-Belle.'

Yes. Maybe we would find something there. But there was something else I had to ask her. What was it? I frowned, thinking. 'What were you telling me before I fell asleep, Rimli?'

Rimli paused while brushing her hair, and looked at me from the mirror above the dresser. 'Roy and Daniel's pictures. We should show them around tonight. You have them in your bag, don't you? Maybe, someone might recognize them?'

Akriti Gallery was a set of small rooms lit by fluorescent tube-lights. A smattering of people in long cotton kurtas and printed saris were dutifully doing the rounds of what seemed to be prints and chiaroscuro drawings of slum children and prostitutes. A waiter approached with hot chai and cold lassi. I was appalled. So unlike a Mumbai gallery opening! Anyway wine was a no-no now that I was pregnant. Still, a chilled juice or a mocktail would have been nice. 'Ramendra Singh?' I asked a man standing near the entrance. He pointed to a tall, white haired man in a rust-coloured kurta, biting into a samosa and chatting with a group of younger men. I went up to him. 'Professor Ramendra Singh?'

The group around him dispersed, and Rimli and I introduced ourselves.

'Yes, yes, Manasi Sheth. You're the Mumbai ladies who had called this afternoon. Not that I could recall Manasi, but then I teach only printmaking. But after your call, I asked a colleague of mine. He remembers her *very* well,' he said grinning wolfishly.

Ramendra Singh led us to a short man in violet-frame glasses whose colourless shirt rose above his protruding belly, and introduced him as LM Gajendra, a professor of Art at the FFA. 'Manasi Sheth? She was my student, yes.' LM Gajendra scowled. 'Who wants to buy her paintings? Tell me and I shall talk some sense into them!' He laughed at his own joke, a high-pitched hyena-like sound. 'But seriously, that girl had good technique, a really steady hand, but lousy conception. Zero originality. She would come up with these brilliantly executed strokes, but overall every composition would be total pastiche, absolutely flat. Or, she would copy other painters. I told her to go into graphic design or something. But no, she fancied herself an artist. Temperamental too! With men hanging around her all the time! The way she dressed and acted! She invited all this. Loose morals in a woman, and look what happened.' He was all sanctimonious, his fat face scowling disapproval. 'Could not take the truth, and went psycho...' He made a gun shape with his fingers, and rolled his head sideways.

More corroboration, then, of what Rimli and I had concluded from the few conversations this afternoon. Manasi Sheth was not a promising artist. But there was a phrase that caught my attention in LM Gajendra's dismissive monologue. He had said, *she could copy well*'. I had the sudden feeling we were onto something. 'Can you think of anyone else who knew her?' I pressed, earnestly.

'Many,' the professor sneered, and I wondered if he was also one of the men who had the hots for the deceased and beautiful Manasi Sheth. 'In fact, I can see one here,' the professor announced. LM Gajendra walked up to a tall, long-haired young woman, elegantly draped in an off-white patola sari. 'Shruti,' he said to the young woman. 'Meet these ladies from Mumbai. They are looking for works of Manasi Sheth.'

'Shruti?' I ventured, exchanging a quick glance with Rimli. 'Shruti Pethe?'

The woman nodded, her eyes suddenly large in her long thin face.

'I think we spoke to you this afternoon...' I said, curious why Professor Gajendra thought this woman was a good friend of Manasi's when she herself had told us this afternoon that she did not know Manasi well at all.

'Good, good, you know each other,' the professor nodded and moved on.

'Yours?' Rimli asked Shruti, pointing at a sketch beside her and she nodded.

I looked behind Shruti – the charcoal sketch beside her was particularly grim. A slum child with a severed

266 • amrita chowdhury

leg, a car rushing away. More of the social realism I had discussed with the artist couple in Kolkata. Surely there was too much pathos in everyday Indian life for artists to reflect it in their work. Even if it was an Indian art trend fifty years after it had become passé in the West, it was probably needed here. Well executed too, but not the type of stuff I liked to have around. I turned away, unable to stomach the bleakness of the picture. 'Listen,' I said, anxiety tingeing my voice. 'It's urgent. I need to find out something about Manasi.'

'I don't know much about her death. We were just classmates,' Shruti demurred.

'Please...'

Shruti was silent. I knew she knew something. If only she would tell me.

'The photos...' Rimli nudged me.

I got the photos of Daniel Leibowitz and Roy Jordan out from my bag and held them before Shruti. Did I imagine it or was there just the slightest stiffening in Shruti's form?

'Sorry, don't know. Can't help,' Shruti said blandly and turned to walk away. Rimli extended her arm, halting Shruti mid-tread. 'Please, can we talk after the show?' But a waiter interrupted us just then with onion bhajias and paneer tikkas, and Shruti moved away.

Rimli and I hung around for the rest of the evening with one eye on the room, and one eye on Shruti. Most of the attendees were associated with the FFA; either lecturers or students. The conversations in the room were totally different from those in the art soirees of Mumbai. One group was avidly ruing the lack of 'PDA' in Baroda, and PDA turned out to be the public display of art, rather than affection. Another set of students, snacking heavily on the samosas and chai, had pulled up some plastic chairs and, oblivious to the other viewers around them, earnestly discussed the role of art, debating whether it should reflect individualistic concerns or respond to the socio-religious-cultural milieu of the society around. Rimli and I were amused at the pretentiousness.

By nine, people had started moving out, and then we noticed Shruti inching towards the door. Rimli and I rushed out too, and caught her just outside the door. 'Please talk to us,' I pleaded with Shruti.

'You are wasting your time, I know nothing,' she said.

'About what?' Rimli challenged her brashly. 'How do you know what we want to know?'

I brushed Rimli aside. 'Please,' I begged Shruti. 'I am pregnant. Someone has threatened my child, my family. Someone connected with selling forgeries. I need to know. I need to know what Manasi knew, what you know, whatever little. It may help...' I exhaled loudly, willing the old panic to stay away, ordering the tears not to gather. But my hormones overtook me – I had that excuse now – and tears filled my eyes.

'Oh, all right,' Shruti gave in, her shoulders slumping, and came with us.

The three of us went up to my hotel room, ordered dinner from the room service menu, and sat down on the messy double bed. 'Okay,' Shruti said, after we had eaten. 'What do you want to know?'

'Everything,' said Rimli.

'Which photo did you recognize?' I asked, laying out the two cuttings on the bed.

'Him,' she pointed to Roy's photo. 'Manasi was in love with him.'

I felt my heart accelerate. I had been expecting this ever since I had learnt about Manasi's Anglo boyfriend.

Then the story emerged. Manasi, excellent at execution and struggling with originality, used to copy the works of other painters for fun, particularly some of the famous Baroda artists. Then, just last year, Roy had chanced upon her, sought her out at a student party where she was being her usual flamboyant self. Possibly she had bragged about an excellent Khakhar reproduction she had executed and sold to a Marwari businessman for pocket money. Roy then convinced her to do paintings for him. Forgeries!

'But how do you know all this?' Rimli asked.

Shruti opened an inner zip of her ethnic embroidered bag, took out a much folded wad of paper and spread it out. Brushed across the water-colour sheet, in varied shades of grey and black, in tip-sizes from thin to thick, was a signature, repeated over and over – a snaky S in the middle of an untidily scrawled *Amrita Sher-Gil*. Like the signature on my painting, on my *Woman in Red*.

Rimli and I gasped.

'So Manasi painted my fake Sher-Gil...' I whispered, overwhelmed by the evidence.

'I don't know,' Shruti looked grim. 'She confessed to fake Khakhars. These signatures, maybe she painted a fake Sher-Gil, maybe she was preparing to fake one.'

'I saw this sheet in her room one day, under her desk! It must have fallen there by mistake.' Shruti shook her head, eyes lost in memories. 'I confronted her with it, and she confessed to working for Roy. I kept this paper, threatening to expose her, but I never did, never pushed her hard enough, and she knew it; counted on my easy friendship. I should have unmasked her then and there, she would have been miserable for a while, but at least she would have been alive!' A half-sob escaped her.

Shruti told us the rest of the story. After some months of going around together, over occasional trips to Baroda, Roy had convinced Manasi to make copies for foreign clients. The first task was an old Bendre painting, slightly modified from his pre-Independence era works, using special colours and wash. The papers authenticating the painting had been sent by a friend of Roy's in Delhi.

Daniel, I thought. *So that was the angle – he was the master restorer, the technical mastermind behind the forgeries!*

Shruti continued: 'By then, Manasi imagined herself to be in love with Roy. Plus he had promised her a solo exhibition in Prague for her own works, a platform that would launch her on the international scene. Manasi fell for it all; fish to hooked worm, or innocent saver to chit-fund seller. Soon she was doing a number of works for Roy: mid-century Hebbar works that Manasi painted from pictures sent by this guy in Delhi; Khakhar adaptations as instructed by Roy. She even attempted a Binod Bihari Mukherjee – such a different style.

'She used to copy signatures when we were students. Just for kicks! Her father's, our teachers', and later artists'! I remember, Chitrita Goswami, who was a visiting professor one summer, found her copying her signature and gave her hell for it. But Roy just used her, turned her youthful pranks into crime! Don't do it, I had warned Manasi when I found out. But I didn't argue hard enough. I was too caught up in my own efforts and struggles...'

Shruti looked frazzled now. She pulled out a cigarette pack, and lit one. 'I feel so guilty. I have been carrying this paper ever since...' Her voice was a whisper, hoarse in the stillness of the room.

'Cigarette smoke is bad for Tara,' Rimli started to say, breaking the moment by rushing to open the window. Shruti moved to the window, exhaled deeply, then waved her hands to dispel the nicotine cloud. Standing by the window, she continued: 'Manasi was totally besotted with him...this dealer from overseas, the handsome firang, flying around the world selling art, flying in to make love to her.' Shruti laughed dryly. 'He knew the right promises to make: vague enticements of a solo show in Prague, an exhibition in Mumbai, overseas commissions from collectors of new artists. She lived on it for several months. Then she found out about some other women in his life, and threatened to expose him if he did not organize the promised Manasi Sheth solo. Somehow it got ugly...!'

Shruti turned away from the window, and looked directly at me. 'She had come to me the night she died, teary-eyed, scared. What have I done, she had railed! Somewhere along the way she had learned that Roy was selling her paintings as high-priced originals to unsuspecting buyers in Europe, not as modest reproductions that he had first said...but she had gone along with it because she was in love with him. When she found out about the other women she was livid. She threatened to expose him if he did not get her a solo exhibition. He'll kill me, she had sobbed. I had just pooh-poohed at the whole thing, accused her of being melodramatic, and suggested she simply stop painting for him.' Shruti was defensive. 'She was so into histrionics most of the time... I never thought... Next morning, it was there in the papers.... Manasi Sheth commits suicide!'

'Did she?' I whispered.

'I don't know...' Shruti replied. 'She wasn't the suicidal type. She loved life too much. Even that night, she had not been talking of ending her own life, rather being protective of it...'

We sat in silence, a three-month late wake, a shared communion for an interrupted soul.

'Roy has cheated me too,' I told Shruti. 'This Sher-Gil I bought from him, possibly Manasi painted it. But I paid a large sum for it, and now my reputation as a gallerist is at stake. I want to expose him.'

'How?'

'There is still no proof,' Rimli said.

'You can't go by my words. There is no real evidence here. This paper proves nothing. These signatures may well condemn Manasi, we might prove Roy was her boyfriend, but there is no professional connection between Manasi and Roy,' Shruti said.

'A tip-off,' I was feeling reckless. 'A police raid on him, maybe some proof will emerge.'

Rimli was thoughtful. 'We have two forgers, both dead. So is Roy's operation over? Or do you think there are other painters in other parts of the country, slavishly producing fake masterpieces?'

'There will be underworld connections...if deaths were organized...' Shruti warned.

Terror seeped in invidiously. There was no stopping it. It came in, not with tidal ferocity, ramming against the wood, battering the meagre plank blocking its path, rather with the ghostly relentlessness of flood waters from a crack beneath the closed door. Silently it rose, inch by inch, carrying with it the scum of the streets, the debris of destruction.

I squared my shoulders, flashing Dutch-courage in the face of panic. 'I have decided. I shall confront Roy.'

twenty-two

Rimli and I changed our tickets from the evening flight and took the morning flight back to Mumbai. By mid-day I was home pretending to my in-laws that my work sourcing art from Baroda had gone exceedingly well.

I was fecklessly excited, feverish in fact, mulling over how to approach the authorities, as I took a shower. But to whom should I speak – the local police? No, it has to be a greater authority, I thought as I lathered in the shampoo and massaged my scalp, attempting to circulate ideas into quick motion. Was there a special branch, an art brigade, someone who looked at matters of cross-border heists, of transactions outside the country, of artworks leaving our shores?

Then there was the whole matter of art export. There were laws. There were taxes and customs duties to be paid; probably not exhaustive, but they did exist. Did Roy and his gang ship these pieces out as originals? Or were they shipped out as copies? Did the paperwork conveniently lose itself somewhere along the way once the painting reached overseas, so that the paintings could be touted as originals? Or were the paintings being smuggled out of the country, without the knowledge of the authorities? Could something like this *ever* be achieved without the collusion of someone powerful in authority? Anyway you looked at it, something was afoot. Something serious!

I came out of the shower dressed in a loose kurta and long drawstring pants. Not that my baby bulge was visible yet, but I would need to dig out my old maternity pants soon.

Gul called as I was hastily gulping down an early lunch of vegetables and hot chapatis. She was curt as she instructed me to sit with the graphic designers today, and chase up the art critic who was going to write the foreword. 'This weekend is going to be very busy, we need to take down Muthu's paintings and start preparing to hang the next set. Please plan on being around.' Then she threw in a final comment: 'By the way, just whom did you talk to about your Sher-Gil? A couple of people have called me to ferret out the details of how you bought a fake!'

If her voice had been any harder, any sharper, it would have chopped the signal waves. Oh no! Lola! She must have confided in someone, who in turn confided in someone else! Gul was mad at me, but matters had gone beyond my control. Now I would have to face the questions full on.

'Please tell Ravi and Sud, before they hear from other sources,' Gul said frostily as she rang off.

So after reminding my mother-in-law and the maids to pick up Rohan at the appointed hour, I headed off to Lower Parel to sit with the graphic designer.

In the graphic designer's tiny air-conditioned office, while she fiddled with the layout – changing fonts, moving text blocks, cropping pictures, readjusting layer transparency – and even as I said yes and no to various alterations, my mind was elsewhere, thinking of whom to call. The CBI came to mind. But I needed a contact there. One visit to the Kolkata police station had been enough to tell me that I needed to go through someone.

Once the revised catalogue began to take shape, I excused myself from the designer's office, set up a meeting with Ravi Uppal and then called up Pheroze Dastur. I managed to get the number of his friend in the Maharashtra Police, a senior honcho, who then gave me a contact in the CBI.

'Come to the office and give us a written statement,' the CBI senior man said, when I called him.

'Can't I just make my statement over the phone?' I pleaded.

Apparently not. The statement provided would need a signature, though as a friend's friend, the CBI chap was gracious enough to suggest that he could send an officer to meet me in Pheroze Dastur's office that evening.

As for the arch villain himself, Roy, was he even in town? In the country? I called his mobile, but he did not pick up the phone. I called the Yacht Club. The register showed he was checked in as a guest, and therefore in town, or at least within the state. I phoned Gul to find me a number for Ayesha – that blonde arm-candy he had been with at our last show – from the Saloniere Star guest-book. When Gul gave me the number I called up Ayesha, who sounded exasperated by the call and said, petulantly, that she had not seen Roy in weeks.

Where the hell was he?

I was so jumpy that instead of going back to the office to help Gul with pre-marketing calls for the Baroda show and working on the million details for our third show of the young Kolkata artist, Anirban, I switched my phone on silent and headed off to the spa for a much needed pick-me-up.

Two hours later, hands and feet in shiny buffed softness, nails freshly coated in Mauve Mania, and hair a chic curtain of freshly pressed strands, feeling calm, confident and in better control, I reached Ravi Uppal's office at the appointed time.

When I got to Ravi's office the receptionist asked me to wait a while. As I sat down with a magazine a stocky man in dark glasses and a handlebar moustache emerged from Ravi's room. 'I'll expect the shipment to reach Dubai next week then,' he said to Ravi as they shook hands.

My eyes almost popped out of my sockets when I recognized the man. 'Was that...was that...one of those underworld goons?' I asked Ravi incredulously as he turned to greet me.

Ravi laughed. 'You have a very vivid imagination, Tara. Tell me, what's the matter? Anything urgent? You had said it was important we meet today itself.'

I told him baldly that I was going to the CBI to complain about a fake Amrita Sher-Gil painting that had been sold to me by Roy Jordan.

'An Amrita Sher-Gil fake?' Ravi was all concern.

Obviously his friends in the art world had not informed him of Roy's nefarious dealings. So I apprised him of matters.

Ravi appeared startled, his thick jowls rippled in quick leathery motion. 'Ring of forgery, Tara? Against Roy Jordan, you say? You have found some proof? You know what the CBI are like, don't you? Do they think you have something worthwhile to go on?' He jumped up and down in his cushiony leather chair as he shot the questions at me.

'Small clues really, little bits of evidence, that point towards a ring of forgery. But I need your help to unearth the rest.'

Ravi looked at me thoughtfully, waiting for me to elaborate. So I poured out the entire story – about the questions surrounding the Sher-Gil's authenticity, about chasing Roy's contacts across the country, about the trail of dead artists all of whom had connections with Roy, and about the threatening call I'd received from some Mumbai underworld type.

Ravi was sympathetic one minute and the next he was questioning me again: 'Has your painting been verified as a fake? Have you asked Roy about it? Maybe there's some confusion – he must have papers to prove attribution. The other Sher-Gil painting he unearthed has been authenticated and the new owners have expressed no reservations about it.' He tut-tutted my worries, offering to give his considered opinion on the painting. Then he added, 'It's not good for the gallery business, Tara, to start talking of fakes! I thought Roy was a particularly good friend of yours. What happened? Is this a *personal* vendetta?'

I flinched, as if making contact with acid. What was he implying? What had he *heard*? Did he know of Roy's little fling with me? 'What do you mean?' I squeaked angrily.

He surprised me by responding, 'Drop this silly pursuit, Tara.'

'What?' My surprise was muffled as a lump caught in my throat.

'You have no proof, Tara. To proceed on grounds of suspicion, well, it may happen in the movies, but in real life you will find no takers. You will only make it hard on yourself.'

There was a harshness in his voice; this was not my friend and my art mentor, not the Ravi I knew! He may be concerned about the outcome of the case as an investor in Saloniere Star, but this hardline stance was much too aggravating. 'Let's see,' I said stiffly. 'If the CBI puts pressure on the framer, he may buckle.'

'That framer probably belongs to the underworld.' Ravi came around his desk toward me, concern creeping into his voice. 'Look, Tara, I can understand how desperate you must feel when someone unknown threatens you. But think of your son, think of your own safety – you take the matter to the CBI and suddenly there will be questions you don't want to answer and a gun to your head. It does you no good.'

He was close, very close, invading my personal space and a fleck of his spit escaped, touched my hair slightly. *Yuck!* I shifted back. 'As long as it does no good for Roy, I don't care about the rest. I have done nothing wrong,' I responded thickly. 'Word will get out anyway, at least I should be seen to be putting up a fight.'

'Don't!' Ravi clasped my shoulder hard, jerking me slightly to drum in caution, anger in his clenched features. 'It will mean devastation for your family, bankruptcy for your business.' His words had a hard edge.

Was he warning me or threatening me?

I forced his hands off my shoulders, and without a backward glance at Ravi Uppal, stormed out of his office.

Pheroze's office was close by, squashed in a suite of rooms in another building in Nariman Point, while his sprawling auto parts manufacturing unit lay on the Old Bombay–Poona highway past Panvel. I had half expected Gul to be present when I went there; Pheroze would have called her for sure. Both to hear what I had told the CBI, and to lend me moral support. But when I entered the smart veneer-panelled office with its wall of sun-control glass, Pheroze was alone. Before I had a chance to ask if Gul would be joining us, Pheroze's secretary walked in announcing a visitor.

CBI Officer Manoj Singh Thakur, an unlikely looking plainclothes investigative officer, was too lanky and too fair to appear intimidating. But, of course, officers have their men behind them, and a holster on the hip can notch up their fear-inspiring quotient.

Manoj listened carefully as I recited the tale again, not flinching as I mentioned the evidence of dead artists, Roy's sexual liaisons with Manasi, the suspicious behaviour of the framer in Kurla, Leibowitz's iffy credentials and dubious dealings, the stories of commissions for copies of paintings by dead painters, and the anonymous threatening phone call I had received.

Without mentioning Shruti Pethe's name, I showed Manoj the paper with the rows of Amrita Sher-Gil's signature on it and informed him that I had a confession from a dead artist's friend about Roy's involvement in the forgery ring. I ended my statement against Roy Jordan with the conjecture that not only was he involved in a large-scale scam involving the duplication of the works of famous artists – that much was clear – but that there was smuggling too, given the fact that most of these paintings were being sold outside the country.

Manoj Thakur sat impassively when I finished. 'You don't have a whole lot of proof.'

'There must be something you can chase up?' My voice went into tremolo. He *had* to help me. I had no other recourse.

'Well, we could conduct a raid on grounds of suspicion, if your contact can give us a written statement that an artist was being asked to do forgeries.'

'Won't my statement do?' I insisted, feeling the need to expedite matters. Even if Shruti agreed to give an official statement, she was in Baroda. It would take time to get a signed statement from her. It might take days to get through the bureaucratic process after that. 'And what about that framer? He looked very suspicious,' I said, shuddering as I remembered my encounter with Asgar.

Pheroze looked concerned as he exchanged a how-do-we-tell-her look with Manoj Thakur. 'It's best to let the matter go, Tara, that would be best for you. These workmen have a naturally rough, bullish attitude... maybe you mistook it...'

I gave Pheroze a withering look, but he took no notice.

Manoj Thakur looked into the distance, as if gathering his thoughts, then said, 'There may be something to it... Links deeper than you may imagine... Mafia links, political links. There always are.' He squared his shoulders and looked at me: 'Here's what I propose to do. You write out the statement and I shall ask my Commissioner for a raid on Daniel Leibowitz and Roy Jordan. No guarantees. In the meantime, I can ask the customs department to report to us if they find anything suspicious about Roy Jordan. Fair enough?'

It was the best I could hope for. I agreed hurriedly and hand-wrote a statement on an A4 sheet I picked up from Pheroze's printer. Manoj Thakur checked my phrasing of the statement, then I added my signature at the bottom and gave it to Manoj.

I was so emotionally and physically wrung out when I reached home, that I just collapsed on my bed. Rohan had not seen me in two days – he was in school when I had come home in the morning – and he came rushing out now, clambering over my half-limp body, demanding stories and playtime. I read him half a story, drugged with hormones. 'Just a quick nap…' I pleaded and fell into a deep sleep.

It was dark when I woke up. Rohan was watching a movie with his grandparents. He cuddled with them when I entered the room, secure in their undivided attention. It pinched my heart, but at least he was not hankering for care and company. I went to the kitchen in search of a snack instead.

Later, after the film he was watching was over and I had read Rohan his bedtime story, Raj called, all concerned about how I was feeling. He had an invitation he had forgotten about, some formal dinner apparently, sponsored by a financial news television channel. It was a bring-the-spouse event. Would I join him please, he asked apologetically. 'I can pick you up in half an hour?'

A formal dinner? Not something I was looking forward to at the moment, but then I wanted to make up lost ground with Raj. 'I'll come,' I told him.

It was comforting, I thought two hours later, to be seated at a beautifully appointed round table under glittering chandeliers in a five-star hotel ballroom in Bandra, Raj's hand hovering protectively on the small of my back, listening to another interminable 'Indian Tiger' story; the uncrushable enthusiasm of the moneyed men of the city as they talked of long-term economic prospects and the need to not worry about short-term storms, reminded me of Rohan and his pals with their Power Ranger toys.

In the lull between the keynote dinner address and the arrival of an outrageously undressed Bollywood troupe for a song-and-dance routine, Mrs Aditi Mewawalla, wife of an eminent seed oil manufacturer turned stockbroker and big art collector, walked up to me, glittering in rubies and a red slithery dress. She was one of my clients.

'The Muthu paintings you picked will be delivered to you this Saturday, after the show ends,' I told her. 'I am sure you will enjoy them.' She had bought two Muthu paintings from Saloniere Star a few weeks back.

'No hurry, sweetie. I have my sights on this gorgeous TV Santhosh I saw at Pundole this week; what do you think of *him*?' she asked, a compulsive prize-seeker who, having spent her dosh, lost interest in her purchase and moved on, her glittering eyes fixed greedily ahead, on the next trophy acquisition. But then she turned to me and stretched her eyes as she exclaimed, 'But what's this I have been hearing, Tara? Some paintings you have bought are *forged*? Is that *true*?'

The next morning, I dressed quickly and waited impatiently till the respectable Indian office start-time of ten in the morning. Then I called Officer Manoj Thakur's mobile phone, again and again, until he responded, to the tenth call, with a brusque hello. But when I inquired whether any progress had been made on the case, he was curt. 'Look, Madam, these things take time, especially when you have no clear proof.'

He was stalling. He was not about to go after Roy and Daniel in a hurry. I had to do something on my

282 • amrita chowdhury

own, get some proof, some confession. Otherwise word would get out, my name would be sullied forever, while the offenders got away. And Roy, that bastard who played with women, with their money and their vulnerabilities, would go scot free.

I called Roy's number again – to no avail. But when I called the Yacht Club front desk, I was surprised. 'Jordan Sir was staying here but he had to suddenly check out,' the man at the reception told me.

'Suddenly?' I echoed.

The man helpfully informed me that Roy Jordan had to go to London on urgent work, and though he had been booked to stay for another week, he had checked out earlier that morning.

London? Had Roy got a whiff of my plans? Was he escaping the country, evading the unsheathed talons of the Law?

I rushed out to the car without thinking, and then came to a sudden stop. I didn't know where Roy would be at the moment. The driver looked at me expectantly, waiting to be told where to go. But I hadn't a clue. Roy could be anywhere – in a restaurant, in a club, in a last minute meeting with a friend or a client.

I closed my eyes and felt the slow ballooning and collapse of my lungs, and tried to visualize what Roy might be doing, what any criminal on the run would do, at the juncture of leaving the country. If he were leaving suddenly, say under the shadow of an imminent encounter with the Law, having been tipped off that trouble might be on its way, would he linger over café lattes? Most definitely not! He would simply pick up his possessions and run to an unknown destination to lie low till matters subsided.

'Fort,' I said on an impulse. 'Dilkhush Manor.' I instructed the driver to take me to the old mansion Roy had taken us to, the one he'd said he had borrowed from a friend as his temporary storage place. If he were fleeing the country, wouldn't *that* be where he would be, gathering his things?

On the way I told the driver to halt at a small electronics shop, a hole-in-the-wall seller of counterfeit stuff, and bought a cheap Dictaphone. The irony was not lost on me. I was aiming to trap a seller of fake paintings using a fake machine. At least, the makers of these meanly-priced machines were not raking in heavy profits, claiming that these reproduced gadgets were originals and supplying fake warranty documents to justify their high prices!

Dilkhush, the Victorian behemoth owned by Roy's friend, stood proud in its tree-lined bylane, a timeless sentinel of years past. The footpath at its base buzzed with activity – the lazy motion of paan-sellers, as they rolled up the betelnut leaves, filling it with sugary coconut mixture and tangy heady masalas; the clutter of book-sellers touting bestsellers cheaply reprinted without permission; the hustle of poster-wallahs, pimping *Debonair* pull-outs and cleavage-popping shots of Bollywood starlets behind calendar deities; the muscled pushcart pushers resting a moment under the tall trees, before they heaved their load of weighty sacks again.

As I climbed up the broad winding staircase past the unmanned entrance, deep into the cool heart of the building, the noise of the street receded. Up on the first floor, I pushed open the heavy door.

The place looked different in the day time. The lights were switched off. Behind the drapes, through the wine-coloured glass in the high wooden framed windows, an eerie light filtered into the room, making me fanciful.

Anything could happen to me in its quiet confines. I could scream and scream for help if I needed to, and none of the people milling about on the street below would hear me. I tiptoed through the room, towards the door leading to the back corridor, and into the store room I remembered from my last visit.

I stepped into the corridor just as Roy stepped out from the storage room, arms curved around rolls of canvases. He froze and I gave an involuntary start. I had been expecting to meet him, and yet I had not.

'Well, well,' Roy spat, lips curling venomously – the same lips that not too long ago had softly whispered in my ears. 'Been sleuthing, have we, Tara? Checking out artist deaths around the country, and trailing fakes! Aren't you scared to be here alone?'

'You sold me a fake, Roy,' I ground out. 'What did you expect?'

'Poor, poor Tara! So much drama for one small painting! What is sixty lakhs in the art market, darling? Peanuts! You will make many times over that sum if your gallery continues the way it has. Besides your husband is so rich...and he has no idea what his precious little wife has been up to with me... cavorting with strangers behind his back... or does he?' Roy clicked his fingers, dismissively. Scorn tinged his cool voice. 'What can you prove, Tara? And at what cost to your marriage? And the CBI commissioner you are entreating, will he do anything without proof?' He smiled cruelly.

Taken aback by the sheer viciousness of his words, I held the smooth wall for support. What would Raj say if he ever found out about my indiscretion? While we were a most modern couple in what we ate and whom we hung out with, were we really modern enough to absorb a storm like this in the marriage? And how did

Roy know about the CBI commissioner? Not Pheroze for sure! 'Officer Manoj Thakur?' I spluttered.

'What do you think?' He sneered at me, moving a step, a menacing look in his blue eyes.

I looked at the alcove behind him, at the god idols in their flowered garlands as the smell of cinnamon dhoop assailed my nostrils. 'Omigod... Ravi Uppal?' I said, suddenly figuring out to whom Dilkhush belonged, as I remembered Ravi's words from yesterday.

Roy just smiled, malice twisting his handsome features.

I could not believe this! The corridor spun around me, reality tumbling in kaleidoscopic twirls. Ravi, my trusted friend in all matters related to art, a senior mentor of Saloniere Star, an investor in our fledgling art business, a well-respected businessman in this city, was in cahoots with Roy! A twin-headed devil deity – feasting upon the very flesh that bowed before it in prayer.

My insides clenched, how could it be? How could I have been fooled so easily and by so many? What about the painting I had bought from Ravibhai, was that a fake too? What about the paintings in Ravi's Alibaug house that he had been trying to convince us to sell through Saloniere Star? Were they *all* a bunch of fakes?

'So is Ravi the last link in the chain of these forged paintings that you and Daniel have been so cleverly producing? You...you miserable son of a...' I goaded Roy, willing him to accept or deny this statement, heaving with emotion, months of anger throbbing in my head, in my mouth, filling it with the hot dense ash of long-held hatred.

This man, these arms which held those canvas rolls now, had made me mindless enough – no, *I* had made myself mindless enough – to stake everything. I had walked into his embrace, forgotten common sense, and opened my purse wide to a calculated act of crookery. If I could have, I would have torn him, limb from limb.

I grabbed at a roll of canvas, the last one of the bundle, already half slipping from the clasp of Roy's arms, and it unfurled partially. I saw a haunted hollow-eyed woman, her vacant stare disturbingly glossy against the bronzed backdrop of paint. *Bikash Bhattacharjee?* Oh my God, was it the painting I had seen in Ravi Uppal's house the other day?

It could be proof. I needed it. I needed to see the entire canvas. I pulled at the canvas, straining to get it out of Roy's fingers, as he pulled back, grabbing the canvas, tugging with all his might, and I staggered back, hands gripping air, feet missing a step. The roll remained in Roy's possession.

'Tut, tut,' Roy said. 'Trying to make me angry, Tara? Trying to make me spill the beans?' He walked forward, an edgy tilt to his gait, and laughed crazily. 'Fuck you, Tara, you spoilt stupid NRI. Go away. You cannot even begin to play this game.'

Anger pulsed through my veins, blanking out my fear.

As Roy coolly continued to put the canvas rolls in a largeish cardboard box, I stepped forward, trembling with fury. 'I can imagine how you and Daniel got into this together – an easy market, soft targets, not enough regulations, little documentation of information – ripe for a couple of counterfeiters to swing into action. Daniel was the mastermind, wasn't he? Selecting paintings to be forged, supplying canvases and materials, scripting out the fake papers, while you gigoloed with every woman in town and beyond, getting them to paint or deal or buy these fricking pieces, these masterfully detailed fakes!'

'You little bitch!' He advanced towards me, holding the box as if ready to strike me with it any moment. 'You know nothing! *Nothing!*'

I cowered against the wall, eyes on him, dreading the impact of the box swinging towards me.

But then he backed off: 'I don't have time to waste with you. I have a flight to catch, because thanks to you and your meddling, I have to go away for a while, let this all die down.' He walked past me, through the door, into the main room.

Hysteria overwhelmed me. I was alive, I was unhurt. So another suicidal move originated from nowhere. I started again, running in front of him, jostling to take the box from him, pushing him, as he shoved me away. I fell onto the hard ground on my back, the cardboard lid of the box fell on me, followed by the tumble of soft canvases, as they scattered around. In a half daze I heard the quick intake of Roy's breath as he clambered onto the floor, picking canvases and shoving them back into the box.

The wind was out of my gut, and I was dizzy – my poor, poor baby in my tummy, my heart caved in dread! But a canvas was lying next to my hand. I sat up, grasped it, and unrolled it quickly – it was the same one I had seen in Ravi's basement, the same one from that London catalogue from last year. I let go of one hand and the canvas slid back into a loose roll.

At the same instant, Roy pulled the canvas from the other side, and we were at it again, in a tussle of wills, his strength greater any day, but with sheer pigheadedness I held out against his strength, not letting go of the paint-hardened canvas.

288 • amrita chowdhury

Roy tugged again, and I slid on the floor, pulled by his brute force, facing a losing battle. He'll get it, he'll get them all. I scanned the floor in desperation, and saw something, a splint of wood, possibly a broken handle or a crumbled part of some furniture, seized it and hit at the canvas, striking it with the splintered wood, as Roy pulled back with greater might than before. He slumped back, canvas roll in hand, and I wobbled back from the impact, doubly giddy, a torn piece of the canvas in my hand.

I heaved myself up, pouring anger into the move as I tried to hide my hand and slip the canvas bit into my purse. 'What I don't know is how you shipped these pieces? How did the paintings go through the export authorities?' My breath was short, my voice came in gasps.

Roy slammed the box on a desk, rummaged through a drawer to get packing tape. As he hastily taped down the box he said, 'You want to know, do you?'

I stepped back, stumbled upon a stool, edged back again, and hit a cupboard. There was nowhere to go. I fumbled inside my bag, and pressed the switch of the Dictaphone, praying that its cheap machinery worked. Roy was upon me in seconds, his breath venomous as his arm snaked up to clutch my hair, raking it, nearly ripping it from my skull, making my eyes smart with the pain.

'I'll tell you,' he thundered at me. There was murder in his eyes; disgust in his voice. 'I'll tell you because you can *do* nothing, you *are* nothing, no more than a useless snivelling snoop, incapable of hurting me, because before you can drag your sorry ass to call that impotent officer of yours, I shall leave this country.'

His voice had a dangerous edge, unhinged with fury, and a crazed look came upon him as I watched, afraid to move, afraid to breathe lest he tightened his grip. A narrow precipice it was, between safety and terror, perhaps between life and death. 'Yes, we forged works of art. Yes, it was waiting to happen, with so little information, with such easy-to-fake provenances, from families that lived large once, and lost it all. So many rotten descendents of families past their prime, ready to pawn off family heirlooms, and so much scope to go beyond it, to create heirlooms where none existed, to duplicate multiple heirlooms where one was available.

'The painters themselves, famous once – Amrita Sher-Gil you know of, yes, but also Bhupen Khakhar, Jamini Roy, Hemendranath Mazumdar, Nandalal Bose and many others – long gone and dead now, but with no way of rising from the ashes to deny anything. My buyers are mostly nouveau riche Indians in far-flung places like Sierra Leone or Alaska or Azerbaijan, unconnected with the informed mobs in the usual art hubs of London and New York and Mumbai; some wealthy East Europeans, some with diplomatic connections to India, eager to collect masterpieces, drooling to be declared collectors, aware enough of artists' names to purchase their paintings, yet unaware enough to suspect anything... Yes, we were doing very well, thank you very much. With Daniel here as a restoration consultant, with years of experience in restoring turn-of-the-century paintings, and mixing new ingredients to replicate old materials – it was just perfect. But Daniel wasn't the mastermind. No, you have that wrong.' He gave out a loud laugh, a feverish hyena-like reverberation.

'Your Romanian pal in Delhi?' I whispered.

'My, my, aren't you well informed!' He mocked. 'A mere cog, since you ask, just another conduit to collectors in the former Eastern bloc. Natasha was quite eager actually, to get her cut, to subsidise her nasty little habit.' He raised his hand to his nose, and made a sniffing gesture, mania in his red eyes. 'How did we ship it, you ask?'

He laughed out loud again, increasing the pull of his hands upon my skull till my eyes swam. I looked at him, his throat vibrating as he laughed, his shoulders convulsing, his nostrils flaring, and I prayed, prayed with all my might, that the mini-recorder in my bag caught some of his words, however muffled.

'How do you think we shipped it?' He laughed again: 'India makes it so easy, you know. A bribe here, some connections there, a discreet phone call from the right number, and it's a cake walk. For most part no papers are ever required, and there are no messy trails to cover up. Simple. Easy.'

He let go of me suddenly, and I fell, knees trembling, hands behind me, sliding against the wall. My scalp was smarting from the excruciating sensation of hair being nearly ripped out. Yet what caused me to crumple was not the pain, but the relief, the sudden respite from violence.

I watched through stunned eyes, barely daring to breathe, as he pulled some papers out from a drawer and stuffed them in his case. Then he picked up his wallet and passport and put them in the pocket of his jacket.

'It's people like you,' I spat at him. 'The unscrupulous few who give art a bad name; create panic among buyers.'

'Well, there is precious little you can do about it. I'm off now,' he sounded jubilant. 'Leaving the country, just like Daniel did last night. Convenient, the way it's been organized by our common friend.' He smiled at me, a mean curl of his lips, wrought in evil malevolence, leaving me in no doubt about the identity of this friend.

'You won't be able to catch me, Tara. All your stupid rants and whirling dervish efforts, tch tch...quite stupid...' He looked at me, ire writ upon his face, and took half a step forward, puckering his lips. 'For old times' sake, then?' He grabbed my arm and pulled me close to him. As he looked down into my eyes I realized what a complete ass I had made of myself. A wave of nausea hit me and I grabbed my mouth feeling the bile rise. Roy stepped back abruptly. 'Or maybe not!' He blew me a kiss, an aggressive gesture mocking my helplessness. 'Ciao, darling,' he said, picking up the case and the box. 'My plane is waiting for me.'

I stared behind him feebly, head muddled. He was going to escape, and the Law, its gait plodding and steady like some tubby-toed terrapin, would never be nimble enough to catch an escaping fugitive. Roy would be gone, and with him, my plans of unmasking his treachery and reasserting my acumen as a dealer of fine arts. All I had was a piece of canvas in my possession, a snatch of fabric with some paint on it, ripped off the edge of a larger composition. But would it suffice as evidence?

I stared at the stone floor where thin shafts of light fell, refugees from the bright world outside, infiltrating through the tiniest chinks in the window. The tape, I remembered, sanity returning again. God I hope it worked.

I fumbled with the zip of my oversized bag, and rewound the mini-recorder a bit and replayed it. Sounds filled the room, suffocated by the cloak of leather, but not too garbled. *'Just like Daniel flew away last night.'* The words were clear enough; there would be more if I rewound more.

Energized, I pushed myself up, skeetered across the stone floor, then down the wide-brimmed stone steps, into the unconcerned hustle-bustle of India, as vendors, labourers, pedestrians, loiterers carried on as usual. As if nothing had happened and nothing of import would ever happen, and watched with idle curiosity the white man just hopping into a silver Mercedes, unaware of his running-from-the-law status. Even if I screamed it out, it would impact them as little as a nuclear explosion stirs cockroaches. I ran to my car waiting under a large peepul tree. 'International airport,' I shouted to the driver who took in my dishevelled air with shock and a certain disapproval. 'Quick. Follow that silver Mercedes.'

In and out of traffic we weaved, getting stuck behind a truck then zooming ahead, then screeching to second gear behind a cycle and swerving to the front, past the brightly blue curve of Marine Drive, shockingly clear on this mad, mad day, and onto the clogged arteries connecting to Pedder Road, in a surreal Bollywood style chase, lopped in typical Mumbai fashion by beggar-kids jumping in front of the zooming car, skinny hands waving for alms and families with babies on scooters slowing us down. While the driver manoeuvred past them all, I dialled the number for Manoj Thakur and played the entire tape for him, the cool AC and a numbing fear making every hair on my arm stand, echidna-like, frail quills piercing the unnatural irony of the situation.

By the time I was off the phone, and getting assurances that a squad would be on its way pronto to the airport, we had lost sight of the silver Mercedes countless times, only to find it again, stuck behind some ozone-slurping Suzuki or an equally sluggish but helpful motorcycle with a side-carrier transporting a florid-faced family.

Once on the highway, past Mahim, despite the hoardings-adorned detours welcoming some visiting Delhi dignitary or other, it was relatively easy to chase the silver Mercedes, as it swerved into the posh avenue of seven-star hotels, hurtling at top speed towards the international airport zone.

'Oh, oh, oh,' I screamed as the car in front took an unexpected turn, away from the roads marked Arrivals and Departures, along a broad unmarked road, and my driver managed to turn just in time, screeching brakes, jerking motion and all. My stomach rose to my throat, ready to spill everything out, and I clutched onto the seat as we veered again.

A gate, I could see a gate. What's this? I was totally fazed, as the car ahead slowed down near the armed sentries, flashed a card, and sped inside. We hurried on to the gate. 'Where's your gate pass?' The sentry accused my driver, as we halted at the gate.

'What is the matter?' I rolled my window down, and demanded an explanation.

'Private area. You can't go in without gate pass.' The man remained adamant.

It was the entrance reserved for the private aircraft zone.

No amount of pleading and smiling moved the guard. I opened my purse to display a thin stack of five hundred rupee notes; but mindful of the hawk-eyed presence of an armed jeep parked on the side of the road, he waved it away, loudly appalled that I could even propose such a thing.

Tearfully, I called up Manoj Thakur and informed him of the latest developments, frantic, as I climbed down from the car, and ran towards the armed jeep across the road, in search for empathy and help.

But the men in the jeep remained unmoved. 'You rich people think you can get around the rules. Let me tell you, Madam, rules are to protect you. No gate pass, no entry – it's simple. If we let you in, and you are innocent, that's fine. But if we let in someone who looks respectable and is a terrorist, then what?'

It was nearly twenty minutes before sirens sounded, twenty eternities of pacing the dusty side of the road, squinting in the brilliantly mellow sunshine, peering at the area beyond the gate. Twenty aeons of cursing myself and the world around before half-a-dozen police jeeps zoomed into view, armed men in mottled khaki hanging off the sides. The first car screeched to a stop, tyres revving up a tornado of red and brown dust. Agent Manoj waved his CBI badge at the men in the airport patrol jeep, and the jeeps behind him swerved ahead and went in through the gate. Manoj shouted out to me, and I ran to his car and hopped inside.

In a commotion of motion we descended upon the aircraft control area, jeeps spilling the somewhat-lost protectors of the law, who jumped out in a flurry of bravado, but then looked around wondering what their brief was, again.

Officer Manoj jumped out of his jeep, barking into his little walkie-talkie, sending men scrambling in little groups onto the tarmac towards the small business jets readying for take-off, towards the rows of private jets still in hangars, emblazoned with corporate regalia, evicting clueless pilots, terrorizing the ground staff, while another set followed him. I scurried after Manoj.

The men stormed upstairs towards the control tower and banged upon the door, only to be quickly led inside by a fearful sentry. They demanded to see the flight logs for names of passengers. No way could this be last minute, Manoj informed me, what with a myriad rules around private aircrafts and careful pre-screening of passengers. So, it had to have been planned earlier, and if Ravi Uppal was in the game, then my meeting last evening in his office was probably a mere confirmation of the rightness of plans already in motion, rather than the primary instigator of a cross-border flight.

Roy Jordan, Roy Jordan, we went through the thin pile of flight logs for private aircrafts, scanning for the name, till we found it. On a Falcon 2000 bound for Dubai.

'Stop this flight,' Manoj brandished a fist at the air traffic controller, who sat white-faced, nervously fiddling with his identity card as it swung on a dark cord from his neck, nearly choking himself in fear.

Manoj shook the man's shoulder, a gentle rocking, to and fro, to rouse him and the man jumped into action, typed in details, and checked the flight's status on a control screen.

'It's gone…' the man squeaked, and we rushed towards the computer screen, to watch a moving dot on the radar screen, airborne toward the Arabian Sea soaring heavenwards and taking with it my meagre hopes.

Flown away? I clutched the back of the flight controller's chair, knocked by the unfairness of it all: the physical abuse of the morning, the mindless chase across town, the unexpected wait, and this futile journey. Tears streamed down my cheeks. What had started as an adventure in art, a heedless fluttering away of multiple zeroes, a whimsy, a half-felt truth, inspired as much by a love for colour, strokes and textured emotion, as by the desire to possess and outshine, and by bitter vengeance, had ended in this – this sorry misadventure of hapless reality. Another stupid case of a naive woman fleeced and a clever trickster who made away with the loot.

'What is happening?' Officer Manoj's frantic shout, accompanied by a sudden tumult of the flight controller's fingers upon the keyboard and mouse, as he rattled keys and ran from one computer to the next, pierced through the miasma of my loss.

'The plane is off the radar...' he said, as a loud noise, like a bullet fired somewhere, a sharp bang, muffled by the distance and the glass window, shook the tower.

We looked up at the sky, at an intense October blue, as it burst into pyretic orange, a hurling ball of flames, a fiery propulsion of combusting paraffin and alloyed titanium, there for an instant, then replaced the next, by the thickest, sootiest trail of black smoke, smearing across the sky.

How quickly my fortunes had changed! I watched in astonishment as the man who had played me for a fool was now dealt out his own exit.

Yes! I exulted, an orgasmic rejoicing rising from my gut, jangling every nerve, the build-up of hot pleasure, at the unexpected justice of this explosion.

With shaking fingertips, I wiped away the odd, remaining tear, and thanked God for Roy Jordan's summary death.

❧twenty-three

The sound of a telephone's ring shattered the stunned silence. The aircraft controller and I sat transfixed by the fading orange glow of the sky and the whorls of black smoke quickly wisping away to a jumble of thinning grey strands, while Manoj Thakur answered his phone. 'Yes, yes, good, okay,' he punctuated the pauses, ending with, 'We'll be there soon.'

Sensing Manoj Thakur's gaze, I turned away from the aerial melodrama beyond the window to the inside of the control chambers. Against the bank of computer monitors, flashing data or displaying psychedelic screensavers, Manoj stood still and firm-eyed.

'My team conducted a raid at Dilkhush. They have found something. Let's go.'

Leaving the stunned airport staff behind, we climbed down the Control Tower and got into Manoj's jeep and whisked back to South Mumbai as soon as we could.

Soon enough the stupor would vanish, and tongues would move faster than the air traffic radar, spreading the word of the cops-and-robbers chase, avid media-mongers would join in, digging delicious details from Roy's life and speculations about the world of art. The name of Saloniere Star might be dragged into the fray, or we could get lucky.

Numbness gave in to fear, a delayed primal reaction against the savage violence of the morning. I sat in the car and hugged myself, teeth clattering and limbs shivering. Suddenly I was aware of every bit of myself, the dull throb where I had landed on my back, the smarting in my scalp where Roy had clutched and pulled my hair, the place on my wrist where the pinch marks had smoothed out, but the memory of that punishing grip remained. Then there was the fluttery feeling in my tummy, where the baby swam in its amniotic sac. Mumbai sped past, its virulent filth a mere blur, as I stared outside the car, lost in my thoughts, reliving the horrific incident. My innocence had been ravaged, and nothing in my sheltered life would remain untarnished.

Manoj Thakur was all solicitous. 'You look traumatized. Can I call someone for you?'

I gave him Raj's number. He dialled it and spoke to Raj, quickly explaining the incidents of this morning, and gave the phone to me.

'Take me home,' I mumbled to him, still shivering.

'You could have been really hurt, Tara, this reckless behaviour, not telling anyone anything...' Raj said in the gentlest voice, but I could hear his voice catch. 'I'm coming to pick you up,' he said, insisting on making an appointment with the doctor as he took down the address for Dilkhush.

The que sera sera moment would happen, reality would have to be dealt with, but at this instant, curiosity overcame fear. I asked Manoj about the raid, it was the first I had heard of it, and he said he had ordered the raid as soon as he had listened to the taped conversation between Roy and me.

Some paintings had been uncovered in the mansion, not in the spare room used to store paintings where they could be expected, but hidden inside a broken teak armoire stashed behind stacks of disintegrating furniture in one of the other rooms, before any of Roy's cronies had a chance to shift them. 'We've called in some experts.'

'What will happen to Ravi?' With Daniel escaping the country and Roy escaping Life itself, the only other link in this chain could be Ravi Uppal. Except there was nothing that actually linked Ravi to Roy – if those canvas rolls held any clues, they were all charred specks in the Arabian Sea, twenty miles from the coast, unable to tell their story.

'Nothing,' Manoj shrugged, and gazed outside the car window, at the city speeding past behind us. 'Not unless there is any concrete evidence.'

The scene at Dilkhush was very different from the morning. Lathi-toting men in khaki guarded the door to the building. The pavement-dwellers sat erect, on high alert, conducting their business in upright stances, very aware of the presence of the constabulary, surreptitiously trying to conceal their contraband gadgets and their illicit posters, while taking in all the details of the proceedings on the floor above.

Manoj jumped out of the car, and I rushed behind him up the stairs I had tottered down just hours ago, and re-entered the wine-windowed hall, now full of uniformed policemen, bustling about, breaking the ominous loneliness of this morning. It was a weird feeling being back at the scene where Roy had bashed me around and nausea threatened to overwhelm me. Bracing myself, I followed Manoj Thakur.

'Sir,' a tall young officer snapped to attention and led Manoj through the corridor to a back room, stuffed and grimy, with armoires, dressers, settees, and chests stacked atop one another, pushed close with bare inches to squeeze past, in a hotchpotch overlay of walnut, teak, cherry and rosewood. Through a narrow path between the furniture, the dust of days now freshly anointed with a police tape in yellow, we reached a large inlaid armoire at the back. Within its cavernous inside were some paintings, about ten odd, canvases stretched but without frame borders.

I reached out a hand to touch one.

'Later,' Manoj barked, stopping me, and gave orders to his staff to take them out into the main hall. We moved back to the main hall to greet the expert called in by the CBI folks. Policemen started bringing out the paintings one by one, to line them against a long wall.

Raj rushed into the room just then, and drew me into a deep embrace despite the sniggering stares of the constabulary. 'Thank God you're safe!' he exclaimed into my hair. 'Now let's go, get the baby checked out, the doctor wants to see you immediately. She will be in her a clinic within the hour. Let's go.'

'Just in a bit...' I said.

'You're pregnant, Mrs Malhotra?' Manoj Thakur frowned, astounded. 'You should have told me. You should not be here, doing this.' He shook his head, so concerned, that I wondered if he would have taken my word at face value and caught Roy yesterday itself, had I played the teary pregnant woman.

The paintings seemed a mixed collection from across decades, from landscapes to abstracts to figuratives, signed by artists from Nandalal Bose to Dhurandhar.

'I don't know what to make of this set,' the expert, brought in from the National Gallery of Modern Art, said. 'I can discuss these with my colleagues. We might need to do some tests, cross-reference against listed works. Just looking at them, though, I cannot say if they are real or fake.'

The last painting arrived, a dark Bikash Bhattacharjee, oddly juxtaposed doors and arches hanging upside down in grey clouds with a flaxen haired baby doll. It offered no instant revelations to the expert. 'The Doll Series,' he muttered, polishing his bifocals.

Hot fluid waves suddenly clenched my insides. That scrap in my purse, that little piece of canvas I had managed to tear from the painting Roy was carting off this morning! The one I thought was the Bikash Bhattacharjee I had seen in Ravi's Alibaug bungalow just days ago. Wiping the sweat off my upper lip, I half-ran to a large desk, and emptied my bag to retrieve the precious bit. The painted torn triangle did not have a signature, just the vividly dark backdrop. Not enough to go by. Still, I called Manoj and showed the bit to him, and mentioned seeing the painting in Ravi's beachside art vault and also in the catalogue of a recent London auction.

Manoj pursed his lips, consternation furrowed his forehead. 'Ravi is too well known, Tara, a powerful man. I have to step carefully.' Quickly he shouted out orders to his staff to find out who owned the upper floor of Dilkhush, and called up sources at the Enforcement Directorate and Customs for information on Ravi Uppal.

The frail fist of the Law, which I had always imagined to be too slow and too feeble for effect, suddenly seemed amply robust as I saw Manoj Thakur in action. The Enforcement Directorate, he told me while on hold between conversations, was an agency created to track foreign fund transactions of business houses and individuals, a routine mapping of money in and money out, to ensure legalities and discourage money laundering. Most big businessmen were monitored, so quite possibly Ravi Uppal's business was within the radar as well.

'What? The government has *databases*?' I stared at Manoj astonished, finding it impossible to imagine government agencies having sophisticated computer systems and data mining processes to keep track of suspicious activities.

Manoj shot me an annoyed glance, one hand covering the phone, still waiting for response from the other end. 'Interdepartmental tracking may not be as good as in the West, but of course we have computerized data within each department.'

❧twenty-four

I was starved for news by the time I had the morning tea and biscuits Raj brought in. I was all on edge, wondering what had happened yesterday after I'd left Manoj Thakur. Seven in the morning was too early to call, but I rang Manoj Thakur's mobile number anyway; it went unanswered.

But before I could try Manoj again, Raj snatched my phone, and leaned forward to press me back against the pillows. Massaging my belly, he told me that my parents were flying in this morning and would be here just after breakfast. He moved back just as Rohan barged into the room, followed closely by my in-laws.

Family solidarity was all very well, quite the blessing and all that, but I was chafing for news, real news. Like, did the Enforcement Directorate reveal anything and whether anything pointed at Ravi Uppal's involvement with Roy Jordan. I kept trying Manoj Thakur's number but there was no response.

Rohan went off to school and my parents arrived in a bustle of hugs and tears and subdued jubilation over the grandchild-to-come. I sat at the breakfast table amid the general loud concern of Raj, my parents, my in-laws, Gul, Pheroze and Rimli. I was dying, ready to

pass out from an overdose of cosseting and an acute
deficiency of news. 'Where's the newspaper?' I asked,
changing the topic.

'No,' my mother-in-law and father-in-law said at
the same time.

'It hasn't come,' said Raj, biting into his omelette.

I looked from one to the other, when the maid
rustled in, holding a sheaf, 'Paper, Madam. Sir kept it
near the bin by mistake.'

I held the sheaf warily, aware of everyone's eyes on
me, and unfolded the paper. There it was, the anchor
piece on the front page:

The Daily Post, Mumbai

   October 28

   *In a dramatic incident yesterday, a Falcon 2000
private jet bound for Dubai, crashed over the Arabian
Sea soon after take-off. 'The left side of the plane was
on fire. Smoke filled the sky,' a resident by-stander
in Vakola reported. 'We are still investigating the
matter,' a spokesperson of Mumbai International
Airport Ltd (MIAL) said, refusing to comment upon
the matter further, but a ground staff member in
the private aircraft area near Kalina informed us
that CBI officers had turned up soon after the plane
took off.*

   *The sole passenger of the plane, Roy Jordan,
a British National, died in the crash. Roy Jordan,
an art dealer, had come into the limelight last year
when he found an Amrita Sher-Gil painting, a major
discovery feted by Indian art collectors. The painting
was sold privately to an industrialist in New Delhi for*

*an undisclosed amount of several crores. It is alleged
that Roy Jordan was escaping the country with rare
artefacts. Along with him, the pilot, Inder Singh Gill,
also perished.*

*The private jet, belonging to generic
pharmaceutical manufacturer Care Pharma
Enterprise Ltd., was used for occasional private
charter, a company spokesperson informed. The
plane, made in 2001, was purchased second-hand
by the Indian business group two years ago and was
insured by GG Financial Services. 'We will conduct
a detailed investigation into the cause of the crash,'
a Care Pharma spokesperson said.*

*This incident is likely to focus attention on
the use of private aircraft in India, especially for
foreign travel and by foreigners. Recently, British
officials have expressed concerns about terror-based
organizations using private jets, and unnamed
contacts in Aviation Authority of India have expressed
similar sentiments.*

The article carried a long shot of a plane with smoke
trellising above, below and around it. Not as bad as I
thought. At least, there was no mention of Saloniere
Star.

Then Gul said, 'Let's discuss some other matters,
Tara. The gallery will be okay. We'll manage the business.
But we need to get Ravi Uppal out of the picture, return
his money, and get our gallery away from his influence.'
Needless to say, Pheroze and Raj sat up sharply, agreeing
with her, and within minutes Pheroze reorganized funds
and called up his bank manager to put money into an
escrow account, ready to be transferred to Ravi Uppal's
account as soon as we spoke to him.

*

My phone rang and I rushed to it like a desert rodent to the oasis.

It was Manoj Thakur. 'I have news from the ED.' He was stiff-voiced as usual as he told me that as he had expected, the Enforcement Directorate had Ravi Uppal's transactions under surveillance. They revealed the usual periodic transfers to and from certain accounts associated with spindle-makers and hosiery-spinners and button manufacturers, as well as some one-off money transfers for purchases from art galleries overseas. No transactions were tagged for selling art overseas. All perfectly reasonable and seemingly above board for a textile businessman who also forayed into art business. Except for a few unexplained deposits, four times in the past two years – possibly related to Roy Jordan, possibly not. A simultaneous raid had been conducted on Daniel Leibowitz's flat in Delhi but it was found empty, cleared of everything except the furniture.

'Nothing against Ravi, then,' I sighed. It had been too much to hope for. 'What about the paintings you found in Dilkhush?'

'Nothing clear – other experts have been called in. They believe some of the retrieved paintings might be real, while four are suspect.' Manoj said that the experts were going to talk to other experts, do some cross-referencing, which might take a week. 'There is one other thing though,' he added.

'Yes?' I replied eagerly.

'Customs has found some records of paintings shipped by Roy. I will round up the shipping agents. But I need help sifting through the documents to see if there is anything suspicious.'

'I will come,' I said instantly – ignoring Raj's protests – when Manoj said that he would send an official car in the afternoon to escort me. Then I turned to Raj: 'Please understand, I'm in too deep to let go now.'

An hour later, a young officer rang the bell and I left with him for the Commissionerate of Customs in the CSI Airport in Sahar. It was a long drive in afternoon traffic – was it just yesterday that I had chased after Roy and time had shrunk in the heat of the chase?

Arriving at the airport, I was effortlessly whisked through a special entrance with a pre-organized special visitor's pass and within minutes, I was on the mezzanine floor occupied by the Customs department. Manoj Thakur met us at the entrance and the three of us walked through the corridors to arrive at the office of the Assistant Commissioner for Exports Mumbai III, where the AC waited, flanked by two younger officers.

The AC, Divakar Rao, a short, straight-backed person with thinning hair and a luxuriant moustache, shook my hand gravely. 'Thanks to your complaint we have unearthed a scam.' He nodded his head in approval and I felt a ray of hope – we had some proof then! 'Show Mrs Malhotra, Ashish,' the AC told one of the juniors.

Ashish, the officer, quickly opened some documents on an ageing grey PC on Mr Rao's desk, typed in some searching tags and showed me a list of shipments documented against the shipper name, Roy Jordan. 'We have an automated record system which logs data on all packages shipped from Mumbai airport. Some of these go back two years,' the officer said. 'But we have printed out details for a few.' He pointed to a thin stack of detailed export declaration forms and airline shipping documents.

'As I told you before, Officer Thakur,' AC Rao took over in his deep serious voice, 'of these ten items, seven have been shipped to individuals tagged as "Gifts". Can a dealer gift so many paintings? This is tax evasion!' The AC looked vehemently aggrieved, his nostrils flaring softly in anger.

Only ten paintings shipped over two years?

It was too few, but I remained quiet.

'The others?' I asked, deflated. Tax evasion by Roy Jordan might perhaps be a scam legally, but it did not implicate Ravi or suggest a ring of forgeries.

'The other three went to a gallery in Ibiza,' Ashish read out the details from the computer. 'See, they have declared the goods: three paintings by NS Bendre, valued at 37 lakhs total.'

'Could be valued right depending on the size and vintage of the paintings, but most probably, I'd say this lot is seriously undervalued!' I said to the AC, and his face took on a triumphant there-you-go look. 'Just curious, I know Roy sent a painting for a Sotheby's auction this year. Can you check on it?'

I spelled out Sotheby's and Ashish ran another search, but of course, nothing came up.

'Maybe he used aliases?' I was ready to give up; it could have been anything – shipped under other names, shipped to a third party as a gift to someone, who then gave the piece to Sotheby's, shipped under the name of the original seller of the piece. Or it could have been hand-carried by Roy or by a private courier. How many other paintings were sent outside India unaccounted?

We tried other searches – against Daniel Leibowitz, against Natalia Balogh – and came up with nothing. Ravi Uppal came out clean as a whistle.

'What now?' I glanced at Manoj, feeling shorn of hope.

'We will study these records,' Manoj told the AC.

'Of course, of course,' the AC ushered us out of his room, and Ashish took us to an empty meeting room. 'The three shipping agents Roy used over the past two years will be here by five,' he said as as he left us.

Manoj asked Ashish for a print-out of all records for Roy. We sat in the tiny meeting room on grey chairs under a flickering white light and pored over the papers, noting with dismay that many paintings were listed *Untitled*, and logged meagre descriptions against individual shipping agents. After several cups of sweet tea and a quick break – where I managed to use a smelly bathroom without throwing up – we had detected nothing unusual.

Just a few documents remained to be cross-checked by 5pm, when Ashish came to call us. We followed him, papers in hand, to a large meeting room where a panel of high-ranking bureaucrats, including AC Rao, another AC for Anti-Smuggling activities, a senior from Customs Preventive, officers and aides, stared at the three shipping agents, who looked distinctly uncomfortable as questions were shot at them from all sides. There wasn't much to learn, the men were just cogs, ground-level doers in the world of transworld shipments, who simply greased low-level palms and ensured the safe passage of goods from the shipping office to the plane cargo hold. They knew as much as Roy had told them to write on the submitted paperwork.

It was a bleak exercise. The AC screamed, the aides threatened and asked about painting shipments from a dated list. I looked from face to face, at the bored faces of the two officers who were not screaming. Manoj was busy talking on his mobile.

Asish looked at the agent sitting in the middle – a colourless man in a colourless shirt – and asked about a painting which, for a change, listed a title, an unusual one at that: *Caliente* by SH Raza gifted to a Mrs Leyla Shahtakhnova in Baku – a surefire defrauding of the government! Who *gifted* a Raza worth a pop?

The agent on the right, a youngish fellow in a foppish striped shirt, responded, 'Baku? I thought I shipped *Caliente* to Australia.'

The sleepy room woke up to commotion, and the agent gasped anxiously, worried about what he had let slip. The documents were scanned again, no double mention of *Caliente* was found anywhere.

'I must have remembered wrong,' the agent Ramesh Rastogi suggested.

But, it was such an unusual name. Ashish was sent off to run another check, and people clumped around the table discussing possibilities, shooting accusing glances at Rastogi. A few minutes later, Ashish returned and jubilantly showed another record dated 2006 for shipping agent Rastogi, and a piece titled *Caliente* by SH Raza shipped to a Mr Ankit Uberoi in Perth. The shipper was Farishta Gallery in Colaba.

'Let's go,' Manoj said briskly.

A camera bulb flashed in my face as soon as we stepped outside, and I jerked my hand instinctively, covering my face with my arms, just as a young girl in jeans and a flowery kurta thrust a mike in front of Manoj Thakur and said, 'Sources say Roy Jordan was smuggling precious art out of India and the CBI has found some evidence of this in Colaba?'

'No comment,' Manoj replied, and propelled me ahead, towards the jeep by the kerb-side.

The reporter trailed us with questions: 'What is your link to the case, Madam? Did you know Roy Jordan, Madam? Do you think there is an underworld involvement in his death?' There was a brief curious snigger from onlookers. It's easy to blame all on the mafia in Mumbai. It's like the joker in the pack, the twist in the tale, a quick scapegoat, when other explanations fail.

I sat listlessly in the car as the driver navigated the thick evening traffic. Reporters were sniffing about already, how soon before the story broke and the fact that I had bought a fake from Roy made front page news? But then, there were the two paintings with the same name, shipped out of India over two years ago. Was it the same piece sold twice, or were they copies? Were there *Caliente I* and *Caliente II*, part of a series?

Manoj's phone rang. 'Hello,' he answered in a tired voice, but a few seconds later, sat up, said a brisk yes with a decided hoot in his voice. 'It was ED. We have something on Ravi,' he exclaimed excitedly. 'It's a lead!'

Dilkhush was owned by a family trust, which also held majority holdings in Ravi Uppal's textile business. In other words, a convoluted, legally permitted way of accumulating assets and saving taxes. Still, if Ravi owned Dilkhush and Roy was using the place as his temporary base in India, there was a connection. Enough to sanction a police inquiry, but not enough to issue a search warrant for Ravi's premises.

'By morning, I will have men stationed near his houses in Cuffe Parade and in Alibaug, waiting for orders,' Manoj told me. 'I will go and question him, and if anything suspicious emerges, we'll take it from there. But it's best if we don't involve you in this process.'

*

Gul was waiting for me when I reached home. After I told everyone about all that had happened at the Customs office, I took Gul aside. 'There was some confusion, about a Raza painting called *Caliente*,' I said. 'It was shipped twice with a year's gap, to two different people. Ever heard of the painting?'

'No,' Gul frowned. 'Shall we Google it?' We did but found no mention of a canvas named *Caliente* by Raza. 'I will check in all the folios I have,' Gul said, and told me about what had happened in the gallery over the last two days. Muthu's paintings had been taken down, and Jai's men had been in the gallery painting some walls eggshell blue and some walls cream bisque. Today, on the portion of the wall painted yesterday, two paintings had been hung up.

'We'll hang the other paintings tomorrow,' Gul said.

'There was a reporter at the airport today, Gul,' I leaned forward, looking furtively at my family, but they were sitting on the sofa watching TV, probably relieved that the authorities were getting into the act. 'She was asking about my involvement with Roy.'

'Don't worry about it, Tara. It's beyond your control now.' Gul's lips thinned, but her eyes were wide – not warm, but not mad either; a forced neutrality. 'Let's focus on the mundane,' she told me. 'Tomorrow I will come to pick you up and we'll go to the gallery.'

I smiled, probably for the first time since morning. It sounded like a plan. I said goodbye to Gul and went on with my own mundane tasks for the evening, organizing an extra bed in Ro's room for my parents to sleep in, while my in-laws stayed in the guest room and Ro bunked in with us. Mundane, that's the key. Little details mattered.

Mundane mattered little next morning, when the doorbell rang in the wee hours and I woke up to the sounds of a verbal scuffle, Raj and someone else. I gathered my gown, and sleepily walked out of the bedroom, twisting my tousled hair into a messy knot, to see the maid hovering in the hallway, my father-in-law and father looming behind Raj, and beyond Raj, in the landing near the lift, a young man in stiff hennaed spikes and goatee, waving a paper, screaming in Hindi.

Raj closed the door on the young man and huffed into the room.

'What happened?' I asked, suddenly wary.

'Nothing,' Raj scorned, 'creeps on the chase.' He flung a cheaply printed broadsheet on the table. *Naya Jagat*. A two-bit daily. And there on the front page was a picture of me and Manoj Thakur leaving the airport, my face partially hidden in my hands and Manoj's arms in front of him as if shoving someone away. *Vimaan Mein Sansanikhez Maut!* blared the headlines, promising sensational scoops. I did not even want to read further, to find out what they'd reported and what they'd implied.

'It's only a rag,' Raj shook his head. 'Probably no one pays attention to it.'

But he was wrong! By mid-morning, I had calls from several reporters – from English dailies, Marathi dailies, the lot – asking for comments, for the inside story behind the escape and death of Roy Jordan, about the implications of paintings found in Dilkhush, about the painting *Caliente* and if I knew how Roy had acquired that painting. Each question was more preposterous than the one before.

Who was feeding the press? More than that, was it this easy to track my name and number, when there were no White Pages to speak of, no directory listings which an ordinary caller could turn to? Each new call on my mobile made my panic level rise. But what could I say to these reporters, when I had no clue who they were and how they would distort my words. 'No comments,' I told them all, and hung up.

Then Mrs Aditi Mewawalla called at 11am, 'What's this I hear, Tara? Are you involved in forgeries?' She sounded more shrewish and high-pitched than she usually did. 'I have invested good money in supporting artists, but I don't want my investment surrounded by scandals!'

All that effort in unmasking Roy, and now this! There had to be some way out.

'I should make a statement, don't you think?' I called Gul frantically, on the verge of tears.

'I'll get someone I know,' Gul said, saying she would speak to the PR agent who had helped us before.

Raj had taken the morning off, but he emerged now from the bedroom in his jogging gear. 'I'm off to the gym, I have to go out and clear my head.' he said crisply. 'I'll be back by the time Gul arrives.'

'Will this affect your Ellerman Jones India project?' I asked, blinking back the storm of horror building behind my eyes.

'Now don't think of tangential matters, Tara,' Raj gave me a side hug, rubbing my shoulder in a reassuring gesture. 'My clients are overseas. Of course, word gets around and reps matter, but we'll deal with that later.

Just your name being mentioned in the papers does not imply scandal.'

Then Rimli arrived and Gul followed, an hour later, with a reporter from the *Times*, a kind-faced, well-built woman of medium height, in a non-descript kurta and pants and a name which must take up a lot of type space: Sharbani DattaGupta Rajaraman.

In a clear, cultured voice, Sharbani assured us, 'These events happen, Tara. There was this case involving a gallery in Kolkata a few years ago. A gallery in Delhi was held culpable last year. But news tides over and unless the gallery owner has frauded clients, the story dies down and gallery owners eventually go back to their business.'

Eventually. I threw a worried glance Gul's way. As a new gallery, did we have the luxury to pick up our business eventually?

'But Tara's the defrauded party here, Sharbani,' Gul interjected vehemently. 'You must tell her side of the story, make it known that Saloniere Star is in the clear.'

Sharbani apologized and said, 'Of course, let's hear your story, Tara. You give a statement, the true story as you say, and your name is dragged in the mud. You don't control how every copywriter and every editor views your story. You have to be prepared for the storm to blow over; just hope it's a squall, not a tornado.'

'Go on now,' said Gul softly.

I brought out the untitled *Woman in Red* from my bedroom and placed it on the dining table propped against a vase. The long-limbed figure in red leaning against a market cart, at the centre of all this upheaval, looked at us pensively, unaware of the commotion she had caused.

Sharbani switched on her mini recorder and I told her how I had bought the painting from Roy in a private sale, and that later, after art experts had doubted the authenticity of the painting, I had challenged Roy. There was no real way to explain the CBI involvement without going into conjectures over the artists' deaths, over Daniel Leibowitz's credentials, and hinting at some as yet unrevealed mastermind. But I omitted those details.

'So you challenged Roy, he denied it, and tried to escape and you got the CBI in?' Sharbani summed up.

'Yes,' I shook my head urgently, hoping she delved no deeper.

'What was he escaping with?' Sharbani looked up at me, eyebrows raised. 'Paintings, of course – but whose paintings, who supplied them, who was buying them – there are many unanswered questions here. Did you find anything?'

'No,' I sighed.

Gul spoke about Saloniere Star, and how we represented young artists and how I had bought the Sher-Gil painting for my personal collection; that it had nothing to do with the gallery.

'Picture time, then,' Sharbani said, and I posed, stiff-faced, forcing my lips into a smile, holding my Sher-Gil. Raj walked in just then, and Sharbani rounded him up too, and took some more pictures of the two of us: holding the Sher-Gil fake, and others around the house with our Husain line drawing and the huge Chitrita Goswami canvas. 'I don't know which painting I'll end up using for the piece,' she said, as she packed away her camera and recorder and took leave.

The bell rang soon after and I rushed to open the door. Manoj Thakur walked in, fury in every step, and took a

318 • amrita chowdhury

position in the middle of everyone. 'What a morning!' he barked, chewing forcefully on a piece of gum.

Ravi had vehemently denied knowing that Roy was involved in anything shady. He had admitted to buying paintings from Roy and selling some from his collection to him. 'He was furious, threatened political action against the department and called up his senior pals in the Police. The Police Commissioner said it was just courtesy questioning and no action would be taken without evidence,' Manoj said and added that apart from Ravi's Cuffe Parade apartment and the Alibaug bungalow, he had a fleet of eight Mercs, one Audi and one Carrera, as well as his yacht, *Moonsong*, moored near the Gateway. Then there were the textile plants on the Mumbai–Pune highway. 'Who knows what's hidden where.'

'What about the Bikash Bhattacharjee canvas I'd torn a corner of, from Roy's stash?' I asked.

'Hah, if that was evidence, it's perished with Roy,' Manoj bit out.

'Can't you search the Alibaug house?' Rimli exclaimed. 'Verify if the painting is still there?'

'Not without a warrant.'

'But did you *question* him?' Gul's voice hit a high note. 'Did you *show* Ravi the canvas scrap Tara had torn?'

'Yes, as a matter of fact, I did,' Manoj said. 'He said *he* had the original and it was intact. He shrugged off any connection with Roy, except the most obvious one – that he knew the man socially, had availed of his services as a dealer, and offered Roy a place to use as his temporary office in lieu of payment for a painting bought from Roy. What Roy did in his business, if and how he and Daniel produced and sold fakes was beyond

Ravi's knowledge. Ravi said that if Roy had forged his Bikash Bhattacharjee, it was without his knowledge. He said Tara was mistaken – it could be another painting from the same series.'

'What if...' Gul sat up, twining her fingers in her messy hair. 'What if Ravi is correct, the painting he has *is* the original and the painting with Roy was a copy? It's a fantastic theory – but either Ravi was made a fool of, which I doubt, he is quite known for his shrewd business ways! Or if not, then Ravi knew about the forged painting and was involved in the creation of the fake...' Gul's voice trailed off.

There had to be some *four hundred* paintings in that Alibaug house, not counting the stash in the Cuffe Parade apartment. Some of them were fine examples of modern Indian art. What if many of these had been copied and sold as originals to remote collectors, while the masterpieces remained stored in an Alibaug basement, to be taken out after a forgettable period of time? The spectre of masterly forged creations, floating in salons across Eastern Europe, the Middle East and Africa, wavered before me. There could indeed be a lot more to it, beyond the obvious involvement of Roy and Daniel.

'There is no proof,' Manoj Thakur reminded us. 'No way to prove anything, till we can actually get two copies together, and prove the sales path for the fake went through Ravi Uppal. Till then it's just a story.'

'Why would Ravi even get into forgeries?' I asked, puzzled by Ravi's visible success in the textile business, which did not match up with this connection to forgers.

'The ED tells me that there has been trouble in paradise for the past few years,' Manoj Thakur shrugged derisively. 'Exports gone sour, hedging bets diving against the dollar. Maybe he just needed the cash. Plus his family business had collapsed in the 80s and though he revived it, it never reached the glory of its heydays. He might have needed cash to inject into his businesses, an easy inflow on the side. Maybe he just seeks illicit thrills. Whatever it is, we have no proof.'

However long we debated and however many inferences we drew, there was only one thing to be done – pay out Ravi Uppal's share in Saloniere Star. 'Let's do it tomorrow,' I told Gul.

My painting was in the papers the next morning, a small pixellated photograph, along with the story of how a newbie gallerist had been duped by a rogue dealer. As per script. But would it convince anyone?

'Forget what's happened, Tara,' Gul arrived at noon in a bluster of motion, and dropped a thick wad of printed contact lists on the table. 'I've been busy calling up people since morning, telling them how Roy duped you. We need to clear the air, that's all. Put the episode behind us. Carry on as usual, focus on business, all that. Come on now, Tara,' Gul added. 'We have an opening scheduled for next week.'

I drove down with Gul to Saloniere Star.

'What the...' Gul muttered, as she pressed the key into the lock, and the front door swung back on its own accord. And then she gasped, stunned, slamming her face into her hands as I stepped up from behind, shocked to see the state of our gallery: the newly painted walls gouged out, the light sculpture smashed to smithereens with shards littering the floor, the cover of the leather chaise ripped out and two paintings by artists Shreyas Waghle and Nibedita Sinha slashed to shreds.

'Oh God!' Leaving Gul frozen by the door, I raced inside to the other room, and took in the mutilated walls, the plaster ripped out, and beyond the room, in our office, Gul's folios scattered on the floor, pages torn, covers wrenched off, her laptop smashed, its top and bottom part hanging loose, wires revealed in serpent-like coils.

I dropped my bag and laptop case and slid onto the floor, on my knees. I plugged the wire into the laptop, jammed the top and bottom pieces together, and repeatedly hit the start button. I peered at the broken machine, willing it to start, not understanding this shadow of violence that had doomed our gallery. But the laptop was a gone case.

The store room! I ran through the kitchenette and with trembling hands, pushed open the door, which looked like a cabinet door, but led into the storage room in the back. Canvases stood stacked against one another in the darkened room, the remaining works by Shreyas and Nibedita and Pulak Parikh, undamaged, waiting to be hung.

'Thank you, thank you, thank you, God!' I sank back against the wall, one hand on my thumping heart, perspiration soaking my body as a tremor of seismic proportions rose from my toes and ended somewhere deep inside.

I gathered my breath, and walked back into the main room where Gul stood dazed, inspecting the slashed paintings. 'We can do nothing.' Her eyes looked large and haunted in her tanned face.

'The other paintings are safe, Gul,' I whispered.

Gul raced to the back room, and looked, tears in her eyes, at all the remaining paintings safe from whoever had broken into the gallery and trashed it.

Luckily Muthu's paintings had already been sent to their buyers earlier this week. There would have been no way to replace the sold paintings. As for the financial loss, that was another matter.

'I'm scared, Tara,' Gul said, glancing back behind her shoulder, and shivered.

'I'm calling Manoj,' I said, walking back to the office room where I had left my bag on the floor, and took out my mobile.

'Stay there, don't open the door, I'm coming over immediately,' Manoj said when I told him what had happened at the gallery.

I sat waiting for him, head hung low, and the strangest thought came to me. We had not yet paid out Ravi for his investment in our gallery. Pheroze had put all that cash in our account the day before, and we had tried getting an appointment with Ravi, to tell him we planned to buy his stake out. But that was then.

'There's something we must do, Gul. *Now.*' I looked at her, determination in my eyes. 'We need to return Ravi's money, put the cash back in his account. All that we owe him.'

'Yes,' Gul replied, wiping her palms down her face in a tired gesture. 'I don't know how I forgot to tell you, but I spoke to Ravi this morning. I told him that we had come into some cash and wanted to buy out his share in Saloniere Star.'

'Really?' I exclaimed. 'What did he say?'

'Oh, he appeared fine with it, twenty lakhs is just loose change for him he said, and added he would have offered that we keep it for a bit longer if it helped with our cash flow. But with your name in the papers now, he was happier removing his name from our gallery.'

'The two-faced bastard!' I burst out. 'Did you say we were okay without his cash?'

'What do they say, about rats leaving a sinking ship?' Gul smiled grimly. 'But I wasn't outright rude, if that's what you're asking. I did say we were certain we wanted to take the gallery forward on our own. And that we would stop by his office and sign the documents formally ending the partnership.'

I stood up, squared my shoulders and walked back to the office room. Fishing out my laptop from my bag, I cleared away the torn glossy folio pages from the desk, and placing my laptop on it, logged onto the internet with my wi-fi aircard. With Gul standing over my shoulder, I went into my webpage favourites to open our bank's homepage, typed in the account number and password and opened the online bank account for Saloniere Star.

I checked the balance – there it was, in a long string of zeroes, the money Pheroze had put in. I typed in Ravi's bank details, his account number and BSB number, which I had saved in a file from before, and made the money transfer. A type and a click, and there it went, in a virtual arc of cash, all that money, dot-dot-dotted away from one node to another.

'Done.' I logged off, and switched off my laptop just as the doorbell rang. It was Manoj.

'Woah!' Manoj exclaimed, taking in the room. 'You have to lodge an FIR, we will take it from there.'

'But we don't know who did it, remember?' Gul responded, her voice sharp.

'Any guesses?' Manoj snorted. 'I need a way to catch that bastard!' His eyes zoomed from my face to Gul's and swivelled back to stare at the slashed painting behind Gul.

'But he's an investor in our gallery, rather was...' Gul said. 'Why would he do it?'

I explained to Manoj that Ravi was a part-investor in our gallery and that we had decided to put his money back into his account, from the money lent to us by Pheroze. Manoj nodded thoughtfully. Financial dealings with a suspect are never good, and I scanned his face, reading it for conspiracy theories.

But he said evenly, 'He did it to distract attention from himself, to punish you, to scare you.' Then he shrugged his shoulders. 'Could be anything, really. There are many loopholes here, Gul, Tara. The ED has been suspicious about Ravi's dealings for a while, just that they have not found solid proof. The paintings found in Dilkhush – by the way, experts now think they could all be fakes – is another loose string connecting Ravi to Roy. But I need more concrete evidence. My guys ran a check against the two credit cards Roy Jordan used to settle his Yacht Club bills over this past year. They were paid from some bank account in Monaco. I have involved the National Central Board in Delhi, that's the Interpol division in India, and they have spoken to their counterparts in Monaco, to check Roy's bank records, to see what transactions were made over the past year. There has to be something, some trail of money exchanging hands, some evidence which we can use to search Ravi's properties.' Manoj looked at me, pointedly. 'One mistake from Ravi, that's all I need, one mistake...'

'What do you mean?' My voice sounded freakishly hollow to my own ears.

And so we laid out our plans.

*

Gul called her driver inside and, ignoring his frightened gasps and shudders at the mess, told him to stand guard in the gallery, pretending we needed to go to the police station to report the incident. Leaving the whimpering man behind, we went down the few steps, past a foul-smelling rubbish truck that was supposedly collecting the garbage. We quickly climbed inside Manoj's waiting jeep and drove towards Nariman Point in the light mid-morning traffic. A warm breeze whipped us from the open windows, ruffling hair and flapping loose clothes, and despite the warmth of the day, little tremors of dread mixed with thrill chilled my hands and feet.

'Here,' Manoj said, handing me a tiny, black, button-like object as we were about to alight. 'It's a transmitter, a listening device, so I can hear your conversation.'

Outside Ravi Uppal's building in Nariman Point, Manoj pointed out two open-top jeeps unobtrusively parked on both sides of the road. 'My guys,' he said reassuringly, and climbed down with us. Beyond a slight bend in the road, the sun beat down directly on the cusped liquid greyness of Back Bay, turning it into a sheet of antique gold.

Signing up in the lobby, we went up the elevator, refusing to look at each other. Manoj stepped out on the tenth floor and went through the staircase exit door to check on his men already stationed on the two nearest landings. Gul and I went to Ravi's office area and announced ourselves to his personal assistant.

'Do you have an appointment?' the efficient looking dragon frowned, peering at her computer calendar.

'Tell him it's urgent – about the sale of an expensive painting,' I said in my most imperious voice; nothing works better in India than the impression of power and the mention of money. 'He'll meet us.'

The woman capitulated, walked inside to apprise Ravi of our arrival and then led us into his inner chamber.

Well, well, well, the celebrity is here,' Ravi mocked me, rising up to bow slightly, in a loose white shirt which nevertheless strained around his middle. His office smelled of cinnamon dhoop. I looked for and spied the puja alcove tucked into a shelf, where little silver deities presided in their flower garlands.

'I was expecting Gul to come alone. What brings you both here?' He sounded curt. The last time I was here, I had stomped out on him.

But then, the last time I was here, I had not known of his involvement with Roy.

I flushed. We sat down across from him, uninvited.

'Ravibhai, a lot has been happening,' I smiled my best placatory smile, but he did not smile in return.

There was an awkward silence. My heart sank. How should I phrase this? I looked at Gul, trying to read her expression, but her face gave nothing away.

'Indeed, a lot has been happening,' Ravi scoffed, scorn tipping his voice. 'I just got an email alert from my bank – you have transferred 20 lakhs into my account. I gave you cash and I would have preferred cash in return. But, well, now that you have already transferred the money, let's move on. I'm assuming you are here to sign a document to cancel the earlier MOU.'

Cash transaction – was Manoj listening in, I wondered.

'I do have a basic letter here,' Gul glanced at me, and produced a folded sheet from her purse. 'See if it's okay.'

Gul handed the sheet to Ravi, who cursorily scanned the short para and signed it. After Gul signed at the bottom of the document, she passed the paper on to me – a legal Saloniere Star document that I, a partner in the gallery, was seeing for the first time! But then I had done so many things without telling her about them either.

Glancing briefly at the document, I signed it.

There, it was done. The formal severing of Ravi Uppal from the Saloniere Star account books!

'Okay then...' Ravi drummed his fingers upon the table and looked pointedly at the door

Gul cleared her throat, and started to speak, softly but steadily: 'We are here for another reason today, Ravi. A client of ours has asked us to find an early twentieth-century Bengal School painting, and we immediately thought of you, you would surely have something in your lots.'

'Why?' Ravi stood up belligerently, and glared down at Gul. 'Why this sudden change of mind? You didn't want any of my paintings two weeks ago.'

Gul looked taken aback and gulped.

A chilly silence descended. Ravi looked annoyed.

I could sense Gul's agitation, her usual manner was frank and forthright and I did not want her blurting out the real purpose of our visit. I held out a hand, steadying her arm, and turned to Ravi, trembling inside, but pretending to be calm. 'The opportunity just came up, the client called yesterday,' I said. 'Plus, there was more trouble at the gallery today, Ravibhai.'

'Hah, I had warned you about that,' Ravi bit out. 'No more than what you could have expected...'

'But it *is* more than that,' I said, voice aquiver, trying to mask my anger at how calmly he sat in front of that puja place, pretending all this was *my* fault. 'I was wrong in approaching the CBI, Ravibhai. I should have listened to you. Now matters have gone out of hand, our gallery was attacked this morning, everything was trashed, the paintings on the walls were slashed through...' A catch, a real one, gruffed my voice and I took a deep, juddering breath and went on, looking at Ravi's large body as he sat down again, hulked upon the table, elbows planted firmly on the table top, thick be-ringed fingers intertwined, veins ramming out in his large fists.

'Not happy to be notorious, hain?'

'I wish this would end, Ravibhai. I'd do anything for it to end...'

'You should have been careful when you could have.'

No hints here. He was giving nothing away. 'I just never imagined Roy was so deep into forgeries,' I changed my tactics. Maybe Roy's name would draw a response. 'He always told me he had borrowed the Dilkhush office from a friend, he never mentioned it was you.'

Ravi narrowed his eyes, ever so slightly.

I continued, heedlessly, heart hammering at my own audacity: 'I met him that afternoon, you know, the afternoon before his plane crashed... so providentially. I challenged him and he hinted there was more to it than I knew, a grander scheme, a higher-up invovement...'

'Get out,' Ravi suddenly shouted standing up and snarling into my face, his breath garlicky, his eyes bulbous. My heart stopped. 'Get out before...' he screamed again.

He had no weapons, but did he need them? A phone-call would suffice – his henchmen lurked everywhere. What would happen next? What had

I unleashed now? My head swam. I scrambled up, pushing my chair back clumsily, and took half a step back, into Gul.

The door burst open at the moment, and I jerked around and stared dazed as two uniformed policemen ran into the room, revolvers in hand, screaming *'Don't move!'* followed by a man in badged khaki, and with them *Chitrita Goswami*.

What the...? thoughts flashed through my mind in psychedelic order. Had Manoj informed these people? Did those policemen even know Manoj was stationed outside? And what in God's name was Chitrita doing here?

'DCP Mangesh Desai of Mumbai Zone 1,' the officer flashed his ID casually, staring at Gul and me, trying to assess our involvement, his roving eyes taking in the plush office with the teak desk, the leather chairs and the large paintings on the walls. 'We have allegations against you, Mr Uppal. Ms Goswami here has just confessed that she has painted several fakes – commissioned by you.'

I stared at Chitrita in disbelief.

'All lies,' dismissed Ravi. 'How *dare* you come here again, barging in, hurling accusations? Don't you know who I am? I have friends high up in your department!'

'The EO Commissioner himself has sent me today, on request of the EO Joint Commissioner in Delhi, a friend of Ms Goswami's here.' He pointed to Chitrita with a flourish. 'Ms Goswami?' The DCP invited.

Chitrita Goswami had an ethereal air about her – a rarefied other-worldly presence, totally detached from this seedy scam she was engaged in. She looked Ravi calmly in the eye and said: 'Ravi Uppal here commissioned me to paint fakes in 1972. I did over seventy pieces for him in the period between the seventies and early eighties, works of everyone from Nandalal Bose to Raza. There wasn't the money in Indian art then as there is now, but Ravi always was a far-sighted visionary, a savvy businessman. He knew this market would soar.'

'Your art career is finished, Chitrita,' Ravi burst out savagely. 'Who will buy your works once you start making false accusations against dealers?'

'False?' Chitrita roared, her large eyes flashing red and deadly against the silvery chopped mop on her head. 'I'm not scared of you, Ravi. Not anymore, not for my career, not for anything. You almost killed me when I refused to paint any more fakes for you. But then my intrinsic worth had begun to grow. Now you could blackmail me to give you my originals at no cost. But that didn't stop you from silencing the others, did it? But you can't touch me now. I'm dying anyway.' Her cultured voice heaved and broke. 'Cancer – in the terminal stage. A few weeks, that's what the doctor has given me. My son... you remember Gautam? The little boy I struggled so hard to make a life for? He died last year. Nothing holds me back now. Nothing,' she said thickly, as if every syllable created a cosmos of void, of utter blackness, devoid of any hope, any love, anything to clutch onto.

'When I saw the name *Caliente* in the newspapers yesterday, along with news of Roy Jordan's death, I knew I had to come clean. Did you get Asgar and his henchmen to kill him too? Or is sabotaging a plane something you reserve for your better-heeled goons? I should have spoken up when Manasi died. She was an admirer of mine, you know – she had come to me for professional advice a year ago. I knew she was caught in the same trap I was, but I couldn't bring myself to open up to her, for fear of the consequences.

'Today I have come to claim my mistake as my own. I painted *Caliente* thirty years ago, when I had no money, when my husband threw me out on the streets with a young sick baby, my little boy with Down's Syndrome, and I was so desperate, so in need of support, that I got lured into your web. You wouldn't sell Chitrita Goswami paintings then – but you were happy to peddle Chitrita painted fakes.'

I stared at Chitrita, at this vision of elegance in a pale peach chiffon sari and slim bangles around her frail wrists, at this artist whose style I so admired, whose painting I owned, at those long thin fingers which had painted fakes once, unable to reconcile the two sides – the artist and the forger.

Could her life really have been that bad? Memory flashed, Rimli mentioning a news article from months back about the art fundraiser she had organized in Delhi for Down's Syndrome awareness. It had been a personal mission then! Turned out of her husband's family home sometime in the seventies for giving birth to a child with Down's Syndrome, she must have been really alone, desperately in need for cash to shelter her baby. Still.

Was Manoj listening to all this from outside, I wondered as I turned to look at Gul and held onto her hand.

'What rubbish.' Ravi was saying and hastily walking towards the door.

'Not so quick,' the DCP reached out a hand from far and grabbed his arm.

Just then Manoj barged in from outside, a triumphant look on his lean thin face. 'We've got you, Mr Uppal, we have evidence enough for a search warrant.'

Ravi halted, hatred twisting his face. 'It's her word against mine. That's no proof.'

'*Caliente*, such an unusual name, no?' Chitrita's laughter reverberated in the stillness. 'Did you ever wonder, Ravi, how I came up with that name? I was already an artist then, not selling much, but I had my own style. I never wanted to copy masterpieces, so I created a smaller painting in a master's style. Do you even remember what *Caliente* looked like?'

She looked at Ravi, a look that combined great revulsion and great dispassion. 'It combined two phases of Raza's style, in fierce red and intense ochre. My first forgery. I remember how I cried...' her voice broke now, and I stared at her anew, horrified, relieved, amazed.

Chitrita gathered herself, her lovely eyes heavier and redder than before. 'I had just learned Spanish, and I called it *Caliente*, after hot, after fire, because that's what I was doing – playing with fire.'

'Good fiction, that's what it is, officers,' Ravi raised his fat face imperiously, feigning unconcern. 'Drivel. Rubbish.'

'What about the Sher-Gil whose picture I saw in the papers today?' Chitrita interjected. 'I painted that too.'

'What?' I burst out. Chitrita had painted my untitled *Woman in Red*?

'Yes,' Chitrita turned to where I stood in the corner, acknowledging me for the first time. 'Yes, Tara, I painted that Sher-Gil. I was always influenced by her style, loved her craft, her women who epitomized loneliness, solitary even in a crowd. I mixed her style from different phases – a lone woman from her earlier phase with the background detail from a later phase.'

Oh My God! I sank to my knees, trembling. The final curtain-raiser. Her words echoed all that I had been told before by the numerous Sher-Gil enthusiasts and scholars I had met ever since I had bought the painting.

'What about Manasi?' I exclaimed, perplexed. What about that sheet Shruti Pethe had given me with Amrita Sher-Gil signatures practised in paint?

'Manasi?' Chitrita looked sad. 'Poor girl. I should have warned her about getting involved with Roy and Ravi. But I was scared she would find out about my own involvement. She could never do a Sher-Gil.'

'Manasi wasn't even a good enough forger,' spat out Ravi.

'What?' the DCP sat up, while Manoj hooted in manic we-have-you laughter, and moved at super-hero speed to wrestle Ravi's fat arm behind him and twist it inside a hand-cuff held by the DCP's subordinates.

'They would have got you anyway. I have proof too, Ravi,' Chitrita's eyes were shimmering jewels, liquid against her papery skin. 'I have transparencies of each and every painting I did for you.'

DCP Mangesh Desai and Officer Manoj Thakur led a suddenly subdued Ravi away.

Chitrita gathered her thin sari tighter about her slim shoulders, head held high, only the barest tremor of her lips betraying emotion. I went up to her now and took her hand.

'I bought that fake Sher-Gil painting from Roy Jordan,' I said. 'I call it *The Woman in Red*. She speaks to me like no other painting has ever had. She gave me comfort and strength when my own world was falling apart. Her loneliness is supreme, but it's invincible. I drew my courage from her regal bearing. I identify with her. She liberated me. It's not a fake painting if the emotions it elicits are so genuine.' And the tears spilled out, hot fat drops of relief and peace that it was over.

Through the haze of my tears, I saw Chitrita gather me to her frail body. 'And you, Tara, it was your courage that liberated me.'

❧epilogue

I *wake up feeling amazingly refreshed. Ah bliss, I flex my feet, wiggle my toes and languidly press the bedside bell for the morning tea and papers. As I do so, I grin toothily at* The Woman in Red *– my Amrita Sher-Gil fake and Chitrita Goswami original, hung prominently above my bed – and give her a thumbs up sign. Mmmm. Life is good.*

Last night, a month after the raid in Ravi Uppal's houses, Saloniere Star opened its pre-sold third show, showcasing the Bengal school artist Anirban Ghose to an impressive set of attendees. Our second show – the group exhibit of three Baroda artists – had opened a week late because the salon was in slight disrepair; it too had drawn many visitors.

Roy's death and my fake Amrita Sher-Gil had hit newspaper headlines and were discussed threadbare on the national news. As I sat in the news studios answering questions, the flowing kurtis I wore concealed my baby bulge but not the glow on my face. The authorities had done their bit too and revealed forged paintings commissioned by Ravi Uppal. Links were found between Roy's bank accounts and Ravi's undisclosed offshore accounts that Indian authorities had no inkling of. A picture emerged of Ravi's deeply entrenched system of selling fakes to nouveau collectors over the decades, first on his own, and then, when Indian art prices exploded, through a hired accomplice ie Roy Jordan. Accounting discrepancies were found in Ravi's textile business, dodgy art deals propping up turbulent cash flows. As for the plane crash, who knew what happened? Stories abounded – engine malfunction, crow caught in the engine, pilot error. But the aircraft was buried deep in the Arabian Sea. The CBI indicted Ravi Uppal on multiple counts of fraud, forgery, and money-laundering and invited injured parties to come forward if they had been swindled by Ravi Uppal, but only two did. How many, after all, wanted to confess publicly that they had been duped?

Gul and I had spent immensely long hours calling up collectors, meeting with the cognoscenti and the art community, explaining the circumstances, converting sympathy into sales, and transforming the general lack of trust into understanding. Long days and longer weeks for me, as I longed to put my feet up, but had to go round and round, reliving my story, quite enjoying the ooh and aahs it invariably generated.

Still, the great global machinery of art goes on, and while some ill-fitting cogs jam the wheels occasionally, they are quickly greased and the motion continues unabated, like the gears never froze and the wheels never stopped. And I? I have learned my lesson – to never buy anything on blind trust, but to do my own checking and double-checking to ensure that what I've bought is authentic stuff.

Chitrita passed away last week in Delhi, defeated by the cancer which had inveigled itself from organ to bone. I spent a lot of time with her, this past month. Alternately crying and laughing over the whole episode, which had marred a few months of my life, but had shadowed hers for decades. Before she died, she re-signed my painting with her signature, authenticating it, turning it into an Amrita Sher-Gil-inspired-Chitrita Goswami. I still lost money on The Woman in Red. *But the sense of identity I feel with the figure in the painting is complete. Like* her I have been forced to stand up for myself, to scale the depths of loneliness. But there is an added dimension to it now.

Of despair and repair.

Of a woman who stumbled, but fought back.

As a Chitrita painting, it is valued far less than a Sher-Gil, and Chitrita's value came down after the scandal of the forgeries broke, but then duly rose again when her tragic story hit the headlines after her death.

For me, it was, is and always will be, my most treasured painting.

The maid brings in the tea tray and I reach for the morning papers. There is a picture of Saloniere Star's event from yesterday, with glittering fashionistas smiling next to consular types and attending artists. A smile plays upon my lips, as I relive the triumph of last evening, my Gauri and Nayanika dress revealing the soft swell of my belly as I pose next to Raj.

Raj walks out of the bathroom, just then, freshly showered, a thick brown Egyptian towel wrapped snugly about his lean hips, a lopsided smile softening the angles of his face as he sits beside me and caresses my belly, and the little girl who sleeps within. We have decided to name her Chitrita. Now Raj is looking at me, desire in his eyes. But this is Mumbai, the door is open, anyone can walk in any minute – Rohan, Raj's parents, my parents, Gul, Rimli, the maids, the driver, the dhobi...it's an open house.

I laugh, bending forward, warm in his love, secure in my family's embrace, kissing his shower-softened lips, breathing in the fresh musky smell of him, noting a little drop of water, a silvery ball, as it falls from his wet hair down his angled cheek onto his bare chest and below. 'Tonight,' I promise against his ear, and lean back against the pillows, eyes aglitter with excitement.

'I love you,' I say softly, putting down the paper, as Raj raises one eyebrow, amused.

Then I laugh and add, 'And I love my life here.'

✵acknowledgements

I am deeply indebted to:

The wonderful world of contemporary Indian art for being so inspiring – the artists, the art sellers, the art critics, the art writers, the art bloggers – true champions, all, of the beauty in Life and Art – and for providing valuable information, which I could embellish and fictionalize.

Amrita Sher-Gil, artist extraordinaire – she left behind a limited legacy of paintings. But imagine if there was something else out there, undiscovered! Well, I took the liberty to imagine just that. I salute her passion, her courage and her artistic determination.

Yashodhara Dalmia for her biography of Amrita Sher-Gil; the non-stop, super-charged, spirited city of Mumbai, perennial Muse to writers, for being such a fabulous backdrop for my book; Alpona Banerjee for the precious gift of Time, and for sharing thoughts on everything from Modernism to Miller-Modigliani; Ranjana Mirchandani-Steinrucke for deep insights and ideas over long drinks; all my friends whose funny coming-to-India stories I shamelessly borrowed; my early readers – Alpona Banerjee, Leena Godiwala Deubet, Neha Mullick, Nitin Pachare, Swarupa Pachare, Ranodeb Roy, and Sumit – for ploughing through those painful first drafts and horrifying me with comments like, 'Wow, what a colourful life you lead.' *It's fiction, guys!*

Nandita Aggarwal, my amazing editor, for that instant karmic moment of picking up my book, her astute fashioning of my prose, and calming me down on many an occasion. The entire team at Hachette, including Shivmeet Deol and Anurima Roy, for all their efforts.

Mugdha Sawant for endless technical support. Alaknanda Kumar and Mahesh Patil for my website www.amritachowdhury.com). Subhabrata 'Rontu' Basu for introducing me to Andrew Go, and Andrew for sending that email to Thomas Abraham.

At various stages, for ideas (in alphabetical order): Angeera, Preeti Ambani, Ananya Banerjee, Beth Citron, Yashodhara Dalmia, Deepak Das, Samit Das, Yashwant Das, Anil Dharker, Madhulika Gupta, Advaita Kala, Bose Krishnamachari, Brinda Miller, Sanchit Mullick, Khorshed Pundole, Sharmishtha Roy, Arun Sahu, Sajal Sarkar, Indira Somani, Harriet Vidyasagar, and all the collectors and connoisseurs I know, for general art chit-chat.

The Breach Candy Club for providing air-conditioned kid-free spaces to work in.

My parents, Dr Mohan Lal Verma and Dr Purnima Prasad, for giving me big dreams and the tools to make them come true. My brother Chetan, my in-laws, my grandmother Ammiji, and my entire family for their acceptance of my wayward skedaddle chasing yet another dream, the Muse. Friends on five continents for monthly 'Are you done yet?' reminders, thus keeping me on track.

Shoumik and Aishani for making my life scatty and fun, all at once.

Finally, but most of all, Sumit, for simply being there, for his unending support, for believing in my dreams when I didn't believe in them myself, for his incredible sense of humour, and, of course, for underwriting my shopping habits without too much ado.